ACCLAIM FOR
THE END OF ALWAYS

"Evocative descriptions of the Wisconsin landscape and Marie's intensely felt love serve as a balance to the harsh reality of her life...A moving story with skillfully crafted characters."

—*Library Journal*

"A powerful story of a woman's desperation and brave efforts to escape a brutal heritage, to end the family violence and help set a precedent for other woman in the future. An intense statement to the power of determination and hope."

—**BookLikes**

"Deeply affecting."

—*Booklist*

"A gritty yet hopeful tale about a young woman determined to escape her family's legacy of abuse...An accurate commentary about the times that, sadly, may still apply behind the closed doors of many households today."

—*Kirkus Reviews*

"A well-written family history that finally has the female protagonist standing up for herself! Randi writes so well about difficult situations. This novel will appeal to historical fiction lovers as well as book clubs for the range of female characters portrayed and their different reactions to hard times."

—**Flyleaf Books**

THE END OF ALWAYS

ALWAYS

a novel

RANDI DAVENPORT

Inspired by Actual Events

TWELVE

NEW YORK BOSTON

For all the Reehs women everywhere

Twelve
Hachette Book Group
1290 Avenue of the Americas
New York, NY 10104

www.HachetteBookGroup.com

Printed in the United States of America

RRD-C

Originally published in hardcover by Hachette Book Group.
First trade edition: May 2015
10 9 8 7 6 5 4 3 2 1

Twelve is an imprint of Grand Central Publishing.
The Twelve name and logo are trademarks of Hachette Book Group, Inc.

The Hachette Speakers Bureau provides a wide range of authors for speaking events. To find out more, go to www.hachettespeakersbureau.com or call (866) 376-6591.

The publisher is not responsible for websites (or their content) that are not owned by the publisher.

Library of Congress Cataloging-in-Publication Data

Davenport, Randi
    The end of always : a novel / Randi Davenport. — First edition.
        p. cm.
    ISBN 978-1-4555-7307-3 (hardcover) — ISBN 978-1-4789-7743-8 (audio download) — ISBN 978-1-4555-7306-6 (ebook)
    I. Title.
    PS3604.A94265E53 2014
    813'.6—dc23
                                        2013030539

ISBN 978-1-4555-7308-0 (pbk.)

All the greatest things are simple, and many can be expressed in a single word: Freedom; Justice; Honour; Duty; Mercy; Hope.
—Winston Churchill

1

When my father came to America, he brought my mother and my sister Martha to Waukesha, Wisconsin, where I was born and grew up. Then as now, the town stood on a vast tableland of grass west of a lake so broad you could not see from coast to coast. Indians were here first, and the value of this land to the Menominee came from its proximity to the lake, which also made it a gathering place and later a trading town. Eventually, the place was overrun with traders who bartered with the Menominee for furs and skins and anything else they thought they could get for cheap. The traders all seemed to believe that prosperity came with opportunity, but like all men, the traders meant their own prosperity, their own opportunity. This is the American way.

A long trolley line ran through the middle of town and then on to Milwaukee, but in those days Waukesha was not so big that you could not walk the length of it if you had to. The richest people lived in houses on the limestone bluffs that over-looked the river. We lived on the other side of town in a plain house on a plain street. We had a kitchen at the back and a sit-ting room in the front and a little room next to that that I used as a bedroom even though it was just big enough to get a bed into and only had room for one window on the wall. In between our house and the houses on the bluffs lay the town center. This was where the business of the county was conducted, where ledgers and accountings and sales and foreclosures were kept and practiced and written and traded by men in dark suits and white shirts, their trousers held up by suspenders that fastened at the waistband of their pants with buttons made out of mother-of-pearl.

Once you got outside of Waukesha, there was farmland. You might see a farmer with his plow, the furrows opening up like rounded slits in the ground and falling away behind the blade as the axle passed over. Just beyond the farmland came the forest. This was my land. This was where I walked. Up under the trees where the earth seemed to curve away and the sky opened over me like a bell. That was where I could breathe. That was where I could think. That was where I felt free.

When he arrived in Waukesha in 1888, my father had every intention of buying land. *Land.* This was my father's word for our future. There was no land for him on Rügen, only emperors who came and went, dividing and redividing the country to suit their own interests. Every so often, the island changed hands. It was a fierce land of fierce people, and I believe a good part of my temperament does come from the character of the place, even if I have never set eyes on it. Rügen belonged to the far north and along with its almighty determination apparently had enchantments entirely its own.

Martha insists that she has no memory of the trip over the ocean, but this is not the only thing for which Martha claims amnesia, so you will forgive me if I do not entirely believe her. Willie and Hattie and Alvin and I were born here, which made us Americans. I often felt that we stood on the other side of a line my mother and father and sister could not see and did not

know existed. When I was small, my father would open his atlas to show me the route they had taken, but all I saw was a flat
blue page printed with the word *Atlantic* and the gnarled edge of
Europe, which did not appear any more real to me than a page
in a book, which is not the same as a country where someone
could actually live. America, on the other hand, was the land
beneath my feet. I walked America every day.

The year I turned seventeen, summer burned like fire. Heat lin-
gered even after sunset and the air did not cool, not even in
the blue shadows under the trees where the ground went black.
The lake turned brown at the shore and the stones on the beach
burned hot and branches lost in storms were cast up on the
rocks, where they went white and then fell to dust. It did not
rain and the creeks faded and the Fox River shrank between its
banks.

One night in August, I swept the back porch and watched
dry lightning flare over the horizon. Behind me, Martha clattered the supper dishes as she put them away. Then she came
outside and stood next to me and wiped her forehead with the
back of her arm. "It's so hot," she said. "I don't think I can stand
any more."

We stood and watched the lightning.

"How is he?" I asked.

"Mother thinks he's better." But she sighed deeply and
pushed her hair back from her temples, a gesture so quiet and
oblique I knew she disagreed.

"Isn't that good?"

She didn't reply but only watched the sky. It paled and went
dark and paled and went dark. From far away came the low
rumble of the interurban.

"I'm not just going to stand here," I said.

Martha did not look at me. "Do what you want," she said.

At the top of the stairs, yellow light made a slit in the dark hallway. I tapped on the bedroom door and then leaned against it and stood in the doorway. My mother lay on the bed with Alvin stretched out on her chest. Even from across the room I could see that his pulse beat in his temple like something inside of him was desperate to get out.

My little brother carried a name my father had picked out. He thought the name had a certain ring of newness to it, a certain American sound. My mother thought it sounded like the name you give to a horse. But she had to live with the choice. We all had to live with my father's choices. He ran our household like he was the king and we were his subjects. His hand had the final say, and there was no word more certain to compel our obedience.

When Alvin first got sick, my mother thought he was teething. She rubbed whiskey on his gums to settle him. But a fever came on, and my mother had spent most of the day before walking Alvin up and down or trying to get him to sleep or laying wet rags on his head. By this morning he merely slumped in her arms and stared up at us with a hard sparkle in his eyes. Now his eyes were closed, and he did not even seem sweaty in the heat but lay as still as the toy babies they sold at the dry-goods store. My mother rubbed his back.

"Is he better?" I asked.

Before my mother could answer, Alvin made a guttural sound and began to fling himself up and down like a fish fighting a line. My mother cried out. After that, the only sound in the room came from the small whumps Alvin made as he pounded his head against my mother's chest. When he finally went still, my mother touched his forehead and listened for his breath. It came in harsh, shallow waves. "Tell Martha run and get the doctor," she said then. "I do not know what else to do."

My mother had already buried one son, her first child, who died before he was a year old. She and my father had left him behind when they left Rügen. When she told us about him, he was so far away and never to be seen that it seemed he had never existed at all. Then, the summer Willie turned fourteen, my father sent him out to work. My father told us that work in a mining camp would turn Willie into a man. What it really did was turn Willie into someone we never saw again. The day he left, he packed a comb and a clean shirt and set out from our front porch. I watched him until he disappeared, but he never looked back and certainly did not look back at me, even though I had been closest to him and had often lain awake at night while he sat on the edge of my bed and talked to me about how things would be different when he grew up. His house would not be like this one. He would get away and stay away. I could count on that. Later, when he did not write and did not return, I told myself he must be out there somewhere. But I felt a hard hurt whenever anyone said his name and then a kind of flattening, as if the mystery of what had happened to him had to be turned into a sheet of paper that I could fold and put away.

The doctor rolled his cart into our drive and tied off his horse, which stood blowing and swatting flies at the fence rail. He called to Martha to hold on, for he'd be right there to help her down. Then he came toward me out of the dark with a cheerful expression on his face. "Hot as Hades," he said as I led him upstairs. "I don't believe it can get any worse than this." But then I pushed the bedroom door open and he saw Alvin and he did not sound so jovial after that.

"Elise," he said. "You just lie still. There's no point in moving that child. Let's see if we can't get a good look at him where he is." He sat on the edge of the bed with the tubes of his stethoscope protruding from his ears. He moved the silver disc across Alvin's back and curved his palm around the back of Alvin's neck and let his hand rest there. "Not an exact measurement," he told my mother. "But I find it usually gives me a good idea."

Martha and I stood shoulder to shoulder in the doorway. I watched the doctor as he touched Alvin and then I watched Alvin, who did nothing but lie on my mother's chest and did not even open his eyes. He seemed to be disappearing by the second, and I wondered how long it would be before he vanished entirely. Even now, he did not seem to be Alvin but instead seemed to be the memory of Alvin, still tethered among us, but who knew for how much longer. My stomach lurched at the thought and I looked at my mother, who was now openly weeping, and my throat closed and then I felt tears come to my eyes.

The doctor said that Alvin's illness was not uncommon. You often saw it in the summertime among children whose mothers fed their children things they should not have fed them, meat that had been cooked but not put on ice, something left over from breakfast. He wished these women would do a better job, but what was he to do about it? There was nothing he could do. And where Alvin was concerned, the illness would have to run its course. It would have the predictable result, and my mother should expect that by morning. Then he put his stethoscope back in his bag and told me he'd left his hat on the kitchen table and he could pick it up as I showed him out. He'd send a bill next week.

After the doctor left, my mother remained on her bed with Alvin still stretched out on her chest. But the doctor was wrong and Alvin did not die by morning. He lay like that for another half a day, and Martha and I took turns bringing my mother water so she could drink. Hattie sewed a little doll from left-over felt and tried to interest Alvin in this, as if a toy would pull him from the place he'd gone. When he died, we were all in the room together. We heard the rattle of his breath and then the silence that followed.

My mother laid Alvin in his crib and then she put on a hat and walked into town, where she hired a photographer to take his picture. She insisted that his eyes be left open until the picture was done. The man stood my brother in his box against the wall, and my father stood in the doorway next to it, his hat in one hand, his other hand in the pocket of his trousers. In the picture, this was how he appeared, as if only part of a man, his head missing and his dark legs disappearing, his suspenders loose over his unruly white shirt. Martha was nineteen that day and Hattie was twelve. My mother was thirty-eight. After that, with Willie gone and Alvin dead, my father was left alone with daughters and a wife, a house full of women he could do with as he pleased.

The only one to follow my parents from Rügen was my mother's brother Carl, who sailed from Hamburg on a ship called the *California* the year after my parents left. He was a tall man with red hair and a red mustache. I had no trouble picturing him on deck, his hair blowing and spray rising from the sea. When he got here, he took a job at a dairy. When he grew tired of that, he went to work on a farm, and when he wearied of that, he made a bed of blankets on the floor and lived in our front room. He left his work boots on the front porch until someone stole them and my mother had to appeal to my father for money to buy a new pair. Not long after that, he took a job at a machine shop and moved into a boardinghouse in Milwaukee.

My father disliked Carl but I could not understand why. I

loved Carl. He did card tricks. He brought gifts for my mother when he came to see her. A bottle of lavender water. A pair of beautiful white lace gloves, which she kept in a box and took out to look at but never wore. But if Carl tried to give us paper dolls or jacks, my father would take the toys away and give them back to us on our birthdays, with a card made out of a piece of folded newspaper and signed with his own name.

My father was not a godly man. To my knowledge, he never set foot in a church after the day he married my mother. Instead, he worshipped at the altar of socialism, that font of good wisdom that poured over Waukesha and brought us laws about clean water and education, which I suppose can be said to have done some good in the end. My father, for his part, talked about the rise of the workingman the way someone devout in other ways talked about Jesus. My father had his heart set on the idea that men live in chains.

The word *land* seems to have a simple definition but it can mean more than the obvious thing. It can mean the ground under your feet, the place you walk, the place you pitch your tent or build your house or find at the edge of a body of water that would otherwise take you whole. But it can also be the place you come to, the way my parents landed in Waukesha. For my father, land was the one thing he wanted above all else. For him, *land* was the word for desire. What he would not do for land, he would say. Practically nothing at all. He could already see the cows lined up at the barn at milking time. The buckets he would decant into a tank. All of us at work to make sure he turned out rich. A dream of land that he was sure would turn solid under his feet: a white farmhouse, a bank of raspberry bushes, a stream that never ran dry.

But when my father got here, he found that he was more

than half a century too late. The towns and cities were not settlements but places with buildings made of brick and stone and farms already developed. The small amount of cash that he carried was not sufficient to buy. His first job in Waukesha was in a flour mill where the miller still spoke German. When my father had learned some English, he moved on to an ironworks where the fires from the foundry singed the hair from his face and the hair just over the tops of his ears. It grew back but he did not know that it would. For a time he raged about working conditions that permitted a man to be scorched like that, right down to the skin. Then he took a job as a barman at a saloon on St. Paul Street. He worked nights and came home at dawn to a house he rented from a man who owned three hotels and a livery stable.

2

By September our small yard had parched and the weedy grass had baked dry. The ground crunched underfoot and sent a haze of dust and grasshoppers and desiccated seeds over us. We spent every day filmed with grime and even the washtub seemed always to have a layer of silt at the bottom. My mother complained that the dust got into the house and she could not keep up with it. For my part, I pictured our house like a veiled thing, secreted and unknown behind its shroud of heat and powdered earth. This thought made my throat close.

At night, when my father went to work, my mother told us stories about the life they had left behind on Rügen. The way she talked made it hard for me to understand why they had left. She said it was a beautiful place. She said it was a magical place. But I guess bad things were always happening there. You could be out alone on a road at night and a horseman could come upon you and that would be the end of you. You were never supposed to stray too far from home.

On that island there were hills shaped like giants and cliffs littered with swallows. Dwarves were as common as squirrels. We were bereft of dwarves in the woods of Wisconsin, so this fact alone was of great interest to my sisters and me. On Rügen, the white dwarves flew around in the shape of little birds or butterflies. The brown dwarves were handsome and wore brown jackets and brown caps and shoes with red laces. Sometimes they would leave gifts for children, but sometimes they would steal children away. The worst of all were the black dwarves, who wore black jackets and had red weeping eyes.

Whenever she told us about them, my mother always leaned forward and whispered loudly that if you did not attend, your life could be ruined forever. Dwarves were dangerous. You had to be careful at all times because you walked among them whether you could see them or not.

If I voiced some skepticism about how invisible dwarves who might also take the shape of insects could ruin your life, my mother seized the moment to assure us that what she said was true. She herself had known someone who had forgotten this one rule and had paid a very high price indeed.

Here is what she told us happened: My mother and father came from a town called Garz, which had been so named because it once guarded the island from the Vandals, who made a happy mission of roving and plundering its eastern shores. When my parents lived there, there was a guard tower and the remnants of a large stone wall that some long-ago architect must have imagined would stave off the hordes. There was also a temple still in place for the worship of an ancient goddess, but everyone had forgotten her in favor of St. Petri, in whose church my parents had married. That was the German influence.

A miller lived in Garz with his beautiful young daughter. Her mother was gone, perhaps drowned in the sea or dead in a field, it did not matter, that was not the point of the story. The point of the story was that the miller knew that anything could happen if his daughter strayed from his sight. There were charms and wonders aplenty on that island. So he kept her by his side. Night and day, they were together, and she was never permitted to go anywhere alone. Whenever she left the house, he had to go with her. If he could not go with her, she could not go.

They lived like this until the girl was fifteen or so. She was restless but there was nothing she could do. But there came a day when the miller was forced to send his daughter on an errand alone. No matter how many times she told the story, my mother did not ever recall what the errand was. Perhaps she did not know. She only remembered that the miller told his daughter to run fast and when she had completed her task to go straight home. He would walk down the road to meet her.

The girl had other ideas. She was young, so she felt brave and free. She finished her errand but then she walked by herself in a stony lane. Above her the open sky. Around her the spreading fields. Ahead of her a road that she had chosen all by herself, far away from her father's house, as if their paths were meant to diverge from the very beginning and all she had to do was discover this.

She passed a meadow of rippling grass where a boy knelt to tie vines to a frame. The boy looked up as the girl came by. (Here my mother said that the girl could not be blamed for anything that happened because she had no idea that this chance meeting would change everything.) The boy stood and came down the hill and looked the girl in the eye and touched her hand. Of course they fell in love on the spot. After that, they spent all of their time together. They held hands and walked in fields full of flowers or let the waves chase them on the beach under the cliffs. According to my mother, there were beautiful white cliffs on Rügen, and people came from all over to see them.

You might wonder what the miller thought of the girl spending all of her time with this boy. The answer is, he did not know. He was away at work so much that many things escaped his attention. Perhaps this is why it did not take long for the girl to grow bold. One day she decided to go for a walk by herself. She let the door close behind her. She turned the key in the lock. She made her way across the field behind the mill. She slipped into the forest. The pine needles covered her tracks and the sky opened out above the trees and she walked in great purposeful strides, which made her feel strong and powerful.

She did not come back. Her father and the boy she loved looked for her everywhere, but all they found was her absence. It was as if had become a maid of the mist, a sylph now just a sliver of water in a stream that ran away. They could not find her. She was gone.

When five years had passed, the boy went up into the hills. The moon lit the night and he found a hundred brown dwarves dancing in a ring. One dwarf took his cap and tossed it into the air. The boy caught the cap and put it on his head. When he saw what had happened, the dwarf wept and begged the boy to give him his cap, but the boy reminded him that when a dwarf throws his magic cap away, he must serve whoever finds it. The dwarf gnashed his teeth but he knew the boy was right. So he led the boy to a glass door at the top of a mountain and then down a long stairway to a hall so vast that it seemed to be another country below the earth. That was where the boy found the miller's daughter, surrounded by gold and jewels of every description. She had grown pale and her hair had turned silver, but the boy knew her right away. He held her to him and kissed her and the color came back to her cheeks. He said he was there to save her. He told the dwarf that since the girl had been forced to work for him for five long years, she must be paid. He still had the dwarf's magic cap, so the dwarf was compelled to do as he was told. And that was how the girl and the boy came to fill their pockets with treasure. They took it with them when they returned to town, where they married and lived, wealthy and happy to the end of their days.

Still it did not rain. I stood under the white sky and clipped shirts by their tails to the clothesline. Hattie stood by the basket and handed the shirts to me one by one. These were followed by the flour sacks my mother used as kitchen towels and then by Hattie's white stockings, ripped and mended where her braces snagged the threads at her knees. Bees vibrated in the stick pile and Hattie hummed a little song with them, a tune I did not know. From far off, the sound of wagon wheels rumbled along the road that ran in front of our house. The sound got louder as it came closer and then it disappeared. Stillness came over me like the world had stopped. No wind and yet I had the feeling that the grass around us seethed like a sea.

I pinned my clothespin to the line. Hattie walked up to the drive and looked down into the street. Then she came back to me, stepping in her leg braces like a doll with hinged joints. "Marie," she said, her voice like the voice of someone who is about to fall from a high place. "It's Mother."

They carried her around the side of the house and my father opened the door for them and then they carried her inside.

By the time I got there, they had arranged her on her bed. I did not think that bundle of bloody clothes could be the woman who had told me to hang the shirts and help Hattie with her bath. Not with her hair plastered to her head. Not with her face gray as the dusk.

My father stood at the window, his face turned away, his hair separated into greasy strands. Across the room, Martha knelt

on the floor by my mother's head. She glanced up when I came
into the doorway.

"Help me," she said.

There were flour sacks packed over the wound, but these
were saturated with blood. Martha pulled them off and dropped
them to the floor, where they fell with a wet sound. She tried
to unbutton my mother's dress but my mother cried out.

I leaned against the doorway as if the floor could not hold
me up.

"Get the sewing box," Martha said.

The space before me turned a strange, hazy gray.

"Will you do something right?" Martha shrieked. "Just this
once?"

The men who had carried my mother inside stood between
the sink and the stove. I could tell they were not going to explain anything. They had already closed ranks, their faces set in
the same expression, like a panel of witnesses who have taken a
vow of silence.

"What happened?" I hissed. But all they did was shuffle
their feet and look everywhere but at me. Behind me, the cicadas buzzed in the trees. Even if it was just their wings that
brushed together, they were louder than the men in that room.
Our yard was littered with cicada shells, and the town paper
printed a story about the molting. The writer wrote about this
act as if it was familiar and nearly human and that every seventeen years we, like the cicadas, should expect to leave a part of
ourselves behind.

Finally the tallest man cleared his throat and looked at his
hands as if he had forgotten he was holding his hat. "It was an
accident," he said.

There were four of them and that was all any of them said.
They did not care that I was angry. They did not care that I was
scared. They did not even wait for me to ask again. The tallest

one just reached over my shoulder and pushed the screen door open and then shoved past me and they all filed out, all except the last one, who was younger than the rest, with dark hair and light eyes. He wore a black shirt and light canvas work pants with dim stripes and a black fedora and brown boots laced up over his ankles. When his eyes met mine, I felt the world empty out of me. He was handsome with the face of a man who has done things, even though he was still just a boy.

"Fräulein," he said gently. His gaze was bright and piercing and he held his hand out to me, the gesture of a man with something to offer, of a man who knew more than words.

My father came down the hall and walked by without a word and without a glance. He took his hat from its hook in the mudroom and stopped in the doorway and squared the hat on his head. Then the back door slapped behind him. His footsteps on the gravel drive came back to me, and white light came through the window and pressed on the room like the flat of a hand. A sound I did not want to recognize rose, and I listened to that sound even as I told myself not to think about the way my mother lay on her bed or cried out or did not sound like my mother but sounded like a woman calling and calling from a world I did not know and never wished to enter. But when Martha screamed my name again, I picked up the sewing box and turned toward her voice. I had always believed I knew what the word *horror* meant, but on the day those four men carried my mother into our house and left her bleeding on the bed, I found out that I did not. Not really.

People do not believe that a girl's life can change in an instant, but it happens all the time. Look around. You are surrounded by girls who have just learned that no matter how careful they have been to do exactly as they have been told, never to question, never to show their underthings, never to speak unless spoken to, their lives are not their own.

In the living room, the windows were open but the curtains did not move. Two women passed by in the street, a tall one with a small blue hat on her head, and a shorter one, whose hat was shaped like a holiday platter. Their voices faded as they passed.

"Martha?"

Hattie limped toward me, her face a pale planet in the falling off of day. A faint aroma, like the odor of something decaying, came from her leather straps.

"No," I said. "Only me."

"I thought it was Martha."

She swayed as if she was held up by things beyond herself, a spindly board blown by an invisible wind. The braces were my father's idea. He decided that Hattie's legs were bowed and he found a doctor who agreed with him. But Hattie had grown three inches since winter and soon would be as tall as me, and now the braces did not fit properly and she limped when she wore them and walked like anyone else when she did not.

The light in the windows began to fade. A great wave of sadness washed through me and then seeped away.

"I was waiting," she said.

"I am sorry," I said.

She took hold of my arm. "Can I go in there?"

I shook my head. I did not want her to see our mother on that bed, waiting for the doctor to come back with the morphine, the tears on her face and the blood on her belly spreading.

"She is my mother, too," Hattie said.

"I know," I said. "But it will be best if you leave this to Martha and me."

She wiped her eyes with the backs of her hands. "What happened?" she said.

"No one knows," I said. But of course that was not true. My father knew what had happened. My father knew the whole story.

No one called it murder back then. That word has grave weight but I am willing to say it. Martha does not agree. To this very day, all she will say is this: *the day Mother had her terrible accident.*

Hattie picked up an edge of the limp curtain. She wound it around her hand and let it fall. "Is she going to be all right?" she said.

"The doctor is coming back," I said. There were no words to explain what was about to happen. To see our mother put down like an animal whose time is done. To imagine our mother as one of us right now but in the next minute gone. I could not say any of this out loud.

"And then she will be set right?"

"He has something he needs to do," I said. I touched her shoulder, her hair. "I am sorry," I said. "Hattie. I thought—"

She bent away from my touch. "Stop it," she said.

We stood in the last light from the windows. My mother's wedding portrait hung on the wall behind Hattie. No older than me when this picture was made, and then carried in the hold of a ship from a place she would never see again to a place she had never seen before. In between, days on the ocean, the world rising and falling. How terrified she must have been. How much trust she must have placed in my father.

When the sun was down, I heard the doctor's cart roll to a stop out front. Behind me, a faint aroma, the metallic tang of blood as Martha tried to wash the flour sacks. From very far away, the clang of the interurban. I pictured its sparks showering down like blue fireflies.

3

When the days finally cooled, dusk came before the end of the day in the woods around town. Some days I escaped my father's house and walked in that early darkness, black branches rustling above and the air coming cold and moss already rich and damp on the north sides of the evergreens. I stepped over chuckling streams and ducked under branches and held them so they would not whipsaw back and hit me in the face. When the moon rose, it hung dull and yellow in the dark blue sky and I whispered little poems and songs to myself like one grown wild with spells and incantations. Walk into the sun, I murmured, my whole, my heart. Walk with me into the far away. Burn down my life and be my love forever.

Then a wind came up overnight and knocked branches down, and where the branches had remained intact, the lesser pieces of the trees had fallen instead. Martha said these could be used as kindling if we only troubled ourselves to pick them up. I sat on the back steps with my elbows on my knees while she zigzagged under the trees, bending and straightening, dropping sticks into a sack she made by pinching the folds of her skirt together. In the growing darkness she looked the way my mother would have looked had she been the one to gather and reap. I felt something catch in my throat. Then Martha started across the grass toward me and was just Martha again, thin as a stripped stick. But she looked pretty in the near dark with her hair falling in pieces over her neck.

"Help me," she called. She shook the bag she had made of her skirt as if this would convince me.

The man who lived behind us stepped out onto his porch and dumped a bucket of kitchen scraps into a bowl. He whistled for his dog and stood back and watched Martha with her sticks and sack while the dog ate. His wife's white sheets were still pinned to the line but wilted as no ghost would be.

The screen door rasped. My father passed me on the steps, his axe in hand. He stood the axe on its poll and let it balance while he peeled his shirt over his head. When he set the first log on the chopping block and centered the splitter, the black blade caught the light and I wondered if this was the last thing my mother saw, this or something similar, another cutting edge or perhaps a knife or a sharpened shovel or the out-flung hook that she would suddenly realize was the scythe that swept the tall grass, as though she herself was a stalk that needed to be trimmed and tamed.

I closed my eyes and pressed my chin harder into the heels of my hands.

The sound of the interurban came over the yard and then faded away. Waukesha used to be like this all the time, wheels grinding, trucks rattling, engines rumbling, everything around us in inescapable forward motion. The future seemed to be right at hand, measurable hour by hour, and I thought surely we would be flattened, for no one could withstand that much progress. But the year my mother died, times turned hard. You could not open a newspaper without reading about another failed bank, another shuttered mine, another machine shop gone quit. The newspaper said that seventeen banks had collapsed in Milwaukee alone between August and the first of November.

I tried to picture this the way that you might picture a house of cards coming down, but I was not successful. I had been to Milwaukee several times. Most recently, my mother took my sisters and me there to see her brother. Carl took us to an opera house with painted cherubs on the ceiling and blue velvet seats where a small orchestra played music. From what I knew, Milwaukee was standing just fine.

My father grunted every time his blade struck wood. Someone rustled in the grass close by and I opened my eyes. Martha shook her skirt over the kindling box and let the sticks fall. She sat down next to me.

"It will go faster if you help," she said.

The lights of town came on. Some of our neighbors had their windows open and dishes clattered in their kitchens.

"Where is Hattie?" I replied.

"I did not ask Hattie," she said. "I asked you."

I reached over and brushed bits of leaves and twigs from her skirt. She caught my hand by the wrist and pushed me away. But I leaned my shoulder against hers and rested there for a moment and she did not draw back.

"Martha," I whispered.

She twisted to face me. "What."

My father's house behind us. My father in the yard in front of us.

"What are we going to do?" I said.

"I do not know," she said. "Stop asking me."

"We have to do something," I said.

The breeze blew and acorns rattled on the roof of the house and dropped into the grass with a sound like hard rain.

Martha sighed. Then she said, "You can sit out here all night if that is what you want. I am going inside."

But I shifted and let my head rest once more against her shoulder. I reached up and twirled a piece of her hair through my fingers. She stiffened.

"Martha," I said again.

She put her arm around me. "She is gone," she said. "Nothing we do can bring her back."

"You do not care," I said.

She dropped her arm to her side and pushed my hand from her hair. "Close the subject," she said. "Promise me?" When I did not reply, she put her hands on her knees and stood up.

I held her skirt. "Martha," I said.

She pulled away. "Stop it," she said. "I said no."

The screen door smacked behind her. After that, the window filled with the kitchen's faint glow.

My father set another log on the tree stump and tested the weight of the axe. Then he hoisted the haft with both hands until the axe was high over his head, where I watched it gleam again in the late light.

When he was finished, he pushed past me into the mudroom and hung the axe on its hook. He came back down the steps and went to the pump, where he washed with a great deal of snorting and shivering. Then he bent down and retrieved his shirt from the grass and put the shirt on and stood buttoning it in front of me. He reached into his pocket and pulled out an envelope.

"I need you to take this to Otto Muehls," he said. "Tonight."

I stood and brushed the seat of my skirt. The envelope was damp and the writing on the front had blurred from being in his pocket while he cut wood, but I could see the address. I could count the coins through the paper. Two nickels and a dime.

Otto Muehls kept traps and went into the woods and then hung the carcasses of the animals he snared from the limbs of the trees out behind the chicken pen. Perhaps he meant to remind the poultry of the order of things. One day he showed me a trap he used to catch raccoons, the horseshoe shape of the jaw, the teeth he sharpened with a file, the short cable that held the spring in place. He told me to touch it, go on, it could not hurt me. But when I moved toward it, it hammered shut and nearly took my hand. He pretended to be shocked but I knew he meant to trick me.

We bought our eggs from Otto Muehls's wife, who tended the chickens in the pen. The eggs were pale blue and green and sometimes pale yellow, like the inside of a lemon rind. My mother said the pale yellow eggs were the best, but I could not tell the difference. To me, an egg was an egg. Something could not be other than it was.

My father watched me. "I would go myself," he said, "but it is late and I do not feel up to it. You can go in my stead."

I did not say anything.

"You can go in my stead," he repeated, his voice rising. "Do not stand there agape. Get on your way."

When I was halfway to the street, I heard his voice behind me. "Do not dawdle," he said. His voice had its familiar edge. "Mind you come straight home."

I took the river road where I could look back at the twinkling lights of Waukesha and out at the patchwork of farmland and then at the forests, where I liked to think that a few of the Menominee still lived in their ancient bark houses, cradling their babies on backboards, as if the wild limned the borders of the things that were most familiar. Beyond them, the dark-moving water of rivers and lakes, the dark trees, a dark land that turned colder to the north.

Just up ahead, a whitish stone glittered in the roadway, the point shaped like an arrowhead, the vein of quartz a river that cut and faded. I leaned down and picked it up. When I was little, I kept a box filled with leaves and sticks and acorn caps under my bed. I picked up stones as white as a dead woman's eyes. These were my treasures even if they were not the currency of the land. I walked everywhere, and everywhere I saw things that could be gathered and sometimes these things were not stones or sticks but pictures that stayed with me. Once, down by the river, I saw a woman no older than Martha walking barefoot, her skirt hanging in shreds around her bare calves. Some mornings, an old woman came to our back door and asked for food. She carried her boots in an ashen bag slung bandolier style across her chest. Another woman was hit by a train as she gathered berries by the railroad tracks. They said she lived in an empty house, for she had burned all of her furniture for heat.

The prospect of any woman wandering the land does not sit well with me. I can be much agitated by the idea. But in those days, that kind of rootless drifting was exactly what happened when a woman did not have money and did not have the protection of a man. Either of these things alone could devastate. Together they were fatal. My mother always fed any woman who came to our door, even when we barely had enough to feed ourselves. She made sure my father did not see. But she always had something on hand, even if it was no more than a piece of bread spread with a spoonful of lard.

The lights were out at the Muehlses' house. When I walked up the steps and looked in the front window, all I saw was my own face floating before me. I considered knocking but I knew that the only person who would come to the door would be Mr. Muehls. He'd be in his nightshirt, his spindly legs white and hairy below the hem of his shift, with his rifle cocked and ready. That he would shoot into the yard just to have his fun was something I would not put past him.

I stuffed the envelope between the edge of the door and the doorframe and walked quickly back to the road.

Across the water the shore was dark. I kept on until I came to the bridge by the mill, where I leaned on the rail and the reeds hissed and the wind picked up and a log as rounded and stiff as a body slid through the current. Something dark bent against the wind. A tree, perhaps, or maybe a single lady slipper, its stem bulging like the goiter on an old woman's throat, or even a fern as long as a broom, its roots no bigger than my foot.

And then a match flared. Down in the darkness, someone cupped the tiny light. He turned his face up to me and I could see his dark hair and his light eyes, the dark brim of his hat. I thought he had disappeared with the men who had carried my mother but he had not. He was on the river with me in the night. In just that instant, the match went out. But he lit another and looked up at me again. I looked back, breathing. When the match light went out again and did not return, I realized he might be making his way along the dark shore. He could rise from the dry weeds and I would take the sound of his movements to be the sound of the wind, the scraping of an earnest branch. I turned and walked away from the bridge as fast as I could, along the river road where waves slapped the grassy shallows, past the houses where contented people slept, running just a little when my own house came into view, as if I already heard the sound of footsteps behind me.

4

The next day my father took the train to Price County. This was the sixth time since July that he had taken the train to Price County, but just like the other times, he kept the nature of his interests in Price County to himself. I don't believe it would have occurred to him to tell us what he was up to. As far as he was concerned, his business was no business of ours.

He was gone for five days. When he returned, he told me he'd decided I would go out to work. He knew that banks were failing and families were starving, but jobs still remained for a girl like me, silly jobs, jobs that did not take much sense, jobs that no man would be expected to take. He was so eager to tell me this that he did not even take off his hat before he sat me down to give me the news.

We were alone in the kitchen. I did not reply. I knew my father could do as he pleased. And the idea that I would go out to work seemed to make him happy, as if his heart had lifted with the perfect solution to a long-simmering problem. He beamed and slapped the tabletop and finally took his hat off and poured himself a drink. He said that I was lucky that I would not have to work half as hard as a man but I would still earn money. Workingmen were the ones who had it bad. Workingmen were the ones who felt the heel of the boss man's boot.

Then he said that he would take the money I earned and use it to benefit me and my sisters. In that way, I would contribute to the well-being of the family, which was the least I could do, since he put a roof over my head and clothes on my back.

That night, he asked around at the bar and right away, a man stepped up and said he knew of a job that would be perfect for me. I suppose they made arrangements there and then. I never knew the specifics. All I knew was that within two days of my father's return, I started work at William Oliver's commercial laundry on Seventh Street, a place I had never heard of or seen until I walked through the door, a place my mother would never have permitted me to work if she had still been alive, a place that was downtown and as far away from anything I had ever known as it could possibly be.

Three large vats stood on stoves that rested on brick platforms against the rear wall of a large room, and four of us worked at washtubs on a table that stood in the middle of the room. Big windows looked out over the dirt yard and a door led from the main washroom to the front of the shop, where William Oliver handed over parcels and took money. All day long we scrubbed napkins and tablecloths and towels and sheets and underpants and shirts and collars and stockings on washboards and squeezed our pieces out through wringers we turned with cranks.

I had a spot near the end of the table and Ella worked next to me. She had been at the laundry for so long that her arms had taken on a shiny and smooth look, long glistening patches of scalded skin now white as waxed paper. She tied her hair on the top of her head with a piece of string the color of ash and wore shoes that she made from pieces of cardboard jammed into an old pair of men's leather slippers. You could foretell her entire future when she slapped toward you across the floor.

Johanna worked across from me. She had the demeanor of a beaten dog and dark marks circled her forearms and a purple and yellow mark on her cheek renewed itself week by week. She would not look William Oliver in the eye when he came to inspect our work.

Inge worked next to Johanna. She had come over when she was twelve, which meant she had landed in Waukesha in 1867, when things were still wild, she told us, and savage Indians killed women in the streets. If you went outside, you had to go in a pack or risk vanishing altogether. "You cannot imagine the terror we felt," she said, but she did not sound terrified. Then she said that in all the years that followed, she had not seen anything to impress her with the idea that Waukesha had endured improvement save for the simple fact that the women of the town were now safe.

In a small room off to the left, there was a stove with plates to heat the irons, and two mangles and three ironing boards and a large table with a wooden jig that permitted clean shirts to be folded without flaw after they were pressed. A spool of brown paper hung from the wall and all you had to do to package an order was roll the paper out on the table, cut the paper with a razor blade that was kept there on a string for that very purpose, fold the paper around the laundry, and tie the package with a piece of twine. The flat workers kept to this room and I never got to know any of them. I do know there was one who did nothing but turn fresh laundry into brown paper parcels from morning until night.

There is no diversion in laundry work. There is the weight of the water and the weight of the basket and the weight of the soap and the weight of the hand agitator and the weight of the wet wash and the weight of the wash on the lines and then the weight of the water again, a long slow cycle that runs again and again across the length of the day. But laundry work fails to distract. It cannot take the place of the things a girl thinks.

I hunched over my washtub. I did not care to handle stockings that strangers had worn nor did I care to touch their undergarments, but this was my work and my father had arranged it and there was an end to it. Every day was the same: I walked into town and then up the alley and after that into the yard behind the laundry, where I set my lunch pail under the steps. I took my washboard from its place on the shelf. I levered burning wash into my basket. I dumped that wash into my tub where the water was scalding hot and picked at the boiling cloth until I could take hold of a shirt collar, a hem, a cuff, and rub it up and down on the board. I dipped bibs and aprons in the rinse water and turned these through a wringer and blistered my hand on the crank. The soap stung every inch of skin gone raw and burned the places the water had burned already, but Ella told me not to worry. After a while, she said, the burns would scar over and would not hurt anymore. But if you have ever washed clothes in this way, you will not soon forget the experience.

Paint peeled in long curling strips from the walls and the windows steamed and the light in the yard turned hazy, but I could still see a piece of the sky. There I looked while the others talked about the girl who had hung herself after her brother did something to her in the barn and about the servant girl who had just come over from Germany and jumped down a well when she found out she was pregnant. I watched clouds roll in and fade away and then I watched the sky brighten and darken. I tried to think of what the forest would be like, its trees whispering songs and the limestone jutting up from the path under the hemlocks where I had walked untamed, beyond the reach of town. But the trees and wind and birds, the rocks and streams and woods, were now so far away I might as well have seen them on a postcard and just imagined what it was like to walk there, the way you do when you see a distant place on a travel poster.

I trawled my wash water for another long black stocking and used it to dab at my washboard.

"If you do a bunch at a time, it will go faster," Ella said. She pointed at my single stocking.

I swirled the stocking through the rinse water and then cranked it through the wringer.

"Suit yourself," Ella said. "But he won't like it."

I ran two stockings through my wringer and dropped them in the basket at my feet. Ella hauled a towel from her tub and fed the towel through the rollers of her wringer. Water ran in rivulets over her slippers but she did not seem to mind. She turned the crank and asked if anyone had heard of the girl who had run away from her father's house and married her own true love, which seemed like the thing that most girls would want to do. Nothing like marrying the boy you were put on this earth to marry, and we should all expect that this would happen because the good Lord had His ways. But on the day after her wedding night, this girl learned that her own true love was already married to a woman who lived in Chippewa Falls. That wife drove a horse and cart all the way to Milwaukee to fetch her husband. When she found him, she did not care what kind of ruckus she made at the hotel or in front of his new bride. It was an unholy scene, end to end. After that, the girl was disgraced. Her own mother would not let her come home.

Then Johanna said that that was nothing. She herself once knew a girl who was made a promise but the promise was not kept. That girl was later found incoherent and wandering the streets of Watertown. No respectable family would have anything to do with her. She was forced to marry a man who did not care for her and showed this to her daily.

I took a deep breath and dipped my hands into the wash

water and rubbed the stockings against my board and dropped them in the rinse water. I did this again and again, until pain stabbed my thumb and I stepped back and looked down at the cut, where blood ran in a straight line to my palm. I sucked my thumb and looked at it again and then sucked it again. The taste of blood on my tongue was meaty and familiar, salty as tears.

Just before lunchtime, William Oliver came into the laundry room and stood with his hands in his pockets. He was not yet old but he was no longer young. He kept his dark hair long and had a short beard that came to a point. He looked like the devil pictured in my father's atlas. That devil also had a pointed beard and floated in a balloon over a caption that provided advice in Latin, his band of winged consorts in flight behind him.

William Oliver walked to the stoves and took two steps up onto the ladder and looked into the boiling water. Then he jumped down and walked back to the shelf where he kept the record of the supplies we used. He counted my entries twice and then set the paper back on the shelf. I could feel him walking up behind me.

"Mary," he said.

The first day we met he said that I reminded him of his aunt Mary, who grew to a fine old age despite having gone blind in one eye and deaf in both ears. Aunt Mary had to use a trumpet and yell "What?" whenever anyone spoke. But then he said I was nothing at all like her because Aunt Mary had never married, even though she was a woman of upstanding character and let everyone around her know it. Anyone could see that living as a spinster on the beneficence of my relatives was not to be my fate. *Fate.* That was the word he used, as if that was the word for my future and he had something to do with it.

Now he leaned close and looked over my shoulder into my

washtub. I believe he must have had sausage for breakfast, for his breath reeked of onion. He said my name again. Then he said he had a special task for me and I must come with him to his office. I looked around but the others were bent over their tubs and acted as if they had not heard anything at all. So I followed him around the side of the building and up the alley between the laundry and the lawyer's office next door and through the front door underneath the bell that rang whenever a customer came in. Then William Oliver opened a wooden door behind which stood a flight of dirty stairs. In the room at the top, his suit coat hung from a curved hook on a tarnished brass stand, his hat on top of the stand.

"Sit down," he said, and pointed to the chair that faced his desk. The desk was a door laid over two sawhorses.

I hesitated.

"You have nothing to fear," he said. He turned and stood with his back to me and studied the street below. I listened to the sound of a wagon and team as it moved by the building, the rattling of the harness and the grinding of the wheels. I sat.

There were papers laid out across the desk and a ledger book with a green paper cover and a tin can out of which stuck two yellow pencil stubs. A loud sound came from the street, and William Oliver stepped back from the window. But still he looked out at the sky.

"I was born and raised in Tennessee," he said. He spoke like someone speaking to a friend, but I was not his friend, and I did not like being alone with him in his room. "I got some money when my daddy died and I came north," he said. "It's an old story. My eldest brother got the land. I got something to tide me over. I carried the New Testament, John Bunyan's *The Pilgrim's Progress*, and *Huck Finn* with me. Before he died, my daddy said that each of these would offer advice for the road ahead. He has not been wrong." He turned to consider me. "Your father is raising you right?" he said. "Some sort of social training? Some expectation that you will rise?"

I did not reply.

He came toward me and sat down across from me and twisted in his chair and reached for a metal flask that stood behind him on a shelf. "I don't suppose you'll take a drink."

I shook my head.

"Of course not," he said. "But you won't mind if I do."

"Mr. Oliver."

"William," he said. He poured two fingers of whiskey into the flask's cap and raised the cap to his lips and drank its contents in a single swallow. Then he lifted the cap and gestured at me. "I know your father," he said. "I have met his wife. The beautiful Elise." He looked at the cap and then lifted the flask, poured, and drank again.

"My mother is dead," I said in a flat voice. *My mother is dead*, I thought. *She is dead.*

"I know," he said. "Such a sad day. Such sorrow across the land. But I guess it was bound to happen." He leaned back in his chair and put his hands behind his head.

The way he spoke of my mother made her seem like someone who did not belong to me. "I do not know what you mean," I said.

He eyed me. "I find that surprising." He dropped his hands to the table. "I believe if you give it some thought, you'll find that you know exactly what I mean." He raised the flask and jiggled it. Then he set the flask down and rocked gently in his chair.

"Mr. Oliver."

"William."

"William," I said.

He watched me.

My hands shook and I took a shallow breath. "Did you want something?" I said softly.

He twirled the cap from the flask. "Now that is a very philo-sophical question. Let me ask you. Are you a philosopher?"

I shook my head.

"Are you sure? In my experience, questions of desire, of longing, are almost always philosophical questions. What one can have and cannot have. What one will be and cannot be. What one wants and why. All questions for the universe. And that is the realm of the philosopher."

A cold draft came in under the eaves. I shivered.

He cleared his throat and then leaned over with his fist to his lips and coughed. When he was done he looked up at me.

"My doctor tells me I need to go west for my health," he said. He wiped his hand with a handkerchief he withdrew from his pocket. "The cold is no good for me. But here I am." He put the cloth back in his pocket and lifted the flask in the air. "To the bright and limitless future," he said. He took a long pull and set the flask on his desk and laid his hand on the table be-tween us.

"I have a need to restore an order to its owner," he said. "I can't trust the others. I suspect they would open the parcel and distribute the contents among themselves, all in the name of equality. No man better than the next. I'm sure you are familiar with this dreary rhetoric. It's ill-informed, to say the least. Of course one man is better than the next. This is what the world is about." He coughed again and leaned hard over his knees.

When he was finished, he cleared his throat and told me that the package was on the counter by the cash register. "The ad-dress is written on the front," he said. He paused. "You can read? I don't know how you people raise your children. You could be perfectly illiterate."

"I can read," I said fiercely, and stood up. "Do not concern yourself."

He lifted one eyebrow and stood up, too, smiling. I do not

know if he was more amused by my tone of voice or my haste. He hooked his thumbs in his suspenders and contemplated me. "I do not worry, Mary," he said. "But I do think of you. This is what you must bear in mind."

It was lunchtime. I picked up the package and followed Ella and Inge and Johanna out into the yard. One by one they fetched their pails from under the steps. They sat on the cold bare ground in the raw light and ate. The daylight moon had swung past its midday high to the leading edge of the western sky. I could see down the alley to the street. It was now a week until Christmas and the town businessmen had strung gold garland on the lampposts to encourage us to shop. As the breeze came up, the garland glinted and fluttered like the ruffle on a dress.

My mother used to boil our clothes in a pot on the top of the stove. She hummed while she worked, an old tune her mother had hummed, and her mother before her, a song she tried to teach my sisters and me as if we were just the next in line. One day she saw me in the doorway and told me to bring the blueing from the mudroom. The shirts in the pot bloomed white almost as soon as the blueing touched the water.

Now we wait, she said. She sat down at the table and I sat down across from her. I thought she would tell me a tale of Rügen. But when she began to talk, it was only to tell me a story that she had heard from Mrs. Muehls. A woman named Mrs. Hiram McDonald had become deranged with religious excitement and then had grown afraid of everyone. She thought her husband and his friends were out to get her. Eventually, she attacked her children. She broke all the furniture and windows in the house.

The window over the sink filled with steam. My mother

rubbed at a spot on the table with the tip of her finger. She looked out the window. I tried to picture what our house would be like with all the windows and furniture broken. I wondered if the glass would fall inside or out, if it would be hard to tear the legs from the table. I imagined it would be difficult to do these things, to break everything inside a house into pieces.

She rubbed the table again. She looked like someone trying to inscribe a circle with the tip of her finger, like she wanted to mark a place for everyone to see. Then she leaned over her lap in the way one does when one's belly hurts and inhaled deeply and sobbed one single sob.

I froze.

Of course she gathered herself before she went any further. She straightened and caught her breath. She stood up. She went into the mudroom for the pail. She went down the steps and crossed the yard and levered the handle until the pump came to life. Then she stood in the shadow of the house as if she had forgotten what she had come to do. She let the water gush in a white froth onto the ground.

I watched her. When you are only a child, you do not offer your mother a hand. She always stands beyond you, on the other side of a dividing line that you cannot cross. So I have to confess that I stood there dumb as a post while she wiped her eyes on the back of her sleeve. When the light moved across her face, she looked years younger, as if she was still a girl.

Down by the brewery, two boys used a blue rubber hose to rinse brown bottles in the delivery yard. They stacked the crates of empties by a hatchway. Across the street, the plate glass window of a haberdasher's shop, straw bowlers arranged like a landscape at the foot of a dummy who sat with a felt fedora on his head. The river out ahead then, in a wide space unmarked by trees.

The road sloped down. I passed the post office with its American flag curled up like a chrysalis, and then I passed the train depot where a man in a wool flannel hat had drawn a map on a piece of newsprint and was showing the map to the stationmaster. The stationmaster kept shaking his head but this had no effect. The man with the map stayed fixed on his subject and his voice carried clear out into the road.

Up ahead, a girl who looked like Hattie stepped along the railroad tracks. She was barefoot. A girl who must have been her older sister walked behind her with her feet swaddled in burlap bags tied off with twine. Every few feet, one or the other bent down and picked up a piece of coal and dropped the coal into her apron. Fires burned in the shanties below the railroad station and columns of blue smoke stood in the air. When I breathed out, I could see my breath as if my very soul kept escaping. I did not mind this at all.

The railroad fell away behind me and then the river was only a smell in the air. The road turned and a tall house came up beside me. It sat apart from its neighbors and at one time must have been white but now was mostly bare wood. A rusty gate stood at the foot of the walkway. The gate was not hinged to the fence but leaned against the pickets like a bicycle someone had forgotten.

I turned the bell and waited. When no one came, I walked up and down on the porch and watched my breath cloud in the cold air. The porch had seen better days, just like the house. It was littered with old webs and brown leaves, and the desiccated carcasses of last summer's beetles dangled legless from the windowsills. I was just about to turn the bell again when a man in a worn black suit cracked the door. "Full up," he barked. "Try Mendota."

I hesitated. I knew what everyone knew about Mendota. It was the name of a town and it was the name of a lake, but whenever anyone said Mendota, the only thing he really meant was the state asylum for the insane. People were said to go inside and be held for life, as if a person were a thing that could be captured and kept, like a mouse in a jar.

I held the package up so he could see it.

"I have a delivery," I said. My voice cracked a little. "William Oliver sent me."

The man in the greasy black suit looked at me and he looked at the package. Then he held the door open and I stepped into a dark hallway with dark carpets and dark walls. A staircase disappeared to a second floor. The place reeked of human filth: used chamber pots, unwashed clothes, flop sweat unending. The man acted as if he had not noticed or did not mind. I put my sleeve over my mouth and breathed through the cloth.

"This way," the man said. He led me past the front parlor, where a short man balanced on a settee, his wooden legs holstered in leather rigging he wore outside of his trousers. A thin woman sat in a chair under the window. She was attached to the chair by a rope that snaked over the upholstery and ended in a knot bound to a ring in the floor. A young boy stood by the window and looked out at the street. He was covered with so much long silky hair that he looked like a dog. An old man was chained by one wrist to a bolt in the wall. When he saw me, he raised his free arm but his arm ended in a flipper, its three fingers curled roots of what fingers ought to be. And then I saw that he was not an old man but a boy. He opened his mouth and all I saw was a black gash.

A tall, thin young man paced the length of the hallway. He wore old-fashioned clothes, a shirt with a broad collar, one point up, one point down, like a crooked wing, trousers that laced with rigging at the waist, a vest that did not fit him. His hair fell over his eyes but he was handsome, with an oval face and large green eyes. He stepped back when I passed as if I had gotten too close to him. Then he strode toward the front door. After that, he came back toward us and stood in the doorway of the kitchen while we conducted our business.

"They come here when they get out of Mendota," the man in the suit said. "Or they come here instead of going to Mendota. I'm glad to say that we are able to give them a place to stay."

Long before the lunatics arrived, Indians had lived where Mendota stood. They built magical earthworks in the shape of animals, and the woods grew up around the animal shapes like a queer wild fence. The state had left the old Indian earthworks alone when they built the hospital. I had once seen a picture on a postcard. Two wide towers capped with roofs like hats and a huge cupola shaped like a bell. But in the shade, a heave of earth that might have been the leg of a bear or the long spine of a running deer or some other wild thing that came close to the place where wildness was meant to be vanquished.

I set the package on the table and the man in the suit told me his name was James Pulliam. There commenced a wailing in the front room but he just shrugged. "She cries for her baby but she never had a baby," he said. "Never mind. We can do nothing for her."

The room stank of decomposing potatoes and urine, and a canopy of greasy cobwebs swayed in a draft overhead. The boy in the doorway swung his arms and watched us. I caught him looking at me. I smiled at him and he ducked his chin.

James Pulliam reached into his pocket and lifted three bills from his purse and counted them out on the table. "I will oblige you for a receipt," he said. He stood back and crossed his arms over his chest.

"I do not have anything to write on," I said.

He sighed and looked around. "Here," he said. He cut the twine on the package with a pocketknife and opened the brown paper and folded one edge and ran the dull side of the blade along the fold, which he then opened until the crease lay along the table edge and he could tear a piece of paper away. This he folded in half and tore again. He handed the two pieces to me along with a pencil stub he pulled from his waistband. "William Oliver will want a record, too," he said.

Through the window in the back door, I could see a small room where coats hung on hooks and then through the back door out to the yard. The boy in the doorway took a step toward us.

"I'm busy now," James Pulliam said, and the boy stopped. James Pulliam watched me lean over the table. "Don't be afraid," he said. "He's harmless. He suffers from curiosity."

"He is all right where he is," I said. I knew this boy was not like other boys, but I did not think that curiosity could be an illness. His defect must arise from something hidden, a wound or twist so deep that it showed itself only in his lonely smile or in the duck of his chin or in his fearful and hopeful approach or in the way he backed away when bidden. None of these alone would be sufficient to account for his family's despair—something that must have mounted such that they finally caused him to be sent away to live here. But taken together, these things made the boy into someone apart. For a moment I felt a pang for him. He was not covered with hair nor did he need to be tied to a wall. In fact, he did not look so different from the rest of us. But here he was, in a house with a moaning woman and a strung-up dwarf, with a little boy who seemed more fish than child, with a boy more dog than man. Perhaps I felt for him because he showed me the way we measure the quality of difference. It is true that I have been attentive to such arithmetic ever since. None of us is so without flaw that we ourselves might not be accounted for in just the way that someone had accounted for this boy.

Now he stood in the doorway and swung his arms.

"Edwin," said James Pulliam in a warning voice.

Edwin took three more steps back into the hallway. But I could see him yet, his green eyes, his dark hair, his oval face. He grinned and ducked his head again.

"Three dollars for the two weeks," I said, writing as I spoke. "This week and next."

When I was through, James Pulliam followed me to the front door. In the parlor, the woman tied to the chair still mourned the baby she had never had. The boy with hair like a dog rested an accordion on his lap and the bellows huffed and the first notes clanged and then he played with his eyes closed. The man with the wooden legs pushed himself up from his sofa with the palms of his hands and stepped into the center of the room. When the accordion was at full pitch, the man began to dance, or do something that must have been dancing, because it could not have been anything else. I saw him reflected in the hall looking glass, the top of his head bobbing up and down in time to the notes, and the sound of his wooden pegs like the tapping of a coal miner trapped in a mine.

James Pulliam opened the front door and held it for me so I would have to pass beneath his arm. Edwin walked up to me and reached out and touched my sleeve. James Pulliam said, "Edwin," and Edwin dropped his hand to his side. I stepped onto the porch, where the air was cold and clean and my thoughts ran away.

Edwin watched me as I walked up the road, but when I turned the corner, he dropped out of sight. I could still smell the stench of the place and taste it on my tongue. I held on to a lamppost and leaned over and spat. When I raised my head, I saw a dark bird rising high on the wind and then turning in spirals up beneath the clouds. It might have been a hawk or it might have been a vulture with a plucked head, but I pretended it was an eagle, a bird so majestic that the very idea of it cannot fail to inspire thoughts of what it means to be free.

I got my coat from its nail and Inge followed me out into the yard, where a thin wind blew the weeds against the buildings with a sound like a snake sliding through leaves. The stars began to appear on the horizon and spread over the purple sky. I picked out the Big Dipper and then followed the darkness to the Seven Sisters and counted the six who danced and the dim trail of the seventh who used to dance but now had vanished. We passed the druggist and the brewery and the new telephone company building, and the lights of town came on around us, yellow forms shaping the black silhouettes of houses. To my left, I saw a shadow move and still and move again. It bore no definite shape but moved when I moved and stopped when I stopped. For half a block I told myself that the shadow was nothing, the long arm of a tree branch waving in the wind, a sheet left flapping on a line. But as I walked, the shadow kept pace and moved across the snowy ground until it finally disappeared against a line of dark trees, all moving in the dry cold wind.

Inge pulled a cigarette from her pocket, pinched it between her lips, lit a match, and leaned into the flame. I turned my face away so I would not have to breathe the smoke.

At the corner, the interurban came up on its silver tracks, its sparks falling like comets, its glass walls shimmering, its steel wheels rumbling with a sound that made me think there could be no home in this world. Men and women in dark clothes were arranged on wooden seats inside, and the conductor in his blue coat and peaked hat leaned against a pole at the front of the car. A dark-haired boy with a dark hat turned toward the window just as I turned toward him. Our eyes met and he put his palm flat against the glass, as if he could touch me through the window. I turned away out of shyness and then looked back but by then the clacking cars had gone and the light was gone and the boy behind the glass had disappeared.

Inge sucked deeply on her cigarette and the smoke rolled away in the wind. Finally she said, "It is a terrible thing, what happened to your mother."

I nodded.

"I thought you could explain it," she said.

I shook my head. I did not trust myself to answer politely. Inge always pretended to take a motherly interest in me, but I knew she just wanted to ferret out my story as if it was an animal she could flush from a hole.

She held the cigarette between her thumb and her forefinger like a man, turning it so she could study the burning tip. "It is not just to satisfy myself that I ask," she said. "The others were also wondering."

I held myself still. I did not want my mother to become one of the stories that Inge and the others told over their washtubs. The spurned girl who drank carbolic acid and died where her lover would be sure to find her. The woman who drowned herself in a rain barrel, as if that were even possible. The bride who ate the tips of four boxes of matches. The young married woman who suddenly disappeared.

What was there to say? I thought of my mother on her bed. Martha had finally cut her dress open. When the doctor stitched my mother, the sound she made was so bad that I had fallen to the floor with my arms over my head. But what a man does to a woman is the same, here or there.

Old leaves rolled over a roof and fluttered silently to the ground.

"She had a terrible accident," I said at last.

"What kind of accident?" Inge leaned toward me. "What happened?"

I did not reply.

People used to hang glass chimes from the eaves of their porch roofs, just by the front door, and in the evening when the breeze blew, their tinkling sound was everywhere.

Inge peered at me. "I do not know what to think of you," she said.

I stepped into the street and she followed me, smoke billowing behind her until she pitched the last of her cigarette into the gutter. Down the road, the lamplighter made his way toward us. He carried his wick on a long pole and paused at each of the gas lamps, where he touched flame to pilot and the glass bloomed with yellow light. I could not see his eyes for the deep shadow cast by the brim of his hat, and then he disappeared behind us as if passing into darkness. When we got to the far corner Inge put her hand on my arm and stared at me, her gaze intense. Then she shook her head and put her hands in her coat pockets and said good night. I made my way along the road that ran above the river. A shadow flickered along with me, keeping pace through yards and streets and pausing at the corner where I stood to let a drayman's wagon pass. Up ahead, the street was a long dim chain of thin-pooled light.

5

My mother always made sure we followed the old ways. She walked into the woods early in November to find a Yule log. On Christmas Eve she put this in the fireplace and kept it burning all night. In the morning, she sprinkled the ashes around the house to protect us from those who would do us harm. She decorated the tree by herself and kept it hidden in the front room until late in the afternoon on Christmas Day, when she rang a special bell to summon us. We filed into the room and saw the tree for the first time, as if she alone could summon magic. She told us that when she was a girl she could hear the silver church bells from the great town of Veneta, which had been lost when a flood came over the Baltic and everything had been submerged. All that was left were the smooth sands without a stone bigger than your fist, and the color of seawater as it washed over sand, and the weeds and the biscuit-colored sails of the boats, or the red sails of the little clippers that plied the harbor, and the beaches with their pebbles and crushed shells, and a stone pier decorated with flags and lanterns that stretched far out to deeper water. On Christmas Eve, she stood on the edge of the white cliffs in the

complete darkness of early night, waiting for the golden seagull, which was said to sparkle even more brilliantly than the
stars in heaven.

Now Hattie and I stood shivering in the front room and
watched Martha hang nuts and apples on a spindly tree with
thread from the mending box. I thought we should build up the
fire in the stove but Martha said no. She always took my father's
side. I imagine she felt that the weight of trying to be a mother
to Hattie and me was a considerable weight indeed.

I picked up a walnut tied in a bow with a twist of red yarn.
"Here," I said. But she put one finger up and glared at me and
said, "Put that back."

Morning light came up around us and ice lay in long glassy
black stripes on the road where the wagons had passed. As I
watched, a car glided slowly past. I did not know who would
bring an automobile out in this weather. Cars did not have
heaters and you had to drive with a robe over your knees for
comfort. Or this is what I observed. I had never yet ridden in
a car.

Hattie turned her back to the tree and wished out loud for
mittens. Martha told her she had better be careful when she
went out, because the ash man dressed in his animal skins and
plaited straw might find her and demand whatever she had. If
she did not give it to him, he would steal her away to his house
of twigs and leaves and she would never be seen again. But
Hattie made a face and told her to shut up because this was Wisconsin and there were no ash men here.

We celebrated that night without a goose. My father had
gotten an old hen from Mrs. Muehls. I singed its pinfeathers
and washed it and stuffed it with bread and a little sausage and
onions and a few mushrooms I had picked in the woods and let

dry on a twine I strung up in the mudroom. The bird was surprisingly passable to eat. There were many things Martha and my father might say about me, but they could not contest that I could cook.

After supper, my father handed each of us a brown packet containing a fresh pair of black stockings, a paper with a new needle pushed through it, and a new spool of black thread. He seemed very pleased with himself, even if my sisters and I were disappointed with his choice.

He reached for his cup and looked into it and then let the legs of his chair drop back to the floor. He stood and went to the mudroom and came back with the newspaper and a bottle, which he uncorked with one hand. He sat down and leaned forward and ran whiskey into his cup. He lifted the cup and drank.

I sat very still in my chair. Martha glanced at me quickly and then looked away.

My father read the paper quietly for a time. Then he said, "This man Ira Miller was arrested last night on the charge of killing his own horses. Not two days ago this same man went to his barn to feed his horses and found two of them dead with their throats cut. He also found a note saying that there are too many horses in the world and all of Ira Miller's horses were going to have to die. He has fifteen horses, so this must be the work of a madman. But now we know better. Now we know Miller was insured. All he wanted was the money." He paused. "Only a very stupid man will kill for money," he said. He took a drink from his cup and cut his eyes at me. "That is the best way to get caught, and when it is over and you are sitting in your prison cell, what do you have? Nothing. It is better to kill for principle because principle will never leave you. Twenty years later, you will still know that you did the right thing."

He lifted the bottle and poured a little more whiskey into his cup. He had turned his shirtsleeves up to protect the cuffs and his arms were large and well muscled. I looked at his wrists and at the width of his hand, the breadth of his palm, his unmarked skin. Always the same, one thing laid over another until the one fact that I had was too big for me to ignore.

I never doubted that he killed my mother. I had no question of it. I had seen him beat her so badly that she had to stay in bed for days afterward, her face split like an overripe peach. I had seen him kick the chair out from under her. I had seen him crack her over her back so hard with a piece of wood that splinters flew through the air. It was not at all hard to think that on the day my mother died, my father had just gone too far. Pushed her into the sharpened end of an upended spade. Plowed into her with his knife. He tossed that knife around often enough at home and never failed to get my attention when he did so.

I stood and picked up his plate and dropped it into the dishpan and watched it sink like a flat stone.

"Second," my father said. His voice drilled into my back. "You need witnesses if you are going to take a man's freedom. Without proof they don't have a thing. This is the way things are in America. A man's life is his own. It don't belong to anyone but him."

He stood and dropped the paper to the table. "I'm going to work," he said. He shrugged into his coat and looked around for his hat. And then he snapped his fingers as if he had just remembered something and put his hand on Martha's shoulder.

"I saw that boy, that George Kolb, on the street," he said. "He was coming this way. I told him not to bother. I told him your place is here. So we have seen the last of him, good riddance." He narrowed his eyes. "I make myself clear?" he said. "You understand?"

Martha nodded but she looked like someone had kicked her in the stomach. And when my father was gone, she sat at the table with her hands over her cheeks and eyes so I could not see her face, but I knew that she was crying. George Kolb had been her beau for almost a year. He was a mild-mannered young man who worked in a bank and wore tiny gold-wire spectacles and carried a leather case that contained nothing but his lunch but which he was sure would one day contain the important papers that befitted an important man. It did not seem possible that anyone would love a boy with such a high hairless forehead, but Martha said she did.

"George will never put up with this," I said. I did not believe that but I had to say something. "George will be back. You know George will be back."

She cried harder.

"It will be all right," I said.

She lifted her chin. "How?"

I could hear Hattie murmuring a song in the front room: *My handsome winsome Johnny.* "He would not have to know," I offered. "You could meet him on the sly."

But Martha just cried harder and reached over and gripped my hand. "I cannot!" she said. Then she fell to sobbing again.

Hattie came down the hall. Her braces made the squeaky sound they made when they had gotten wet and were beginning to dry. She looked at Martha and then she looked at me. "Why is Martha crying?" she said. But of course there was no explaining it. Martha and I might talk about our father, but we never talked about him with Hattie. I suppose we wanted to protect her. Now I think she knew as much as we did all along. She lived in his house after all.

"Shush," I said. "Bring the cards."

When Hattie came back with the deck, Martha sat up and blew her nose on one of my mother's handkerchiefs, which she took from her pocket. Her eyes were liquid and her cheeks were red but she told Hattie to deal her in.

Our Christmas supper dishes went unfinished. Darkness came up around the house and the kitchen window went black. We played Old Maid, passing the single queen among us like a ghost, until it was well past Hattie's bedtime. Outside, the wind moved through the evergreens, their dark boughs rustling and rustling like the waves of some shoreline long forgotten. The pale stars surrounded and surrounding them, the stars.

The next day I left the laundry at lunchtime and walked into the center of town, where the new courthouse stood in an open square. Its huge tower resembled a spire rising into the blue Wisconsin sky, as if justice was a kind of heavenly supplication to the things we all thought we believed in and could count on. This is an American concept. We pray for justice above all else, even if we do not love the law and do not love our lawyers or our litigation. We like to think that everything we do is based in fairness. This is our most dearly held illusion.

On the day we buried my mother, the grave diggers set up an awning over the open pit and we waited in the shade. My father stood with his back to us. Martha stood silently behind him. Hattie wept and touched her braces through her clothes. Down below the bluffs, the river burned silver in the sun and cut between the dark trees of the woods and then disappeared under the limestone cliffs that ran to the east of town.

The preacher read from a book he took from his pocket. Halfway through, he stopped and took his coat off and laid the coat on the ground at his feet. My mother told us that one day God would call us back to Him and we would live as angels amidst the finery of the sky. But there was nothing uplifting or beautiful about the open pit in the sun-parched ground, the dry grass unbending to the shovel's touch. You might imagine that I felt this way because I had grown skeptical of reverence, but I think anyone standing on that hot piece of ground on that blistering day would have felt the same. I do not think my lack of faith is all that unique. We all have our reasons.

Toward the end, towering thunderheads began to build on the western horizon. A wind came up and lifted our clothes, and the canvas awning flapped and rippled. My sisters held their dresses down with their hands, and my uncle Carl held the brim of his hat.

My father leaned over and took a rusty spade from one of the grave diggers. He lifted the spade and moved the first clods of dirt into the darkness. When he handed the spade to Martha, tiny shards of red paint from the spade's peeling handle stuck to his hands.

Around us, a rolling field of basalt angels and blocks of granite and stone. Carl stood the spade in the earth and the grave diggers came up behind him with their shovels. My father put his arm around Hattie. He put his arm around Martha. They leaned into him and he dropped his chin into Martha's hair. Then he stepped back and walked down the hill. The sun passed behind the great slope of clouds and the grass flattened and the first large drops of rain came.

Now I walked up and down in the street in the cold shadow of the courthouse. It had courtrooms above and offices below. Down a set of gray granite steps that must have been quarried just west of town where the earth gave up stone in slabs, the words *Police Station* were painted in an arc on a set of frosted glass doors, *Police* on one side, *Station* on the other. I watched a thickset man in a black coat come up the steps and square his hat and then unwrap the reins for his horse from the hitching rail and lead the horse down the street.

I turned my face to the sky. "Help me," I said. Someone passing by might have thought I was talking to myself or to no one in particular or maybe even to God, since my words sounded so much like a prayer. But of course none of that would be true and certainly not the idea that I would talk to God. I was talking to my mother, whom I imagined stayed somewhere where she could see me still. I did not really believe this but I told myself it was true so that I would not feel so alone.

My father killed my mother. I tried the words out under my breath, as if I already stood in front of a policeman behind a counter, as if he had a pencil in his hand and was ready to take down the things I said. I had to imagine myself speaking at all, for I was not sure I would be able to say anything, even if I was sure I knew what the words should be. All at once I imagined my father in his jail cell, weeping. I thought of the terrible pain I would feel, to see him there and in his suffering know that I was the cause. Even in the bright light of day, that picture caused a searing sensation in my chest. I wrapped my arms around my waist and felt tears start behind my eyes. I angrily brushed them away. Girls were taught to appeal to men in all things, but I could not be two things at once, not the angel of justice of whom I dreamt, and not my father's daughter to boot. No one could do that.

Men were out having lunch and some of them looked curiously at me as they passed by. I slipped on a slick of ice and steadied myself.

Up on a hill, men climbed among the raw yellow beams of a new house, knocking boards together. The coppery smell of snow came on the wind and the choked rumble of the interurban unfurled across town and blue clouds incandescent in a wash of sunlight brightened overhead. I was surprised to see construction going on when the day was cold and the earth was frozen, but I realized the foundation had already been set and the men worked in the rafters. Walking one of the planks, a boy with dark hair and light eyes, who balanced perfectly and then jumped from the joist to the ground.

He wore the same canvas pants he was wearing the day he carried my mother into the house. I tried to recollect where he had touched her, whether under shoulder bone or hip bone, her body a parcel that did not belong to him. But all I remembered was the way he turned to look at me as he backed out through the door, the last of the men to disappear in the shimmering heat.

Now some trick of sunlight made his face seem luminous. The wind ruffled his hair. He looked up from his board and patted his pockets as if he was searching for something. Then he caught sight of me and a look of surprise came over his face. He held up his hand. "Fräulein," he called. "Wait."

No one called me fräulein. Not even my mother, who otherwise thought it might be useful for me to learn the ways of an island I had never seen and that had already passed into history. I lived in America. I was born here. This was a place where all men were said to be created equal and therefore entitled to be free. I took these ideas seriously. The word *fräulein* belonged to some other girl, and I looked over my shoulder as if I expected her to come up behind me.

The boy trotted down the hillside and stood in front of me. He pushed his black hat back on his head and grinned. He was a little out of breath and his eyes shone and his cheeks were covered with stubble.

"Fräulein," he repeated. "What's your name?"

"Marie," I said, but I spoke so softly that I thought he would not hear me. He nodded.

"I am August Bethke," he said. He pronounced his last name the old German way, so it sounded like *Bait-ka.* "Pleased to meet you." He picked up my hand, limp as a dead fish at my side, and pumped my arm up and down. My hand went with his in a way that made me feel that it no longer belonged to me. He laughed and squeezed my fingers.

What love feels like is no secret, but it is hard to put into words. You will know this to be true if you have ever fallen in love, and who among us has not? Girls are trained to fall in love. This is the one thing at which they must not fail. Failure means they are doomed to become mannish, with brusque phrases and sharp tongues and weary clothes that have been passed down to them by their married sisters. I was reared to distrust a mannish woman. In fact, I was reared to distrust all women, with no woman more untrustworthy than the woman who has failed at love.

August dropped my hand.

"Where are you going?" he said.

"Nowhere," I muttered. My face felt hot. My tongue felt thick. I blushed again. I thought of Martha, turning beet red whenever George thrust some stupid bouquet of daisies at her. We were surely cut from the same cloth.

"Nowhere? Out here by yourself? You are very brave." Once again he touched his fingers to my hand. The nape of my neck tingled and a wave of sparkles rose behind my eyes.

The sound of hammering came from the house.

When I was seventeen, the things I knew about boys came from the boys I knew in school where they stayed among themselves and only ventured close to girls when they had something disgusting to drop down our dresses. I had that experience myself, visited on me by a heavyset boy named Charles Miller, whose family came from Bavaria and ran a butcher shop in the center of town. Charles divested himself of a frog and was disappointed when I was happy to find the thing in my chemise. I did not mind frogs and thought to make a pet of this one.

At lunchtime the boys ran out onto the playground and sat in a circle in the dirt and traded their food, bargaining and jeering, until the best among them felt that he had improved his lot as much as he could and the others crept away to eat their poor crusts in defeat. The girls stayed inside and dutifully stuck with the items our mothers had packed for us.

When you got right down to it, my father was the only boy I had seen up close in a regular way. He was the one who teased me. He was the one who chased me around the house with a spider. He was the one who took my hand as if he intended to shake it and then rolled the bones together until I dropped wailing to my knees. He was the one who laughed at me when I cried.

August looked at me with interest. I realized he was waiting for me to say something.

"I am going back to work," I said. "I was on an errand."

He looked me up and down, taking in my skirt, my blouse, my ratty old coat. I felt my face burn again. It was as if he could see through everything I wore, down to my bare skin.

He gestured up at the skeleton of the house. "My father has a company. I work with him."

He was much taller than me and I felt the way he stood over me. Just behind that, I felt William Oliver's laundry drawing me, or maybe it was William Oliver himself, exerting his great magnetic pull. On this day, I did not want to return late. I did not want to be fired. I did not want to find myself in front of my father with no explanation for how this had come to pass.

"I need to get back," I said.

August smiled. He had very white teeth, each a perfect shape. "You should see yourself," he said. "What a mess." The gentle way he said *mess* made me realize that he meant just the opposite. He smiled again and brushed my hair back with his bare fingers as if he was already familiar with every part of me.

He leaned toward me. "I know you won't believe me," he said softly. "But I remember you."

A man stepped around the corner of the house. He held a hammer over his head and he waved it in the air. "Augie," he yelled. "Hey, Augie."

I looked up at August. "Augie," I said. I smiled. But my skin felt as if it had been stretched too tight. I already held August's name like an ache I wanted to touch again and again.

He grimaced and shook his head. Then, very tenderly, he cupped my cheek with his palm, his hand heavy and steady, and I leaned in until I was nothing but that hand, that weight.

"I wanted to help you," he said. He paused as if he could not find the right words. Then he brushed my hair back again and dropped his hand to his side. "It bothered me," he said at last. "It bothered me a lot."

I tried to picture August thinking of me, but I could not picture the look on my face when I saw him with my mother in his arms. I could only know the sound of my mother's terrible cry. The rest ran away.

In the far distance, a crow called. A second crow answered. *Two for joy*, I thought, and my chest lifted in just the way it would if something inside had come alive. August stepped closer and I pushed at my hair and then I smiled at him and reached over and took his hand. He gripped my fingers hard and looked down at me with a look so raw that I thought I might fall to my knees. We stood like that for a moment, but then the man up at the house yelled August's name again and I knew I had to get back to work. Still we did not move. After a time, a faint whirl of snow showered down around us. The snowflakes sparkled like glass.

When I lay in bed that night, I could hear Martha pacing the floor. Up. Back. Again. Again. It seemed impossible for a thin person to have such a heavy foot but she did, as if with each step she could stamp the thing that ailed her out of existence. I listened for a long time. I knew she was thinking of George. I knew she was the one of us who always obeyed. I knew she got no reward for that, either.

No one knows why we are drawn to the ones we love. Perhaps the things that happen to us when we are children explain everything that comes later. Perhaps after all the mistaken ideas our parents have about us we feel that we have met someone who recognizes us for who we are and who will hold our spirit like a flame. Some things just lack definition. Love is not always like a love song. It is the darkest emotion and has to masquerade as joy or else we would never dare swim in its river.

Just past midnight, Martha dropped heavily onto her bed. I watched the tree outside my room, its branches black against the black sky. Just through the window glass at the edge of the curtain, the star Vega burned through the night. I thought of August. I felt my heart rise.

6

Not far from where my mother grew up, a ruined castle stood on the hillside above a deep black lake. My mother said that she had seen this castle herself many times while walking in the hills of Rügen. Not much remained, just the foundation, a weedy pit, and a half wall with the shape of one window open in the stone.

Very few people ventured near that castle and almost no one went into the lake. Everyone knew that eerie things happened there. Some said a devil lived in the water. Some said a goddess. My mother was sure it was the latter. On bright moonlit nights, she said, you could see a beautiful woman come through the woods and down to the lake. If you stood quietly, you could see her strip to her skin and then slide into the water, which itself became luminous as soon as she submerged. She was surrounded by a host of pretty girls—her servants—and the girls followed her into the lake. There they all disappeared. Eventually, you would hear them as they splashed. When they appeared again, they would be dressed like brides, long white veils streaming behind them as they made their way back into the trees.

My mother said it was very dangerous for a man to watch

the beautiful woman. If he saw her, he would be drawn to touch the water where she bathed. If he touched the water where she bathed, he would lose all of his power. If he lost all of his power, the lake would swallow him whole. If the lake swallowed him whole, he would never be heard of again. These were known facts on Rügen. Everyone discussed these things openly.

Still, a long time ago, several men decided the warnings were silly. These men had grown up on Rügen and should have known better, but they felt they were modern and therefore entertained modern ideas. They believed they could hold these particularities in contempt. So they brought a boat to the lake and left it to float overnight. When they returned in the morning, it was gone. After a long search, they found it tied in the top of a beech tree on the far shore. They knew it was the woman in white who had taken it. And soon after that, one of the men went missing. But only one. The others went back to town and did what men always do. But you never caught them near that lake again.

When my mother told us this story, she told it in such an intense way it seemed that she had delivered a secret message, something that she wanted us to be sure to remember. But my sisters and I paid little attention. We asked about the dress the beautiful woman wore before she went into the lake. We wondered if her hair was white or golden. Hattie wanted to know if her feet were finned like a fish. And my mother smiled and petted our hair and told us not worry about such simple things. Her voice sounded sugary but I knew she was irritated by our questions.

I don't think it would have been possible for us to understand. The lakes of Wisconsin were deep but nothing emerged from them, certainly not magic, and certainly not women who trailed light behind. Our lakes had rocky bottoms, and if you swam to the limit you would find nothing but a barrel or a

wagon wheel or some other piece of trash. No men went fishing and disappeared, except for the men who got drunk and
fell out of boats. There was no accounting for such behavior,
but I suppose they had better drown and hurt only themselves
rather than bring their drunkenness back to their wives and
sweethearts.

In the morning, I woke early. Snow had fallen overnight and
it was too cold to sleep. My quilt had dropped to the floor and
I lay bunched and shivering under an icy sheet. I could see
my breath in the bedroom air. My father never did have a free
hand with the stove wood and I used to dress under the covers
on winter mornings. This day was no different and I saw no
point in remaining in a cold house. I put a piece of bread in
my pocket and set out for work, where at least it would be
warm.

By the time I reached the mill bridge, the horizon radiated
pink. To the north, the farmland grew faintly white in the rising
light and the river slid away like a great ashen whale. It seemed
the world in all of its cold emptiness belonged only to me. This
feeling brought me no gladness.

Just as I came up to James Pulliam's house, the leading rim
of the sun appeared behind the trees and the snow turned blue.
Edwin stood in the front yard, his breath curling around his
head. He should have had a coat but he was outside in his
shirtsleeves. He tossed something to a squirrel waiting on its
haunches under a tree, but when I came up, the squirrel cocked
its head and stiffened. Edwin looked back over his shoulder
and saw me and then came across the yard in swift, pushing
strides. I stopped and waited with the fence between us.

His lips moved and he turned to gesture at the air beside
him. "Where are you going?" he said. His voice was low and

clear. His forearms were bare and his hands were raw and red in the cold. He leaned toward me and flicked his thumbs against his index fingers but he did not scare me.

"Work," I replied. I smiled.

"Where do you work?" He did not meet my eyes when he spoke but looked past me to the pink sky.

"William Oliver's laundry," I said.

He made no comment about that but just started off along the fence that stood between us like a line in the land. I followed him on the other side. He looked thin and cold.

"Are you hungry?" I asked.

He nodded. I reached into my pocket and pulled out my slice of bread.

"Here," I said. "Take it."

He ate quietly and carefully. He did not appear to want one crumb to go to waste.

"Better?" I said.

He nodded.

We came to the end of the fence. The world became brighter and colors appeared, the pale yellow siding of the house next door, the red harness on a horse that jingled past pulling a wagon behind, the driver humped over, a green blanket spread across his lap.

Edwin stared intently at something beyond the trees. Then he turned and strode away without a word. When he got to the porch, he began to walk up and down. He kept his gaze trained on the sky, as if he saw something none of the rest of us could see.

I waited and waited but when he made no move to return, I went on my way. Houses began to send smoke from their chimneys and the smoke rose white against the sky and the familiar smell of coal fires filled the air. A jay stood blue on a fence post and then flew in a blur into a black tree where snow fell. The wind rose. My hairpins threatened to come undone like threads unraveling.

I heard him before I saw him, his footsteps pounding in the dirt, and then he fell in step beside me. He swung his arms and looked at me through the hair that fell over his eyes and every so often stared at the sky, where he would scan the horizon for unknown things.

The sky just looked like the sky to me, the clear blue you sometimes get after a snowfall, the morning sharply drawn under all of that glistening light, the whole of the country coming awake at the same time.

We passed the place where they sold ice cream in the summer. Its blank windows rattled in the wind. Just on the other side, Edwin stopped and put his hand on my arm.

"There is a war," he said urgently. "I am the angel. I am the light."

I stopped. "Edwin," I said.

He looked down at me.

"What do you mean?" I said. "I do not understand."

His expression flattened and he bent down and looked me in the eye. His lips moved and he stared at me for a moment. "You are in danger," he said. Then he dropped his hand to his side and turned away and made his way back up the street, his shadow thin on the snow.

I tucked my chin into my coat collar and pushed my hands deeper into my pockets. A wagon came around the corner and I stepped out of the way. The horse dropped steaming horse apples into the road while the driver clucked to him as they passed.

By the time I got to the laundry, William Oliver's man had the fires lit and three kettles simmered on the stoves. I hung my coat on its hook. Then I took up the first duffle and unbound its cord and pulled the sheets into my basket and hoisted the basket onto my hip. I climbed the wooden ladder to one of the vats and began wrestling the sheets in one by one, stirring after each addition just the way you stir when you make a cake. William Oliver stood in the doorway and watched me.

"You are here early," he said.

I nodded. I dropped another sheet into the water.

"I do not pay overtime," he said.

I did not reply.

"Mary," he said. "Did you hear me?"

I turned to look at him and I nodded again.

He sighed. Now he stood in the doorway and watched me stir the wash. I did not like to be caught alone with him. I did not like the feeling of his breath on the back of my neck or the faint brushing of his fingers when he touched my hand. He always pulled his hand back, so I suppose he meant for me to imagine that his touch was inadvertent, an accident. But I knew he touched me on purpose. And when he could not touch me, he watched me, and it felt as if his gaze was another kind of touch.

When my basket was empty, he came over and took it from me and then took my hand and helped me down from the ladder. He would never have dared do this if the others were there, but he had me alone and there was nothing for it but to go along. I shrank from him but he did not notice or if he did, he did not care.

"Who says chivalry is dead?" he said. He was very pleased with himself, as if it took a big man to take the hand of a girl whom he has frightened. He knotted his fingers in mine. I tried to pull my hand away. He tightened his grip and walked with me to the wall, where another duffle waited. The first had come from the Hotel Vanderbilt, which was a mean little place that gave itself airs, and the second came from a private household, for it was tagged with a surname. I knew it would be filled with underpants and all the other things I did not like to touch. But it gave me a good reason to pull free of William Oliver's hand, and this time he did not try to stop me. I squatted down and unknotted the cord on the duffle and lifted it and shook it out over my basket. There is such a thing as the greater of two evils.

I found only sheets and pillowcases. William Oliver watched me. He rocked back on his heels and when I lifted the basket, he took it from me and put his arm around my waist and propelled me over to the ladder. His hand was heavy on my hip and he bent his cheek to my hair and sighed deeply. My heart pounded. I did not know what time it was. I did not know when anyone else might come. I had no idea what he wanted. But that was not true, for I knew exactly what he wanted, or at least I thought I did.

In the end he returned the basket to me in great haste and made for the soap bucket, as if all along he had had no other intention but to study his inventory. I looked out to the yard and saw Inge in her dark gray coat walking toward us, her lunch pail glinting in the sun.

7

Of all the stories she told me, my mother never said anything about how she met my father. She never said anything at all about love. She told me about dwarves who lived under the hills or crowded the beach in their merry thousands, terribly dangerous to the girl who came upon them alone. She showed me a garnet bracelet she had brought with her from the island, its little faceted stones set in gold. When I was little, she had me convinced that this bracelet had been made by the white dwarves that flew around like tiny birds when they were not busy making jewelry. But the bracelet disappeared when my father lost his job at the mill and my mother never mentioned it again.

Mrs. Muehls raised geese along with her chickens. If you went to her house in the daytime you would see the geese facing each other with their red bills nearly touching and their gray feathers flat as a smoothed sheet, too stupid to move out of each other's way. Mrs. Muehls also raised two daughters, both so short and thick that it looked as if their shirtwaists had been upholstered to their backs and then stitched down at the waist so that nothing could escape. The girls were married now and gone from home, but Mrs. Muehls made sure they returned to her house every week for Sunday dinner, where my mother said Mrs. Muehls lectured them on their shortcomings while insisting that all she meant was that she was concerned for their well-being.

Now Mrs. Muehls stood on our back steps with a sugar sack in her hand. Her shape stood out sharply against our white yard, her breath frosty around her head. When Martha opened the door, Mrs. Muehls held the sugar sack before her and explained that her daughters had outgrown their skates and Mrs. Muehls had been just about ready to throw them away when she recalled that we were here, poor motherless lambs, and at just that moment she decided not to throw the skates away but had brought them here for our use. "The Lord shall provide," she said, and it was clear that she saw herself as part of the Lord's supplies. Then she craned her neck and tried to see the inside of our house.

Martha must have been skeptical for she stood in the doorway with the edge of the door in her hand and let the heat out and acted like she did not understand. Perhaps Martha, like me, had had enough of the Lord's provisions. I do not know what Mrs. Muehls hoped to see. No doubt she imagined she would come away with a tale to tell.

I suppose you could not blame her. When my mother died, my father had not even run a notice in the paper. Under these circumstances stories were bound to arise, especially after he had a stone put up over her grave that said *Mrs. Herman Reehs* and thereby sent her into the afterlife without a name of her own.

When Mrs. Muehls gave up and went away, Martha laid the skates on the kitchen table. There were three of us and only two pairs of skates, but Martha said she had no interest in skating. She said she would spend the morning with Mary Johnston's *To Have and To Hold*. This was a novel about kind colonists and noble Indians. Martha loved that book. I imagine she believed that if she memorized it, the story would belong to her.

I turned to the table and unwrapped the skates. They were heavy old-fashioned things, boots with blades and laces. I picked them up and carried them into the front room, where Hattie lay on her stomach with her feet in the air and her paper dolls spread out before her.

Outside, the fields were white. The sky was white. The roofs of the houses were white. The dark woods that spread out around Waukesha were white. The river snaked below the bluffs under a white mantle, as if nothing living had ever passed this way. We walked up the road from our house and crossed the mill bridge and followed the road out of town until we came to a church and a field that had flooded and frozen. Skaters moved in a circle around the field, and barrels of orange and blue fire stood in the snow, heat shimmering upward in trembling veils. A man with a fiddle walked up and down. The music came to us and then disappeared and then came again. Soft white ash turned in the air and twisted away, the church gray against the cold gray sky. A bony brown dog moved along the edge of the ice and boys pulled sleds up a hill and skaters slid by and music wafted away.

I set one blade on the ice where the snow ran out and the ice took over and trapped yellow grass below like frozen hair. I pushed off, and pushed off again. I watched one foot and then the other. My breath caught in my throat and I clutched the air with my hands.

Hattie followed me. She started out slowly but soon skimmed past, her coat blowing like a bell over her skirt.

"Marie," she called. "Come on. Keep up."

She slid away from me and I pushed off with my left foot. I could not get my right foot to move at all. My dress clung damply beneath my coat. Little boys flailed their hockey sticks at me and girls skating in pairs split to go around me and gave me annoyed looks.

In Waukesha in winter you can see many days without snow, but when snow comes, it comes for hours at a time, and when it ceases the world is soft and white. When you walk outside, you see nothing but that whiteness. On sunny days you can be blinded. You have to squint until your eyes get used to the bright light, and it will be painful until your eyes adjust. It helps to wear a hat with a deep brim so you can shade your eyes. This was just my condition, snow-blind and sweaty, when I saw August Bethke on the far side of the field. He was just a shape at first, his dark coat and his dark hat and his light canvas working-man's trousers, but I steadied myself and squinted and he came into focus. I looked around for Hattie but she was far away. Then August leaned over and said something to the two boys nearest to him and they glanced at me and shrugged and skated away. When August came across the field and slid to a stop in front of me, his gray eyes shining, his hair caught under his black hat, a package of Cracker Jack poked out of his coat pocket, creamy except for its bright red lettering. He smiled and took my hand.

"Come with me," he said.

He put one hand on my waist and took one long step and I felt my feet go out from under me. I grabbed his coat to keep from going down. He laughed and took hold of my forearms until I could steady myself.

"Okay," he said. "I will teach you. Just take long steps. Pretend you're flying. Right? Pretend you are a bird who can fly. Like this. See?" He pushed off and showed me three long, smooth strokes. Then he took three strokes back to me.

"Okay?" he said. "All right?"

I pushed off. Below the dark green ice, fissures of white where the water had thawed and refrozen, and below that, the dark gray of the wild fields frozen over.

He watched me. Then he came up beside me. "Use both feet," he said.

I wobbled. He grabbed my elbow.

"Look," he said. "Do what I do." He took one of my hands and put his arm around my waist and propelled me away from the tattered edge of the snow. His coat smelled of wood smoke. His shoulder pressed mine. I felt the moving muscles of his thigh. I felt each stroke as he pushed off.

Across the field, Hattie waved to me and made a perfect round O with her mouth and then grinned and skated away.

August held me closer. "Who is that?" he said.

"My sister."

"In the blue coat?"

I nodded.

"She is pretty," he said. Then he put his mouth next to my ear. "But she is not as pretty as you."

The sound of his blades on the ice sharp and crisp. The wan fields and the white sky and our breath in clouds around our heads. Everything a rotating blur and my spine tingling from his touch. My heart lifted and I stretched my arms wide and he pushed me and the air parted and the wind stopped and nothing had ever happened but this moment. I began to laugh and it seemed to me that I laughed against my will and then it seemed that I could not stop laughing and all because I sailed under August's hand.

He put his mouth in my hair again. I felt myself go nearly limp. "See?" he whispered just above my ear, his voice moving through me like a swell. "It's easy. We're flying."

The fiddler dropped his violin to his side. He went to stand by a barrel of fire. He laid the violin on a blanket on the snow and stamped his feet and waved his hands over the flame in just the way a magician uses his hands to conjure something out of thin air. The skaters kept skating in their slow spiral around the center of the field.

August kept one hand at my waist and I stepped unsteadily, feeling his hand palm down at the small of my back and the snow under my skates. We picked our way over to an old board that had been laid between two upended farm pails. He brushed the board with the edge of his hand. "Here," he said. Then he sat down beside me.

He told me that he had been born in Pomerania and had sailed to New York from Hamburg on a ship called the *Polaria*, arriving on a hot night near the end of the summer. He had been almost four when they arrived, and he remembered the steel floor of the ship with its bolts as big as baseballs and the black water and white foam passing far below and the smell of the docks when they came off the boat in New York, the press of people around them, and the hazy heat on the wharf with the sun a hot, dim sphere rising in a white sky. Their heavy clothes. The crying seabirds overhead. He came with his father, Wilhelm, who was a carpenter, and his mother, Auguste, who kept house for them, and his little sister, Olga, still a baby on the boat but who now worked as a dressmaker. The ship also carried his father's younger brother, Karl, and his father's mother, Johanna, who helped with things for a time but died when August was eleven.

Hattie turned in a circle, her coat open over her knees.

I told him that my mother was dead and no one knew how. Then I went quiet. He had been there that day so I imagined he had seen the whole thing. That he was well aware of who my father was and of what he had done and how he had managed to get away with it. But I did not say any of that. I dug the blade of my skate into the snow and traced a line and then another line and then drew crosshatches through that.

August said that the day he had first seen me, he had been moving a load of lumber from the yard down by the train station to a building site on the north end of town. And then he started to look for me but he could not find me and when he did, I vanished. I disappeared into the shadows that night by the river. I ran away from him up the road just as the snow began to fall. His brothers told him to forget about me but he could not.

I turned my blade flat against the snow again and smoothed a flat sweep of snow and then stabbed it with my toe.

Down the road my father's house, spare and blocky and filled with secrets.

"You do not know me," I said.

"I know you," he said. He touched my sleeve, my wrist. He turned toward me. He took my head in his hands and leaned forward. Our foreheads touched. "We know each other," he whispered.

I could not believe that he would be this bold out here in the open air while the skaters slipped by in their circle, while the daylight came down around us and the afternoon turned flat and broad and bright, while Hattie skated across the field and every so often cast looks our way. But I did not stop him. I could not stop him. If he wanted to be reckless, I would be reckless, too.

His eyes gleamed. I could feel his breath on my mouth, his fingers in my hair. I wanted to kiss him but I forced myself to turn my face away. Then he reached over and picked up my hand and squeezed it.

Far away from us, the fiddler started on a polka. The skaters moved in their measured ring, the men in trousers tied off below the knee and round hats, the dark skirts of the women blowing out behind, their little hats loosening and growing jittery on their heads.

"You will change your mind," I said.

"Never," he said. He leaned against me. I felt the shock of

him again and watched his bright face grow tense and his eyes darken. "I will never change my mind," he said. "Not about you."

"August," I said. I stopped. How could I ask him? How could I not? He held my hand and I thought of my mother in his arms and Hattie on the ice. The day rising over us like a faded dome. It was impossible to put my question into words. For his part, August watched me and waited and did not speak.

Finally I stood up and brushed the snow from my skirt and he stood up next to me. "We should skate some more," I said.

"If you call that skating," he said. And then he laughed.

Far out across the field, August's brothers skated up and back among a pack of youths. One reached into his pocket and un-screwed a flask and drank from it and then wiped his mouth on the back of his hand and skated away. Hattie glided toward me, her cheeks red, her skirt ruffling. She stopped at the edge of the ice. She watched August's hand on my back and his hand when he took mine. She looked at me.

"Hattie," I said. "This is August."

He dropped my hand so that he could reach for hers. "I am very glad to meet you," he said.

"August who?" she said. She stood with her hands burrowed into her pockets. Her breath made a veil around her hair.

"August Bethke," I said. "I met him." I stopped. There was no way to explain how I had met August Bethke.

"I see that."

"Do not be suspicious," he said. "I am in love with your sister."

"Really?" she said. "In love?" She poked me in the arm. "With Marie?"

"Why do you laugh? I am very serious." He took my hand in his and held it palm down over his heart.

I stood next to him in the daze made by his heat and by the

feeling of his shoulder pressed against mine and by the scent of his warm breath and by the cold air and by the sound of the music that came across the ersatz pond below the mean little church on the edge of the great wide world. *August*, I thought. *August Bethke*. At that moment, his name contained all of the answers. I felt certain I could walk next to him and away from my father and away from my mother, or the ghost of my mother, which flickered through our house like a shadow without a name.

"I am going to give your sister a skating lesson," said August. He smiled at Hattie. "You come, too."

"I'll watch," said Hattie. She turned toward me. "And then we need to go." She did not try to conceal her concern.

"I know," I said. "I promise to be quick."

It was late afternoon when Hattie and I made our way home, over the bridge and past the burned-out shell of a farmhouse, where I could smell the blackened wood under the cavernous cold air. When we got closer to town, we passed a box of a building where two young men in rough coats and caps squatted beside a galvanized steel tank and used a black rubber hose to decant a colorless liquid into a washtub. They watched us as we came by and one of them stood up and leaned against the wall and after a minute lit a cigarette and stared after us as we made our way away from him.

The road curved toward the river and the water lay before us for a time, glinting with a leaden sheen like an object gone dull in the fireplace's ash. We passed the park in front of the biggest springhouse, and the path to the front steps was broken by footsteps that turned into black holes in the snow. A man and woman walked together, her hand clasped in his and her dark green skirt dragging behind her and her hem blackened with a fan of water, like she had been walking for a while and the snow on her skirt had had a chance to melt in the sun. Even from the street, I could see that it was Martha. Even at a glance, I could tell that it was George. They did not see us. They just walked away from the road with their heads bent together and crossed into the blue shadow next to the springhouse. The park road rose along a shallow slope and then turned at the top of the hill. They followed the path and passed back into the fading light and started up the rise.

"Martha," I muttered. "You are such a liar."

Hattie turned around to face me. "Did you say something?"

I shook my head. "Go on," I said. "Never mind."

When we got home, I put the sack with the skates in it on a shelf in the mudroom. Hattie hung our coats on their hooks. My father sat at the kitchen table, the newspaper open over his lap, a bottle beside him on the table. He turned toward us when we came in. "Did you see this?" he said.

"We're cold," I said. "Can't you let us warm up first?"

I had not thought before I spoke. I had simply spoken. I had merely said the words.

He let his paper fall loosely to his knees. He squinted at me.

"You watch your step, girl," he said. There was no mistaking the edge in his voice.

It hardly mattered. August told me that he looked for me on every street in town. He walked up and down the main roads. He searched for me along the sidewalks in front of the drugstore, the bank, the police station. He never forgot the look in my eyes when he saw me standing in the yard. One day he thought he saw me when he was riding in the front car of the interurban. He put his hand flat on the glass, just in case it was me.

When he took me out on the ice I felt his thigh on mine. I would have done anything to make sure he kept touching me like that. He did not cross our arms in front of us like two people on a promenade. He put his arm around my waist. He showed me how to skate, stroke by stroke, until I pushed off when he pushed off, and let myself glide when he did. We picked up speed around the field, and he leaned into me to show me how to take the corners, each stroke warm and hard and alive.

In the trees behind the church, a flock of starlings gathered in the branches. When the wind picked up, Hattie waved to me from the snowy slope and a cloud passed in front of the sun. The birds lifted from the trees. I felt August beside me, his body, his heat, the absolute truth of his heart.

Now I turned my back on my father, on his hard voice, on his hard eyes. I could not believe I had said what I had said. Still, the fact of the matter was that I had talked back to him and I had not died. The fact of the matter was that I was entirely alive.

8

When my mother was a girl, she waited for the equinox, when it was said that eggs would balance unbroken on their broad ends and animals would talk. But she had never been able to stay up late enough to hear her mother's chickens tell stories in the dirt lot next to my grandfather's house. Spring came with planting and she mostly remembered walking behind my grandfather as he dug the holes for potatoes. She dropped an eye into each hole and then covered the eye with dirt.

I suppose this is why she grew potatoes in our yard. Don't we always do what we've always done? It seems our habits are set in this regard in our own long-ago times, before we have even become aware that our behaviors are being fixed in place.

I stood over the rusty barrel and let the contents of my dustpan fall in a gritty cloud. When I turned to go back inside, August stood before me, a match flickering in his cupped hands. The cupped match went out and he popped another against his thumbnail and the flame flared and lit his face.

"Marie," he whispered.

He seemed to hold the yellow flame in his fingers. I looked back over my shoulder. Martha was a shadow who moved around in the kitchen light.

"You should not come here," I said, but I said this very softly. I did not want him to leave.

"I had to see you," he said. His breath came in misty waves and rose in clouds and disappeared.

I could hear him breathing. Our neighbor next door stepped onto her back steps and held the screen door open. Her dog ran out to the fence and lifted its leg on a post. She pretended to watch him, but I knew she had her eye on my garden, where I stood with August Bethke. After a minute, she whistled to her dog and the dog ran inside and she followed it and closed the door. August let the match in his hands go out.

He wore a long woolen coat that came down past his knees and a soft hat. He reached over and brushed my hair from my eyes. Then he took my hand.

The frozen night road was dark and cool and the fields fell away on either side and the woods lay before us in a great black shape. The lights of town glittered like the lights of a ship rising and falling far away on the sea and then dropped behind us. We left the world of fields and houses and walked with the woods crowding up beside the road until we came to a break in the trees where the parted way seemed as a split in the world, darkness on each side but the trail and the sky beyond glowing with the first light of moonrise. August tightened his grip and helped me step up onto a fall of logs. He held a branch back until I had passed. He stood in his boots in the shallow torrents of a stream and held my hand while I stepped from rock to rock. He lifted me over a stretch of wet earth.

———

He came for me again and again, even though I told him it was not safe. But the truth was simple. I did not want him to stay away. One night he took me to a low cave in the bluffs. He lit a fire and then took a burning stick and held it up to the walls, where thin charcoal outlines of pregnant deer and huge birds with broad wings and narrow men drawing bows at the deer had been left by some long-lost Indians when they were in charge of this land. The little figures were scorched and plain, stick figures with large bows, bulbous deer looking back over their shoulders. The men had square heads and large astonished eyes.

Another night we came to the top of a rise. August led me by the hand into the center of the clearing. He took his long coat off and spread it on the dead grass like a blanket. He lay down next to me and held my hand. He told me that he intended to build a good house for himself. He told me about the work he did with his father. He could not wait for me to meet his sister. He planned to make a trip in summer to a place up north where there were said to be a thousand lakes for fishing.

The sky brightened and darkened, just the way in sunlight a cloud casts a shadow, and then an evenly curved arc of blue-green light extended from horizon to horizon and to the very top of an endless curve of sky. It rippled like a curtain under a breeze, as if a whirlwind had come from the north with a fire folded in on itself and a strange brightness all about it. The world seemed infinite then and all because August was with me.

I shivered.

"You are cold," August said. He rubbed my arms and smiled and tickled me and pulled at my hand and I fell down with my head against his shoulder. He put his arm around me. "I need to warm you up," he said.

The metal smell had gone from the air. Spring would come and then summer and then it would be a year since the doctor had come and scolded my mother about Alvin, who had died anyway. And three weeks after that, it would be a year since my father had come behind the men who carried my mother into our house and laid her in her blackening dress on the bed. A year since my father held the door for those men, one of whom was August, who lay next to me now.

I propped myself on my elbow and asked him if he remembered. He sat up and pulled a long piece of sweet grass from the ground and sat chewing it thoughtfully. The sky flickered above us in undulating bands of green and blue.

He said he remembered the day. He remembered carrying her. But he did not remember anything else. He did not remember how she came to be there. He was sorry but he did not know what had happened.

"Why do you want to take his side?" I said.

"Whose side?" He seemed confused. He pitched his piece of grass into the night and turned to me and hugged me closer.

"My father's side."

"I am not taking your father's side," he said. He put his face in my hair. "I do not know your father's side."

"Then why will you not tell me?"

He sighed and nuzzled my hair again, and I went stiff with something I could not fail to identify as irritation.

"I cannot tell you because I do not know," he said then. "I was driving a load of lumber. A man stepped into the street and waved me down. That was your father. That was the first time I ever laid eyes on your father. He said he wanted to put a woman in the back. She was bleeding. So we took her. He sat in back with her. He was talking to her but I could not hear a word he said. We drove to your house. We carried her inside. He never said what happened. He told us there was an accident. That was all he ever said. I do not know anything else. I swear to you. I would tell you if I knew."

I listened to August breathe for a minute and then I stood up. I could see a yellow glimmer in the woods far off to the south, where someone must have had a house, a shed, a barn. Someplace they had made for themselves. Someplace where they intended to be safe. Maybe they had come across an ocean to put their house in that very spot. The grass rustled behind me and I heard August get to his feet. He shook his coat out and came to stand behind me. He put his coat over my shoulders. He turned me to face him and he put his arms around me as if he would warm me to my core. He told me he loved me. He told me he would always love me. He told me he would keep me safe. I leaned into him, into the warmth of him, into the scratchy comfort of his wool coat. He reached down and took my hands in his. Then he gripped them so tightly that the bones moved beneath the skin and I nearly cried out, and then I did cry out. He smiled a little and said that I must like that and then I grew angry and leaned into him harder and into the bottom-less pain that felt so familiar and so much a part of me that I knew he truly loved me.

If I smiled to myself at the laundry and Inge and Johanna and Ella watched me with open curiosity as I turned to my work, I did not care. I climbed the ladder and stirred the vat. I dipped the pole and swung steaming sheets into my basket. I scrubbed the sheets until my hands bled. I saw William Oliver. But I was in the laundry room with Inge and Johanna and Ella and all he could do was come and stand next to me and examine my work. When he gave up and walked away, I smiled and shook my head and sometimes laughed. One day when I did this, he turned in the doorway and fixed me with his stare, one eyebrow raised. I ignored him. But he stayed in that doorway for a long time.

If I stood on the back steps and watched the deliveryman

load the brown paper parcels into the wagon while the western horizon turned rosy with the light at the end of the day, it was only to see that night was coming. August was coming. I felt an ache in my chest like a string wound taut and taut until it is so tight and wired that it cannot slacken except if it is plucked by the right hand or else snapped in two in the waiting.

A slice of blue moonlight lay across the bottom of the garden and the wires for my mother's bean plants carved a thin shadow across the back fence. Everywhere the night, still, cold. I worked my broom under the kitchen table. Reached down and fished a button out of the dust. Martha hummed while she washed the supper dishes. *Wait till the sun shines, Nellie.* My mother's clock ticked in the front room. Hattie went up the stairs and after a minute, I heard her braces fall to the floor.

Something tapped on the glass over the kitchen sink and Martha bent over the dishpan to peer out the window. She was wearing an old skirt that had belonged to my mother. I do not know when we started to go into her room, when we started to take her things and wrap them around ourselves, but we had. We did not talk about it. We just did it. Hattie wore my mother's old blue coat. Martha had her skirt. I wore her shoes. The day I took them, I told myself I was just borrowing them, that it was foolish to let a perfectly good pair of shoes go to waste, but I found a reason to wear them every day.

I could see August through the window, his shoulder and a wedge of his arm. Then he stepped away and the window went blank and glassy. I made one last pass with the broom and carried it along with the dustpan to the mudroom, where I set the dustpan on the floor. I lifted my coat from the nail by the door. Martha stepped into the doorway.

"Who is that?" she asked.

"It is nobody," I said. "Do not think about it."

She looked at the coat in my hands. "Where are you going?"

August tapped on the glass again.

Martha reached out and touched my sleeve. I could see that she meant to calm herself, as if self-control was something she had practiced so long and so hard that she fell into it the way another woman might fall into a bath. But she was not entirely successful. "I hope you know what you are doing," she said. Her voice went up a little in pitch when she spoke and that was the giveaway.

"You do not need to worry," I said.

She rolled her lips together as if considering what she might say, but she could say nothing that would matter. I was not to be stopped.

"You make that hard," she said at last.

"Pretend you do not even know."

"But I do know," she said. "I do not know everything but I do know something."

"Pretend you do not," I said again. And all the while I was thinking: Pretend you never saw him. Pretend I go out to fly through the night. Pretend I haunt the woods by myself. Pretend I am just wild. Pretend you do not know me.

She watched me button the last button on my coat. Behind her, August stepped off the porch and stood in the yard with his back to us. "What if I tried to stop you?" she said.

"You can try," I said. "But I am going." In my mind, I was already gone. I was already running through the darkness holding August Bethke's hand. I was already kissing him beneath some tree only he knew about.

"Do you know what will happen if you get caught?"

"I won't get caught," I said. Confident as death.

The house creaked like a ship coming undone from its moorings.

"At least tell me who he is," Martha said.

"A boy," I said. *My boy*, I thought. *My August.*

"I can see that," she said in a cutting voice.

I smiled. "A carpenter."

Her eyes narrowed. "What is his name?"

"August," I said.

"August who?"

"Bethke," I said. I pronounced it the way August did so it sounded like Bait-ka.

"Bait-ka," she said slowly. She stood in the doorway and turned the name over in her mouth, but this time said August Bethke and pronounced the last name the way Americans would say it, so it sounded like Beth-key. She repeated the last name again with a puzzled look on her face.

I reached for the doorknob but she suddenly took hold of me and tried to pull me back into the kitchen. "Stop," she said, her voice urgent and fierce. "Please stop. Do not go with that boy."

I pried her fingers from my arm. "Cut it out, Martha," I said. "I am going." I heard footsteps on the porch steps. August tapped on the glass again and said my name and I turned toward his voice.

"Please," she said.

"You cannot stop me," I said. "Do not even try."

We walked out into the night. August took my hand and I felt the great shock of him jolt my bones. When I turned to look back, Martha stood on the porch and watched us, her thin frame tall and narrow against the dim clapboard of the house, deep shadow falling between us, my mother's skirt blowing around her knees.

Down by the river, August led me over a gravelly beach to a small wooden boat. In the daytime these shores were bright with dry yellow reeds, and red-winged blackbirds trilled in the tall grass. At night under the moon the river shallows were gray and foamy and the marsh grasses crackled and settled and no birds flew. The river glinted silver. August pulled the boat into shore and once I stepped in, he waded into the river to lift the anchor. Then he hoisted himself over the side and dropped into the hull. He took up the oars. With even strokes he pulled us out to where the current caught us. His dark hair fell into his eyes and he pushed it back and he reached over and put his hand on my skirt. In one quick gesture, he ran his hand up my inner thigh. He let his hand rest there. I felt nothing but the thrill of that gesture and the weight of his palm. When he smiled and lifted his hand and leaned back and put his hand back on the oars, I could still feel the heaviness of his hand on me and the weight of its promise. The boat creaked beneath us.

He stroked downstream. We slid past the tall brick machine factory and the town park with its circle of benches and then past the biggest of the springs, where the springhouse was closed up tight for the night but where in the morning people would walk to take the waters for their health or have themselves driven there in wagons and in cars. August pulled the oars into the boat and dropped them into the hull and we floated in silence. He pulled a candle stub from his pocket and lit the wick. He poured some of the wax onto the seat beside him and stood the candle in the wax. The flame flickered and went out. He popped another match against his thumbnail and lit the candle again. I wondered what people along the shore must have thought when they saw us, a boat the same dark color as the night and so invisible and yet a single light moving gently along the surface of the water.

The candle went out again and this time he did not relight it. When we came around a curve, he searched the shoreline. Then he pulled us out of the current to a rocky beach that was more shore than sand, just tall grasses waving and small stones and the dark pines falling away. He threw the anchor into the water and let the boat drag against its weight. He crawled over the bow and tested the line. Then he stepped to the side of the boat and took my hand. I cautiously stepped onto a rock and then another and then down until I stood next to him in the shallows, my boots wet, my stockings wet, my skirt wet almost to the knees.

He had brought us to rest in a tiny cove that seemed carved by some ancient hand from the determined lines of the river-banks. He told me to wait and then he crossed the beach and stepped through the branches into the woods. I was left by the river in silence, wringing the water from my hem, my shoes soaked and my hair coming unpinned. The wind tossed the branches and tossed the trees where August had disappeared. I could not see him nor could I see the place where it seemed he had stepped off the face of the planet. No light or house or farm or factory nearby, only the dark, moving river and the boat bumping lightly against the gravel.

I stood under the stars and breathed in the watery river air and waited for him to come back. I felt myself all the more alive because I was alone and waiting. I felt myself all the more free because the river breeze lifted my heart and sent it sailing. My father was like bad news from a faraway place and completely missing on this early spring night. When I stood on that beach, it seemed to me that I had never met him and all I knew was the wind and the water and August.

He led me across the grassland to a faint trail that led upward under the trees. We climbed past old limestone shelves that ran with trickles of water and grew dank with moss. We climbed above the shelves to a place where the forest floor softened with fallen pine needles and drifts of leaves, all brown and dry and yet still yielding, August's hand on mine as the trail rose steeply into the night. At the top, he stood breathing and I stood breathless next to him. We looked back over the way we had come. He put his arm around me and I leaned my head against him. He told me that it was not much farther and it never seemed this far in the daylight. I nodded. Far below, I saw something glint in the grass by the boat. August turned away from me but I hung back. He turned toward me and asked me what was wrong.

"I saw something," I said.

We stood together and looked over the limestone cliffs to the grassland below the woods.

"Do you see the boat?" I said.

He nodded.

"It's by the boat."

He squinted into the darkness.

"I do not see anything," he said.

"Wait," I said. And just then in the darkness a small flash of light, like a reflection in a tiny mirror on a bright day.

"I see it," he said.

We watched but the light did not come again. The grass near the boat rippled and flattened and the wind pushed against us.

"Let's go," he said. "It is nothing."

"August."

"It is nothing," he said.

We stood on top of the cliffs and looked down into the river. The grass moved and the boat rested and no light came.

"You see?" he said. "Nothing."

He pulled me after him and I followed him along the top of the rocks to a place where the trail disappeared and nothing but a great dense wall of brush and undergrowth and tall pines stood before us. And then we stepped into the brush and there was a shed. When August lit a match and put it to another candle stub, I saw that the shed was fitted with a slatted board door that hung by hinges made of strips of raw deer hide. A

crude window had been papered over with greasy butcher paper. August let the match burn down and then shook it out
and put it in his pocket. He stepped forward with the flame
of the candle stub before him and pulled the door open. It
scraped dirt and then the inside of the shed bloomed with a
dark yellow light.

We sat on a pallet made out of tattered ticking and straw
that someone had pushed against the back wall. Nothing before
us but the dirt floor and the candle stub standing in a puddle of
wax on a tin plate. A pile of leaves blown up into the corner, as
if the door had come loose in the fall and stood ajar long enough
for some of the forest to come inside. August told me that this
was a hunting cabin built by his father and his uncle. They came
up here when they did not have work. They used the boat to
bring back the deer they had shot. In town, they would hang
the carcasses from the limb of a tree behind their house until
the deer were drained and done. Then they would skin them
and butcher the meat. They would make a fire in the middle of
the yard and lay thin slices over the smoke on a chaffer they had
taken from an old combine. While the meat smoked, they pack-
aged the roasts in bags made of flour sacks, which they bound
with twine and hung from the rafters in the root cellar under
the stairs. He said the roasts tasted best right before they turned.
He always looked for the pieces that had been brined and hung
and dried and had developed a crust of blue mold, like a country ham. That might be six months after the deer was killed, if
the root cellar did not get too wet. He stopped.

"I do not know why I talk so much," he said. "Maybe you
make me nervous." He picked up my hand and held it up in
the candlelight. "Poor thing," he said. "Poor hand." He ran his
thumb over the healed scalds now white in the dark light. He
stroked my red and weeping wrists. He flattened my hand between his two palms as if the heat from his hands could heal it. I

felt the heat and the pressure and the thick, smooth calluses that crossed his palms.

"When we are married, you will not have to work like this," he said. "I will take care of you forever."

He put his arms around me and held me in the flickering light of the candle and then he kissed me. He kissed me until I felt my blood and bones and skin and muscle turn to shivering water and the water that I had become flooded toward him. He kissed me harder and I surged around him, as if I had become a tumult of currents and deep places. I made a sound that I had never heard before and we lay down on the pallet and he moved over me. His face was fierce and tender. His eyes suddenly dark and intent. I felt his hand at my waist, his fingers on the buttons of my blouse, my blouse rising under his hand until he could slip his hand under my chemise. My heart pounded and I closed my eyes and my spine became a tight wire arcing, with my hands on his back.

"August," I said, and my voice surprised me because it was full of tears and yearning.

"It's all right," he said. He kissed my neck. "Let me show you."

At the first sign of light, we stood and dressed and I turned away from him but he pulled me back to him and said my name. By the time we reached the boat, a steady rain stippled the surface of the river. August took his coat off. He held it over my head, his breath frosty and blue in the early light. I stepped into the boat. He followed me through the shallows, leaning his shoulder into the prow and then hoisting himself over the side. He shivered and sat dripping. He picked up the oars. Then he rowed us against the current back to town. He let the boat rest under the mill bridge so I could climb out in shadow. I found the street and tried to look like I had just come out of my own house and was on my way to work. Like this was any other day. I gave him his coat when we touched shore and he kissed me and I kissed him. The world shuddering with life. I climbed up the bank and stepped out onto the street in my soaked dress and my drenched hair. I pushed my hair back and walked away from him but turned at the last minute to watch him pull the boat away from the shore. A woman in a green dress with a hat pinned to her hair came out of her house and stood on the front porch and watched me as I made my way up the street. She stared at me hard and went back inside. I walked with my unhooked boots and my dragging wet skirt and my dripping and draining hair all the way along the river road and then nine blocks to the laundry. When I came inside, I sat on the wooden floor and fastened my shoes. Then I stood and picked up a basket of dirty clothes. I measured a scoopful of soap flakes. I climbed the ladder next to the nearest vat. I dropped shirts and aprons in, one by one. The air hot and heavy and my clothes soaked and cold, the floor wet where I had dragged my skirt behind me. Inge and Ella and Johanna watched me and said nothing. I bent over the vat and stirred the steaming water. I watched the clothes turn and sink and rise and listened to the sound of the water boiling as if it were the sound of wind in the treetops on a high cliff overlooking a river only I knew about.

9

I dreamt of my mother, who came to me as wan as a wraith and bloody still. She sailed cloud-like under the dark trees with her terrible dress and her terrible wound and her terrible secret. She smiled when she saw me but when she could not put her hands on me, her face turned cold. Then she moved away under the trees. I saw that she was not alone but rose and fell in the midst of other shimmering women, pale in their pale gowns, their light faces turned back to me without expression. I tried to follow her over the soft trails and high rocks of the woods, past a stream that ran over a white cliff, past the tall waving grasses of a river. But she grew fainter and fainter until she finally evaporated. I stood alone on a vast plain where a blue lake glittered. Nothing made a sound save for the rising wind.

They left me alone. My wet dress clung to me. My skirt made a broad swathe of water across the floor, dripping and trailing the river behind me, and the rain, and the wild woods. I carefully climbed the ladder to the last vat on the line. The weight of my skirt reminded me of August and I said his name to myself and said it again. I pumped the hand agitator. Inge bent over her washtubs and pretended to sing to herself, but I knew she was watching me, just as I knew Ella was watching me while she cranked canvas trousers through her wringer.

The flat workers came at noon. They hung their coats by the back door and went into the room where the ironing boards waited. Then Inge and Ella and Johanna broke from their work and went down the back steps into the yard. They pulled their lunch pails out from under the stairs and stood by the delivery wagon and ate. The laundry room went silent and sunlight fell in a square on the floor. I sat in the hushed light and leaned my head against the wall and slept.

By three o'clock my dress had dried stiff as a board and smelled sour. Dried mud flaked from the hem as I walked from the vats to my washtub. When Inge could stand it no longer, she told me to come with her. I followed her out onto the back steps. She wielded a clothes brush and went over my skirt until most of the caked mud was gone.

"It is the best I can do," she said.

"Thank you." I shook my skirt out and let it fall over my shoes.

She slapped the clothes brush against her hand. "Where have you been?"

"Out."

"But where?" she persisted. Her voice had an irritating wheedling tone. This did not make me any more predisposed to answer.

Women like Inge ask questions with their faces composed in a studied mix of fake empathy and raw curiosity. They see themselves as acting on behalf of the common good. They generally have high opinions of themselves and their busybody behavior. Invariably, I do not share these. It will not surprise you to learn that I hated Inge's suspicious face and her cajoling voice. I hated her clothes brush and her assistance. I hated the prying she thought she could pass off as pity.

The deliveryman led the horse by its harness out of the alley and the horse pulled the delivery wagon into the yard. The horse lifted its head when it saw us and rolled its eyes and stepped away. The deliveryman yanked on the harness and slapped the horse hard on the neck and the horse stilled. It stood breathing while the deliveryman unfastened the traces and bundled the reins. He turned the horse and led it back down the alley.

"If you were my daughter, I would skin you alive," said Inge. Her voice was calm but she tapped the back of the clothes brush against her open palm, as if she hoped my skirt and skin would become one.

"Then it is a good thing I am not your daughter," I said. For the first time I thought: *I am no one's daughter. Not anymore. I belong to August and he belongs to me.*

She picked at the bristles on the clothes brush and then bent and swiped the brush at the back of my skirt again. She moved as if she was trying very hard to restrain herself. Once someone has said she thinks you ought to be struck, I imagine she will have a hard time refraining from the act.

"You remember Lydia Berger," she said. She straightened and let her hand fall to her side.

I shook my head.

"Fifteen years old. Lived just north of here." Inge waved in the general direction of the river. "Lydia wanted to stay out all night and go to a carnival. Of course her father would not permit this. She went anyway. In the morning, he whipped her within an inch of her life. This was the right thing to do, in my opinion. You cannot have a young girl running all over the countryside. A girl has one thing and one thing only and when that is gone, it is gone. There is no getting it back."

A black cat made its way across the edge of the yard. It

passed the double doors over the coal chute and sat in the waning sunlight and washed its front paw. It looked over at us with its paw still in the air and then licked the paw quickly and set the paw on the ground.

"A man, of course that is something different. It is almost expected of him. But a girl cannot afford this. You cannot afford this." She picked up my hem. "If your mother was here, she would say the same."

I watched the cat, so perfect in its independence. The only thing to do when someone wishes to lecture you is to offer a look of complete innocence. I knew that she did not know anything. I do not think it was just my natural impertinence that made me wish that she would leave me alone. She did not know anything. She ought to leave me alone.

"Lydia burned her father's house down," Inge said. "When the neighbors took her family in, she burned their house down, too. Her mother told her to go and wait at the Wisconsin Lake Ice Company, where the family kept horses in the barn. Lydia did as she was told. Also in the barn were sixty-four tons of hay. Lydia took the horses outside and tied them up. Then she burned the barn down. When the sheriff arrested her, he asked her why she did it. She told him that she wanted to take revenge on her father for whipping her." Inge pointed the handle of the clothes brush at me. "Of course he had the right. She was his to do with as he pleased. She stays in jail to this day, though. Maybe she did not think that part through so well."

Someone had tried to hang wash on a line that ran the length of the back porch of the building behind the laundry. A man came out and looked at the laundry. He leaned on a tree branch that had been whittled into a walking stick. He limped over to the wash and touched the sleeve of a shirt. Then he turned and limped back into the apartment. The door closed with a loud bang.

"What happened out there?" Inge said. She tried to make her voice sound sympathetic but I knew she was not sympathetic. To this day, I do not expect to find out that Inge ever showed sympathy to anyone.

I lifted one shoulder and let it drop, as if to say that whatever this was, it was of no concern to anyone. It could not matter and should not matter. I was not ruined. I was alive.

She eyed me. "Maybe he took advantage. If you want to say so, now would be the time."

"Nothing happened," I said. I tried to keep my voice even. Nothing was the water. Nothing was the river running through me. Nothing was the dark and endless night.

"People talk," she said.

"They do not have to," I said. I met her gaze and she quickly looked away.

The clang of the interurban cut through the air. I thought about the people riding inside, on their way to homes they loved, as if everyone in the world was in love with someone and lived their days with what that felt like.

"We have to run a good place here," Inge said.

I shrugged again. I started to inch away but Inge put her hand on my arm.

"We could lose our jobs," she said. "All of us."

I moved my arm but she reached for it again.

"Do not be so selfish," she said. "If he loses business, what do you think happens to us? He will not hesitate. He will not keep us without work."

Later, just as I was leaving, I saw her standing at the front counter, talking with William Oliver. They leaned together while Inge whispered and moved her hands.

I took the river road home. Black leaves against the wet sidewalk. The rutted road ran out before me. A rank smell rose from my dress.

I got to my street just in time to see my father come down our walk. He took his hat from his head and creased the crown and then put the hat back on. His coattails flapped. He swung his arms as he walked. I hung back. Martha stood at the kitchen window and stared out into the yard. She turned when I came in. She took in my awful dress and my wild hair and said nothing. She lifted my supper plate out of the food warmer. She carried the plate to the table. She opened a drawer and found a fork and a knife and a spoon. She set these beside the plate and told me to sit down and eat. A pot of water simmered on the stove.

"Do your dishes when you are through," she said stiffly. "Do not look to me."

Outside, a steady rain. I imagined the rain as it streamed over the limestone cliffs and made its way to the river, and then I imagined the shed and the place inside the shed where August and I had lain all night. I thought of him as he stroked us back through the dark river upstream to town. I wrapped my arms around my waist.

My wrecked dress hung on the hook on the back of my bedroom door. My unraveling boots dried by the stove with crumpled newspaper balled up in the toes. I wore a dark skirt and a dark blouse and my mother's shoes.

Martha leaned over and lifted the latch on the stove door. She let the door swing open. A sudden heat warmed the room and blue flame rolled over the last log.

"I do not know what you expect me to say," she said. She sat down at the table across from me and swept her hand along its surface and then her hand went still.

"I do not expect you to say anything," I said. "You do not have to worry about this."

"You are asking me to lie for you," she said.

"I am not asking you to do anything."

"If I know about something and I do not tell him, that omission is the same as a lie." She ran her palm across the table-top again.

"Do not be ridiculous," I said. "Do not take things to extremes. If you do not say anything at all, you have not told a lie."

"What if he asks me straight?" She dropped her hand into her lap. "What am I supposed to say?"

"Tell the truth," I said bluntly. But I knew this was easier said than done.

"Marie," she said.

Rain streamed over the dark kitchen window. The fire popped and faded and the blue flame flattened and died away.

She stood and hiked her sagging skirt and dragged it behind her to the sink, where she brushed her hands over the drain. I thought I could count her ribs under her shirtwaist, as if she had begun to vanish before my eyes. These days, she practically disappeared when she turned sideways. The wind came up and murmured like children crying in the eaves. Then it fell away and she turned to face me, her face as tight and chiseled as the bones in a Halloween mask.

"What do you know about this boy?" she said.

"I know enough."

"What does that mean?"

I knew August's mouth on mine, the taste of him, the smell of him, the weight of his body, the shuddering that came when he was through. I knew he made me feel strong and whole, and when I was with him, I knew that I had never before been myself and had only become myself after I met him.

"I know him," I said. "Believe me."

"What about his family?" she said. "What do you know about his family?"

He had an accent just like my mother's. He had two brothers. He had a sister named Olga who worked as a seamstress. "They are just like us," I said softly.

"How do you know that?"

"I just know," I said.

She snorted.

"We are just like you and George," I said.

She stiffened in her chair. "It is not the same at all," she said.

"It is exactly the same."

"No," she said. "It is not."

I leaned over and lifted the iron poker from the firebox and jabbed at the coals. They brightened and a single yellow flame licked up out of the ash. "I know you meet him in the park," I said.

She folded her arms over her chest. "That's right," she said in a prissy voice. "We meet in the park. But it is not the same. For one thing, we are engaged."

"Engaged?"

"Yes."

"Does *he* know that?"

"Who? George?"

"Not George," I said. "You know I do not mean George."

She smoothed the front of her apron. "George and I will tell him when the time is right," she said stiffly.

I leaned forward and poked the anemic fire again. I did not dare put another log on the coals even though the kitchen would soon be dead cold.

"How do you think he will take it?" I said. I stirred the embers. "He told you that George was to stay away."

"We will tell him when the time is right," she repeated.

"Just like you will ask him what happened to our mother when the time is right," I said. I gave her a nasty look.

She held still. I could see that she had not expected me to bring this up. "That's right," she said.

I stabbed the coals with the poker until they smoldered, an undulating red that moved as if it breathed. *Ashes to ashes*, I thought. *Dust to dust.*

Rain fell in a sudden rushing torrent and then slowed.

"Even if it takes forever," I said.

"Yes," she said tightly. She bit her lip.

"Why don't you just ask him?" I said.

"Why don't you?" she said, her voice tart. Then she went silent.

The rain beat against the kitchen window.

She wiped her hands on her apron and crossed her arms over her waist. "I hoped I would not have to tell you this," she said. The skin on her face pulled taut as a drumhead.

"Tell me what?" I thought she was going to tell me something about our mother, some piece of information that she had discovered. I knew she must have wondered. One day, right after the funeral, I caught her going through my mother's purse, looking at my mother's comb, her spool of thread, the three Mercury dimes she always carried with her, no matter what. Martha jumped when I came into the room and dropped the dimes on the floor and one rolled under the bed and she had to lie entirely flat and stretch her arm out in front of her in order to reach it. Despite this, we never spoke of what I had seen and I had never seen her do anything like it again. But I knew what she was up to. I knew she was looking for something other than the bald truth to explain the world.

"There is a family," she said carefully. "I have heard of them. Everyone has heard of them. This is not a good family."

I listened to the rain. I imagined myself in August's arms, his face pressed into my neck. I felt myself stir at the memory, rising as if he called me to him.

"You do not know that it is the same family," I said.

She reached for my arm. "Last name Bethke. That is what I heard."

I turned the poker and slid the point through the last of the fire's light. I lacked patience for gossip. Pretty is as pretty does and Waukesha was full of stories. Everyone liked to talk. Everyone thought they knew everything.

The kitchen had begun to go dark around us but neither one of us had bothered to light the lamp. Rain sluiced over the window and the yard and the town and the sky disappeared. I did not want to listen to Martha's theories about August or August's family or any of it. Bethke was a pretty common name. In German, it was nearly as common as Smith. If she had things to tell me, it was just because she wanted to hurt me.

"You do not want me to be happy," I said. "You want me to be as miserable as you."

"That is not it."

I thought of August's mouth on my breasts, his hands in my hair. The way I felt when he said my name, as if we spoke to each other in a secret language and he would be the only one ever to reach me. We did not belong to Waukesha and Waukesha did not belong to us.

"You know what will happen if he finds out," she said.

I tapped the iron against the stove and watched ash fall back into the embers but I did not say anything.

"Tell me you will stop," she said.

I shook my head. I could not stop seeing August any more than I could stop breathing or stop my heart beating.

"Tell me," she said again. "I insist."

"I cannot," I said.

"Why not?" She clenched her fists. "Of course you can."

I tapped the iron against the stove again and it clanged loudly.

"Stop that," said Martha. "Hattie is already asleep. You do not seem to understand. I am not asking you, baby sister. I am telling you. You are to stop."

"It is you who does not understand," I said. My voice pitched up. "You have no right to tell me what to do."

"I am the oldest," she said sharply. "You have no choice but to do as I say."

I leaned the poker against the stove and pushed at the stove door with my foot. There was nothing for it but to tell her the truth.

"I cannot stop," I said. "I *will* not stop. I love him and he loves me."

"Oh God!" she cried. She stood up so fast that her chair fell over. She clutched at the air in front of her the way a woman might try to keep a dish from falling. "Stop and think," she said. "Just stop and think. He will kill you."

I swung the stove door with my toe and then let it bang shut.

"I thought you said it was an accident," I said.

10

William Oliver stood in his shirtsleeves on the back steps of the laundry. When I came through the wet yard, he lifted one hand to his head and ran it through his rumpled hair and then stroked it over his beard. He watched me walk toward him.

I stopped at the foot of the stairs. The sun rose and light spread across the gray sky and the clouds still churned along the horizon.

He contemplated me for a minute and then waved at the wide expanse of sky. "Sometimes," he said, "you can wait all day and never see anything alive. Not a bird. Not a rat. Not one thing that moves. Other days, the sky is teeming with pigeons and the roads are glutted with squirrels. Why is that, do you suppose? What makes one day different from another?"

"One day is the same as the next," I said plainly. "It is only the seasons that change." I was tired. I had not slept much the night before. I had gone to bed when Martha was finished with me, but I had lain awake a long time, listening to her move around in the kitchen, and then listening to the beating of my own heart.

"Ah," he said. "The philosopher arrives."

"I am not a philosopher."

"But you show every sign of being a philosopher." He rolled back on his heels. "You arrive late to work. You sleep on the floor at lunchtime. You come in here looking entirely disreputable, like someone who has lost her way. Are these not the actions of a philosopher?"

I shook my head.

"They aren't?" He held his hands out, palms up. "And now, rain," he said. "If we stay here, we will be soaked. I know this is a state that brings you pleasure but I do not find it nearly so agreeable. Get inside."

We went up the dirty stairs to his office. He told me to sit down and then he sat across from me. He put his boot heels up on his desk. Rain pattered on the roof and the wagons that rolled by made a soft wet sound in the street below.

"Better keep your coat on. The man is late with the fires this morning," he said. He looked me up and down. "Perhaps taking a page from your book."

"Mr. Oliver," I said.

"William," he said.

"William," I said.

He held his hand up to stop me. "The thing that remains to be decided is what to do with you," he said.

I waited. When he did not say anything else, I cleared my throat. "I do not understand," I said.

"I believe Inge told me the whole story. I believe I have all of the facts."

"Inge is lying," I said. Inge's facts were not my facts. Inge's facts were something she had dreamt up all on her own.

"Have you explained this to your father? He is the kind of man who would be extremely interested in your experiences, if I am not too much mistaken." William Oliver smiled at me through his billy-goat beard. "No? No explanations for your father? Well. I guess I am not really surprised." He leaned forward and dropped his heels to the floor. He stood up and began to walk up and down in front of me. "It is understood that a girl like you is going to have adventures," he said. "This is unavoidable. But certainly not the kind of adventure you are having now. Certainly not some lout, a boy who can barely read and write, who drags you out into the woods and throws you down on the ground to have his way with you. Surely not. This is nothing but common. Nothing but coarse." He stopped in front of the window. "I would think you would want better than that, Mary. I would think you would hold yourself in higher esteem."

"It is not like that," I said, protesting. William Oliver knew nothing of August Bethke. He knew nothing of the way August held me.

"No?" He turned and looked at me. "What is it like, then?"

"Not like that."

"I believe Inge has a different opinion."

"Inge is lying," I said again. "She has no business talking about something she does not understand."

He folded his arms across his chest. "Mary," he said. "Inge is a neutral party here. Why would she lie? She has nothing to gain. I can rely on her to tell me the truth."

"She is lying," I repeated. "You are not being fair."

"Fair?" he said. "Fair? I'll tell you what's not fair. It is not fair that you come to work late and expect to be paid. It is not fair that you sleep on the job and expect to be paid. It is not fair that you show up in a dress so misused that you threaten to make the place infamous all by yourself. That is what is not fair in my humble estimation."

"I do not expect to be paid," I said hotly. This was more than I could bear. What were we talking about? My night with August, which was certainly none of William Oliver's business, or my pay?

"Is that so."

"Yes."

"Did you come and tell me that?" He looked around the office. "I do not remember that conversation, Mary."

"I did not think of it," I said slowly. This was true. And if this was all that William Oliver wanted, I did not mind. I would gladly forgo all my pay if only this conversation would stop.

"Your thoughts were elsewhere, no doubt."

I stared at my hands.

"I can assure you that I thought of it," he said. "I can tell you that Inge thought of it. I feel quite certain that all of the girls thought of it. They are arbiters of equity, after all. This is practically all they talk about." He waved his hand at the street. "In our kind of market, which is not yet a socialist market, no matter what men like your father might say, we work from basic principles. You work for wages, which I set. I also set the work that must be done for those wages, the terms and conditions. It is a simple economy. Do you understand?"

I nodded slowly.

He glanced over his shoulder and met my gaze. "Of course," he said, "money is not the only thing that can be exchanged. But whatever the exchange is for, in order to maintain harmony and equilibrium, the contract between the two parties depends on the equation I have described. Which is why it is so easily undone when a girl like you does not follow the most fundamental rules. Which is why your adventures have really upset the apple cart."

He turned away from the window and walked back to his desk, where he sat down and reached into his shirt pocket for a cigarette. He patted his chest in search of a match and then stood up and fished around in his trouser pockets. Finally he found what he was looking for and scraped the match across the underside of the desk and rolled the cigarette in his teeth until the tip poked into the flame. He watched the flame for a brief moment and then shook it out and dropped the match into a porcelain cup. He drew hard on the cigarette and then exhaled.

"It comes down to you," he said. "You have put all of this in motion. You have suggested a new equation. You have laid out a new set of rules." He picked a piece of tobacco from his lower lip and flicked it away. "I think I will be happy about this, in the long run," he said. "When we look at the greater scheme of things. And I know that you wish to be happy as well. The question is this: How do we take the next step?"

"I do not know what you mean," I said.

"I think you do."

I knotted my skirt in my lap.

"I often visit that tavern where your father works. Surely he explained this to you. That this is how you came to have this job. That it was my suggestion."

I felt the air go out of my chest. "Please," I said. "Mr. Oliver."

"William."

"William."

He waited but after I said his name, I said nothing. Naturally, I wished to dispute everything he said but I could not find the words. I had thought myself strong and full of ideas that needed only to be put into practice, but when I sat in William Oliver's office, it seemed a suffocating passivity had settled over me. Only a child raised to be silent will know what I mean when I say this. You can want to speak but then you cannot. The truth of the matter was that I could not afford to lose this job. I could not go home to my father and tell him I had lost my place of work. And I did not know how to balance that need—which in any case I felt to be more of an affliction than a need—with William Oliver's thinking.

I knew what he was asking. I knew that I would never do it. What I did not know was what would happen after that.

He lifted his heel and ground the spent cigarette against the sole of his boot and then dropped it in the cup with the match. He raised his gaze and looked at me. "I would not be too quick to say no," he said. "Not understanding things the way a bright girl like you understands things. What good is all of that philosophy if in the end you cannot answer this kind of question?" He sighed. "Mary," he said. "You will see this as a problem that does not have a solution, for that is the way the young always think, as if the only road is the one they would have chosen for themselves. They fail to see the possibilities of roads that are chosen for them. I believe that I have offered you a plum opportunity. We two can share quite a bit of pleasure. I will make it pleasant for you and you will come to enjoy it. But I can see that you do not yet share this view. That is fair. I will give you some time. I think it will not take long for you to come to your senses."

I worked beside Ella and Inge and Johanna until quitting time. They eyed me when I came back from William Oliver's office, Inge with a smug, self-satisfied air, Johanna quiet as a cipher, Ella far away. But I said nothing and did my best to keep my distance. At lunchtime we stood in the yard but they turned their backs to me and talked among themselves. I should not have been surprised. Water will seek its own level. I walked across the yard and sat with my coffee tin on the doors of a coal chute and unwrapped my slice of bread and half a pickle. These I ate sitting alone in a long oblong of sunlight, my skirt tucked under my knees.

That afternoon I stood on the top step of the ladder and looked at the burbling water and the sheets that swirled like strange billowy fish. I thought about the girl who had been at the laundry before me and how it must have been when she slipped, what she must have known the minute she felt herself going in.

I stood on the back steps at night and watched the stars blink into position and waited for August, but he did not come. At first, I wandered between my father's house and William Oliver's laundry in a state of disbelief. I could not imagine August would stay away. That was the hardest time. That was the time when August suddenly began to seem entirely unreal, just like a boy in a dream, and then the things we had done began to seem unreal also. But I knew those things were true. There were words for what we had done. We had made our way in the dark. We had climbed the luminous cliffs and up under the black evergreens and along the top of the bluffs. We had followed the long escarpment that ran from the foot of the river all the way east to the great falls just as if we had walked the long spine of America. We had reached the little house tucked into the woods. We had disappeared from the world. And when I thought he was gone, you will easily understand why I at first churned like the plates of the country itself, deep below the surface, wrecked and ready to split apart. If he did not come back, I would never be the girl I had been again. That thought was too terrible to put into words.

Only when I was finished with that did I start to feel righteous and angry. His absence did not seem to fit with all the things he had said and done. It did not seem possible that he would leave me just as soon as he had shown me that cabin in the woods. But I knew that this was the kind of thing that happened to other girls. I knew that it could happen to me.

Martha came out onto the back steps with her broom. She put her thin arm around my shoulders. "Is there a moon?"

I shook my head.

"Too bad. I would have liked to have seen the moon tonight."

I turned toward her and raised my eyebrow.

"Sometimes you just want to see the moon," she said defensively. "You are just in the mood for it." She paused. Then she squeezed my shoulder. "I saved you some soup," she said.

"I am not hungry."

"You need to eat."

"I must be coming down with something."

She frowned and stood her broom against the rail. Then she sat on the step and patted the stair next to her. "Sit next to me," she said. "Just for a minute."

I sat. A furry gray moth fluttered over the yard. I had hopes that she would be kind. I did not want to say so but I longed for her sympathy, as if that would prove she understood and did not hold anything against me. I sat with my hands open in my lap, palms up and fingers wide. I suppose you could say it was some sort of supplication, but I would not go so far as to say it was a prayer.

The man who lived in the house behind ours came out to the yard with his pile of newspapers and trash. These he dropped into the barrel at the foot of the garden. He leaned into the barrel and lit a match. After a few minutes, yellow flame licked up the insides of the drum and he searched the ground for dry leaves and twigs. He stood feeding these to the fire.

Martha stared off at the flames. Finally she heaved a sigh and put her hands on her knees. "I need to know," she said flatly. "Is he coming back?"

I shook my head.

"Oh my God," she said. She grabbed my arm and dug her nails into my skin. "He is not coming back?"

"No!" I said. "Stop that!" I pulled away. "That is not what I meant. Of course he is coming back!"

She softened slightly. "What did he say to you? Tell me everything."

"He said that he loves me."

"Of course he said that he loves you," she said. "They all say that. What else?" My sister had a way with contempt. It was her constant companion, like an imaginary playmate.

"That he wants to marry me."

"Indeed." She knocked against the broom and it fell into the yard. We both looked at it.

"Yes," I said.

"That is not much. He owes it to you to marry you." She made it sound like August had stamped and canceled me like a transaction at the bank.

The night sky bright with stars then and the air soft and cool and my sister beside me stiff as a bone, barren and dry as if eaten by animals, unable to see what I saw, unable to feel the things I felt.

"What if I do not want to marry him?" I said slowly. I did want to marry August. I wanted to marry August more than I had ever before wanted anything. But the idea of not marrying August suddenly came over me and provoked a weird elation, as if I had by my own choosing done something that was mine and mine alone.

She froze. "What are you saying?" she said. "What do you mean?"

"Never mind," I said. I knew I could not explain this. "Forget it."

She reached down and pulled a long weed from the edge of the steps. "I do not understand you," she said fiercely. Then she tore the weed to shreds.

The man in the yard behind ours knocked a stick against his barrel and little orange sparks flew up into the air and circled away above us. I watched them disappear. Then Martha put her arm around me again and I tried to pull away. But this time she held on.

"He was asking," she said quietly.

I straightened. "What did you say?"

"Nothing," she said. She squeezed my shoulder and then let her arm fall back to her side. "He wanted to know if you always go to work."

"Of course I go to work!"

"He said that William Oliver had come into the bar and he asked him how you were getting on. William Oliver told him that you were working out fine."

I imagined my father behind the bar, towel in hand, and William Oliver with his drink in front of him, maybe raising his glass, maybe singing my praises. He would say that Mary was a good girl. He would say that Mary was a hard worker. He would say anything to get my father to believe that he had my best interests at heart. My cheeks burned when I thought of the two of them, leaning together as if they were in cahoots about me.

"He should have been happy with that," I said.

She nodded. "Yes," she said. "But then he asked me if you go to work when you are supposed to. He wanted to know if what William Oliver said was true."

I went cold. When my father was before me with his fist raised, it was as if I did not belong to him. Then it was as if I belonged to him too much. "What did you say?"

"That you always get to the laundry on time and that you always come home on time."

"That should have satisfied him."

"He did not believe me. He raised his eyebrow. You know how he does that."

I shivered.

"I told him again," said Martha. "But he said that someone

told him they had seen you down below the mill bridge at night. Or a girl who looked like you. And you were not alone."

Smoke curled up from the barrel and drifted away on the small breeze. I wrapped my arms around my waist and rocked silently and studied the wooden step under my shoes. My mother's shoes. A dead woman's shoes, as if her every footstep would turn into my own.

"I do not know how you think you are going to get away with this," Martha said. She pushed herself up with her hands. "But I wanted you to know."

"What did you tell him?"

"I told him that the man who said this was mistaken. I told him that you were here. I told him that I saw you with my own eyes." She began to cry. "You have made a liar out of me."

"I did not mean to," I said.

She wiped her eyes with the hem of her dress. "You are arrogant and selfish," she said. "You have put me in harm's way."

"The responsibility for that lies with someone else," I said.

She wiped her eyes again. "You are being very foolish," she said. "All this for a boy you hardly know."

"I know him," I said.

"Then where is he?"

"I do not know," I said. I thought she would reply but she just turned from me with her face wet. She climbed the steps and went into the house.

The next night, I waited on the porch again. My father came from the kitchen and gave me a hard look, as if he knew I had done something wrong, and then thumped down the back stairs. He went briskly around the side of the house and I heard his footsteps fall away as he passed from our yard to the street. Night was falling, and after a minute I followed him down the drive and stood at the curb and watched him until he disappeared. Then I turned up the road and went the other way.

I walked to the lonely church where August and I had skated together across a flooded field. The church door gave a little when I pushed against it but it was locked. I leaned my forehead against the wood. Above me, in the stained glass windows, apostles turned to their work with great purpose, in scenes gone glittery gray under the starlight. Behind the church, the graveyard shimmered, its faint tombstones a fence between this world and the next. I followed the gravel path into their midst and then sat down and leaned against a headstone and looked up. I followed the stars until I found Polaris, a pinprick of light high atop the vault of the sky like the sharp point of a far arrow. But it showed me no road. My mother was forever beyond my reach. My father went about his business without scrutiny or inquiry, as if this was the just way of things and did not even bear mention. He was entitled to do with her as he pleased, just as William Oliver thought he was entitled to do with me as he pleased.

I could not read the inscriptions on the headstones around me, but I knew they marked someone's beloved, the lost one more loved in absence than they had ever been in life, as if this was the true condition of all families, as if this was the place love invariably arrived. Deep in the heart of my mother's stories was the long-shot promise that we could make our way out of the forest. Each tale offered the same idea: even when hope ends, hope survives. But she was gone and I could not see how.

Something rasped along the path behind me. It could have been leaves blown along the dirt in the wind. It could have been a dog on its way home. The sound came again but no wind moved the trees. I held still. I heard footsteps. When he walked up to me it was as if he already knew where I was. I got to my feet and brushed at my skirt.

"Edwin?" I said.

His lips curved. A smile.

"You frightened me."

"You come," he said.

"Did you follow me? Have you been following me?"

He patted his thigh with the flat of his hand. "You come," he said.

He led me to a door under the church. He jiggled the latch and pushed with his shoulder until the door gave with a thump. We stepped into a room where rakes and scythes leaned against the wall. A cot in the corner, with a crate next to it, and on the crate, a dirty china cup. Edwin picked up the cup and reached into his pocket for a piece of candle. This he stood in the cup while he searched his pockets for a match. Finally he pulled a paper box from his trousers. His hands shook. He turned and held the box of matches out to me and I lit the candle and stood the cup on the crate between us.

He sat down on the cot.

"This is your house?" I said.

He nodded.

"I thought you lived at that house in town." James Pulliam's house, with its fetid odors and gloomy rooms and cold, dank kitchen. The room under the church was clean and dry and smelled only of earth.

"Prison."

"That house is a prison?" I felt like I had to translate everything he said.

His face stilled and he looked away. "They have an executioner," he said. "They kill children." He tapped his thigh and moved his lips and looked hollow-eyed. Then he grinned. "I saw you." He ducked his head.

A wind came up and fell away and the trees out in the churchyard shifted and creaked. The candle tipped in its cup and began to smoke. I reached over and straightened it. There were stains on the brown blankets, a threadbare rag rug on the floor. The cot was the only place to sit. But when I sat down next to him, Edwin stood up. He made a pile of blankets on the floor. He lay down on his side and propped himself on one elbow. His thin face looked strange and theatrical in the flickering candle-light. He watched me.

"Where do you come from?" I said.

He gestured at the walls. "Out there."

"Waukesha?"

He shrugged, as if to say, Waukesha or elsewhere, it did not matter.

I lay down on my side and pillowed my head on my arm. The cot gave a little beneath me. We lay facing each other with the floor between us. I could hear the trees groaning and crack-ing outside. Spring always came like this in Waukesha, a great uncoiling of roots and leaves and buds, a crackling and sinking of ice on the river, the calling of birds and dogs, the humming of early rising insects in the newly warm air; a noisy symphony without a conductor.

He smiled at me and suddenly it all ran out of me like blood from a cut. I told him about my mother. Then I told him about my father. I told him that my sister was in love with a boy my fa-ther would not let her marry. I told him that Hattie wore braces but she did not need them and my father made her wear them just to torture her. I told him that my mother had been mur-dered and that my father was the one who had killed her. I told him that because of this my father would never tell us what had happened to her and the truth of the whole thing lay some-where beyond words and all we were left with was my sister's way of saying it. *The day Mother had her terrible accident.* Then

I told him about August and the day we met and the way we went skating over a field as if we could transform solid earth into anything we wanted. I rolled up my sleeves and showed him the burns on my arms. I told him about William Oliver and the thing he wanted from me and what he would do if I did not say yes. And then I told him that I had not seen August for almost two weeks and I was afraid that he was not the boy he had seemed to be, that he had used me and left me, like I was one of those stupid girls we were always hearing about. And I was not one of them. I was sure I was not. And then I started to cry.

Edwin reached over and gingerly patted my arm. Then he put his hand under his cheek. He gave me a look so tender I knew it could not be a mistake. I sat up.

Edwin sat up, too. Finally he said, "I can take care of you."

I rubbed my eyes.

"We can live here."

I looked around.

"At my house."

"Oh," I said. "No. Edwin. No."

"I can take care of you," he offered softly. Then he lay down again, his head on his arm in a pile of blankets on the cold floor, his thin frame nearly too long for the room. The candle flame wobbled and the light pitched around us on the walls. He looked up at me with his shiny eyes. He said my name. I hesitated but then I lay down. Edwin leaned forward and blew out the light.

In the morning, the birds began to call in the trees, single calls at first, low like the whistles of schoolchildren and then like the crying of young animals. When I stepped outside, I found Edwin sitting on a bench as if he were waiting for a train. He smiled when he saw me.

The sun was not yet up but the woods had begun to take

shape in the fading darkness. When we got to the road in front of the church, he put his hand on my arm. He stared hard at my face, as if he could organize his thoughts and find a way to come to me across a deep and wordless river. I waited. His hand rested on my arm. Finally he said, "You go."

"Edwin."

But he had already dropped his hand to his thigh and was striding away through the colorless tombstones.

I felt queer and light, as if I had unpacked a bag and left the contents strewn on the open ground and did not care what became of them. No one I knew would have let me go on and on like that, without interruption, attending to the things I said as if they mattered. I do not think I had ever said so much at one time.

I waited in the yard until Martha saw me. She opened the door and held it open the way you hold the door to let a dog inside. She took a plate from the food warmer and set in on the table. She told me to eat. Then she touched the side of her face. I saw the red mark that had begun to fade, as if the blow had come sometime before.

"I am sorry," I said. I wanted to reach for her but I did not.

"Yes," she said. "Well." She touched her face again.

"It should have been me," I said.

She stared at me. "Yes," she said bitterly. "It should have been you." She dabbed at her eyes. I felt my heart sink.

I looked at the cold toasted bread on my plate. I picked up the knife and stabbed the butter and then set the knife down. I felt the kind of anger that comes from shame, a thing that belonged to me alone.

Behind me, Martha picked up a plate that stood draining next to the sink. She dried it and put it on the shelf. Then she wiped her hands and hung the towel on the edge of the sink. She told me I could do my own dishes.

"Where are you going?" I asked.

"I have things to do," she said. Her voice like a blade.

I could not blame her. She was right to hate me. But I wanted to find a way to make things right. I wanted to go back in time and be the one who stood before my father. But I did not have a way to do that. For a minute I thought about going into my father's room and waking him up to tell him to hit me instead, but I knew that when he hit me, the mark of his blow would still be on Martha's cheek.

And then I realized that I had thought of the room where he slept as his room, not as my mother's room. As if he had taken her last acre and thrown his fence around it at last.

She reached over and straightened the dish towel. "I hope it was worth it," she said.

There was nothing in the world that would have been worth my father hitting her instead of me. Not even August.

"I was not with August," I said.

She closed her eyes. Opened them. Looked at me. "Where were you?"

I thought of the candle's little flame and the light on the basement walls. The leaves in the corners. Edwin's face. The stillness I felt when I put my head down on my elbow and watched him blow out the light. And the sleep that came like a deep river flowing.

"I did not mean for anything bad to happen," I said. "I made a mistake."

"Where *were* you?" she said again.

"I went for a walk," I said. "I met a boy. He took me to a room under a church. I fell asleep. When I woke up it was morning. So I came home." I felt the night slipping away from me.

She covered her face with her hands. Then she began to weep.

"No," I said, startled. "No. It was not like that. This boy

is not like that." There was nothing about Edwin that I would have compared to the average boy. He had odd ways. He was gentle and peaceful. He listened to me when I talked. "He is different," I said. "I think he has been following me around." I stopped.

She dropped her hands to her sides. "Do you know what you sound like?" she said. Her voice filled with disbelief, as if she could not imagine that I could be so stupid. "They are all like that."

I picked up my table knife and examined myself in the blade. Then I put the knife down. I could see that Martha was trying to regain her composure, but it kept moving out of reach, like a boat drifting away.

I could never tell Martha about Edwin. She had no compassion for those who were different. We had once seen a baby in town with a head so misshapen his skull looked like a bag of balls. And behind him, with her hand on the pram, came a woman dragging her dress, her hair uncombed and her face wild. When we saw them, Martha had crossed the street.

I did not agree with her. Edwin seemed as human as anyone I knew. The boy with hair like a bear coat had looked at me with the most lonesome expression that I had ever seen. He was human. They were all human, even the boy chained to the wall with the flippers for fists.

She would never understand. She would only believe that I had done wrong.

"Two nights in the woods," she said, as if she could read my mind. "Two different boys."

"I fell asleep," I said again. I spun the knife on the table and watched the metal gleam and dull and gleam again as it turned through the light from the stove.

"You have to stop," she said. She unfolded a pocket handkerchief and blew her nose and wiped her upper lip and balled the handkerchief in her hand. Her eyes were red rimmed and sore looking. "Please."

I slowly turned the knife next to my plate. "I do not see why you concern yourself," I said. My words hung in the air. Even I could hear my tone.

She took two steps across the kitchen and slapped me as hard as she could. The blow rang through my head. My ear on fire. Tears started in my eyes. I touched my cheek.

"You make it my business when he hits me," she shrieked.

"Stop trying to protect me," I said. "That is what gets you in trouble."

"Oh God," she screamed, and hit me again. And then again. Each of her blows was like a familiar thing traveling back to me. I did not resist. I just fell under her hand and forgot about Edwin. I thought of August in the dark, moving above me, his love and his strong grip, the way he turned my fingers in his hands until I thought he would wrench my bones into a new shape and I could in that pain give up the shape I had always known.

11

When I left, Martha was down on her knees with her skirt hiked up so she could scrub the kitchen baseboards with an old toothbrush. I stepped down into our bare yard and came along the side of the house. Lavender light lay behind the clouds on the horizon. When I reached the street, I felt my breath come easier. The terrible aching in my throat began to subside.

My hair was still damp but I had brushed it and pinned it and washed my face and hands and no leaves trailed behind me. I wore a wrinkled dress pulled from the mending basket, too tight at the waist and its hem coming undone, but it was clean. At the corner, I saw Mrs. Muehls, her fingers pinching the brim of her hat as if she walked in a wind. She carried her shopping net with its bunch of carrots and its cut of meat wrapped in white butcher paper. She looked at me and then stiffly turned her face away.

In the empty lots, boys rolled hoops and pitched pebbles in the dirt. In the distance, the bank turret flashed in the early sun. The interurban clattered past and men and women looked out at me. None was August Bethke. The brown boards of the livery stable rose and the liveryman stood in the street and unbuckled a team from an old phaeton with curtained windows. He dropped the clinking harness and led the two horses on heavy hooves onto the dull wooden floor of the barn, where the horses drank from a trough. The laundry's delivery cart came up the alley and the driver slapped his reins on the horse's rump. In the window above, William Oliver stared down at the street.

He got to me before I could get inside. We stood in the shadow of the laundry, where a cool black trapezoid cut into daylight.

"Mary," he said. He ran his fingers through his hair. He wore shirtsleeves and charcoal gray wool trousers, his white shirt without a collar and open at the throat, as if he had been up all night trying to sleep in his clothes.

"Good morning," I said quietly.

"I suppose you imagine we will now have some sort of barbaric scene," he said. "Is that it?"

"I do not know."

"You do not know."

"No," I said.

"Do you know nothing about me?" he said. When I did not reply, he sighed. "I do not know why I assume anything," he said. "You are the one with all the ideas. The philosopher. I am merely your humble servant."

I shook my head and looked away. I put my hand on the wall. I imagined I could feel the heat from the laundry, which seemed to me more pleasant and welcoming than it ever had before.

To say I was weary was to leave most of my fatigue unspoken. I could see how everything had been my fault, but I could also see that in all of it, the things I had done had seemed right, first one thing and then another until added together they made a sum that no longer made sense. I longed for August but August did not come. I longed for my mother but she was dead.

The deliveryman led the horse into the yard behind the laundry. William Oliver glanced down the alley and then turned back to me.

"The question remains the same," he said. "This should not surprise you."

I bit my lip and put my hands in my pockets. "Mr. Oliver," I said.

"Do not start that again."

I looked down.

"The one thing we will not do is stand here in the street," he said. "That is one thing I will not abide."

He walked behind me as we climbed the dirty wooden stairs to his office. When we came to the top he pushed past me and opened the door and walked into the room. The warm wet air of the laundry rose through the floorboards. His dark Bible lay open on his desk and he saw me glance at it.

"Do not look so surprised," he said. "Even a great man requires guidance from time to time. The rest of us must also consult those with wisdom far beyond our own. With all due apologies to your philosophical turn of mind, I find that I lack any such individual in my life. So it was John or Samuel Clemens and John won. At least, he won today." He held the book up. "Revelation. How the world will be made new. Consider yourself lucky. I might have been reading Darwin and then where would we be?"

His words bewildered me. "I am sorry," I said. "I do not—"

"No," he said. "I don't suppose you do. Your father is something of a Vandal, isn't he? I doubt he's seen to your education." He waved his hand at the wooden chair before the desk. "Sit down."

"My father," I said.

"Sit down, Mary."

I sat.

"Your father," he said. "He is not well liked by the better class of people. You are aware of this?"

The Bible's pages, dog-eared from the places where he had marked pages by turning down corners. The smell of the laundry swelled over us.

"Let me illuminate. People see your father as something of an ill-bred thug. He lacks—what is it?" He searched the air above his head as if the word might fall on him suddenly and with great weight, like an anvil. "Grace. For lack of a better description." He walked to the window and looked out. "He is just one of the teeming masses yearning to breathe free and that is no recommendation at all, I am afraid." He turned to face me. "Of course, you know that I am counting on these very qualities. Especially when you seem ready to go feral on us."

My mouth pulled but I said nothing. He made me feel stupid and then I felt ashamed and then I fell even more silent than usual.

"Feral?" he said. "No? It means wild. A child of the woods. A nymph of the forest. Raised by wolves. Romulus and Remus. Does this mean anything to you?" He stared at me. "No?" He sighed. "Your mother would surely fix this but your mother has left us. This must please your father. It certainly pleases him that men like me can no longer approach her and say the things we tend to say. Do you know that he punched me in the nose one night when I said something to her on the sidewalk? He did. The next week we had a drink and he told me that everything would be fine, as long as I left her alone. If I did not—" He lifted his hand to his neck and slashed it across his throat.

I stared past him. I was not going to discuss my mother with William Oliver.

He studied me. "Did he kill her? Has that thought crossed your mind? Perhaps we should consult a spiritualist. Call her to us and ask the question."

"Mr. Oliver—"

"William."

"William."

"What." He smiled at me, a smile unmarked by joy.

I shrank a little. "Can I go to work now?"

"Do you work here?"

I flinched. "I thought—"

"So we come back to that."

"To—"

"To the question," he interrupted. He stroked his beard and his eyes were warm and brown and hard. "We come back to the question, Mary, as we are always going to come back to the question." He reached into his shirt pocket and pulled out a pocketknife with a blackened bone handle. This he began tossing in the air and catching.

"Do you know what I did night before last?" he said. "I was thinking of you so I went up to see your father at the bar. I asked after his family. This is what men do, you know, because they have to work very hard to conceal the fact that at any moment they will fall on one another like a pack of wolves. And do you know what he said? He said that you were all fine. And he had that sort of Teutonic blankness about him that is unique to your tribe. You can be a cold and emotionless lot. So I believe the question is still in play."

I stood.

"Where are you going?" he said. In three steps he stood in front of the door. "Sit down."

I sat. He tossed the knife in the air again and again. Each time he caught it, it slapped against his palm and the hard muscles of his forearm flexed.

You always wonder what you will do if someone threatens you. You think you will be brave. You imagine that you will get away. But in the actual moment, you sit and watch the knife slap into the palm of his hand and slap his palm again and you listen to everything he says.

"I'm a patient man," he said. "But my patience is wearing thin, Mary." He flipped the knife as if it were a toy, a thing of no consequence, rather than what it was, which was the biggest thing in the room. I thought of the way all men carry knives; my father carried the pocketknife his father had carried, and even my brother Willie carried a knife from the age of six. My father gave it to him for Christmas one year, his only present.

"I do not have to ask your permission," William Oliver said. "You should be grateful that I was raised correctly and could not live with myself if I did not show you this kind of courtesy. But you can see the truth of the matter. We are here right now and there is nothing to stop me but my own good manners."

He studied me.

"I must say I am a little surprised," he said at last. "You are a very daring girl in every way. I did not think I would have to do so much persuading."

I took a deep breath and stood up. I would not let him do this without a fight.

"Oh," he said. He smiled and snapped the knife shut. "I see. Our interview is over."

"I am going to work now." I pushed the words out as if they were punches.

"Right," he said nastily. "You need this job. Your father. Your poor motherless sisters. That penniless boy who says he will marry you. And all the rest of it." He gestured at the air as if he might make my whole world visible. But he made no move to stop me. I walked past him and opened the door and came down the dusty stairs and opened the wooden door that led out into the street.

Above me, he lifted the sash and leaned out over the sidewalk. "Do not fail to recollect," he shouted. "End of day Friday. I will wait on you."

When I got home that evening, Martha stood on the back steps like a stone angel, her face grim and her arms hard around her waist. Then the light shifted and she looked like my mother. The mark on her face had faded and I knew she had spent the day washing the floors and making the beds and trying to figure out how to keep everything as normal as possible, as if she could create a house where all of us would be safe. But she knew differently. I knew she knew differently.

She came down into the yard and put her hand on my arm. "He is waiting for you," she said in a low voice.

I knew where I would find him. I walked as if propelled by something outside of myself, a magnetic pull as tense as a tightwire. Up the back steps. Through the warm kitchen. Down the dark hallway. Into the front room where he sat polishing his boots. When he saw me, he put the boot in his hand on the bench beside him and told me to come in and sit down. His voice mild-mannered, the tone of a man who plans to discuss something pleasant. But his look cut through me. I did as I was told.

He picked up the boot and spit on the toe and began to work on it, moving his rag in circles and stopping every so often to look at the result. Then he picked up a brush and turned to the heel.

He wore his work clothes. He wore the shirt that I had ironed the night before, and he wore the black trousers that I had washed and hung on the line on Monday and then pressed on Tuesday. He wore his blue necktie and his black coat and his mended black stockings. He sat with his legs wide apart so the dirt he brushed from his boots would fall between his knees. His hair was wet and combed.

Even if my thoughts had not flattened and disappeared, taking my words with them, I knew how hopeless it was to struggle against him. When he got an idea in his head, it stuck like something nailed in place. Once I had been singing a song when he came in from work, just a small song, *Go tell Aunt Rhodie the old gray goose is dead*, and I was just little then, could not have been more than eight, and he swung at me as soon as he came through the door and then made fun of me for crying. He worked at the flour mill in those days and he wanted the house quiet when he came home.

"Where have you been?" he said.

"At work," I said.

"I see." A clod of dried mud fell to the floor. "All of this time at work?"

"Yes."

"From yesterday until today? At work?"

The dirt on the floor. The sound of his rag.

"No?" he said. "Not at work?"

"I went for a walk."

"Like a hure." He looked at me, his eyes small and round. "You know what that is. A whore." He said the word *hure* in the American way, so it was exaggerated and sounded like a word spoken by some other man. He held the boot in front of him and turned it so he could brush along the side.

I swallowed, choked the way another person might have been choked by mud in a landslide, water in a drowning.

"That is right, yes? You have become a whore?"

I shook my head.

"No? That is not what I hear. I hear you go with many men. That you have a fine business for yourself up there in the woods."

I cried and shook my head. The air in the room thinning out and vanishing like I would never breathe again.

"And why should I believe anything you say?" he said. He put the brush down on the bench next to him and spit on the boot and held the boot between his knees and began to rub it with his rag in straight strokes. "I know you are a liar, so." He rubbed the boot hard and then waved it through the air between his knees and looked at it. "I do not listen."

Tears rolled down my cheeks. The sound of the brush on the boot heel again. The house silent as Martha waited as quiet as death in the kitchen.

"Do I not provide for you?" he said. "Is this not my house?" I could not speak.

"And I am your father." When I did not reply, he stopped rubbing the boot with his brush and looked at me. "You answer me when I talk to you, girl," he said.

"Yes," I said. My voice strangled.

"And these things are clear to you?"

"Yes." I blinked and looked around.

"And what I say goes?"

"Yes," I said. And swallowed a sob. I knew weeping would only make things worse. He would tell me to stop my crying or he would give me something to cry about. And then he would.

He put the boot on the bench and picked up its mate and studied it. "So," he said. "Now comes the question. What do we do with a hure? Can a decent house keep her? Can she go out among the neighbors?" He ran his finger along the edge of the boot and looked at the tip, testing for dirt. "No. No. These are not things for a hure."

I felt the word ripple through me. I was not a whore. I was nothing, just a tiny speck in the whole wide world, cast about by things I could not see and could not control, but I was not a whore. August loved me. He loved me. And Edwin was just a strange boy with strange ideas whom I had somehow come to know. I took a very deep breath. "But I—" I said.

My father stood up and slapped his rag onto the floor. "You shut up when I am talking to you," he screamed. "You shut up now."

"But I am not—"

And then my head jolted through black and there came a million pinpricks of jittery white light. The color in the room receded. The sound in the room disappeared in the shushing inside my skull. Everything around me vanished. I could not lift my head.

After a few minutes, the room began to brighten. I tasted metallic blood in my mouth. Now I could hear the bench creak. Now I could hear him breathing. He stopped next to me and I saw his spit-shined boots through the little space between my elbow and the floor.

"Next time, you are out on the street," he said. "I will not have a hure in my house." Then he kicked me and I cried out. He lifted his boot over my face and for a moment I thought he would stomp me into nothingness, into even less than I was at that moment. But he put his foot down without touching me and I lay breathless and weeping while his footsteps went down the hall. The back door slammed and he was gone.

Martha wrapped a cold towel over my cheek and tied it on top of my head but it did no good. My head pounded and my face pulsed and my mouth throbbed. She had washed my mouth but dried blood still flaked from my lips when I moved. A little trail of me left behind, pointing out that I was nothing but a whirling particle of earth. My father raved about equality and justice and freedom and the workingman, but in the end, that was all he cared about. Justice but not for us. Mercy but not for us. We were not citizens of his land. We were the land itself, something to conquer and master and turn to his hand.

I sat up and pulled the towel away. I touched the swelling along my jaw and flinched. I tried to pull my knees up to my chest but felt a sharp stab under my ribs and so let my knees drop. I lay down and wrapped my arms around my pillow and stared into the dark. I wished I had something that belonged to August so he would be with me. But I had nothing. In the flickering light of the hunting hut he had built a fire in a stone pit that stood under a makeshift flue and carefully unbuttoned my dress and pulled it over my head. He had let his palm slide down over my belly. He had lifted my chemise and pulled that over my head. I stood before him motionless while he unbuttoned his own shirt and then unbuckled his belt and let his trousers fall clinking to the floor. He held me against him before he kissed me. The light moved over the walls and the smoky fire filled the air with the smell of burning wood. The night did not fall away but grew larger somehow and deeper, as if the span of stars and the light of suns far distant and the moving of the earth we walked on were all new and we were alone among them, the first, the bearers of this unbearable secret, and joined together forever because of it. I knew that he would come back. But I did not know when and I grew worried in the waiting and then I told myself to have some faith in him and in the telling I knew that I had lost all faith. I listened to the throbbing in my head as if a terrible river of blood pounded against a different shore.

Something dark moved on the far side of the fence. The houses were still and our neighbors were not out in their gardens. No one bundled trash into the barrel behind the fence and no smoke curled to the sky. The dark shape moved again. I left my bucket at the pump. Edwin crouched at the end of the woodpile. When he saw me, he grinned and stood up. He reached over and patted my arm.

I thought of my father, not home yet but liable to come up the drive at any moment. "You cannot be here," I said. "My sister will kill me." *My father will kill you*, I thought, *if he even lays eyes on you.*

He squinted at me. Then he raised his hand and touched my face, very lightly, right along the jaw, where my father had struck me.

I leaned away. "Do not touch me."

He pulled his hand back.

"You have to go," I said. I looked around to see if we were being watched.

His arms flapped helplessly. "The armies that march come upon us in the open," he said. "They ride dark horses and they come upon us in the fields and I was there and I saw what happened when the armies," he said. Then he stopped. "I fought in that war," he said miserably, and his face darkened. "I fought in that war, too." He gazed past me to the open sky and searched the long line of horizon that ran out to the prairie and then east to the gray lake. His lips moved. Then he looked back at me. "What happened?" he said. He pointed at my jaw.

"It is nothing," I said. "My father."

"Why?"

I swallowed. How could I explain any of this to Edwin? It was impossible. So I said nothing and Edwin waited and watched me. Finally I said, "He says I am a bad girl." And felt the truth of this drive me into the ground.

"You come," Edwin said.

"I cannot," I said.

"You come," he repeated.

"No," I said. "And you must go. You cannot be here."

"*You* cannot be here," he said. "You come." He worked very hard to make the words. He leaned forward and patted my arm. "You come," he said. "You come."

"Stop it," I said. "I cannot go with you."

Edwin took a step toward me.

"Maybe I can come and see you later," I offered.

He patted my arm and patted my arm, his face sorrowful.

"If you do not go," I said. And then I stopped. I did not want to hurt Edwin. I did not want anything bad to happen to Edwin at all.

"Please," I said. "You will only make things worse."

He dropped his hand back to his side. He turned and walked in his long loping stride across the neighbor's backyard. When he reached the street he looked back at me, his haunted face still, his hand moving against his thigh. Then he was gone.

The grass was heavy with dew and the air reeked of wild onion and the forsythia bloomed in frilly yellow hedges, broken branches, the promise of flowers everywhere in the antic green shoots under the trees. Spring.

Martha stood on the back porch with her arms folded across her chest. I waved but she did not move. I crossed the grass to the pump and picked up my pail. When I carried it up the steps, she stood back and let me pass.

"I do not suppose you will tell me who that was," she said.

12

Three nights later I carried my dustpan into the backyard and August stepped out of the shadows. He said my name and I dropped the dustpan and my knees turned to water. He smiled and reached over and took my hand. I felt his touch pitch through me, the same warmth spreading like liquid through my chest, the same bucking of my heart, the same idiotic smile like something I could not control. He was here. He had not forgotten me. He had come back.

He took my hand and led me out of the yard and through the trees on our neighbor's lot. He held my hand with one hand and held the branches back with the other, and I let him lead me into an open space where he put his arms around me. I leaned into him and lay my head against the coarse wool of his coat and stood breathing him in as we swayed in the dark. From far away, the sounds of the night in the city.

He put his mouth against my hair and said something I could not understand. He tightened his arms around me. I pulled away. My ribs throbbed, the bruise like something that had split open and begun to bleed again.

He took my arm. "What's wrong?" he asked. "What is the

matter with you?" He looked at my face and then looked closer and raised his fingers and brushed them against my blue jaw. "Jesus," he said. "What happened?"

"Where have you been?" I said.

"What?" he said.

"You did not come."

"I wanted to. I could not."

"You could not? Or you would not?"

"I could not." He ran his fingers through his hair. He usually wore a hat and one night he had dropped it onto my head when I was cold, and had slung his coat over my shoulders and I had walked next to him, feeling the warmth of him in his warm coat. He had pulled the hat down over my eyes and laughed.

"Where is your hat?" I said. I reached over and touched his hair.

"Lost."

"Lost?"

He sighed. The clearing was very small and quickly ran out into the underbrush and beyond that, the backyard of the next house. "We should walk," he said.

"No," I said. I glanced at my house, visible now only as a faint square with dark windows through the trees, a block of light cast from the kitchen window into the yard. I knew that Martha waited for me inside. "I cannot," I said. "We must stay here."

"Then sit down. Here." He gestured around us and then took his jacket off and spread it on the grass so I would have a place to sit.

The ground was cool and damp. We sat with our legs crossed. August picked up a stick and dug at the grass and scraped through the dirt by his boots. I sat very still and tried to breathe through the pain in my ribs. Finally he tossed the stick into the underbrush and leaned forward and took my hand.

Then he dropped it and put his arm around me. I winced and pulled away.

"Stop," I said.

"You are very mad at me."

I lifted one shoulder and let it drop. I was angry but more than that I was ashamed of my pain. I thought it did more than hurt me but marked me and I did not want August to see that I was marked. I did not want him to see me as my father saw me, a girl who could be easily crushed. I wanted August to be in love with the girl I wanted to be, a strong girl who had been made out of the love we shared.

"You should be mad," he said, off on the wrong track but he didn't know any better. "To keep you waiting like that. You are right."

I swallowed hard. "You do not understand," I said.

"Every day I wanted to come to you," he said sadly. He leaned forward over his knees, the shadows making his eyes seem dark as sockets, his mouth just a dark slash, his face unknown in its details. In that moment he did not look like August at all but looked like a stranger come to me under the trees. He picked at the grass and then sighed and looked straight ahead. In a very flat voice he said that he might as well tell me the truth. He might as well get the whole thing out in the open. He had not wanted to stay away so long but it was all out of his control. He had been in jail. It was a terrible mistake. The police thought he was someone else. They had been looking for a pair of men who had been seen boosting lumber from construction sites around town. The night after he brought me home they found him walking with his brother Alfred out on the edge of town where some new houses were going up and they took them in for no reason at all, just for walking down the street. He and Alfred had been locked up in the new city jail for days. They had tried to run and they would have gotten away if they had not come up against a barbed-wire fence that some farmer had put up to keep his dairy in one place. When they turned, the police were right behind them. The police had billy clubs. Which they had used and then dragged the brothers back to the road.

They rode in the paddy wagon into town and stepped out into the light under the street lamp in front of the courthouse and then the head policeman led them into the police station and down a long corridor to the jail. For two days they were the only ones there and August began to wonder if they would ever get out. But finally his father hired a lawyer. The lawyer had come to the jail under the courthouse and the man who kept the keys had unlocked the door to their cell and swung the door open just wide enough to let the lawyer in. The lawyer had sat there with them on one of those hard wooden pallets that pass for beds in a jail and had asked them to tell him everything they knew and of course they did not know anything. All they had done was go for a walk after dark. Just the way he had walked with her. Exactly the same. This was not a crime, was it? And the lawyer had listened and had written some things down on a piece of paper he had clipped to a board, including their names and dates of birth and where they usually worked and their home address, and who their employer was. He told them to be very quiet and not say a word to anyone and to keep their own counsel at all times and to give him a few days and he would see what could be worked out. And that was what they did. They followed the lawyer's instructions to the letter and sat in the jail cell and did not say a word except maybe thank you when the woman who cooked for the prisoners brought them their meals. Very polite, to show everyone that a mistake had been made. But very restless because they knew their father could not work without them and they were losing money every day. And of course he wanted to get to her. That was the main thing, really. He needed to get to her.

They did not have to stand trial. And of course there would not have been any point because they were dead innocent. The lawyer talked to the prosecutor and they made a deal. The lawyer paid some money that their father put up. August and Alfred walked out of the jail that very afternoon. The first thing he did was go home and take a bath and find some clean clothes. Then he had a meal. When the sun went down, he sat with his brother on the front porch and watched the neighbors come home from work. He imagined the happy scenes behind all of those windows. Dinner to be eaten. Maybe sister would play piano after the pie. The women would all be fresh and pretty and the men would be turned out in nice clothes. Things like that. He liked to think about things like that. When it was full dark, he left Alfred smoking on the porch and made his way to my house. Watching the window of my house. Watching Martha at the sink. Watching a shadow behind her he thought must be me.

"And now I see I should have come here sooner," he said. "Something has happened." He picked up my hand and put it down. "Did he hit you?" he asked quietly. "Bad?"

I lifted one shoulder and let it fall.

"Just here?" He touched my jaw lightly and I flinched.

"And here," I said, swallowing. I lay my palm flat over my ribs.

"He punched you here?" His voice tender, disbelieving.

"He kicked me," I said.

"He kicked you?" He sat up straight.

I nodded.

"Because of me?"

"He said I am a whore," I said simply. The word the judgment of a prosecutor from a land to which I did not belong, a far distant land I lived in every day.

"Because of me?" August rolled up onto his knees and put his hands on my legs and looked at me. "Just because of me?"

"Yes," I said softly. "Because of you."

We sat in the dark. I did not mind that August had been in jail. He had explained it in such a plain and straightforward way that I knew he must be telling me the truth. Another girl might have stopped short and perhaps I should have. But I did not. I held his hand in the dark. I understood prison.

After a time, August began to walk up and down in front of me.

"I will go and see him," he said.

"You cannot," I said softly.

He stopped and stood with his hands shoved deep into his pockets. He looked at me, at my injuries, and he slammed the heels of his hands into his eyes. As if my pain was his pain. As if he could not bear to see me suffer.

"It is what I have to do," he said.

"You will make it worse."

"No," he said. "No. I will make it right." He held out his hand and I took it and he helped me to my feet.

"I am afraid," I said, but I did not tell him what I meant. Afraid of a sun that would explode through the sky and rain fire down upon me. Afraid of a great maw in the earth that would swallow me whole. Of course August would not know what I meant. He thought the world was the same for all people and all of those people were just like him.

He put his arms around me and ran his hand up and down my back as if he were trying to quiet an anxious horse. "Do not be scared," he said. "There is no reason to be afraid."

I pressed my cheek against his shoulder. I thought of leaving my father's house and leaving my sisters and leaving the place I had lived with my mother and leaving the things that remained of her, that table, this chair, the pinch-waisted vase on the table in the front hall, her wedding picture in the front room. I felt the ground fall away when I imagined going with August, the ground and the sky and the great turning of the world itself. But he rubbed my back and told me not to worry. He told me to trust him. He said that everything in the world was hard but in this case things were simple. He wanted to kill my father for the things he had done to me but he would not. He would go to the tavern and he would stand before him. He would introduce himself. He would tell him that we were going to be married. And that once we were married, he would be the only man in the world who would be entitled to touch me. By morning, things would be fixed forever.

13

The light from the kitchen window cast a dark radiance over the yard. I turned my face away from August's shoulder and he kissed my forehead the way you would kiss the head of a child. I smiled a little and let my arms fall to my sides and let myself rest against him. I could feel his heart beating.

He gently cupped my face in his hands. "I would do anything for you," he murmured. "You know that." He kissed me again. Then he pulled his coat collar up until it stood around his throat. "I will come back soon."

The fire had burned to coals in the stove but Martha still sat in her straight-backed chair. She looked up at me when I came in. "Are you all right?" she said. "Where have you been?" She stood and crossed the floor and brushed the leaves from my hair and crumbled them into the sink. "You think only of yourself," she said. "Not of us."

"I was just outside," I said.

"Then you know that boy was here."

"August?"

"No," she said curtly. "The other one."

"What other one?"

"The lunatic," she said. She pointed at the back porch. "He came right up onto the steps. He came right up to the door. When he saw me he ran away. I do not know what he expected. But he was out there like the bogeyman, right there on our back steps." She hugged herself. "He cannot come here," she said. "We have a child in this house. What if Hattie saw him? What then?"

"I know," I said. "I told him." I reached up and fingered my hair and found a twig and twisted my hair until the twig was free.

"Make it your business to tell him again."

"I will." I tossed the twig into the sink.

Martha looked me up and down. "You should see yourself," she said acidly. "No wonder they talk. Fix yourself. Straighten your skirt."

I pulled at my waistband until my skirt was straight and combed my fingers through my hair. I did not want to be fixed. I wanted to be outside with August, running away through the night.

Martha sat heavily in her chair. "I have to ask you," she said. "I think I have a right to know. Is it true?"

"Is what true?"

"Do you go into the woods?"

Did I go into the woods? Of course I went into the woods. I went into the woods every chance I got. When I was a child, I went into the woods to find acorns and stones. When I was older, I went into the woods to draw pictures of ferns. Once I caught a tiny dusty toad and let it hop across the palm of my hand, its eyes bulging and its throat fluttering like its heart beat under its tongue. I went into the woods and counted the eggs I found in a robin's nest and learned to identify the calls of the wood thrush and the oriole. I looked up at the sky and longed to float free with the hawks that sailed in long slow circles above me. I stood in a place that belonged to no one but me.

"It is not what you think," I said. I brushed the seat of my skirt and bits of grass fell to the floor.

"Look at yourself." She leaned back and studied me. "Covered with leaves and dirt and sticks. No decent girl would allow this."

"So you think I am a whore," I said. I had no idea how quickly and easily my sister would think the worst of me.

"Do not use that word."

"Why not?" I said. "That is what this is all about. You have such a low opinion of me that this is the first thing you think when you wonder what's going on. That I must be a whore. My God, Martha."

"What else am I supposed to think?"

"I have no idea," I said slowly. "I guess you are going to think what you want to think. No matter what I say."

The embers popped and shifted.

"Do you want me to count it down for you?" she said. She held her hand up. "One. You disappear from this house at night. Two. You run around all night in the woods. Three. You ask me to lie for you. Four. You make sure that I am the one who takes your punishment when he finds out." She ticked the items off on her fingers like this was a list she had been keeping for a while, one that was familiar to her and even comforting, like a story she told herself so she would know what to believe. "Five," she said. "Strange men are coming to our back door. Six. The whole town is talking."

"So you side with him," I said. I thought of the way she stood in the window and looked like my father, with everything about her uncanny, as if he had taken her and shaped her and made her look like himself.

She picked up the stove poker and hefted it against her palm, testing its weight like she might be considering hitting me with it. Then she put it down again. "I am siding with myself," she said. "Just as you have."

I leaned against the sink. The neighbor's dog barked. A voice called and then a door slammed. I listened to the sounds of life falling away and breathed in the hush of a solitary cell. My father's house. My father's rules. My father's crime. I could not bear another minute of it.

"You are going to think what you like," I said. "I cannot stop you." I made a big show of casually studying my fingernails, as if what I was about to say was barely important at all. "But right now, August Bethke is at the bar, telling him that we are going to be married." I looked up at Martha to see how she would take the news. But she just reached over and closed the door on the stove and pushed the latch.

"He will never say yes," she said. "He will never give you permission to marry that carpenter."

"August is not asking."

She glanced at me then, puzzled.

"August is telling, not asking," I said. "He is explaining how things are going to be."

I felt proud when I said this, and glad of August's strength, glad that I had found a man who was willing to go up against my father. I did not tell her that I was afraid. I did not tell her about William Oliver. I did not tell her about Edwin. Instead I leaned against the sink and told her that August loved me and I loved him. Yes, I had been to the woods and I had spent nights with him and I would go again and again for there was something there that I could never find here and that was love and real love and a man who would protect me. I gripped the sink with my hands. We had found our way to each other as if by spell or fate. We would never lose each other. I was to be his forever and he would always be mine.

I spoke with the conviction of a girl who has never been in love before, never followed its rocky path, never seen that change comes upon each of us, never discovered that sometimes, when a door closes, God does not open a window, nor does he open a door, nor is there a way out. I was massively infected with my own innocence, a disease for which there is only one cure.

Martha watched me, a peculiar expression on her face. I thought she would say something mean and cruel, which would prove beyond a shadow of a doubt that she had no way to refute anything I had just said. But all she did was give a small bitter laugh. "Marie," she said, "you are even more foolish than I thought." And then she stood up and went to bed.

I sat in the kitchen for a long time. Our house was silent. For all the things I had said to Martha, I had failed to tell her about William Oliver. And I should have told her about Edwin. I told myself that she was being ridiculous. She could not understand if she did not have all the facts and I had stupidly withheld these. I counted up the things I should have known and should have done and wondered if the choking feeling in my throat might have gone away if I had been able to get everything out. Then I wondered if she would have believed me even if I had been able to get it all out. The William Oliver story seemed preposterous but then it did not. In fact, it was no more preposterous than the fact that my father had murdered my mother.

Rain pelted the windows and I heard a sound that was not rain. When I turned, I found Hattie standing in the doorway to the hall, a phantom child in her white nightgown. She swayed and caught the doorway in one hand. Then she came and stood next to me.

"What do you see?" she asked. She looked out into the yard.

"Shhh," I said. I put a finger to my lips. "Why are you up?"

"I could not sleep." She folded her arms across her chest. "Why are you up?"

"I could not sleep, either."

"What is that sound?"

"It is the rain," I said. "See?"

We stood at the sink and looked out into the yard.

"It is beautiful," she said.

"Come on," I said. "I have an idea."

I walked out to the mudroom and sat on the bench and took off my mother's shoes and rolled my torn stockings down over each knee. I unbuttoned my blouse and slipped it off and dropped it on the floor. I unfastened the hook at the waistband of my skirt and let my skirt fall on top of my blouse.

Hattie watched me. "What are you doing?" she said.

I turned the knob and let the door fall open and then stepped out onto the porch. Rough floorboards, soft rain, the sound of water in the dark. I looked back at my sister. "Be careful," I said. "Watch for splinters. And keep your voice down."

A pallid mist drifted across the yard and hung under the black trees. If all the souls lost on the earth had stepped out of that night I would not have been surprised. Hattie followed me down the stairs and onto the wet grass.

"Look up," I said.

She turned her face to the sky. The rain fell on us as if we were sightless. I opened my arms and began to turn in slow circles, pivoting on one heel, my toes sunk and releasing in the mud. I turned faster and faster and then Hattie spread her arms slowly, as if testing the air, and then she spun beside me. I did not care if Martha woke up. I did not care if the neighbors turned their lights on and stood on their porches and turned their dogs on us and burned their trash and gave us evil looks.

I laughed and Hattie laughed, too, her hair sleek against her head like the wet pelt of some slippery animal. We were like lost girls then, made of rainwater and the night. I wondered if our mother could see us, if she had taken her place in the sky and could look down at us and laugh at the way we were nowhere to be found but in her absence had become completely free.

Then Hattie ran from me and twirled under the trees and I ran to catch her and she screamed and ducked and dodged until, finally breathless, I caught up with her. I put my arms around her and rested my cheek on her wet hair, her chest heaving and the sharp pain of my own breath under my bruised ribs. I did not care. Rain washed over us and the trees creaked and dripped in the night.

"Isn't it wonderful?" I said.

She shivered. "It makes me feel alive," she said.

I pulled back and looked at her, teeth chattering, hair wet and hanging around her shoulders.

"You need a bath," I said.

"So do you."

"I will fetch the water. You go inside and take everything off in the mudroom."

"You will wake Martha," she warned.

"So?" I said.

"She'll be mad," she said. And then she grinned.

"I do not care," I said.

I rolled the washtub out from under the sink and set it in the middle of the room. I struck a kitchen match and lit the lamp with its red glass shade. When the water had just begun to steam I lifted the copper and emptied it into the washtub. Hattie lowered herself into the water. I gave her an old tin cup and a bar of Fels soap so she could wash her hair. I leaned against the sink and watched her. The smell of rain and earth filled the kitchen. She slid down in the tub until the water came up to her shoulders.

"Tell me a story," she said.

The clock ticked in the front room. I pulled a chair up next to the washtub. The only stories I knew were my mother's stories and I picked one.

I told her about an old nobleman who lived alone near Garz, back on the island that was haunted by the golden seagull and the dwarves and the bells under the sea. I told her that there was a small castle in the woods, with spires and turrets and a drawbridge to keep everyone out. The woods themselves were haunted by black dwarves. You could often see their footprints in the sand, thousands of them, like a band of unruly children had been dancing along the water's edge. The old nobleman lived in the castle. He had once had three beautiful daughters and they were known far and wide as the fair-haired maidens, but he had been cruel to them and they had left him all at once. Now he lived alone. He'd been a hunter and a sportsman but he withdrew from all activities and did only the few things that still pleased him: he sat alone, he drank alone, he ate alone. He spent all of his time thinking about the black dwarves who lived in his woods. They were the worst of their kind and the old nobleman would have been better off afraid of them. They had ways that were unknown to men and they liked to play tricks. They carried hatchets and wore armor that no blade could pierce. If they caught you alone, you might as well say your prayers.

"But, like all dwarves, the black dwarves could be overcome. If you had the cap that belonged to a dwarf, you had his magic. If you had the glass shoe that belonged to a dwarf, you had his power. One day the old nobleman came across a tiny silver bell. He knew what it was right away and picked it up and put it in his pocket."

Hattie sloshed in the bath. "So he rang the bell and asked the dwarf to bring his daughters back," she said.

I shook my head. "That is what you would think," I said. "But that is not what happened. The old nobleman called the dwarf to him and asked for riches. He asked for wine. He asked for a great table laden with meat and fine food of every description. Then he asked for beautiful clothes, a cape and soft leather boots and a set of chain mail made of chased silver. A helmet made of gold.

"The dwarf brought all of these things. But he grew tired of the man's demands, for the man always wanted more. One day the dwarf decided he would turn himself into a bird and fly over the nobleman's castle and see what he could see. This he did. Down below he saw the nobleman sitting in his courtyard, surrounded by his treasure, all alone. The next time the nobleman rang the bell, the dwarf did not appear. Instead, an old woman walked up to the castle gate. The nobleman tried to send her away. He wanted his dwarf. But the old woman said that when he rang the bell, he'd called her. Now he must tell her what he wanted. Of course, the old woman was the dwarf in disguise but the nobleman did not know that. He told the old woman that he did not need to listen to her and she should go away before he gave her something to be sorry about. But the old woman just laughed and stood at his gate and did not leave. She leaned on a white staff and on it there were strange carvings in an ancient language that the nobleman did not know.

"All of a sudden the nobleman stopped arguing with the old woman. A sly look came over his face and he pointed to the sea beyond the castle and cried out, 'Look at them! There must be thousands of them at work!' And he explained that he could see the black dwarves who lived under the hills at the edge of the woods and every day they came down to the sea and caused ships to wreck so they could pilfer the cargo and hide casks of wine and crates of amber and all the best parts of the cargo in their crystal palaces underground. And he could make them do his bidding and they looked to him as their king and they brought him the choicest parts of the loot.

"This story made the old woman angry because the dwarf inside her knew that it was not true. But the dwarf also knew that stories have a way of getting around. If the old nobleman told enough people that he ruled the black dwarves, pretty soon everyone would think that he did. So the dwarf decided to teach the nobleman a lesson.

"'Tell me,' he said. 'How do you make the black dwarves do your bidding?'

"And the nobleman took the bell from his pocket. He explained that when he rang his bell, the dwarf must appear and he must do exactly what the nobleman wanted.

"The old woman took one look at the bell and said, 'Oh, what a beautiful bell! I have never seen anything like it! Will you sell it?'

"But the nobleman shook his head and said he would not sell it, because there was not another such bell in the entire world. He would not give it up for anything. 'And what a delightful sound it has,' he said. 'Only listen, mother. Is there any weariness in the world, any sorrow at all, which cannot be softened by the sound of this bell?' And he rang it again.

"The old woman thought the nobleman could not resist money so she flashed a handful of silver dollars in front of him, a great handful, more than the nobleman had ever seen. Still he said the bell was not for sale. So the old woman held her staff out to him and showed him its strange writing. She began to entice him with talk of the secret arts, and all kinds of charms and wonders, and how these would bring him everything he had ever wanted, far more than the bell could bring by itself. Before long, she could see that the nobleman was wavering. He held the bell in the palm of his hand and he looked at the white staff on which she leaned. She kept talking, telling him of the way that the world would be made perfect and everyone would be the same, but he would be wealthy and held in high esteem and he would never be sad or lonely again, and the island on which they lived would be a perfect land in the middle of the ocean, just the way the old songs said it would one day be. A heaven on earth, she promised, all for one and one for all."

Hattie tipped a cup of water over her head. "He took it?" she said. "Right?"

I nodded. "Yes," I said. "How could he resist? He thought the old woman was a witch and she was offering him what he had always wanted, which was everything just the way he alone always wanted things to be. Who would not want that? So he took the white staff and gave the old woman the bell and it turned out that the old woman had not lied. The white staff brought him riches. His cows and sheep grew fat and he was soon known as the wealthiest man on the island. Everywhere he went, the people bowed to him. He tried to live a quiet life but he could not understand why the white staff never forced the dwarf to do his bidding. But you know why. As soon as he had his bell back, the black dwarf sewed it back on his cap and disappeared underground. The bell had much more power than the staff."

When I finished, I tucked Hattie into her bed as if she were still a very little girl, smoothing the quilt and patting her hair. Just as she turned to go to sleep, she told me she loved me.

"I love you, too," I said. Warmth spread through me. Whatever else might be true, Hattie loved me and the night had chased away all of my worries about Martha and my father. August would soon be on his way back, like someone carried out of the world of dreams.

I closed the door and came back into the kitchen and

poured a little more hot water into the tub. I stripped and stepped in and sat with my arms wrapped around my knees. I thought of a black dwarf drilling down into the ground like a snake sliding into its hole. I dipped my hands into the water as if I could raise from the tub the sounds of the river at night, and the soft sounds of the oars as August pulled us toward shore.

In the morning, the trees dripped. I lay awake fully dressed with the blanket pulled up over my clothes as if I were already in exile from a land I did not love, as if a clear road were laid out before me, or a river that would take me to an ocean I had never seen. Then I heard someone's hand on the glass, tapping lightly. I threw the blanket from the bed and went to the window. August stood in the yard looking up at me and my heart lifted fast when I saw him. He grinned and beckoned and then pointed at the yard behind the house. I smiled and held up one finger. Behind me, Martha stood in the doorway, a small black valise in hand. She lay this on the bed and put her palm flat on my back.

"Let me help you," she said. She picked up my brush and began to brush my hair while I fastened the last two buttons on my dress. I could not bear to leave August waiting for one more minute in the yard. "Hurry up," I said.

Martha laid her hand on my back again. "I can pin it if you stand still," she said. Her voice was sharp but she smiled a little. It seemed that even she could not help but catch some of my excitement.

When my hair was twisted and pinned and my dress fastened, she sat on the edge of the bed. "This is your choice," she said.

"Yes."

"And you can make no other?"

"No."

"Do you really think he said yes?"

"It does not matter."

"So you will leave your family?"

I did not reply.

"Your responsibilities?" she said. She picked at the sheet and smoothed it and turned it and turned it. "Your duty?"

"What about his duty to us?"

"He does what a father is supposed to do," she said.

"Martha," I said. "He hit me. He kicked me."

"You are not the first. And you will not be the last."

"But that does not make it right," I said. "Mother—"

"Shut up about that," she said. Her voice rose. "Just shut up."

"It was wrong," I said.

"It was a terrible accident."

"It was?"

"Yes," she said. "It was."

"Because that is what he told you."

She made a smothered sound and began to weep. "Because that is the way of the world," she said. "This is just what happens. You have to accept these things."

"Do you really think that?"

"Do you really think that it will be different out there?" She waved her hand toward the wall. Her voice was thick, wet. "When you leave here?"

I felt my throat close. "Yes," I said.

She groaned and mopped her face with her skirt. Then she reached over and unbuckled the peeling clasps on the valise and lifted it so that it spread open on the bed. The cloth on the inside hung in tatters. "Here," she said. Her eyes were watery and dim. She had given up on me. "You can put your things in here."

August sat smoking on the back steps. When he saw us, he flicked his cigarette into the wet yard and stood up. Then came the cries of what seemed to be hundreds of distant dogs. I looked up and saw an enormous *V* of geese winging north, each body dark against the wan light. The sound of wind which was not wind but was the sound of their rustling wings as they passed by the hundreds overhead. August took my suitcase and Martha put her arms around me. I leaned stiffly against her thin frame and she told me in a weak voice that she was sure I would be able to come home someday. Hattie came into the mudroom in her nightgown and asked what was going on. I leaned down and gave her a hug. She asked again. "What is going on?" she said. She pushed at the suitcase with her toe. "Are you going somewhere?" Then she leaned against the doorframe and Martha put her arm around her. August picked up my valise and took my hand and we walked out over the wet grass. I lifted the hem of my skirt so it would not drag in the mud and we turned and came along the side of the house. August squeezed my hand and I smiled up at him. I felt the wind rush through me as if it would lift me higher and higher and in that wide-open sky I would fly and never come down. It was almost impossible to believe and yet it was really happening. I had escaped. I was getting away. I was finally going to be free.

Out on the road in the early morning light we surprised a lone deer standing on the crest of earth that rose between the muddy wagon ruts. She stood and stared at us with a blank expression and then leapt away and flipped her white tail as she bounded into the underbrush. The world was filled with the sound of birds.

14

We followed the road along the interurban rails. The river gleamed silver as it snaked below the bluffs. We passed the ice factory where in midwinter men had laid out their iron grids and cut blocks of ice from the river and hoisted the blocks by wagon team onto the banks and from there dragged them to the sawdust rooms of ice cellars, where the blocks would stay whole until June. August took my hand as we came to the apothecary with its awning furled tight as a sail and then to the greengrocer's, where the canvas was also rolled away and no barrels stood on the sidewalk. All of this was as unfamiliar to me as the shore of a new country. The place I would live with August. The place our lives would begin. Everything seemed strange and new and the world I had always known was now made up of parts that no longer fit together. My heart skipped and I skipped a little, too, just to keep time with it, and August laughed.

The sky grew brighter. The rain had greened the grass overnight and the trees that had been bare the day before were filmed with new leaves. Just past the bank, August turned into a narrow road and we walked past wooden buildings that grew smaller as we moved away from the center of town. Finally he stopped in front of a tearoom and set my valise on the ground.

"Are you hungry?" he said.

I shook my head. I had become too unreal in my escape to feel something as common as hunger. I was unanchored from everything, liberated from my father's world. I did not want to spoil it with eating.

"Come on," he said. His eyes sparkled. He took my hand and pushed on the door until it opened. "Just some coffee."

We were the only ones there. We sat at a table with a blue-and-white-striped cloth under the front window. He ordered coffee and sweet rolls and then stretched his arms over his head and yawned. Then he looked at me and smiled and reached across the table and took my hands in his.

"Okay?" he said.

I grinned. "Okay," I said, and laughed.

He looked around. "This is nice," he said. "Right?" When I nodded, he smiled. "This is my plan," he said. "I have a place for us. And before we go there we will go to the courthouse. It will all be legal." He gave my hands a little shake and started to laugh. "We will be happy forever," he said.

The idea flickered through me and grew stronger, like a promise already kept. The woman who ran the tearoom brought two china cups and two saucers and set these down in front of us. She came back with a coffeepot and a pitcher of milk and a bowl of sugar on a tray. She set the tray down between us and poured the coffee and then carried the coffeepot back to the rear of the tearoom, where a large stove was already hot. She stood at a table and pinched yeasted dough from a ball resting in a bowl. She laid the pieces out in front of her and flattened them into rectangles, which she spread with a mixture of cinnamon and sugar. She rolled the sheets into logs and twisted the logs into clover shapes and laid the shapes on a metal sheet. Then she slid the sheet into the oven.

Out in the street, men in work clothes began to pass by. A dark carriage rolled past and then an automobile, its bright windows gleaming in the morning light. In the distance, the sound of the interurban as it began its morning run. August held my hands and gave them a squeeze. Then he dropped them and sat over his steaming coffee and stirred milk into the cup. He held the pitcher out to me.

I spooned sugar into my cup and realized that for the first time in my life I could have as much sugar as I wanted. I tossed in an extra spoonful just because I could. Only someone long imprisoned could find so much joy in such a tiny thing. Then I added milk and stirred the coffee with my spoon. A man in a business suit came in and nodded at us. He took the table next to ours and the woman came over and took his order.

All of a sudden I was starved. When the woman brought our sweet rolls, I gobbled mine as if I had been famished all of my life. August watched me and laughed and ordered two more. Outside, the traffic on the street thickened. Men came along the sidewalk, in work clothes gone gray at the knees, in black suits with pin-striped vests and crisp white shirts, in dungarees and in canvas trousers, wearing shirts without collars and the plaid flannel and dark twill trousers of the Menominee. Men everywhere and the world belonged to them, and always had, and always would, and the very fact of this blinded them to the rest of us.

The clock tower across the square struck once, for seven thirty. Across town my father would have come home. He would be ready to go to bed. He would have let Martha have it when he learned that I had left. A tiny bit of joy rolled away from me when I thought of this. I set my roll on my plate. "August," I said. He smiled when I said his name. "Tell me what happened last night."

"Last night?"

"When you went to see my father." A small knot tightened behind my ribs.

"At the bar, you mean."

"Yes."

"It was no problem." He smiled at me again. "Like I said."

"But tell me," I said.

He lifted his cup and finished his coffee and then got the attention of the woman by the stove. He twirled his finger over his cup. She brought the coffeepot and poured. She looked at me and I nodded and she refilled mine. Then August said that he went to the bar directly from my house. He spent a few minutes combing his hair and straightening his clothes before he went in. The people who passed him on the street looked at him strangely, but he did not mind because what were people's opinions anyway but their own misguided ideas about things? Meaningless. When he walked up to the bar, he thought right away that my father had been waiting for him. He took his apron off and led August into a back room, where there was a padded table and around that four chairs and a mirrored bar that was much smaller than the bar out front but stocked with better brands of liquor. My father held out a chair and told August to have a seat. Then he took two glasses from the bar back and filled them from one of the bottles. He brought these over to the table. He said that he knew this day would come and so he had been looking into things and had learned all about the Bethke family. Had learned all about the Bethke family ways. Knew that the family wasn't the best but had quickly figured out that they weren't the worst, either. Maybe not quite like everyone else but not so bad that they could not have a drink and entertain the future. That was what he said. Entertain the future.

August knew that what he meant was a very particular future and he said that this was why he had come to the bar on

this rainy night, to have this very conversation. But he refused
the drink. Once accepted, it would change things between them
and he did not want that change to come before they had conducted their business. And so they had left the glasses untouched
while they discussed what was to be done with me. My father
pointed out that he had already told me that my days of wandering in the woods were over. August told him he could not agree
more. If my father was surprised by this, he didn't show it. He
simply said that he was glad they were in agreement. But August
knew that they were not yet in agreement and he said so and
my father's eyes hardened. He tried to stare August down but
this was a ridiculous enterprise and had been tried by other men
and they too had come to nothing with that approach. So August merely looked back at my father and eventually my father
dropped his gaze and returned to the drinks, which he offered
again. Still August said no. Still he said they had business to conduct. And my father raised his left eyebrow and asked what that
might be.

And my father, much as August expected, did not burst out
laughing when August said what he had come for, nor did my
father say no. He merely drummed his fingers on the padding
on the tabletop and explained that this was a place where men
came to play games of chance—poker, mostly—and in this way,
the whole room had the feel of a gamble about it, like any place
where you could come and roll the dice or try your hand with
Lady Luck. That dreams could come true here but they could
also die. And he asked August which he preferred. August said
that he did not gamble, for that was a fool's errand, and he preferred things that had a great deal more certainty about them.
And my father told him that there was nothing in the world
that could assure certainty among men. He smiled in a superior
fashion when he said this, and August realized that my father
thought he had found the flaw in August's thinking and things

would naturally proceed from there. But that was not the way things were going to be. August told him that in this way of thinking he was very wrong, for there was one thing that would always bind one man to another and this had everything to do with the possession of certain things, and in particular, the possession of something that one man had that the other man wanted. This bond often meant the working out of exchanges. There was always a way to strike a bargain in such cases and this was what he was prepared to do. And he mentioned that perhaps my father had some need of a carpenter around the house.

August smiled when he said this. He explained that he had offered this first because he did not want to play his whole hand with the opening bid. As August expected, my father said that he had no need of someone who would only come and spend half his time sneaking into corners with his daughter. So right away they came to a dead end. August had waited for my father to make a counteroffer but my father had just fiddled with the rim of padding along the table edge and watched August. Again he offered him a drink and even took one of the glasses and moved it closer to August. He appeared to think this was a time of merriment rather than one of great seriousness. But August dismissed the glass. He said that they were like the two men he had described, already tied by something and my father well knew what it was. And my father had done exactly what August expected, which was not to mention my name at all but to go directly to the thing itself. He drummed the tabletop and then he stopped. He said something like, I suppose you mean money, and August nodded, and my father said, You think she is for sale. And this was a surprise because August had not thought that my father would be so blunt about the whole thing. On the other hand, if he wanted to speak plainly, that was fine with August. He shrugged and reached into his coat and laid a black leather pocketbook on the table. He asked my father what it would take to solve this whole dilemma. And my father looked at August and looked at the wallet and looked at the table and said there was no money in the world that could buy his daughter. That was when August told him that he was not trying to buy his daughter because after all he loved his daughter very much. Instead he was there to make the whole situation easier, to share what he had with a fellow workingman, to make it clear that he wanted what was in each man's best interest. He did not intend to take anything away without bringing something to the table. That was all. It was not a matter of making a purchase. It was a matter of making something unequal equal, and each should take something that would make his life more pleasant. He would waive all claim to a dowry and he would walk away as soon as my father accepted the situation.

He was not surprised when my father picked up the pocketbook. The clamoring from the bar had gotten louder and he had taken to looking over his shoulder. He knew he had to get back to work. He knew he could not stay away forever. He had to complete the transaction there and then or give it up for another night.

He told August that he wanted to hear of a wedding as soon as possible and that he should take good care of his daughter just as he himself had done for all these years. She was his treasured daughter and he would not stand it if he should hear of some mistreatment. And then they drank their drinks and shook hands and that was it. From the bar, August walked to meet his brother. Alfred told him that he had been to see their cousin as planned, and he did have three rooms to let at the back of his house, and this was where we would make our start.

"And of course, there was one more thing," August said. "Your father did not wait for the final offer." He grinned and reached into his coat. He pulled out an old brown leather wallet thick with bills. He dropped this on the table between us. "You see? All this could have been his." He winked at me.

I do not know what I expected. Perhaps for my father to refuse or to threaten to lock me in my room or to track me down and beat me to a pulp. But I had not expected my father to give in so easily. To take the money and shake August's hand, as if I were a horse or a head of lettuce.

William Oliver was wrong. The arrangements among men had nothing to do with physical might. Men were not wolves. They were bankers, adding and totaling and betting on margins and cashing in chips and swapping credit slips and taking loans and deeding property to each other. A passage of cash like this was an ordinary day. The man who came out on top was settled by determinations of value. Money was everything. People like me? We were nothing but objects to be passed hand to hand.

August tapped the top of the wallet. "Plenty more where that came from," he said. He slapped the table once, for emphasis. He was pleased with himself and pleased with the story and he thought that I would be pleased with it, too. Perhaps he imagined that later we'd tell jokes about the way he'd gotten the best of my father and proved that he was the better man.

"You paid for me?" I said. "August?" My voice was so low that even I could barely hear it.

"What?" he said, startled. "No. No! It's just that I could do it and so I did. I figured your father for exactly the kind of man he is. I greased the skids. I saved us some trouble. I set it up so things would work out fine." He paused, a stunned expression on his face. Clearly, he had never for a moment considered how I might understand the story he had taken so much pride in telling, and it had never occurred to him that I might understand it this way. And then he drew himself up to cover his hurt but that did not work because I saw through him and I saw that my words had stung him. "I do not know what you think," he said. "But I do not own you. If you want to go, you can go." He waved his hand at the street. "There is the door."

The man at the table next to ours used a roll to wipe up the grease from the last of his sausages. He sipped his coffee and looked past me out into the street and squinted at the passing scene. He sat so quietly and with his attention directed so fully elsewhere that I knew he had been listening to everything we said. I wanted to scream at him to mind his own business. To stay out of this, for the things that passed between August and me were private and belonged to no one but us.

But I knew that was not true. If anything, nothing about this was private at all. My father and August, establishing the rules and measures and boundaries of their trade, working out the details, figuring their gains and losses, locked in their dance: these in fact marked out the world in definite and definable ways. And the man sitting next to us had clearly recognized the story. It might have been his story for all I knew, and if not his exactly, then similar to ones he knew well. Surely he had paid for something he coveted himself. Surely he had put cash in the bank.

"Do you want me to go?" I said.

"No, I do not want you to go," August said. He took my hands in his and rolled the bones in my fingers until I bit my lips to keep from crying out. He let go of my hands. "I want you to stay forever," he said in a wretched voice, the words coiling slowly out of him as if he could not bear to say them. "The way we said."

When I did not reply, he stood up and came around the table and dropped to his knees. He wrapped his arms around my legs. He buried his face in my lap. His voice was muffled but he told me that he had loved me since the very first day he had set eyes on me. All he wanted was for me to be happy. All he wanted was to go to the courthouse and stand in front of a justice and get on with it. Then he said that if my happiness meant that I should leave him right then and there, he would not stop me. He would step back and let me go. He would never darken my doorway again.

He said all of this in a very dramatic way and I was embarrassed. I am not the kind of person who calls attention to herself in public. The man at the table next to ours cleared his throat and signaled to the woman at the stove that he wanted to pay. A man in grimy overalls opened the front door and after him came two older boys with jackets slung over their shoulders. They stepped into the tearoom and looked at me and looked at August on his knees with his face pressed into my lap and then stepped around him and took a table near the back. I felt the damp heat of August's words when he breathed them through my skirt. He was new to me again and I wasn't sure I liked this part of him. But then he began to stroke my calves under my skirt, his palms gently cupping the curve of my legs, his fingertips lightly brushing my stockings and then sliding between my knees, and I felt that same quiver run up my body that always ran up my body when August touched me. My muscles softened and I sagged a little. At that moment, he was August again and any doubt I might have had rippled away.

Outside, the street had filled with wagons and men in dark hats on horseback and women with parasols, as if they expected the sun to be bright and hot this early in spring. Inside our own world, August breathed warm air onto my thighs and steadily caressed my legs until I told him again that I would marry him. It did not take long.

By the time we walked down to the courthouse, horses were tied up at the long poles in front, their wagons and buggies angled behind them into the street. August pointed to the doorway that led to the jail where he had been locked up, but of course I already knew where it was, since it stood next to the police station, where in the late fall I had stood in the cold, trying to think of exactly the right words to say when I told the police that my father had murdered my mother. As we crossed the road, I thought I saw Edwin moving toward me. But when I looked again, the sidewalk was bare and sunny and there was only a wooden Indian in front of a cigar store.

We climbed the main steps and passed through the wooden doors into a dim lobby with a polished marble floor. When a man dropped his key ring, the sound came over me like a shot. Above, a huge marble staircase led to the second floor. August took my hand and led me up the broad steps and along a wide corridor until we stood in front of a door that was half opaque milk glass and lettered in black and gold with the words *Clerk of Court*.

He squeezed my hand. "Are you ready?"

I leaned into him. I breathed in the smell of him. I put aside everything I thought I knew, the deal he made with my father, the way our future seemed a little less clear than it had before. I did not care about any of it. I just cared about the pounding in my chest. August's touch on my skin. The next thing that would happen, the idea of which shuddered through me, as if I had already seen August naked in the light of day, already felt him pierce me to my soul.

"Yes," I said. He put his arm around me and hugged me tight. Then he opened the door and we went inside.

When Martha and I were little, we played dress-up. We riffled through my mother's trunk and wrapped ourselves in old tablecloths and bits of lace left over from the curtains she'd made. We strapped our waists with lengths of ribbon and fought over who got to wear the white, for there were only two kinds of ribbon in the trunk, white and a sort of ugly navy, and we both knew that brides did not wear navy. We wanted to put on these clothes and feel wholly and completely in our bodies, as if we had traveled through time to the day when we would occupy the places we were meant to stand. We walked around the house with napkins on our heads. We stomped through the yard and sang a song without melody, pretending it was the Wedding March. We had no idea what the Wedding March might sound like or if something called the Wedding March even existed, but we had the idea that when you got married, you marched like a soldier into a land to which you otherwise did not belong. You needed a marching song if you were going to do that. You needed a good strong beat, like an anthem, to drive you forward.

I had no wedding dress, no flowers, no ring, no father to give me away, no sisters dressed in pretty gowns to precede me down the aisle, no mother to weep when I went into the arms of my husband. I did not care. I had August. It was springtime, when everything begins and begins and begins. I felt slightly sick with excitement. I wondered if I could be undone by happiness.

The justice of the peace told us that he tended to keep these things brief and to the point and he hoped we didn't mind. If we did, we might want to wait and go and see a preacher. But August said that we were ready now. The judge picked up a New Testament from the top of his desk and flipped to a place marked with a purple satin ribbon. He read the declarations and the vows quickly and in a straightforward way, without inflection or interest, as if he were reading the directions to a kit. August said I do and I said I do and the justice said, "By the powers vested in me by the state of Wisconsin and the county of Waukesha, I now pronounce you man and wife."

He closed the book and held it in front of his waist with his arms crossed before him. "She belongs to you now, son," he said. "You can kiss her right here if you want to."

August smiled and turned toward me. He cupped my chin in his hands and leaned down and kissed me, a bottomless, watery kiss that made me disappear into him again, my chest aching with pleasure, my hands held dumbly at my sides. When I reached up to hold him and his kiss deepened, the justice said, "That's fine, now, that's fine." And so we stood looking into each other's eyes. And then we began to laugh. We laughed until our breath was nearly gone. We laughed until we could not speak. We laughed until my ribs hurt, and August ran his wrists over his eyes, where tears had sprung up and now ran down his cheeks. We laughed with the justice of the peace looking on and we were still laughing when August threw his arms around me and yelled, "To hell with them! Right?"

When we finally broke apart, he took my hand and led me out of the judge's chambers, racing through the hallway, clattering down the stairs, through the echoing hush of the courthouse lobby, and into the clear light of day. Just across the street stood a huge elm tree and under its spreading branches I saw Edwin. He stared at us and walked up and down and stared at us again and then stood in the shade, wringing his hands. I grinned and waved but Edwin did not wave back.

If just for a moment I thought of my mother, I did not think of her long. I pushed her memory away, the dark red of her wedding dress, the dress plastered by blood to her body on the last day of her life. I nursed my happiness like it was a bubble that could still expand. Much to my amazement, it did.

When the streetcar came along, I climbed the iron steps and made my way behind August, who came along the aisle until he found two seats side by side. He paid the conductor and the conductor dropped our fare into slots in the top of a machine he wore strapped to his waist.

I had never ridden the interurban before. When we pulled out, the hard jolt surprised me. Sparks poured down and we picked up speed and wind whipped in through the open windows. The wheels clattered and the racket inside the car was deafening. Whenever we hit a curve, we all leaned far to the right, or far to the left, until I thought we might tip over. But we did not. We just hurtled along as if we were racing into the future.

August put his mouth against my ear. "Two stops," he said.

The town slid by. People looked up at us as we passed and the gray river came suddenly into view and just as suddenly slipped away. August pulled the cord and the bell rang. We came to a stop in front of a dry-goods store. We climbed down and August took my hand as the streetcar pulled away. We walked two blocks to a tall yellow house, where we turned up a gravel drive and came along past the raw frame of a building that someone had started at the bottom of the yard. On either side, houses with white cotton curtains blowing out of the open windows so close you could nearly reach out and touch them.

I looked over my shoulder when August climbed the steps to unlock our door, but I did not see my father pounding up the street. I did not see Martha hovering in her irritating, painful way, her gaunt face reproachful, as if my behavior forced her to suffer endless regret. I did not see Hattie, although this left me with some sadness, for I would have liked to have had Hattie at my wedding. I would have liked to have seen her dance down the aisle the way she had danced in the rain.

But too late now. I had really done it. I had left them all behind. A strange feeling of relief juddered through me, down my arms to the ends of my fingertips, down my legs to the soles of my feet.

The rooms were nearly empty but they were clean. In the sitting room, into which we stepped from the porch, a tiny spindly couch with torn blue upholstery stood against the wall. Two wooden chairs and a worn painted table with a scalloped apron had been placed under a window. Beyond that was a room someone had set up to be the kitchen. It had a large window that looked out on the driveway and a very small stove and an old icebox. A rusty sink. Sunlight vivid on the floor. The door to the bedroom opened off of the kitchen and I followed August as he set my valise on the bed. Someone had made it up with a faded green quilt and two flat pillows naked of their pillow slips. There was a washstand with a cracked pitcher and bowl and a small mirror and a wardrobe with one door hanging open and a bare window that looked out over the empty side yard.

August looked at me and then looked around. "It is not much now," he said. "But you can fix it as you would like."

"No," I said. "I like it."

He smiled and crossed the floor and put his arms around me and dropped his face into my hair. I felt his heart beating in his chest. "What do you think?" he said softly. "Are you tired?" And I shook my head no even though I had never been more tired in my life. I felt his hands slide to my waist. He leaned back and began to unbutton my blouse, each button, one by one. He unfastened my skirt and pulled my blouse from my shoulders and let my skirt and blouse fall to the floor, a pile of green, black ribbons that matched the black ribbons banding my green skirt, like shadows in the forest. I felt his hands on my buttons, my snaps, my hooks and strings, all the trappings that kept me laced and bound and tightened down. He put his hands on my shoulders and very slowly slid them down my chemise, over my breasts, over my ribs, over my stomach, until he could slide a hand between my thighs. He let his hand rest there, still as a stick, and I breathed harder and still he did not move and I breathed harder still and squirmed against his palm, yearning. Looking into his eyes. Breathing harder. Only then did he push me back onto the bed, where my valise fell to the floor. I sat up and pulled my chemise over my head and leaned back on my elbows and watched him. He took his shirt off first and then his trousers and then his drawers. I had never seen him before, but only knew him as a shadow in the darker shadow of the night. Now he stood before me in the slow float of differing light, day-light now and no longer dark, and nothing that was quite his, nothing quite mine, but only a desire that was our whole, then, desire and freedom. I felt light-headed and urgent, restored to myself and new at the same time. He smiled boldly and stood over me, his body light and golden and strong. He lay down next to me and did nothing at first, just looked at me, looked at my skin, my body, my shivering limbs. Then he kissed me and I sank into his kiss. He pulled away and smiled at me and reached down and moved his fingers against me and I cried out and then I was nothing but trembling flooded with blurred light. Only then did he move over me, part my legs with his hands, move me the way he wanted me, move into me. I arched my back and opened to him and then my eyes filled with tears and he kept on and kept on and I had as with a vision the thought that even our dust would be mingled together forever. Each stroke was a seal, a promise, and I moved under him as if against my own will, crying out, and then his voice washed over me, a great jerking groan and I felt him quaking inside me.

In the late afternoon, we finally slept. When it grew dark, the neighbors' dogs began to bark. I woke and heard footsteps on the gravel outside. I sat up and put my hand on August's shoulder. I said his name.

"Do you hear something?" I said.

He smiled softly but did not stir.

"August," I said again. "I mean it. Do you hear something?"

He opened his eyes and looked up at me. "Marie," he murmured. "Go back to sleep."

"Why are the dogs acting up?" I rolled over on my side, the room dark now and everything unfamiliar. I felt fear rise in my throat and knew that even though I had gotten away, that old feeling stayed with me like a snake coiled around my heart.

"I do not know. They are dogs."

"No," I said. "You should go see." I thought of my father, who might have made his way across town, his ideas his own and still all about me. I thought of his fist, knotted like a stone at the end of a rope. I thought of the curl of his lip when he smiled. I felt my belly clench around its boulder of grief. He could walk in the night unseen. He could climb our stairs unbidden. He could come upon us in the dark and he could make us his own.

But August just pulled the pillow over his head and said something I could not understand. I pulled the pillow away and he sat up and in a suddenly sharp voice told me that it was nothing and he was tired and I needed to stop it. I sat very still and held my breath. He punched the pillow and put it back under his head and lay on his back and looked at the ceiling. I exhaled very slowly. Then he rolled over on his side and leaned over the edge of the bed and fished through the pockets of his trousers until he found a cigarette and a box of matches. He sat up and lit the cigarette and then fell back and lay on his back smoking.

"Find me something I can use for an ashtray," he said. His voice milder then, as if he had perhaps forgotten who I was and had now remembered. The tiny knot inside of me unclasped, like a leaf unfurling from a bud.

I brought him a saucer that I found on top of the icebox

and lay down next to him while he smoked and tapped ash into the plate. The dogs kept barking and the evening deepened. I waited for a step on our stairs, a knock on our door, but none came. Whatever worried the dogs, it was not my father.

Finally I said I was hungry. August ground the cigarette out and stood up. I watched him walk naked into the kitchen and as soon as he passed into the doorway, he was August again, the boy I loved, and not the man with the hard voice. He returned with a block of cheese and some cold ham and a plate and a knife and some rolls wrapped in a napkin. I reached for my chemise and he said to leave it alone. I lay back on the bed and felt thrilled by my own nakedness. "There is more," he said. When he came back he brought two thick glass bottles of beer and a metal church key. He opened one of the bottles and handed it to me and then set the church key on the windowsill.

We ate our supper and drank the beer slowly and did not say much. The dusk light made the room dim and we decided against candles and let the last of the light disappear over us. I lay on the bed with a pillow propped behind my head, with the wet bottle of beer making a cold ring where I held it on my belly as if my body were a table. I could just see the first star as it hung in the window, a perfect pinpoint of clear, cold light gleaming in the sky. I thought to make a wish but I did not know what to ask for. It seemed that all of my dreams had come true.

When we were done, August wrapped the remainder of the cheese in the napkin that had held the rolls. He set the plate and the knife and the empty bottles on the floor next to the bed. He said my name and lay down on his stomach with his arm around my waist and his face in my shoulder. He told me how much he loved me. "Are you happy?" he said.

I nodded. I told myself that I could not imagine that every footstep belonged to my father. I could not foretell disaster every time a dog barked. And I *was* happy with August. I did not need to tell myself anything about that.

He sighed and burrowed his face into my hair again. He told me that he had never been this happy in his whole entire life. He had never known another girl like me. He would love me like this until the end of my days. He would take care of me forever.

He stroked me as he talked and I felt the weight of his hand on my bare skin and felt my breath catch in my throat. His hand on my skin smooth and strong. His hand on my breast. His lips on my throat. I reached for him then and he lifted me so I could sit astride him and look down at his shining eyes and his luminous face. I leaned down and let my hair fall over us like a curtain. We kissed with soft lips, as if there was a truth that we could find together. And then he groaned and rolled me over and pinned my hands above my head. He would not let me move, but just held me and that was what I wanted then, that and all the world that was him. His very force like a whirl-wind tearing through me until I thought I would split and die.

In the morning, I woke alone. I stretched and felt the warmth of the sunlight, the soft breeze from the window cracked on the other side of the room, my skin alive, my bones alive, my heart alive. Joy like a stranger I would have to get used to.

Before long I heard the front door open and close. I was embarrassed by my happiness and shy about seeing August, with whom I had traveled so far the night before that by now he must be unknown to me. I rolled on my side and pulled the sheet over my head. August came in and pulled the sheet back. He looked down at me and laughed. He carried a brown paper sack of rolls. He told me he was making coffee and I should get up and get dressed and go down to the laundry and quit my job, for he was going to take care of me from now on. "I order you to do this," he said. He reached down and gave me a gentle swat on my bottom. "As your husband," he said, laughing. His words delighted me as much as they would have had they been the first words of the world. And maybe they were. They felt like words that had made me.

We sat side by side on the little sofa in the front room, my knee draped over his knee. I idly swung my foot and he leaned back and put his hand on the back of my neck. Outside mist lifted from the ground of our new country and vanished. Everything around me as if in a beautiful dream.

As soon as we were through, he kissed me and dropped two nickels into my hand. He closed my fingers around them. He told me that these would be enough to get me down to the laundry and back. Then he stood up and picked up his tool belt and strapped it around his waist. He stood in the door-way holding the door open while I found my coat. He looked like a cowboy I had seen on a long-ago poster for a Wild West show, his tool belt slung around his hips like he carried guns and knew how to use them. I could not believe he was mine for-ever. I threw myself against him and kissed him again and again. He laughed and took me in his arms and warned me in a thick voice to lay off because he had to go to work. But he cupped my breasts as he said this. Our promise to each other. Our secret prayer.

15

William Oliver stood at the front counter with a tall man who was counting out coins. When he caught sight of me, he gave the man his parcel and then opened the front door for him. The man said something to William Oliver, who nodded and said something in return. They both glanced at me. Then the man turned and walked away.

"Mr. Oliver," I said.

"Be quiet."

"Mr. Oliver."

"I think you have lost all bargaining position," he said. He clenched his fingers. "Wouldn't you agree? You did not have that much to begin with, but now you have none. None." He took me by the elbow and walked me hard and fast into the alley. Dark shadow fell over us. In the street, wagons passed in the daylight. "Morning deliveries are almost through, but there is still time," he said. His voice was hard and low. He tightened his grip on my wrist.

"I do not understand."

"Of course you do."

"Let go of me," I said. "Mr. Oliver." I pulled away from him. "I do not work here anymore."

"No?" he said.

"No," I said. I tried to step away but he squeezed my arm. Then he bent my arm behind me, as easily as if this had always been the plan.

"I think you do," he said.

"I do not," I said. "Let go of me."

"We will see what your father says about that." He pushed me hard into the wall, his familiar face queer and twisted in the half-light. "Right?" he said. "Right? Your father will have plenty to say, I can assure you. Two more nights in the woods, Mary. What can you possibly have to say for yourself?"

"Stop it." I pulled away as hard as I could, but he pressed against me and his arm came up across my chest and pinned me against the wall. "It is time, Mary," he said. "I have been patient with you. I have given you every chance. I have waited for you to come to your senses. You have chosen another path. Not my path," he said. "Certainly not the path that any thinking girl would have chosen. But your choice has given me certain advantages. I think you know that your time has run its course. I think even you can see that there is only one thing left to do."

"You are hurting me," I said.

He loosened his grip and stepped back a little. I curled into myself and tried to pull free, but still he held my wrist in one hand. Then he held my arm against the wall over my head.

"Two nights ago, before things had made themselves entirely clear, I went to see your father," he said. "I walked into that bar and I sat down in front of him. And he knows me, as I have said before, so I was not surprised when he greeted me. I was even less surprised when he poured a shot for me on the house. We had that trouble over your mother, as you no doubt recall, but we have not had any since. Some men might even suggest that your father and I are friends. Despite that, I protected your secret, even when that boy who claims to love you came in and sat at the bar. He was there for a long time. He tucked into quite a few drinks. When he departed, he left a pile of cash next to his glass. Not so big. Do not get too impressed. But more than I expected. He is a carpenter, after all."

I drew air in like I was drowning and stared at him. "That is not true," I said.

"No?" He studied me. "You may have even bigger problems than you realize," he said. "But I am sure we can find a solution."

I shook my head and again tried to pull away but he moved as a man in great stillness, which is the way that a man moving with too much force always moves, and shoved my arm back again.

"I am done waiting," he said. "You understand me?"

I shook my head and he slapped me, not hard, just a stinging slap to show me that he could.

"We can do this here or upstairs," he said. "You choose."

I shook my head weakly, tears dripping from my nose. I pushed hard and tried to heave him off of me, as if he could be lifted like a stone or a heavy board, but he just smiled and wrenched my arm against the wall. I turned my face away and he leaned in and rammed his tongue into my ear. He shoved his face into my hair, my neck. He ran his hands over my breasts. He lifted the hem of my skirt and began to fumble with my stockings, his hands on my bare thighs. I tried to let myself fall to my knees: I would crawl away, I would go belly first down the alley, I would get away. But his hand dropped and he tore at my skirt and then, as if he could not wait, he shoved his hips hard against me, bucking in short thrusts until he made a stifled sound and shuddered.

A single blade of grass as sharp and green and plain as day blew slowly in the wind. It ruffled with all the others. There were stones next to it and beyond the stones, a small pool of gray water puddled with a greasy aspect, as if someone had drained cooking oil on the ground. The sound of the interurban came and went and after that the town came back to me. William Oliver stepped back and reached into his pocket. He dabbed at the front of his pants with his handkerchief. Then he told me to get inside and get to work, that I had made my bed and now I must lie in it. He told me that we weren't through, not by a long shot, but when he said this, something in me splintered and fell. I pushed my shoulders back and stepped away from the wall. I told him that I was married now. My father had given his blessing. I did not work at the laundry anymore. He should take any wages I had coming and give them to my father for the upkeep of my two sisters. We would not meet again.

In the street I wiped my eyes and lifted my chin and walked along the wooden sidewalk. A few women watched me, their faces curious and unsurprised and sympathetic and not unkind. They smiled at me as I made my way along the storefronts and nodded encouragement. One reached out to touch my arm as I passed alone among them.

A Menominee woman in a dark blue skirt with fringe at the bottom walked in front of me, a child in each hand and each child bundled in dark red plaid flannel. When I passed her, I saw that her face had been burned and a wide smooth scar lay over one cheekbone, shiny like the skin on my arms where the laundry vats had burned me. I could feel William Oliver's hands on me. I imagined everyone who saw me could see them, too, huge handprints scorched into my dress. I thought that I would now be known to everyone as the girl who had let this happen to her. And then I remembered what the talk had already been, that I went into the woods with men, that I was some kind of a whore, and I knew that no one would have any sympathy for me.

There is only one thing to do on an occasion like this. You must have some sympathy for yourself and then you must get on with things. So I set my mouth and walked in long strides and told myself that everything would soon be all right. I would never see William Oliver again. This hour would be over and behind it would come another and soon there would be half a day and then a whole day between me and William Oliver. Before I knew it, he would be a memory, and after he was a memory, he would be someone I would remember only when something caused me not to forget. I promised myself that this was what would come true.

Of course, I also recognized that I was lucky to be alive. There are many girls who meet a man like William Oliver and do not survive long enough to teach themselves to forget.

When I got off the streetcar in front of the dry-goods store, I passed a tea shop where a woman straightened red-and-white-checked curtains in the window and looked out over the street as she worked. I passed the bakery where August must have bought our morning rolls. I looked around for the greengrocer and found it on the corner, its awning shading barrels of spring onions. Everything neat and clean and happy and fluttering in the sunlit wind, as if this was a place where nothing bad ever happened.

Past the greengrocery, the houses were closer together and painted with milk paint, white and yellow and baby blue. They sat back from the street at the top of trimmed yards, as if each had land to spare for nothing but decoration. Big trees shaded the lawns. A man with a mower whirled the blades through the grass. A baby cried. The woman who must have been my next-door neighbor sat on her front porch.

I saw Edwin at the top of the drive. He sat hunched on the

back steps, but when he caught sight of me, he unfolded his tall thin frame and came toward me. He reached for my arm and I did not stop him. He patted my arm and smiled and said my name.

I looked around at the neighbors' houses, where the windows had been pushed open and clean white curtains blew out over the sills, where the woman sat on her front porch. I tried to imagine what she would say, if she saw me talking to Edwin in the yard. The neighbors would be afraid of him. They would not understand. I barely understood myself.

"You had better come in," I said. "We cannot stand out here."

Edwin ducked through the doorway and looked around the nearly empty room. I flushed and said that we had just moved in and I had not yet had time to fix the place. I gestured at the couch and chairs and he sat on one of the chairs and leaned forward, looking pained and happy all at once.

"Do you want some water?" I said.

He shook his head. "I saw you," he said.

"I know."

"No," he said. "Downtown."

"At the courthouse," I said. "I know. I saw you too."

He gave me a haunted look. "You were coming outside," he said.

"Let me get you some water," I said, but he stood and waved me away with his hand. He paced from one side of the room to the other, moving his lips, patting his leg to a song only he could hear.

Finally he sat heavily in his chair and looked at me. "Did you get married?" he asked.

I nodded.

His eyes were liquid and dark then, his expression that of a man from whom the most important thing in the world has been stolen.

"Edwin," I said. "It is all right. August is a good man. And you will always be my friend."

He groaned.

I glanced at the windows and wondered if the neighbors could hear him. If August would find out.

"Why can you not like him?" I said. "He has many good qualities if you would only take the time to give them consideration."

He gave me a tortured look.

"Edwin," I said. "Please."

He reached over and took my hand. "You come with me," he said.

I understood what he wanted. In the faint candlelight under the church, we had found someplace not even the disciples could reach and were hopeless together in the darkness beneath the earth and in that hopeless togetherness found peace. Edwin could not have been comfortable on that cold floor, but he never complained. He listened while I told him everything. He did not tell me that I was wrong. That I was foolish. That I was making a mistake. That I had bad ideas or ideas I should not have or ideas that would only get me in trouble. He did not tell me I was stupid and he did not tell me to shut up and he did not tell me to get to work. In the last minutes before sleep, when I was suddenly empty and lay on the cot like an unfilled bag of floating skin, my bones dissolved, my organs soft as sand, he made it seem that the world could be a safe place after all. In the morning, he smiled at me and I knew he believed it was only a matter of holding to the thing between us, this single truth.

I pulled my hand from his. "I am married," I said. "I cannot."

"You come with me," he repeated in an exhausted voice.

"No," I said softly. "I am sorry. I cannot."

He started to cry.

When I did not say anything more, he hugged his head in his arms and howled. Then he turned and ran through the door. I heard his footsteps on the gravel drive.

Whenever I looked out my living room window, my only view was into the rooms of the house next door. A pretty young woman lived there with her young husband. She had pictures of dappled landscapes in gilt-edge frames on her walls. A silver tea service on her glossy buffet. A breakfront full of crystal and fancy china. I could even see the picture she'd had made at her marriage, which stood on the top of a gleaming piano. She stood in a column of chiffon, her hair pinned up under a cap stitched with pearls, and gazed out into an invisible world. Her expression was easy to describe. It was that of a woman who is confident that each thing that has happened is certain assurance of the many good things yet to come.

Now she stood at the top of my driveway and waved.

"Come see my yard," she called. She wore a pretty white blouse trimmed with tatting and a navy blue skirt. She had left her shiny brown hair loose under a pink velvet hairband.

She stuck her hand out. "I'm Bertha," she said.

I was very aware of my stained blouse, soiled by William Oliver's hands, and of my shabby skirt, also soiled by William Oliver. My mother's old shoes on my feet still molded to the shape of her step. The shoes had begun to hurt and I felt oafish beside Bertha, like a dumpy girl who does not know how to dress herself. I had not even had a chance to wash my hands.

"I am Marie," I said. I touched her cool, clean skin with my dirty hand and then dropped my hand to my skirt and wiped it on the folds.

She told me that she and her husband had been married for

seven months. Her husband worked for a bank, and they had been very lucky to find this house even though the bank still owned everything but maybe half of the living room because they'd had to take a mortgage. She said that she did not worry about that much because you had to start somewhere. Then she laughed.

Red roses scrambled up an arbor nailed to the porch. I followed her dumbly while she showed me her glads and hydrangeas. She pointed to a garden bed that she'd just had dug. She explained that she would lay out the plants so the pinks and blues would be separated with white, so the foliage would alternate dark green and pale silver, so everything would be orderly and contained. The best part was that she would always know from month to month what was about to bloom. She planned to fill her whole house with flowers. Every room would be resplendent with summer. She repeated this in an enthusiastic voice, as if she liked the sound of the word.

I smiled to show her that I understood what she meant by *resplendent*. I was not just some filthy girl who had moved in next door by mistake. I tried to imagine being the sort of woman who planted flowers to fill the house. The very thought made me shy and a little surprised, as if Bertha had a secret but right away had let me catch a glimpse of it.

We sat on white wicker chairs on her front porch. She served lemonade in tall glasses that she carried out onto the porch on a silver tray. Each glass was topped with a sprig of mint and a stick that pierced a slice of canned peach. She had done the canning herself. She offered me a plate of sugar cookies, each cookie shaped like a heart. She laughed and said how fortuitous it was that she had baked these cookies, in this shape, just that morning.

"Isn't being married wonderful?" she said.

I smiled. I thought of August and the way I felt when he touched me. I thought of our love like a bottomless well, always ready to swamp us with joy. It was more wonderful than I could hope to put into words.

She grinned. "No one ever tells you how good it's going to be," she said. "It's like one big fat riddle that you can't figure out until you've said I do. But the thing is, everyone knows. They all keep it to themselves but they know. I don't know why they don't tell us beforehand." She stretched her arms over her head and then dropped her hands back into her lap. She gestured at the plate. "Have a cookie," she said. She picked up a heart and made a big show of taking a bite. "Delicious!"

I looked out at her manicured yard, where nothing dared step out of line. My own house had crabgrass running up to the foundation. No curtains at the windows. Dissipated gravel on the drive.

Bertha raised her glass and offered a toast to the coming summer. To our great happiness and joy, newly married as we were, starting life together in this good place. We clinked glasses. She picked up the plate of cookies and held it out to me again. "These are so good," she said. "Completely sinful. You should try one."

I shook my head. My dirty clothes stuck to me as if shaped by sweat. I wondered if I smelled.

"You are far too good," she said. "I see I can't corrupt you." She set the plate down and then picked up a second cookie and took a tiny bite. Sugar flaked into the air. "I hope you don't mind," she said. "I'm going to be very bad today. Just don't let my husband find out. He'd hand me a fate worse than death." She laughed.

There was no food in the house and I had no money so I set to work sorting my clothes into the wardrobe. I hung one skirt on one hook and one blouse on another and I hung the green dress with the fading black velvet ribbons on a hook by itself. I left my nightgown and my spare chemise and my underwear and my stockings rolled together in little balls in the valise. I slid the valise under the bed. I took my shoes off and stepped out onto our porch and slapped the soles together so that dust flew. When I got back to the bedroom I took my blouse and skirt off and shook them out hard and hung them from the wardrobe door. I thought about hot water for a bath but I hadn't seen a coal scuttle, nor had I seen a washtub or a bucket. I was very tired. These questions seemed too much for me to answer. I lay down on the bed and rolled over on my side and hugged the pillows. August's scent came to me in a rich wave and happiness rose in me like a tide rushing to shore. I buried my face in the pillow and lay there and breathed him in.

When I woke, it was well past dark. I could see lights on in Bertha's house, and through the filmy sheers over her windows, I watched a man walk from one room into the next and then come back to the first room, where he sat down in an easy chair and picked up the newspaper from where it had fallen to the floor. He spread the pages out before him. I watched for a time but could not see Bertha. Eventually, the man stood and stretched and walked out of my view and did not come back. I imagined the two of them having dinner together in Bertha's gleaming dining room, where she would use her luminous pale china, the plates trimmed with wide gold bands, painted flowers decorating the centers. And there would be a roast and dumplings and a platter of sausages and a big tureen of beets. Afterward she would give him brandied peaches and that plate of sugar cookies and make fresh coffee. They would sit at the table together and talk. He would hold her hand and tell her that he loved her, there in the bright light of that very clean room.

I rolled over and sat up and hugged myself. I was very hungry and the room had grown cold. When I pressed the light switch, no lights came on. When I looked in the icebox, the shelves were empty. I walked back into the bedroom and sat on the bed in the dark and picked up the pillow that smelled of August. I hugged it. I set it down. I picked it up again. Then I threw it across the room.

In the morning, pastel light gave shape to the wobbly washstand and the iron bedstead and my valise now open on the floor. I buttoned my old blouse and fastened my skirt and walked out to the door to pick up my shoes. I sat on the edge of the bed and fastened them hook by hook. My chest felt light and open with anger and fear. I had no idea where August was. I walked back and forth from the wardrobe to the bed and folded my clothes back into the suitcase. I smoothed the tattered fabric and thought of my mother, who must have brought the valise with her from Rügen. What had she really carried and what had she tried to leave behind? She always looked away whenever we asked her about her life before. She just told stories about the horrible dwarves who stole the miller's daughter and kept her locked up and laboring underground. For years and years, underground and in the dark, alone except for the dwarves, who owned her exactly as if she had been a slave.

None of this mattered now. When I thought of August, I felt a doubt that I could not quite manage just by remembering the way I felt when he touched me. For a brief moment, it struck me that Martha might have been right. There was some small possibility that I had not known him well enough to marry him. The idea flickered through me like a flame I did not want to fuel. But it was impossible to ignore. How could he promise to come home and make love to me and then never show up? How could he be the August I loved and also be this other August, a boy who stayed away?

I did not understand anything. I can perhaps be forgiven for my naïveté. There are two things that all seventeen-year-old girls have in common, and one is their naïveté and the other is their belief that they are not naïve. When I was with August, I was like a honey-drunk bee, a dog that has gotten into the beer. When he was gone, I was blank as a bedsheet. His absence was like a nail pounded through a board that had seemed perfect and true. It felt new, an unwelcome surprise that I could not have seen coming.

I closed the valise and buckled its straps and lifted it and carried it to the front door.

He came up to me as soon as I stepped out of the house. He put his arms around me and fell to his knees sobbing. He begged me not to leave. The sun had just begun to rise. I stood in the driveway and let him put his arms around my legs. I let him bury his face in my skirt. I let him cry and say things I could not understand. Finally he looked up at me, his eyes running with tears, his mouth swollen and sticky. He clutched my skirt. He said that he would love me forever.

He was so drunk he could barely walk. He pitched up the steps to our door and fell hard against the railing. I had to grab the back of his shirt to keep him from going down. He stood breathing heavily and swaying by the door so I reached past him and turned the knob. He stumbled into the room and staggered to the couch. He tried to sit on the couch but sat down hard on the floor instead. He fell back and lay there.

Outside, birds had begun to call. Early light made the room gray and then the gray brightened.

"Marie," he said. He slurred the word and gestured at the air over his stomach.

I wavered at the sound of his voice and my anger migrated to a distant place, leaving only a little trail behind, like it was already just a memory of anger and the memory itself would soon be gone. But then I decided I must be firm.

"I am hungry," I said tightly. "I am cold. You left me here alone. I have no money. I have nowhere to go. You are responsible for me. Do you understand?"

He put his hand over his eyes. "It will not happen again," he said.

His words ran together. I could barely understand him.

He dropped his hand to the floor. His hair was matted and plastered to his head. One eye was swollen and glittered through a slit in his purple skin. "Marie," he said.

"Stop saying that," I said sharply. The boy I loved lost in this sloppy man who stank of whiskey and cigarette smoke.

He raised his head and squinted at me. Then he pushed his palms into the floor and lurched to his feet. He stood swaying and breathing before me, one hand balled into the cupped palm of the other, the look in his eyes flat and unfocused, as if he was a man in a walking trance. He took two staggering steps to steady himself. Then he leaned forward and pointed his finger at me, his swollen eye oozing, his good eye hooded and dim. He had dried blood on his mouth. He had dried blood on his hand.

"August," I said. "Stop it."

He breathed in harshly and straightened, like a man who has to steady himself before he speaks.

"August," I said. I stepped back.

He staggered a little, his good eye flat and blank, the other swollen and gone.

"August," I said. "Stop." I put my hand up.

He wrenched the valise from my hand. "You are not going

anywhere without me," he said. His words gurgled together like water running down the drain. He threw the valise at the sofa.

"August."

"Shut up," he said.

"Please."

"Stupid bitch," he said. His chin was down and his words came out low and garbled.

"August," I said. He started to fall and I grabbed his sleeve. He held my arms and steadied himself. Then he straightened and batted my hands away. He jabbed his finger into my chest. "Stupid," he said. He stopped and just stood swaying in front of me, breathing hard. Spittle crusted at the corners of his mouth.

My hand went to my chest. I kept it flat over the spot where he had poked me.

He stabbed his finger at me again. I tried to push his hand away and he grabbed my hand and held it. His fingers crushing mine, as if the bones could be ground to dust at his touch, the veins flattened until the life had run out of them. He leaned down to look me square in the eye and jerked my hand behind my back.

"You are a cunt," he said. "You know that?"

The smell of whiskey, his breath close to my hair, his hand on mine.

"You are hurting me," I said, but he just squeezed my hand tighter.

I put my other hand on his chest and tried to push him back. It is not possible to argue with a drunk. I knew the best thing to do was to try to keep my head down and get out of the way. But he would not let go. He looked at me and I might as well have been some stranger who had crossed him in the road. He stabbed his finger into my chest again and wobbled and took one step to keep from falling. Then he raised the flat of his hand and slapped me hard, a blunt thump I felt deep in my skull, like pulpy meat had shaken loose and now lay shuddering against bone. Tears sprang to my eyes and I fell to the floor.

"Cunt," he muttered again. Then he went into the bedroom. I heard his boots hit the floor as he pulled them off, first one, then the other. The bedsprings creaked as he lay down.

I stayed on the floor for a long time. When the sparkles behind my eyes faded I lay there and cried. Later, when I knew he was asleep, I got to my feet and went into our room. I looked at him laid out before me in the clean morning light, just a man, his face bloodied, one eye bulging and blue, and his face slack. I listened to him breathe. Then I searched his pockets until I found the wallet that had been stuffed with cash. It was empty. I walked back into the sitting room and sat on the couch and pulled my knees up under my chin. My cheek hurt when I touched it. I put my head down on my knees and wept. Sunlight spread in a flat wash across our yard.

Bertha worked in her garden with her back to me and I watched her, her apron strung over her dress, her trowel in her gloved hand, her hair tied back with a pretty blue ribbon. She knelt at the edge of the flower bed. When the breeze blew exactly the right way, I could hear her humming to herself.

The step where I sat was warm in the sunlight. A wagon rolled along the street and then stopped. A man in white pants and a white shirt jumped down and came up the walk. Bertha looked up from her garden when he spoke to her. He wrote on a pad of paper and then turned and walked back to the wagon. He climbed up and slapped the reins and the horse pulled the wagon down the street.

All of this happened as if far away, the world fractured by the geometrics of a kaleidoscope. I did not want Bertha to turn around. I did not want her to see my hair haphazardly pinned in place, my filthy dress. Instead I wanted to lie down and disappear in a hole with no bottom. But I could not. So I sat on the step with my arms around my knees and my chin on my arms and watched Bertha in her yard. I thought of William Oliver and the feel of his weight as he collapsed against me. I thought of Inge, who would have pushed me into boiling water if she had had the chance. I thought of Martha, who I was sure had no comfort for me, nor any sympathy, and who herself slipped away to walk with George in the shadows under the trees in the park. I thought of my father, who terrified me beyond all reason and who terrified her, and our terror sheared away any bond that might have grown between us and left us alone in our common loss. I thought of Hattie and of the way she danced in the rain. She seemed to move in a place that my father had not yet reached. I thought of August when he first came to me. He had felt familiar for reasons I could not explain. His light eyes and dark grin. His hands on my skull when he kissed me. His words in my mother's accent. His love raining down like blows.

For better or for worse, the justice of the peace had said. We had stood in the long rectangle of sunlight on the red carpet and had made promises and taken vows. I thought of August's body on mine. His head resting on my naked belly. The weight of him and the wind in the trees and the darkness and the two of us the center of the world. I could not bear the idea that I would be cast out from that. Even now I feel embarrassed and ashamed to admit this, but I wanted him with me: a man to whom I would always lay myself open completely.

He came outside and sat down next to me. He put his arms around me and rested his face against my neck. Then he leaned back so he could see what he had done. He touched my cheek. He held my head in his hands. He kissed my eyes and forehead and mouth. Then he wept. He told me he was sorry. He told me that he loved me. It was not his fault but the fault of the damned drink. He would cut that out. This would never happen again. He reached down and took my hand.

Our neighbors had their windows open and I could hear laughter and somewhere a woman talking in a very loud voice. I looked up and found a star. I wished that we would love each other forever, just the way we loved each other that night.

We ate dinner at the tearoom near the interurban stop. August took a table on the side of the room, under a high window through which I could see the sky. The door to the tearoom was propped open to catch the evening breeze and I could hear piano music coming from somewhere out along the street.

He leaned across the table and took my hands. He asked me what would make things right. He had not meant for things to go so far. He'd had a long day at work and the crew went out together afterward. Just one beer would do no harm. But he had made a big mistake. He had no explanation.

I wanted my August back. I did not want to see that man again, the one who lay on the floor and slurred my name, the one who came at me out of darkness. But I did not say any of this. The facts seemed beyond words. I told him instead that we needed pots and pans and plates and bowls. I knew the disruption in our housekeeping had not come from a lack of dishes, but I thought we might as well start there. I told him we needed curtains and rugs and furniture. And then I said that he could not leave me alone in that house for a day and a night and half a day again. No lights. No heat. Not even a way to take a bath.

He nodded. "I will give you some money," he said. "Then you can take care of all of that." He smiled and dragged his fingernails across the palm of my hand. "I am no hausfrau," he said. "I do not know what is needed."

"When will you give me some money?" I said. I pulled my palm away. I had not intended for my voice to sound so hard. He gave me a quizzical look.

"Right now," he said. "Right here." He reached into his jacket and pulled out a dull red leather billfold. This he set on the table between us. Then he leaned forward and extracted a few bills. Held them up so I could see them. Laid them on the table next to the billfold. "For you," he said. "Take them."

I had not seen that billfold before. It was not in his pockets when he came home drunk. It rested between us like a piece of poisoned fruit.

He watched me. "Is it enough?" he said. "I have more."

"It's enough."

"Fine," he said. "Good." He smiled and took my hand. "You see? What I said is true. I will look after you." He patted his shirt pocket and found his cigarettes. He lit one with a match just like the kind he used to pop and cup in his hands while waiting for me in the yard behind my father's house. He exhaled a long stream of blue smoke and smiled at me again but frowned when he saw that I was still upset.

"What is it?" he said. "Is it not enough? I will give you more."

"That is not it," I said.

"No," he said. "Here." And he slid more bills out of the red billfold and gave them to me. He told me to put them all away and not to leave money lying around in public. "You are like a child," he said. But he looked pleased. He inhaled and moved his jaw and popped smoke rings into the air between us. "My brother taught me this trick," he said. He leaned back and watched the loops of smoke in the air over his head. Then he waved his cigarette at my plate. "Don't eat all of that," he said. "It's too much."

I put my fork down. The expression on his face suggested

that all was settled and behind us. Our problems had been solved. Now we could have fun.

"August," I said. "There is something else."

He groaned and stubbed his cigarette out in his plate. He poured sugar and milk into his coffee and stirred it with his spoon. "We have better things to do tonight," he said, and lifted his cup to his lips and drank and set the cup down. "All right," he said then, in a tone of voice that suggested I had finally said something to convince him. "If there is more, let me hear it. Whatever it is."

He wore a look of faintly annoyed expectation. I felt a ripple of irritation.

"I want to know what happened when you went to ask my father for his permission for us to marry," I said.

He looked puzzled. He dropped his arms to the table and leaned forward on his elbows. "I already told you," he said.

"That is exactly what happened?"

"Of course."

"Nothing else?"

"Say what is on your mind," he said. "I cannot guess."

I hesitated.

"What," he said. "You cannot even ask a simple thing?"

I bit my lip. Then I told him that William Oliver had been in the bar when August went to see my father. That William Oliver had said that August never went into a back room, never asked permission, but had left a pile of money on the bar and left. And now I thought that my sister might be black and blue across town because everything that August had told me might not be true. Or probably was not true. Then I stopped.

He passed his hand over his eyes and looked away from me and then looked back at me with a drowning expression. "Marie," he said quietly. "What I told you is entirely true."

"But he said—"

"I do not give a damn what he said."

"But he was—"

"So now you do not trust me? What I said is what happened."

"Is Martha all right?"

"I am your husband," he said. "Not William Oliver."

"I know," I said. "But Martha—"

"Why wouldn't Martha be all right?"

"He would hold her responsible somehow," I said. I felt tears come to my eyes. "If you did not get permission. He would take it out on her."

"I got permission."

"Are you sure?"

"Marie."

I wiped my eyes with my napkin and the man who sat alone at the table next to ours watched me. "I am sorry," I said.

"Then stop it," August said. "I did what I said. Nothing different."

When we got to our house, August took me by the hand and led me into the yard. We stood under the stars. He put his arm around me. I felt myself go soft and loose against him. He ran his hand down my back and then looked up. He pointed out Ursa Major and Ursa Minor. I looked up, too, past his shoulder, but I could not really see the constellations as things separate and apart. I just saw all the stars overhead as if they had become one huge field in which we would always walk. When I was with August, I could put the old parts of my life behind me. I could become the girl I wanted to be. I could promise myself that there were a million ways to be hopeful.

Inside, he undressed me carefully and slowly. He brushed his fingertips against my lips. He smoothed my hair. When we lay down, he wrapped his arms around my back and we lay still like that for what seemed a long time. When he began to move, he moved very slowly and gently. I clung to him and said his name again and again and called him back to me, the boy I loved. I let the other man slip away.

The man behind the counter watched me as if he expected me to grab something and run. I smiled at him but this had no effect. I did not mind. It was a pretty day and I had money in my pocket. Let him think what he liked. I would take as long as I wanted to choose my things and he could watch me the whole time. It did not matter.

I walked up and down the narrow aisles, picking things up and putting them down. Silver cans of peas and beans and potatoes and spinach with bright labels all stacked neatly on the shelves that ran to the back of the store and beyond that, a counter with a cash register and cloth sacks of oatmeal and flour and sugar and popcorn. A jar of stick candy striped red and white and another of brown horehound drops dusted with sugar. I looked down at a pile of newspapers on the counter. The headlines screamed about the strikes up north. I could only imagine what my father must be saying. So many men in chains, I thought, all of them enslaved to masters who did not give a damn. It was amazing that any of them lived through the day.

Finally the counterman could stand it no longer. He asked if he could help me.

"Do you have plates?" I said.

He came out from behind the counter and brushed past me. He showed me a low shelf stacked with china, a blue and white pattern stamped on the face of each plate. "How many do you need?" he said.

"Four plates," I said in a soft voice. "Four bowls."

When these were wrapped in brown paper, he looked at me. "What else?"

I fingered the bills in my pocket again. I asked for a skillet and a saucepan and four sets of tableware and a teakettle. The man looked at me as if he did not believe me but he gathered these things and slowly rang them up. He kept glancing at me as if he expected me to stop him. I didn't blame him. I knew I looked like a poor girl who had no way to fend for herself. The bottom of my skirt had begun to come undone and the cloth had torn where I had stepped on it. My shirtwaist was stained. But I did not care.

I asked him to cut six yards of white voile and add a spool of white thread and a packet of needles and a pair of shears. I heard the sound of a bolt being turned as he measured out the yards and then the sharp thwack of the long blade cutting through fabric. When I stood in front of him and counted out the money, I saw the look of surprise that passed over his face and felt deeply satisfied that I was able to pay and was not the girl this man thought I was. It was good to have money and be on my own. Then I stepped out into the street and thought of August again and it seemed the weight of him was something I had known my whole life. Clouds moved over the sun and the wind lifted. The air smelled sweet, like early flowers.

16

The days grew longer and warmer. Two weeks passed and then three and then a month. In midsummer the world was overspread with a calm and even light. Sparrows spiraled up from Bertha's garden and vanished into the trees. In the evening, she watered her beds. In the morning, she cut her flowers. When the days grew hot, she put a fan in the window of her bedroom, where it whirred all night long.

August and I had no fan. We could barely catch a breeze, even with all of our windows open. And with the windows open, mosquitoes rose from the grass and came into our rooms, as well as flies and moths and shiny black beetles that rose into the air with a whirr. We often sat in the dark, just to try to keep the wildlife at bay. But all of this was fine with me. I liked to think the woods drew closer as soon as the sun went down.

Every night when August came in, he let his tool belt fall to the floor. He crossed the room and put his arms around me and held me against him. His clothes were sweaty. His skin was sweaty. His hair was sweaty. He smelled of a long day of work. But that did not matter. I could meet him where he stood. He kissed my hair, my neck, my ears. I touched his face. I felt the long muscles in his thighs. I pressed my face against his shoulder and began to strain against him. I could not bear to wait. I felt his breath hammer through me.

Some nights we fell to the floor right where we stood, with the sky full dark and no light but the light cast by our neighbors' rooms. I wanted nothing more than to be like this forever, to hold August Bethke and have him hold me.

If sometimes I felt a little suffocated by August's desire and thought that in all of his pounding he pressed the air out of me the way you press the air out of a rubber ball, I put those feelings aside. I told myself that I wanted August. I told myself that naturally I would sometimes feel like all of this was too much. That it was all right to feel that way. It was not like I really wanted it to stop. And when he came through the door at night, I had no trouble breathing. I found that the air rushed in and out of me just fine.

I had the voile and the shears and the needles and the thread so I set about making curtains. That summer, each house in our neighborhood was a square with windows shaded against the heat, each lawn a rectangle trimmed within an inch of its life. I wanted our house to look like the houses around us. If every house on the block had white curtains that blew at the windows, we would have white curtains that blew at the windows, too.

I had forgotten to buy a tape measure, so I had to improvise. I walked in the woods until I found a long, straight stick. I laid the stick against our window casements and marked the width and length of each on the bark. I spread the voile out on the floor and measured the fabric against the markings on the stick. I added the length of my thumb to make room for the hem and a very narrow pocket for the rod. I cut each panel and marked the fold and then doubled that and turned the hem under. I threaded a needle and sat and sewed each curtain by hand. It took me three days to finish but eventually I had six panels. I walked from room to room and held the curtains to the windows, imagining how nice they would look once they were hung.

I looked out over the yard and watched Bertha drag a fruit tree on a piece of burlap sack over her grass. A man walked along behind the tree with a shovel over his shoulder. She stopped near the front walk and fished a handkerchief from her pocket. She blotted her forehead and gestured at a piece of ground. The man used the blade of the shovel to mark out a place in the grass, where he began to dig.

My stomach growled. I was hungry but there was nothing in the house to eat. This was the way of things. At first, I thought that August had merely forgotten to give me money for food and he would remember and I would not have to ask. I thought it was his job to take care of me. I thought I should not have to put my hand out like a beggar with a tin cup. In those first days, hunger had even been exhilarating, filling me with a strange lightness, convincing me that I would be pared to bone and in that disappearance I would become the bone that August would always want. But as time went on and still he gave me nothing, or sometimes just a dollar or two, when all we kept in the house might be a bag of oatmeal so I could cook his breakfast, I saw that August meant for me to live on very little. I could tell that he would rather sit on the edge of our bed at night, counting the cash in his wallet, than hand any money over to me. That was when hunger became painful. Without food, my belly was a gnawing jaw and I walked hunched over, as if the rings of my spine were ready to unlatch. When I could get one, I ate an apple, core and all. Once I ate a peach that Bertha gave me and sucked on the pit for the rest of the day. I sucked on pebbles I picked up from our drive, to make myself think that I was eating. That I was full.

But I could not bring myself to believe that August would put his regard for money ahead of me. I told myself that he loved me. That he had promised to take care of me. That he had only forgotten. That my hunger must be some kind of mistake and I just had to wait for him to fix it. Even now, I am amazed at the things I told myself so I would not have to look at him and the way he really was.

Outside, the air was soft and hot. Bees hummed in Bertha's raspberry patch. She saw me and called my name but I just smiled and waved and walked down the driveway. She looked perfect in her perfect yard, as if she had never once been manhandled or turned by the desires of men, taken from herself and turned into something they wanted. It did not seem possible that a girl could walk through life the way that Bertha did, but here was Bertha, doing just that. It was hard to understand.

When I went to her house, she served cake and tea. She never talked about my unraveling dress. She never mentioned my poor shoes. She did not pry about my family. She just sat me down on her porch or in her kitchen and gave me something to eat, a wedge of pie, a slice of strudel. She said they had too much but I knew she thought that I did not have enough. I believe she had taken it upon herself to worry about me, about my shrinking belly, my droopy clothes.

Say what you want, she always said. Don't say what August wants. Say what you want. Above all else.

Her voice was very tender when she spoke. She fed me and told me things that felt like riddles, so surprising to me were they, so filled with ideas that made me blink.

I found a footpath that rose uphill under the pines. No wind moved but the air seemed cooler in the shade. I carried my hunger like an empty bucket. I thought if I kept moving it would not echo and I could ignore the aching bite, the whirlpool that sucked at me no matter what I did.

The trees thinned out near the top. A shallow slope spread out below me. A lone turkey vulture circled slowly and evenly on the updrafts, riding down and then up. I sat under an oak. I drew in the dirt with a stick. I batted flies away from my hair. I collected pine needles and twigs and acorn caps and old burrs and a few small stones—granite, quartz glinting. I lay on my stomach and built a little house and then another. Finally I had a fairy village just like the fairy villages that Martha and I built when we were little.

The turkey vulture disappeared. I rolled over on my side and pillowed my head on my arms. I lay very still. I let myself believe that the emptiness I felt was only a way to get ready for August, who would come home and lie down with me in the dark. I closed my eyes. I let the emptiness be August. I let the dark close over me. After a time, I fell asleep. If birds flew overhead or deer passed behind me on the silent traces in the woods or bears came up from the river or dwarves came out of the ground, I saw none of them.

I dreamt of a ship on the water that came through a silvery mist from a land I could not see and sailed over open water toward a land I could not identify. As the ship sailed, it cast a black shadow on the dark blue water. All around me was the sound of creaking wood and the rippling shudder of the sails. Then there were smokestacks and open decks and no sails at all and the ship was entirely different but in the manner of dreams was still the same and still carried the same cargo. I saw a woman in a dark red dress at the forward rail but it could not be a woman in a dark red dress for the dress was white and the red had come from her and then she and the ship disappeared. I woke with my heart pounding and my breath gone and a sense that I was in danger but of course I was not.

I came down the hillside in the late afternoon, the sun still well above the horizon. I carried acorns in my pocket and a handful of pure white stones. When I got to the road, a man saw me and stopped dead in his tracks. He had a length of rope coiled over his shoulder and a hatchet tucked into his belt. He put his hand to his mouth and backed away and then turned and ran down the road. I looked around and saw nothing. I realized he was afraid of me.

I touched my hair and smoothed the front of my dress. I knew why he ran. But I was no spirit of the woods, no sylph or sprite, no bewitching girl with her hands full of spells. I was a married woman. Still, my dress was soiled and wrinkled and rank. My shoes were dirty. My hair had come undone. I shed pine needles and twigs as I walked. He must have thought I was no good, come to haunt him, the terrible girl who took men into the woods.

But I was not that girl and never had been. I was only myself, hungry and tired and hot and alone.

When I got home, I sat on the back steps and took my shoes off. I heard the sound of creaking bedsprings and then August stood in the doorway. He wore his work clothes. He held his hand out to me, his fingers knotted into a fist. "I have something for you," he said.

He turned his hand over and I pried his fingers open, one by one. A plain gold band rested in his palm.

"Put it on," he said. He smiled. "It is not going to bite you." When I did, a light came into his eyes. He kissed the band on my finger. He said he wanted to prove to me that he could be a good husband. He wanted to show me that he could do the right thing. "Now," he said. "I am going to take care of your bath."

He had already started the water on the stove. He lifted the pot and carried it over to the washtub and filled the tub. He tested the temperature with his hand. He told me to get in.

My hunger disappeared as his words moved through me. I left my dress in a heap and walked naked in the bare end of daylight. I let him watch me, his gaze as if the touch of his hand, as if he had already reached for me. I stepped into the tub and lowered myself into the water. He soaped a washrag. He began to suds my back. I turned to take the rag from him but he laughed and said, "Let me." His voice soft and low and full of wonderment, as if I was something he could not believe he was permitted to touch. Water sloshed onto the floor and he laughed again but his hand stilled on my hip. I heard his breath catch. I knew what would come next. He touched my breasts with his soapy rag and told me to turn and face him. "So I can wash you," he said. I turned.

He took me to a restaurant near the courthouse where the tables were laid with white tablecloths and thick glass goblets and heavy silverware. He liked to hold forth and tell stories about the escapades he and his brother had survived when they were children. He had jumped off a roof on a dare and had broken his arm but that did not matter. What mattered was that he had done it. He had jumped when everyone said he could not. This kind of thing had set him up to be the man he was. He saw himself as fearless and in charge. I saw him that way, too. As we had walked along the street toward the restaurant, we had passed a flower vendor and August had leaned over the crocks of blossoms until he found a tiny bunch of soft pink roses. He told the flower girl to fix them with a pin so he could pin the flowers to my dress. She did not have a pin but he just stood there, staring at her, until she fashioned something with a hairpin she took from her head. She clipped the flowers to my dress. He was not entirely satisfied but she had done what he had asked and so he agreed that it was fine. He paid her a little bit less than the price she suggested and she did not argue with him. I could feel her eyes on our backs as we went up the street. August had taken something from her and it was not just the flowers. It was not just that business with the pin. He had made her feel his power. At dinner he eyed me and said he thought I needed some new clothes. But then he let it go, as if he was determined to have a good time. He took my hand in his and turned it this way and that. He smiled and appreciated the ring he had purchased. He held his left hand out to me and showed me that our rings matched. He told me that the rings were the best he could afford. Even if they were not the absolute best, they were better than the prize that came in a box of Cracker Jack. He smiled again and I smiled at him. I loved our rings. I loved the way they let the world know that I belonged to him.

He had ordered steaks for us and he made sure we had chocolate cake for dessert. A man in a plain blue jacket and black pants sat at an upright piano. He played some soft small song. August pressed his knee against mine under the table and told me I was beautiful. "I can see that others would think you are not so pretty," he said. "But to me, you are." He smiled. I felt tears sharp in my eyes.

Some nights he hit me for no reason. Other nights I seemed to be the cause. One morning he took a razor from his kit and stropped it and then held it next to my face. One night he flicked a knife at me. Afterward, he always said he was wrong.

He always said it was his fault. He always said he wanted to do the right thing. I often thought that if August were president, he could enact a hundred laws against the things he did, but still, he would do them. A hundred years from now, a thousand years from now, I would read newspaper stories about girls who disappeared at the hand of some man. And August would be the same. Law or no law. This I believed to be love.

In the morning he left before breakfast. I opened the sack of oatmeal and saw black things moving. I closed the bag and carried it outside and threw it in the trash barrel in the yard.

He loved me but he hit me. He touched me as if driven by something he could not control. Then he said I was not pretty. He bought me flowers and criticized my clothes. I knew my clothes were shabby. He did not need to point this out to me. I thought that everyone could see how bad they were whenever I left the house. If I caught a glimpse of myself in a store window, I saw a thin girl with clothes that hung on her like sacks.

I swallowed hard. My hunger knew no end and August gave me very little and the more often he hit me, the more afraid I became to ask for what I should have been rightly given. There was no way to ease the hollow or allay the ache and now nausea rose unbidden. I believed that hunger would make you sick and it seemed I was sick every morning, as if my body had chosen to feel queasy rather than empty. And now there was only one thing left to do.

I walked quickly. Two blocks over, a band of boys in short pants and white shirts played stickball on an open lot. Two small girls, no older than eight or nine and dressed in lemon-yellow dresses and red leather boots, pushed past me, followed by their mother, who wore a gray skirt and a gray blouse and a straw boater trimmed with gray silk ribbon. She dropped her gaze as she passed me. I said good morning but she did not reply.

Street traffic picked up. I heard the clattering of the inter-urban and its distant bell and saw its glassy cars and flickering blue sparks. Another wave of nausea moved through me and washed away and then swelled again. After that I was in the center of town. I turned up the road to my father's house. I passed the springhouse and watched the summer women in their white clothes rest on iron benches while they waited for the cure. No water in the world could heal them of what ailed them, if they lived in the same world I did. Four young men on bicycles wobbled along the gravel path and then sped away down the street. I had known this neighborhood as long as I had been alive but now it was unfamiliar, the way that something well known appears in a dream and no longer looks as it did when you knew it in real life.

I stood at the back steps and licked my lips. Then I climbed the stairs and knocked on the door. When no one came I knocked again. This time Martha appeared, frail in her white shirtwaist. When she saw me she fell back. Then she opened the door. She put her arms around me and whispered my name. She was no more substantial than a bony cage.

We sat on the open ground in the middle of the trees between my father's house and our neighbor's place. Insects hummed in the long grass. I told her I was married. I told her about the ceremony at the courthouse and the house that August had arranged for us, its three rooms and the curtains I had sewn using a stick and a spool of thread. I told her about Bertha, who did not have to do anything except play with her flowers and her dishes and her fan. I told her about the dinner at the restaurant and about the roses August had pinned to my dress. I showed her my gold band.

Martha pulled a length of rattling hollow reed from the

ground and split it in half with her thumbnail while I talked. She broke the halved pieces into smaller pieces and let the pieces fall onto the grass.

"What," I said. "What?"

"Are you all right?" She lifted my hand and then let it fall back onto the grass. She stroked my fingers. "You look thin."

I shrugged. "You are one to talk," I said, but she looked stricken. "I am all right," I said. I batted flies from my hair and slapped a mosquito on my forearm.

"It is so hot," she said. She dabbed at her face with the back of her hand. "Let's go under the trees."

We found a place at the base of an old maple where roots heaved up out of the ground and the dirt was cool. I lay down and Martha sat cross-legged beside me. After a short time she straightened her legs and rolled onto one hip and leaned on one elbow. She told me that Hattie had been sent out to work at a neighbor's house, to help with the children. "They have a new baby and two others under three. It will be just for the summer," she said. "In the fall she will go back to school."

"Are you sure?"

"Are you working?" she asked. Then she shook her head. "No," she said. "Of course not. You could not be here if you were." Dappled light fell around her. She frowned. "William Oliver came to the house. He was looking for you."

"August told me to quit," I said.

"It was about something else," she said. "He stood on the front steps and recited something. I think it was poetry but I did not know the poem. Or maybe it came from the Bible."

"The Bible," I said. "I am surprised you recognized it."

I thought of my mother's Bible, printed in Old High German, where someone had recorded the dates and places of our births next to our names and which she kept on a table in the living room and from which she sometimes read aloud, translating the stories as she went, but whose words seemed like nothing to me but distant things that had nothing to do with me.

Martha sat up. "The Bible has always seemed to be a great deal beside the point," she said. "As it has been for you. As it has been for all of us. Suffer the little lambs and all of that." She snorted and picked at the grass. I had no idea Martha felt this way and I looked at her with interest. But she just pulled grass out of the ground and threw it into the yard. Finally she said, "He did not believe me when I said you were gone. He kept asking where you were. He stood on our steps like a man possessed. He was driving the laundry cart and it ended up blocking the street. No one could get by. I told him over and over again that you were not here. Finally he left."

"He is full of ideas," I said. "None of them good."

"Could you have married him?"

The grass was scratchy and I kept feeling insects crawl up my legs. Her question was irritating and beside the point. I sighed. "I do not know, Martha. Maybe."

"Maybe?" She touched the back of my hand. "Did he make an offer?"

An ant marched along a long blade of grass under the tree and came to the end and turned and marched back along the grass in just the way that it had come. I wondered how I might describe William Oliver's offer. It hardly seemed real anymore but of course it had been very real when it came to me.

"He had another arrangement in mind," I said at last.

"I just thought. If you had another prospect." She fingered the buttons on her blouse.

"It does not matter," I said. "I would not have married him."

"You preferred August Bethke," she said. She made his name sound like a curse or a disease.

"Yes," I said. But now when I thought of August, I thought

not only of the way he made me shudder with pleasure in the dark. I also thought of the gun he kept hidden in a bucket under the washstand, which I had found one day, and which he had explained away by saying he needed a gun for protection, although he would not tell me just what it was he needed to protect himself from. And then I thought of the knife he wore strapped to his waist. Of the low sling of his tool belt with its hammers and sharp screwdrivers and something like the talons of a bird rolled into a ball that he could use to pry out nails. Then I thought again of the touch of his hand, the smell of his hair, the taste of him, the sounds he made when he was with me, all of it a confusing world of things that did not add up as I had expected.

Martha lay back down on her hip and picked up a small stick. She ran the point of the stick through the dirt. "Do you like being married?" she asked in a prim voice.

"Yes." But I could not help myself. I looked away and would not meet her gaze.

"All of it?"

"Yes." But I would not tell her about the part I did not like and we would never ever talk about the part I did.

"Everything?" she said. Now she would not look at me.

"You will like it, too," I said. "You will see. When you marry George."

Martha flushed. "I do not want to talk about George," she said. "Not that way."

"Why not?" I said. I could hear the callous tone in my voice. "He is just like all the rest."

She stiffened. "How would you know?"

"Oh, I know," I said, my words suddenly something I wore like a lead vest that would sink me once and for all. I sagged deeper into the grass. I felt old and experienced. I thought I would drown in the things I had begun to realize were true.

Flies hummed under the leaves. The grass smelled sweet and dry and spread away from us in a plaited yellow slope.

"Why did you come?" Martha said abruptly.

"Perhaps I missed you."

"You did not miss me."

"I did." I glanced back at the house and felt a surge of sadness break over me and the world became airless then. "And I missed Hattie," I said gently. "I wish she was here."

"You did not miss us," Martha said flatly. "You need something."

I pressed my lips together and did not say anything. I thought of all the things I needed and the wishes that had gone unanswered and the sharpness of those thoughts ran through me like a knife. I could not understand why it was so wrong to need my family to care for me.

"I miss you," I said. "I think about you every day."

Martha sat up. "For once in your life, tell the truth," she said. "You think I am stupid but I already know why you are here." She waved her hand at my father's house. "What else would bring you back?"

I rolled onto my stomach and put my head on my arms. In a buried and strained voice I told her that I needed some money for food. She did not have to give me much. Just something from the money I had earned at the laundry. Something I could hide in a shoe or under a floorboard and keep for myself. Something that would let me eat. August was so busy, I said. August worked so hard. He did not mean to but sometimes he forgot. That was understandable. He had so much to do. It was like this for lots of new wives. Of that I was sure.

She did not say anything until I was finished. Then she stood up. She waved her hands around her head to dispel a swarm of gnats. She turned to look back across the clearing, where the yellow siding of my father's house made a broken shape behind the trees. "Come back to the house," she said. "I will give you what I have."

In the end, I bought a very small piece of cheese and a piece of a dry sausage and three apples and three potatoes and two cans of peas and a loaf of bread. It took me a long time to decide but I knew I had to pick things that would last. I sat on a bench in front of a cigar store and slowly ate the cheese and half of the sausage and a heel of the bread. I looked in the bag as I ate and counted my things and then tied the bag with its ropey cord.

It rained late in the afternoon and the lights flickered and went out. I stood in the dim kitchen. August had the matches. The wind came up and the trees tossed and the rain seethed along the side of the house and pelted the windows. I listened to the thunder break and roll. I flinched when lightning flashed. I lay down on the bed in my clothes and looked at the ceiling and thought about the rain slashing through Bertha's flowers and about Martha as she pulled the money from my mother's old leather purse and about Edwin, whom I had not seen since the day he held his head in his hands and howled but who was with me every day like the faint image of something warmly pleasant.

I hid my food below a loose floorboard in the bedroom. This I had pried up with the flat edge of a knife. I found a nail where I could hang the canvas bag by its cord so that it was held below the house in a cool shadow. Then I dropped the board back into place. I thought about the food as if it buttressed me against something I could not name. It made me feel better to think that I had carried my own supplies into the country where I now lived and was not so much at the mercy of those who controlled everything, even where I put my feet. Even the air I breathed.

The front windows were pearled with rain and the street was

dark and watery. The lamplighter did not come this far out from the center of town so our road went dark at dusk and the only light came from the windows of houses. I stood and went to the window and leaned my forehead against the glass. I watched Bertha's husband drop his suspenders so they hung in loops at his waist. He stretched and sat in his chair and unfolded his paper over his lap. I could smell whatever it was Bertha was cooking for dinner.

Three nights later, August came home from work. He smiled at me as he came through the door and then he kissed me. I watched him walk into the bedroom, where he dropped his tool belt on the floor. He took the knife out of his waistband and set it on the bedside table. He looked back at me and smiled again and looked at the bed as if I could read his mind. I watched him take two steps toward the basin. I heard the second step squeak. I saw him stop and look down at the floor. I saw him test the floorboard with his toe. He must have felt the board give because he squatted down and touched the edge of the board with his fingertips. He reached behind him for his tool belt and pulled out a screwdriver. He used the point of the screwdriver to pry the board up from the floor. He laid the board beside him. He looked into the darkness under the house. Then he reached down and felt around and pulled my canvas bag out from the shadows. He looked back at me, frowning. I closed my eyes. When I opened them, he'd turned the bag upside down and the contents had rolled out on the wooden floor. Two apples. Three potatoes. The cans of peas and most of the loaf of bread.

"What is this?" he said.

"August," I said.

"What is this?" he said again, louder. He tossed the sack onto the bed.

I lowered my head. "Just some food," I said.

"Just some food," he repeated. He picked up one of the potatoes and tossed it from hand to hand. "You keep this for what reason?"

"To eat."

"What?"

"To eat," I said. "August."

"To eat," he said.

I nodded. "Yes," I said.

"And this is what you buy with my money? Food you keep from me?" He let the potato drop to the floor.

"No," I said. I watched the potato roll under the bed. It seemed unbearable that he would touch what was mine.

"No?" He kicked the apples and I winced. "You have some other money I do not know about?"

"I got some from my sister," I said softly. "August. Please."

"You got some money from your sister?"

"August," I said.

"How did you get this money?" he said.

"She gave it to me."

"She gave it to you? Just like that? You did not ask?" He narrowed his eyes at me. "Why would she do that?"

I wanted to explain but I could not. It seemed too compli-cated to tell him that I had earned money at the laundry, that my father had always taken that money from me, that I was hungry, that I wanted to eat, that I had walked all the way across town to see if my sister would give me some of that money back, that I did not think I should have to ask him for money, that he was my husband and he was supposed to know enough to take care of me.

"August," I said. "It was just a little."

"That is a lie." He ran his hand through his hair. "That is a goddamn lie," he said. He walked up and down in front of me.

"You went begging to your family," he said. "I have that right, don't I?"

"August."

"Did she get his permission?"

"Who?"

"Your sister. The one you went begging to. Did she get your father's permission?"

"It was my money. From before."

"But don't you see what you have done to me?" he said. He tugged at his head as if he could wrench it from his shoulders. "My God," he said. "My God."

"I had to eat," I said. I looked in his eyes. I could not understand how the act of asking my sister for some of my money back had humiliated him, but I could see that he thought it had.

"That is when you come to me," he said. "I cannot read what is in your mind. How do I know anything if you do not tell me?"

My clothes hung on me like empty sacks. I could count every rib when I lay down next to him. He could have counted my ribs, too, had he ever stopped and looked. Instead, he had simply filled me and filled me again until the hunger turned into my longing for him.

"You have not given me any money for weeks," I said.

"Do I know that?" He looked around the room as if he expected the furniture to answer him. "I do not believe I know that."

I had no answer for him. It seemed ridiculous that I should have to tell him to feed me. But August did not think this was ridiculous. He made it seem like I had made a terrible mistake. He made it seem like I should have known what to do.

He bent down and picked up the floorboard he had pried up with the screwdriver. He threw the board on the bed next to the empty sack. He faced me. "What have you got to say for yourself?" he said.

"Nothing," I said softly. Pleading. "August—"

"That's right," he said. "Nothing. There is nothing you can say for yourself." He picked up the sack. "What else do you have in here?" he said. He held the sack upside down in the air before him and shook it up and down as if he expected treasure to drop out. "What else are you hiding from me?"

"Nothing," I said. "There is nothing else."

He kicked one of my apples and I thought that was a shame because the bruise would spread and I would not be able to eat the apple later.

He threw the sack at me. "You make me sick."

"August," I said. I stiffened my back. "What do you want me to do? You leave me here with no food, no money. What am I supposed to do?" I crossed the room and touched his forearm. "I have to eat."

"Do not do that," he said.

"This?" I said. I pressed myself against him. "Don't do this?"

"Stop it," he said. He stepped away. "You humiliated me in front of your family. I don't want to be near you."

"No?" I said. I followed him. "You don't want this?" I pushed myself against him again. I looked up at him. His face had gone dire in the falling light. "August," I said. "August." I lay both of my hands on him. I leaned into him and felt his warm chest beneath my palms. I told him that I loved him. I tried to make him remember who I was. I tried to make him hold me the way he had held me before we were married. I wanted him to feel in his racing heart that we were the same and that he loved me, he loved me.

"Stop acting like a whore," he said. He put his hands on my shoulders and tried to push me away. But I held on to his shirtsleeves.

He raised his hand and slapped me hard across the face. I fell to my knees. Sprays of sparkles stood out before me, white and green and blue, and then came a blow and there was darkness behind the sparkles. I lost sight of the table leg and the foot of the bed. A rushing filled my ears as if the swirling surge of a terrible river and then came another blow and even the river sound retreated. I lay in the blue-black darkness and felt my body move as if I had become a sack of lost and lumpy things. But I did not put my hand up before me. I did not crawl away. After a while I could hear someone far away screaming and then I heard men shouting and someone yelling, "Stop it! You'll kill her!" After that August leaned down through the blank light and the gray shadow and the blue sparkles and the white sparkles. He put his face close to mine. He put his mouth next to my ear. "Understand me," he said. "Next time I will use my gun."

17

Bertha's husband, Frank, and some other men came through the door and pulled August off of me. They lifted me up and carried me across the wet grass to Bertha's house. She covered me with a blanket. I turned my head and spit blood into the grass.

The men put me in a bedroom where there was flowered wallpaper on the walls and clean white woodwork and a lamp with a pastel blue glass shade on the nightstand next to the bed. Then the men were gone. Bertha opened the window and no breeze blew the curtains at the sill. I heard her soft footsteps on the stairs. The night was still and hot. Somewhere below me she chipped ice and put the chips in a clean towel and brought that to me and told me to hold it against my jaw. She set a shallow white basin with a rim of red on the nightstand and used both hands to loosen my clothes. She dipped a washcloth into the water in the basin and dabbed at my face. She put a pillow under my arm so I could hold the ice against my jaw. She sat with me for a long time but I was too ashamed to look her in the eye. Then she went away. I lay in the silence and wished I were dead.

When she came back she carried a vase of dark red dahlias, which she put on the dresser. She had changed from her dress into her nightclothes. She fingered the sash on her wrapper. Her face was weary and sad. I tried to sit up but fell back. Pain shot through my sides, my stomach, my face.

"Lie still," she said. Her voice had a firm, commanding quality I had not heard from her before.

"Where," I said. I stopped. Shattered stars flew up over me in a dazzling whirl and then darkness followed.

"Frank took him to get a drink."

More stars flew up and faded.

"It's bad," she said. "I should get the doctor." She touched my face. "You need stitches."

"No."

"But you could have something broken inside. You look very bad."

Blackness rose and then dropped away and the room sparkled. If I had something broken inside, it was because August had broken it. I licked my lips. Blood. It ran down my neck and into my hair.

"Someone from your family, then," she urged.

"No," I said.

"Your mother?" Bertha smoothed back my hair. Her touch was gentle. "A sister?"

Tears ran out of my eyes into my ears. I stared at the ceiling.

She picked up the washcloth from its basin. She wiped the cloth against my skin. The cloth was cool and wet and she worked gently. Her hair was tied back in a blue ribbon, her robe and nightgown fresh and pressed, her slippers white wool, as if she were a being from a place I had only heard rumored. "Get some rest," she murmured. The cool wet and the stars in my head. "We won't let him in tonight."

———

The first night I dreamt of my mother. She held her hand out to me but I could not reach her. In the morning I lay on my back and stared at the ceiling. I thought about the day August and I got married. They all thought I was ruined already so what did it matter what he did with me? The judge had winked at August like a man will when he shares some secret with another. Kiss her, he'd said, as if he did not know what else had already gone on. Martha believed what my father believed, which made her no different from William Oliver or Inge or any of the rest of them. It was as if they had put their heads together about me and taken my measure and then they had marked that down someplace and my future was sealed. As if I had no say in this and no hand.

Bertha brought a bowl of oatmeal on a tray and set it down on the bedside table. She pulled up a chair. In a kind voice she told me that I should just stay where I was and she would help me eat. She sat there for a time with the spoon poised in midair, but when I would not take anything, she stood up and left. Pain all over my body razor sharp and my ribs hurt like they'd been broken. I lay there and told myself that it would get better. I lay there and cried. When I woke up it was the second day, and Bertha stood in front of me with a soup plate in her hand.

"You have to eat," she said. "Let me help you."

She had made some broth from beef bones. She sat on the chair and said she could feed me if I wanted but I said no. I dug my elbows into the mattress until I slowly came to a sitting position and stayed like that while white pain shot through me. But I smiled at her and took the bowl. I rested it on a tray she placed across my lap and slowly tasted the soup. Nausea lay below the pain, like a thin cloak that seemed ready to strangle me. But I smiled again and told Bertha that I liked her soup, that it was good.

She watched me. "It's not the first time, is it?"

I set the spoon down on the tray.

"Marie." She smiled at me. "These houses are so close together. I don't know what they were thinking when they built them this way."

"They are all right," I said.

"You would think that," she said. She smiled again. "You're just a girl."

"You are not?"

She laughed. "I'm an old married woman of twenty-six," she said. "A great deal older than you. A great deal more experienced in the world, if you must know." She smiled wearily. "Eat a little more. You need to eat if you want to get better."

"I am fine."

"Finish that. I can get you some more."

"No, thank you."

"Why not?"

I did not reply. The smell of the soup had begun to sicken me and I felt clammy and weak. I worried that I would vomit. My ribs throbbed.

"I suppose he wouldn't like it," she said.

"It is not like that."

"No?"

"No." I lifted the soup plate and she took it from me and I fell back on the pillows and knives cut through me. Bile rose in my throat and I coughed and swallowed.

"What's it like, then?" she said in a very soft voice. "Tell me."

"It is not what you are thinking." Something I thought was solid had come unstuck in my head. "We are different."

"All right." She waited.

I thought of August's hand on me, the way he touched me

in the dark and in the daylight, under moon and star and sun. "We are so much in love," I said.

She looked at me as if I were a child.

"I do not know how to explain," I said, and I did not. I could not even explain it to myself, the way August could hurt me and still be my world, absolute and whole.

"Ordinarily it would be none of my business," she said. "But all of this makes it my business." She gestured around the room, at the clean coverlet that lay over my legs and the fresh curtains and the vase of dahlias and the half-eaten plate of soup. "Frank going over there when we heard screaming like someone was being killed. That makes it my business."

"I am sorry." I wiped at the tears that dropped off the end of my nose.

Her clean rooms and her kindness did nothing but make me feel ashamed. That August would do something that meant the neighbors would get involved made me feel ashamed. That now the whole neighborhood would know made me feel ashamed. All of this seemed even worse to me than when I learned that the whole town was talking about that girl who took men into the woods. This was the place I had come to start my life. I wanted it to be beyond reproach. But that was ruined now.

"Marie." She put her hand on my arm. "I'm trying to help you."

"I know." I choked a little when I spoke.

She sighed. "He was here last night. Frank wouldn't let him in." She gave me the towel she'd carried under the soup plate to dab my tears. "You must understand. We've heard it before," she said. "I know that there have been other times. Not as bad as this, of course, but certainly bad enough." She stood up and walked over to the window and looked out at her yard where I imagined she saw roses and lavender and daisies massed in their orderly beds, laid out in perfect measure, blooming only when they were instructed to do so.

"He loves me so much," I said. I heard my voice as if someone else said the words.

"I know that's what he says." She turned from the window. "Do you know who saved you night before last? Frank. And Otto Baum who lives behind us. And Carl Petroski, who came from across the street. And some lunatic boy we've all seen around the neighborhood. Even he came running. They all heard you. These are men who would give you the shirts off their backs. These are good men. And they don't want to see this again."

That lunatic boy. I knew she meant Edwin. I thought of the way he must have bent over me, lifted me, carried me. I sobbed.

Bertha sat down on the bed and laid her hand on my hip. "Can you tell me where your family is? Can I get your mother for you?"

I shook my head.

"This isn't right," she said. She sounded as if she was talking to herself. "You should not have to face this alone. I'm sure they would not want to see you like this."

"Do not be so sure," I said. I laughed bitterly. I thought of Martha, who would probably be glad to see me getting my just deserts. I thought of my father, who would not disagree. He might even wonder why August had failed to finish the job.

She sighed. "You are very tired," she said. "Get some rest. But think about what I said. If I could bring someone here to help you, who would that be? That's the first question we need to answer." She picked up the soup plate. "I'll check in on you later. For now, get some rest."

He came to the front door at first. I could hear his voice down below. Darkness spread over the summer evening and fireflies rose outside my window. The room lit by a single bulb and ashen moths the size of gloves flattening themselves against the screens. August stood on the front porch, talking to Frank in a very polite voice. I could not make out what he was saying, but I felt his voice like a wave that came over me. I imagined him in that room and on the bed with me and the rich smell of him and the weight of his body. "August," I said, my voice the voice of one in a trance or a dream. But Frank would not let him in. August's voice rose in pitch and they argued on the front porch. After that, Frank said something I could not make out and things fell silent. I could hear the cicadas in the trees and then the front door opened and Frank called to Bertha. August stood on the front lawn and pinged pebbles at the upstairs windows without ever finding mine. The front door closed and I heard their voices together again as they moved off down the dark street. I knew they were headed down to the tearoom where at night the woman who owned the place served drinks.

I heard footsteps on the stairs but they stopped halfway to the top and there was a long silence. Then the footsteps descended. I lay on the bed and looked at the screen and felt my body ache. A green moth spread-eagled against the screen and I watched it, its tiny bobbing head shaped like a glassy bead, its long furry antennae rising and falling as if with breath, its lurching blindness in the bright light.

18

Early on the fifth day, I sat up. I slowly swung my legs over the side of the bed. I held my sides and looked at the floor. When my head cleared, I got to my feet. I breathed slowly. The things that pained me came from more than flesh and would last longer than bones that broke or skin that split. August had come every night and every night Frank had refused to let him in. He had come to the back door when Frank had barred the front. He had waited on the grass by Bertha's flower beds. He'd spoken politely at first, but when Frank would not let him in his voice had grown louder and louder, and the awful words he'd used were the sounds of a man who walked freely in the world.

Bertha had scraped the mud from my shoes. She had washed my clothes and had pressed my blouse and skirt and had taken a needle and thread to the torn places. She had laid the clothes out on the chair, where they now waited for me. I stepped out of my borrowed nightgown and lifted my arms and winced as I slipped into my chemise. I breathed and waited for the pain to slide into something I could bear. Then I pulled on my skirt, the sleeves of my blouse. I felt the light in the room dim. I inhaled slowly and then exhaled and then inhaled again. I held on to the back of the chair.

After a few minutes, I made my way to the mirror. The girl who looked back at me could not have been me but of course she was. I touched my swollen jaw and looked at the black and blue and purple and yellow skin around my eyes and the blackened cuts above my brow, across my mouth, across my nose, at my head bruised and swollen like a lost ball. I took a deep breath and closed my hands into fists. From somewhere far away, a lone train whistle sounded.

"It will be all right," I said, and tried to make my voice strong so that I would believe this. Sometimes this is all that is available to a girl. "It is not so bad. It will be all right."

I sat and buttoned my blouse. I waited for the pain in my sides to settle. After a little while, I lay back down and dabbed at the sweat standing on my forehead with the back of my arm.

Sometime later the rain began and I heard a soft tap on the door. Bertha turned the knob and pushed it open without waiting for an answer. Then she stepped away and I saw a tall thin woman in a fraying white shirtwaist and a dark green skirt. She had walked a long way through wet streets and the hem of her skirt was soaked. Her dark hair was pulled back in a bun and lay as tight as a cap over her bony skull.

I pushed myself up on my elbows. "Martha?" I said. My heart rose into my throat.

She stood by the bed and looked down at me. Then she sat heavily in the chair and put her face in her hands. After a minute, she lifted her head and made her back straight. "Look at you," she said. "What have you done?"

I felt the cold inside of me grow colder.

"You have got to quit this now," she said. "This has got

to be the end." She stood up and faced the window. She put her hand on the window frame and leaned her head against her arm. She acted just like I had exhausted her beyond all measure.

"How did you find me?" I said.

"Bertha came."

"But how did Bertha know who you were?"

She turned and looked at me. "It was that boy," she said. "That lunatic."

"Edwin?"

"Is that his name?"

I nodded.

"He told Bertha," she said.

"He could not tell Bertha anything." Edwin could barely string three words together. But he had found a way to warn me anyway, as it turned out, even though I had not listened. I felt a little sob in my spine and I swallowed it before it had a chance to rise.

"But he did," Martha said. She stepped away from the window and sat in the chair again. The lamp burned behind her head and cast its dim yellow light around her hair. "He told Bertha where I live and how to find me. And then she came to see me and told me you were"—she paused—"ill."

"Where is Hattie?" I said.

"At work."

"She still works?"

"Not for much longer. School is coming soon."

I thought of my father. His rules. His policies, his plans, his principles, his priorities, his pain. His insistence on the leveling of everything, which for his daughters meant being leveled right down into the dirt.

"He will never let her go back to school," I said. "You know that."

She did not reply. I suppose she thought that Hattie's work was a different argument than the one she had come to have. She did not know that I was beginning to see that it was all of a piece, like a length of net that my father wove when we weren't looking.

We sat quietly. The trees outside in their black and sodden leaves and the rain coming down in sheets and the dead moths laid out at the bottom of the screen in furry wads and Martha before me in her wet skirt and her slowly curling hair.

"What are you going to do?" she said at last.

"I do not know," I said. In the light of the bedside lamp, her face was all sharp lines and angles, her mouth straight, her eyes deep in gaunt sockets. Some people cannot bear sorrow except as refusal. Martha grew thinner and thinner after our mother was murdered and now she looked like she would disappear completely. I could not tell her how happy I had been. I also could not tell her what it had felt like when happiness fled.

Downstairs, Bertha dropped something. It sounded like the lid from a pot. I listened for the grinding interurban or the rustling birds overhead or the barking cries of geese or just a dog. But there was nothing. Just the faint sound of Martha breathing while she stared at me. The rain beyond.

"Marie," she said. She spoke as if it took some effort for her to keep her voice even. "You have to tell me what you did."

A familiar tiredness rolled through me. "I did not do anything," I said softly. But I thought of the way I touched August and of the way he moved toward me even as he pulled away.

"There has to be a reason," she said. "He did not do this without a reason."

His hands on me in our bed at night and the darkness of love that rippled over me and the way I clung to him when he held me. My breath caught in my throat.

The wind softened. The rain pattered on the roof and then faded and then pattered on the roof again.

"Tell me," she insisted.

I turned my face to the wall. "He found my food," I said.

"All right," she said briskly. "Now we are getting somewhere. And then what?"

"He said that I humiliated him." Tears. I rubbed them away.

She sat back in the chair and thought about this. A wind pushed through the leaves. I watched water fall in spirals to the ground.

"Did he say how you humiliated him?"

"Because I got money from you so I could eat." I sobbed hard and then worked my mouth and tried to stop.

The leaves outside the window showed their silver underbellies. After a time she said, "I can see how he would feel that way. No man wants to have his wife begging in the street."

I tried to stop crying.

"The important thing is that it was your fault," she said.

I dropped my forearm over my eyes.

"It is not as if he is a beast who acted without mercy," she said. "He is not a madman who did this for no reason. You provoked him. So now you apologize. Make sure he is always happy. This is what a wife does. She puts herself last."

"I was hungry," I said tightly. Martha was not going to help me. "I thought I would starve to death."

"Starve to death?" she said. She laughed. "Do not be so dramatic." She stared down at me and shook her head. "I do not know where you get your ideas," she said. "But the important thing is this has been settled. You can apologize. You can go back. Everything will be fine."

After Martha left, I made my way down the stairs, leaning heavily on the rail with every step. Bertha sat in the living room with a magazine in her lap but she looked up when I came in. "Did you see this?" she said. She showed me the picture on the cover, which was a photograph of men in dirty work clothes standing in a knotted bunch in front of a mine. Behind the mine, trees whose trunks were limned with new snow. They must have made the picture before the spring melt. The caption said something about the strikes that I did not bother to read.

The picture made me tired and then it made me angry. No one ever talked about us so that the people who read about us would understand. We were just tantalizing stories told for the reader's enjoyment. Or perhaps we were supposed to serve as warnings. Go this way. Do not go that way. Be the girl we have told you to be. As if we all needed an endless reiteration of what might befall us, should we forget for just one minute. Should we step out of line.

Bertha and I sat on the front porch with plates on our laps. The sun had come out and the grass steamed and the trees dripped. A man in a brown tweed suit came along the street. When he saw us, he tipped his hat and went off whistling. I looked over at my house. The windows were blank and dark. I had never hung the new curtains. I had never planted anything.

When she finished her sandwich, Bertha set her plate on the porch floor and cleared her throat and asked me about my plans. "Since you're feeling better now," she said kindly. "It will be good to have some idea. What did your sister say?"

"She said I should tell him I'm sorry."

"I see." Bertha gazed up at her dripping trees.

I fiddled with my plate.

"Are you thinking about going back?" she said. She spoke very softly. She seemed to think she could spook me like a rabbit in the grass.

I swallowed and swallowed again. "I do not see what choice I have," I said. "I am married to him." I swabbed my face with my napkin. The man who lived across the street came out of his house, looked over at us, turned, and went back inside. You will understand why I had begun to feel that we were always under scrutiny.

My ribs hurt with a boring pain, like someone was trying to screw a bolt right through me.

"You can't go back," Bertha said flatly.

I twisted my napkin into a ball. "He loves me," I said.

"So he says," she said. It was clear she didn't believe him.

"I love him," I said softly. "You do not understand."

"I guess that's true."

"He loves me," I said. I could not comprehend why this was so difficult. She knew what it was like to be married. She must know what I meant.

"I know he says he loves you," she said. "It isn't really the same thing. Frank thinks you need a lawyer. He thinks you should get a divorce."

I winced at the word.

She sighed. Her face pained. "I wasn't going to tell you this," she said.

I heard the clarion blare of a woodpecker's call. "What," I said.

"August has been talking to the men who live around here. He's been telling them what he's going to do when you come home."

I brushed the hair out of my eyes and wondered if it was possible to hurt any more than I did just then. "I know," I said. "He has a gun."

She put her hand on mine. I could not tell whom she was trying to comfort, me or herself, but I grabbed her fingers and she held my hand. "He told Frank that he would use it," she said. "He said that if you ever stepped out of line again, he would not hesitate to do what he needed to do."

A goldfinch flew pell-mell over the lawn, glinting gold and black, rising and falling and rising again.

"A lawyer would get you some money so you could start over," she said.

Tears ran off my chin. I ran my sleeve over my face. "I do not want to get divorced," I said.

"Why not?"

I clenched my hands. I felt August rise and expand around me, a kite still filled with wind that I was not yet willing to release.

"It is shameful," I said. I thought she would understand that. I knew she would never understand why I still loved August.

"What's shameful is what August did to you. That's what's shameful."

"I did it to myself," I said. "That's what Martha said."

It was not just Martha. If something went wrong, it was the fault of the girl. If the man had a knife, she had caused him to use it. If a man had a gun, she had given him reason to fire it. If he raised his fist, she should not have walked into it.

Bertha studied her garden, its armies of roses and its battalions of hydrangeas. "Your sister and my husband have very different opinions," she said, her voice so mild that I knew she had to work to keep it from rising. "Frank thinks you need a lawyer. Frank says that the judge can make August pay." She put her hand on my arm. "He should pay, Marie. For the lawyer and the hurt he's caused you. For all of it." She gave my arm a faint squeeze. "Frank told me you should see someone he knows through the bank. But you need to go today. Frank said things will go better for you if you go while you still look bad."

I touched my face, my swollen jaw, my split skin. The sun sparkled on the wet grass and bees hummed over the flower beds. Everywhere a smell of wet earth. This world was very beautiful, but it was not my world and it seemed it never would be. A bottomless fatigue rolled over me.

Bertha stood and picked up the plates and laid the brightly polished silverware across the top plate and leaned over and picked my napkin up from my lap.

"If we're going to see the lawyer, we need to go now," she said.

A grackle fluttered overhead and then another and another and finally a wave of dark birds skirled through the sky, an undulating wave of black that broke across the vault of blue and split and wheeled away.

Bertha borrowed a cart and horse from the woman who lived two houses away and we drove down into town as the afternoon turned warm. I had seen a woman drive a cart before but the women I had seen were the women who worked outside, digging in the dirt on their family's farms, their bodies thick with overuse. I had never seen a woman like Bertha drive a cart, and I swayed beside her and watched her expertly guide the horse down the hill into town. She told me that she had grown up in Milwaukee in a pretty house with a mother and father and two sisters. Her father had been the chief brewmaster at Schlitz, and her mother had kept house and had taught her daughters to sew and to paint and to play music on a piano they kept in the front room. She had seen to their needlework and their tatting and to their ability to recite the poems of Whitman and Longfellow. It seemed their very futures were wrapped up in the words of a land to which they could only gain entrance by finding love. Bertha shook her head when she said this, as if remembering the love stories told to young girls, these bright tickets to a world that would never be their own. Then she said that by the time she was born her family had been here for two generations and her father was very kind to her, which gave her a sense that the world was kind and she would find kindness in it and so she had. And she had stayed with this belief even though she knew it was more of an idea that anything material. You could not really lay your hands on the real experience of it and in fact were often confronted with its opposite. So as she had gotten older, she had learned that the idea of liberty, especially the idea of liberty that the country had been founded upon, did not entirely apply to her or to any girl and that no woman was ever really exempt from the demands of men. But she had made a religion, she said, out of her belief in kindness.

We came into a street near the courthouse, and Bertha turned the horse toward a hitching post in front of a wooden building with a green canvas awning rolled out over a double plate glass window. On one side of the door, I could see the top part of a man who sat with his back to the window, and on the other side of the door, the top half of a man who walked up and down while another man sat with his hat still on his head. The hat moved sometimes and sometimes stayed still. When we stepped inside, a long hallway ran out before us lined with doors, each fitted with a milk glass window, and we walked along until we came to a door with chipped gold lettering that spelled *Jared Thompson, Esq.*

A clerk just inside the door looked up when we came in. He sat at a spindly desk and worked over some papers and wore a green baize eyeshade. Bertha said that we would like to see Mr. Thompson. The clerk looked us over and said in a superior voice that as far as he knew, Mr. Thompson didn't have any appointments that afternoon. I turned to go but Bertha put her hand on my arm. She told the man in the eyeshade that her husband was Mr. Frank Riewestahl of the First National Bank of Waukesha, and she had no reason to hope that this was true of course but she believed anyway that it might be possible that Mr. Thompson would be able to spare a few minutes for us. "She is in great distress," she said. She spoke in a firm, strong voice and held my arm under the elbow. "Surely you can see that there is nothing planned about this."

The clerk paused and considered me. I wondered how many women like me he had seen before. From the look on his face, I guessed not many.

"I make no promises," he said. He stood and walked over to a heavy wooden door. He knocked, waited, and then opened the door and leaned half of his body inside. The office made me nervous. I leaned over and told Bertha that maybe we should just go. But she shook her head and told me to wait.

Jared Thompson rose when he saw me and crossed the room and held my elbow and steered me into a chair that faced his desk. He was a short man with dark, wavy hair and a clean-shaven face. He wore a black suit and a white shirt, but over the shirt he wore a bright yellow brocade vest, and I thought he must be a man who had a secret yen for fancy clothes.

He asked if I was in much pain. I nodded and he murmured. He appeared to wish to convey to me that he knew better than anyone the nature of my troubles and sat with women who had been nearly beaten to death every day.

He asked me to begin at the beginning and to proceed from there. But the beginning escaped me. Was it my mother laid out on her bed? My father smoking in the street? The men who carried her? The men who carried me? August under the trees? A ship on the sea? I felt it all reel through me like a world that had no exact features and threatened to spin away. My uncle Carl once took Martha and me to ride a carousel. We'd climbed up on our painted ponies and the carousel had begun with a lurch and then picked up speed, and before I knew it, I was whirling and flying, all of the colors around me running together in a dizzying blur, the music blaring, the brass ring going by, and Carl laughing and yelling that we were supposed to try and catch the ring. But it was all I could do to hang on, and when I stepped off, I staggered around the grass as if the world had been upended. I felt exactly the same when I sat across from Jared Thompson and he told me to begin at the beginning. My story had no beginning. My story was not even just my story.

Nausea rose in my throat and I was afraid that I would vomit everything out, August, my father, my mother, a steaming smelly used-up stew of confusion. But I swallowed hard and told Jared Thompson that I did not know where the beginning was. He said I might as well begin with my name and where I lived and my husband's name and who had done this to me, for he presumed that this was why I wanted to see him. After that, I could hear myself talking and the words were my own but they came to me from a distance, the way they would if the story belonged to a girl I had never met, a story that I had heard described by someone else.

When I was finished, he tipped back in his chair and looked up at the ceiling. He tapped his pen sharply against his teeth and then leaned forward and lay the pen down on the desk in front of him.

"I understand your predicament," he said. "But I don't think I can help you."

The room was bisected by light. A small electric fan pushed air around our feet. I hung my head. "I am sorry," I said. "I have taken too much of your time."

"That's all right." He picked up his pen and put it down again and picked it up again. "The problem is," he said, "the law makes few provisions for people like you. Attempted murder of a married woman. If an unknown man accosted you in a dark alley, it would be another matter. He would be arrested.

But you experienced this at the hands of your husband, a man with whom you have a fully executed contract and whom you are bound by law to honor and obey." He looked at me. "You are married to him? This isn't some common-law thing?"

I nodded.

"And the terms of the contract have been realized?"

I did not reply. I had fallen in love and gotten married. I did not fully comprehend what he meant.

He lowered his voice. "What I mean to say..." he said delicately. "You have been with your husband in the way that a wife must be with her husband?"

"Oh," I said. I felt myself go hot. I nodded.

"All right, then," he said. He looked around the room as if he would find what he was looking for in its dusty sunlight. "I haven't seen too many of these cases prosecuted." He drummed his fingers on the desktop. "I'm not even sure I can find a precedent." He studied me. "And you will have to get divorced. Likely that will be the only way."

I flinched. That word again.

"Mrs. Bethke," he said. "If you have the slightest doubt, let's stop right here."

"No," I said quietly. I never felt pushed into any of it but I never felt that any of it was my choice, either. I believed I could make things turn out all right if I just tried hard enough, but it also seemed to me that I had no such power. How could August be two things at once? Or my father? Or any man? I knew that whatever I said from this point forward meant that I would travel to a place that did not include August. But I was suddenly resigned to all of it. I had long ago set out on a journey that I should have realized would bring me here.

I looked at Jared Thompson, with his wavy hair and bright vest. "It is all right," I said.

"Fine," he said. He sat back quietly, as if deliberating. Finally he said, "We might have more success if we set aside the question of attempted murder and pursue divorce on the grounds that you are in fear for your life." He put his pen down and leaned toward me. "Would that be a fair thing to say? That you are in fear for your life?"

The clock tower struck its time. Jared Thompson watched me. "You understand that everything you tell me is something confidential between us?" he said. "That I cannot tell anyone what you have told me here, even if I do not take your case?"

"Yes," I said softly. My chin trembled, whether from the pain of the question or the pain in my ribs, my head, my mouth, I could not say.

"Then tell me." He spoke as if he could wrench the truth from me the way you wrench a root from the ground. "Is it a fair thing to say that you are in fear for your life?"

"Yes," I said quietly.

"And are there witnesses who can testify that you have good cause to be in fear for your life?" His words bored into me. "People who can say that what you say happened is what happened?"

The men who carried me through the night. Bertha and Frank, standing on their front porch, listening to my screams. "I think so," I said.

"You think so or you know so?"

"I know so," I said.

"And who would these people be?" He gazed at me, a level, steady look.

"They had to come," I said. I felt the awful crush of shame. "They pulled him off me."

"How many?"

"Three men," I said. "Or four." My cheeks burned again.

But the fact that there were witnesses did not worry Jared. It pleased him. "Good," he said warmly. His eyes sparkled, two shiny lights. He wrote on his pad. "And did anyone know that he starved you?" His pen poised over the paper.

"My sister."

"Your sister. Good."

I could not imagine what was good about this. "She will not say so," I said. I thought of Martha, who did not want to spare me anything. But she had given me money so I could eat. She had wanted to spare me starvation at least. "She thinks I should go home and be a good wife."

"Is that what you think?" His words made a hole in me, and then everything that had happened poured into me, like water through a funnel. I sagged in my chair.

"I do not know," I whispered.

Jared Thompson set his pen down. "Mrs. Bethke," he said. "If you want to sue for divorce, I am willing to help you. And I can assure you that it is only your very pitiable state that compels me to do this, for it will be difficult. I see you before me, severely injured, but by the time we get to court, these wounds will have healed. Even if we get your friend outside to sign an affidavit today, and I will do that before you leave, these wounds will have healed. And even if we pursue divorce, I think it's far from clear that we will prevail. No one likes to see a case like this come into court. It's too unequal, in point of fact, and because of that, it's hard to argue. Very difficult to get the upper hand. The husbands always seem to come out on top, and who knows but that the law tends to favor them? The law or man, it doesn't really matter which, when you get right down to it. But when I look at you, I know that I have to be willing to try. We'd have no system of justice at all if people like me didn't look at someone like you and say that we are willing to try. You're not going to have any luck at all unless we set this as right as we can. But I do not want to start something that you aren't willing to finish. If you are happy being bloodied in the name of something you call love, that's your choice. But if that's the case, let's call it a day."

The room was bright and hot. The electric fan whirred air around my knees but my legs were sticky under my dress. I could hear the clerk in the front room, banging something out on a typewriter. I thought of Bertha waiting for me. I thought of the horse outside. The long way home. Then the tide rushed in or maybe it was the beating of my own blood. "I want to," I said. My voice caught. "I do. You have to believe me."

But Jared did not seem to feel the weight of this moment or of the things that I felt. He just pushed himself up from his chair and said that since that was the case, he would be glad to proceed. Then he reached over the desk and shook my hand, as if all of this was business as usual. He opened the door for me. Out in the room where the clerk worked, Bertha stood up. But Jared waited in the doorway with the door held open in his hand. "Understand," he said to me. "This is going to take some sacrifice on your part. You aren't going to make any friends. Waukesha can be a hard place. It didn't get carved out of the wilderness on tea doilies and good manners. It promised a good life to people from all over, but a promise isn't the same as a reality. There are dozens of ways life can be hard here. I think you know that." He folded his arms in front of him. "It's the way of the world," he said. "Your own particular piece of ground isn't so good. You've come up a little bit short. But let's see what we can do."

Bertha stood the horse in a set of cross ties and wiped him down and put him back in his stall. She fed him while I cleaned the bit and hung the harness on a hook. We got home just before dinner but I wasn't hungry. I climbed the stairs to my room and lay down on my bed in the fading light. When I slept, I saw nothing. No one came to me and I did not travel and no ship rose below my feet and no wraiths appeared in the trees. If August came that night, I did not hear him.

In the morning, I woke and let nausea roll over me, a gut-wrenching feeling of sickness. I swallowed and swallowed again. My skin warm and then clammy and then some kind of fever washed over me and abated. My hair wet against my scalp. But nothing came up. After a time, the nausea washed away. I could feel the pillows beneath me again. The cool air in the room. I unstuck myself from my nightgown and licked my lips. Then I stared at the ceiling and began to count backward. My own little incantation. My love spell. My chant to keep me safe. It ended when I sat bolt upright and clutched myself around the waist. "August," I said. But of course he could not hear.

I knew it the way you know the sound of your own name. There could be no truth other than this. I was pregnant. That was why nausea followed me unbidden. The nausea meant a baby, and if I did not recognize it before this it was because it had never occurred to me that I could have a baby. Babies were for other girls: The girls who jumped down wells. The girls who had money and rooms painted yellow, waiting. The girls like my mother who had children already. Under the best of circumstances, babies were not for me. And now? Even worse.

The house was quiet. I looked down at my lap but all I saw was my own shape under the nightgown. I told myself that I would have to think about this later. I dressed and came downstairs and took my coffee cup out onto the back steps. I looked at the lawn. I listened for the sound of hammers from the construction site at the foot of the yard, but the morning was still. Blue shadows lay across the damp grass and the wind lifted my skirt and I dropped my hand to hold it in place. "Little one," I said to myself, trying out the words in the way of someone speaking an unfamiliar language. Then I felt silly for saying these words out loud. I put my hand on my flat stomach and wondered at the sea within. Then I imagined the baby like a fairy in the grass flying on transparent wings, glistening silver like the dew. Maybe it would show me what to do. I was sure I had no idea how to be a mother.

I looked again at the darkness on the edge of the yard, where a bank of forsythia bushes bordered the grass and hid the alley from view. The branches moved in the wind and then something else moved and Edwin stepped out into the sunlight. He wore his old-fashioned clothes and his collar was still crooked. He crossed the grass and said my name. Then he said my name again.

"Edwin," I said. "What are you doing here?" What *was* he doing here? He turned up whenever something went wrong, like someone with a magnet in him that was drawn to my misfortunes. You will no doubt understand why this unnerved me. I imagined he would envision himself a knight in shining armor. The next thing I knew he would tell me to come live with him in his room under the church. After that he would howl if I told him to stay away. I took a step back.

"He hurt you," he said.

"Yes." I felt prickly and irritable but I did not blame Edwin for this. He was as hopeless as I was when it came to the world.

I walked with him back to the shadows under the trees. I held my cup out to him and asked him if he would like some of my coffee. He shook his head.

"You come with me," he said.

When I did not move, he said it again, only this time in a louder voice and more insistently, as if I was being particularly stupid and needed to be scolded.

I shook my head. "I cannot," I said.

He frowned and took my hand and pulled me under the trees. "You come with me," he ordered. He dragged me through the trees and out into the alley behind my house, where early morning sun brightened the wagon tracks. I looked over my shoulder at the bare windows to see if August could see me, if his face would rise in the slick glass. But the rooms were dark, the glass blank.

At the bottom of the alley, a cart stood hitched to a brown horse. Hattie jumped down and tied off the reins and came across the grass. My heart stopped.

"You had better hurry," she said.

19

Bertha and Edwin and Hattie took my house apart in less than an hour. Bertha was in her element. She ordered and packed and made decisions: the cups stacked inside the bowl, the skillet packed separately, the dishrags for packing. Hattie came along behind and followed orders. She wasn't wearing her braces and when I asked her where they were, she shrugged and said she just couldn't wear them anymore. And anyway her legs were straight and had always been straight and our father had not seemed to notice when she left the braces in her room. I thought of him and of the way Hattie must have nearly disappeared from his attention, like the phantom presence of a girl from a life he used to live.

She said he was still the same. Still went to the bar at night. Still came home in the morning. Still went to his meetings. But everything around him was different. Hattie took care of the neighbors' children so now she was able to come and go freely. She was surprised at the delight this raised in her and I knew what she meant, for I had felt the same thing, relishing my walk to work, breathing free air, feeling free. She said that Martha snuck out to see George every chance she got, which had turned out to be more and more often. And in the morning, when he returned from work, my father sat in his chair and drank his whiskey and read the newspaper and when he was done, he went to bed. She said he never even took his clothes off anymore, but just lay down fully dressed. His suit coats were ruined, twisted and wrinkled all the time.

All of this came to me as if news from a distant war. I sat on the edge of the bed and tried to see my father as he was now, a man trying to stay the same as his household turned inside out. Then Edwin and Bertha came for the mattress and I moved to the edge of the step outside, just far enough over to be out of their way, and watched Edwin finish loading the cart. The horse stamped and Edwin laid his hand on the horse's flank. The horse stilled. He climbed up and gathered the reins. Just before he got to the street, he turned and looked back at me and waved. I waved back. I thought I had never seen anything as peculiar as Edwin driving a cart and waving, as if he was just any boy.

Bertha came across the grass toward me but then snapped her fingers. She had forgotten something. "Be right there," she called, and climbed the steps to her porch and came back with a sack.

"I made you some lunch," she said.

I took the sack from her. It was heavy.

"And some dinner," she said. She laughed. Then she took my hand and squeezed it and gave me a small purse. She told me there was enough money for fare for the interurban and a little more to help me get started. "Hattie will go with you," she said. "She knows the way." She sat down next to me and put her arm around me and leaned her head against mine. She smelled of lemons, of something green, a faint hint of wild mint. I wanted to sink into her and never leave. But she propped me up and told me that I must not worry. Everything had been taken care of and she would see me when it was all over. "And I can't wait to meet your baby," she said. She smiled and stroked my hair back from my face.

We sat in front in seats right behind the driver. An old woman with a wooden leg sat across the aisle from us and behind her a younger woman with a child in her lap. Every so often, the women leaned their heads together.

We rode past the shanties at the edge of town and then the railroad yard, where bereft men in dirty white shirts and torn canvas trousers stood over a pit of smoldering coal. *There are your workers*, I thought. My father's heroes, passing their bottles around. Filthy and wild-looking men who stood with their legs spread wide, just as men will when they think they own the world. The oily smoke from their coal fire made a faint pall over the blue sky, and I breathed it in as we passed, the smell I had known my whole life.

After that, we rode below the limestone bluffs where I had climbed to the top of the world with August. I squinted and searched for our trail but saw nothing but dark trees and gray stone. We crossed the fields and then we passed over a flat plain, where farmland spread out and white birds rose from the green wheat. This bountiful land. The purple mountains' majesty. All of it America and all of it apart from me, save for the way the country extracted its toll, which came in the form of all of these girls, these dead women, used and discarded, like things with no purchase save as they served to advance the fortunes of men. I never imagined I would meet a boy like August, and as I rode the train away from Waukesha toward Milwaukee, I told myself that I would carry the thought of him like a bone I had found on the forest floor, a beloved bone with a sharpened point. If I lost my nerve, I could touch that point. I could remember the way blood tasted on my tongue. I could stab myself and force myself not to forget.

I listened to the clacking of the wheels on the tracks and felt hypnotized by the clatter. Someone had opened the window next to our seats and hot air poured in. My baby sister rested her head against my shoulder. I closed my eyes. I waited for all of it to pass away.

I followed Hattie from the corner to a red wooden door where she raised her fist and knocked. Next door, a tavern with grimy windows painted black. I could hear the scratchy sounds of a phonograph and I thought of its horn in the shape of an up-ended bell.

We waited until a bolt turned and the lock slid back and the door opened. My uncle Carl stood in the doorway. I had not seen him since the day we stood with the earth open and my mother's box below, when grave diggers loitered like vultures, their pickaxes dirty from someone else's funeral. Now I wanted to fall against him and hold on to his belt just the way I did when I was a little girl and he could pull me up with one hand. I could not imagine how Bertha had found him. I could not imagine that he would want me.

He wore a pair of charcoal gray twill trousers and a clean white shirt with the sleeves rolled up over his forearms. A white band of skin appeared over his collar as if his hair had been cut just minutes before.

"Come," he said. "It is up here," He held the door open. I let myself pass under his arm.

We climbed the stairs. Two dusty windows faced the street. Two battered ladder-back chairs stood in the middle of the room. Someone had bolted a white sink to one of the walls. A small stove was piped to another. The air dry and the ceiling slatted wood and beams, as if this had been an attic before it became the perfect place to hide me.

He put his hand on the small of my back and propelled me to one of the chairs. "Sit down," he said.

I turned. "Where is Hattie?"

"She will wait for Edwin," he said. "He will bring the cart." He dug into his pants pocket and pulled out a felt oval embroidered with orange and yellow flowers, a key tied to the oval with a piece of red twine. "This belonged to your grandmother," he said. "She gave it to Elise. Elise gave it to me. Now it is yours."

I turned the key in my fingers. I felt hollow as a bowl. My world had run out of me when August hit me and disappeared into a darkness that was as familiar as my own shadow. No flower in the world could fix that.

"Thank you," I said.

Carl gestured at the bare walls. "I keep this place for myself," he said. "I come here when I need a rest. Sometimes you just have to call it a day." He smiled at me. "Usually I have some things here. But when I heard that you were in need, I took them out. More room for you that way."

In my mother's story, the girl disappeared and no one found her again. She ran into the earth and sank below the mountain as if she had become a silver stream whose passage could only be known by the thready trail she left behind in the dirt. A small stream here, a tiny rivulet there. But water could also carve stone. It could carve wood. I had heard that it had carved great canyons out west, where the earth disappeared for a mile before you came to the thin river running through rock at the bottom.

Carl sat heavily in the chair next to mine. He picked up my hand and held it. "Marie," he said. "This is a very sad business. I am very sorry to see you this way."

I looked at his hand holding my hand in my lap. Water came to my eyes.

"Did you not see this coming?" he asked in a very quiet voice. The way you would speak to a scared child, a nervous horse, a lunatic. Down below, the rumbling of carts and then a car horn and then a shadow fell in a crooked rhombus across the wall.

"No," he said, after a moment. "I guess not."

Outside, a grinding hum rose and fell away and rose again. I wondered what it might be: a machine shop, a factory, an airplane. I had never seen an airplane but I had heard that they came to fairs sometimes and for a quarter the pilot would take you up for a ride. I tried to imagine myself in the air, lifted like something that has lost all of its earthly weight. But I was no longer sure I would be able to fly without taking a hard fall.

"He is a good man," I said softly, but I did not sound convincing, not even to myself.

"Who?"

"August."

"Ah," he said. "August. Such a good man that he beats his wife to a pulp."

A train whistle from far off but hurtling toward us as if no city stood in its way.

"Martha said it was my fault," I said. I dabbed at my eyes.

"Your sister does not see straight sometimes."

"He loves me."

He gave a bitter laugh. "I can see that," he said.

I looked at the sunlight on the window glass and listened to the city, which hummed below everything around us.

The silence of unspoken things settled around us. Finally I stood and walked to the window. Down below, Edwin and Hattie unloaded my belongings, the bed frame around whose rails I had curled my fingers when August came to me, the mattress where we had spent our nights, our days, our every waking moment, except when he had raised his hand.

Hattie lifted a sack of groceries from the wagon box. I could see the apples next to the tins.

"Do these open?" I asked. I touched the window latch.

"I think so, yes," Carl said. "Well, I guess we will have to see."

20

At six o'clock on the seventh day, I heard the door below open and close and then the sound of the bolt as it slid back into place. Carl's footsteps on the stairs. He knocked on my door and then came into the room and set a canvas sack on the table.

"You look better," he said. "Do you want to get up?"

I did. I felt better and I wanted him to see that I was grateful for everything that he had done for me. That he was still doing for me, day by day. My uncle, whom I had known all my life, could make me shy. He seemed to me to be a stranger but, of course, in a way he was. I had only seen him when my mother was there. When Martha was there. When my father was there, lecturing Carl on his prospects and his stolen shoes.

Carl set potatoes to boil on the stove. When these were done, he drained them in the sink and then set a skillet laid out with slices of bacon over the flame. "You must be feeling better," he said. "Your face looks better. And your ribs?"

"They still hurt," I said. My ribs ached, but the pain that felt as if someone meant to fillet me into strips was dulled now. I really only felt it when I took a deep breath.

"Still?" He glanced at me.

"Not as much."

"All right then," he said. "This rest is doing you good." He dumped the potatoes into a bowl and set the bowl on the table before me. "It is not much," he said.

"It's fine," I said.

"This will be ready in a minute," he said. He turned to the cookstove and flipped the bacon with a fork.

We ate in silence.

"Carl," I said finally. "Did he come back?"

"Who?"

"August," I said softly. I thought of the grass bending under his foot. The darkened rooms. Everything gone. Me gone. "Did he come back to our house?"

"Sure," Carl said. "Yes." He used the back of his fork to flatten his potatoes. "What else would he do? It is the end of his day. He does not expect anything. Of course he came back."

I waited. I thought of the way August had howled outside of Bertha's house, and I thought of the way his hand felt, traveling slowly and surely up the inside of my thigh, the smell of him when I burrowed my nose into his neck.

Carl put his fork down. "He was not a happy man, I can tell you that," he said. "Your father is also not a happy man." He picked up his fork and then set it down again. "He wants to know where you are. He wants to know what he will have to do to make you go back. He says you have made him break his word. He says you have made a liar out of him. He says you are to go back now. And I can tell you one thing for sure. He does not care at what cost. He feels that August has paid and you have run off for no good reason."

"My father," I said, and stopped.

"He has one way of looking at this, Marie," Carl replied. He stabbed the air with his fork and bits of potato fell on the table. "He will never look at it differently." I shrank away a little. I knew Carl was right about my father. He would only ever see things one way and that way was not my way. But Carl thought I disagreed with him.

"I can see that you do not believe me," he said, his fork still in the air between us. "But you can count on this. He is a man very set in his ways. He will always think exactly as he thinks right now. Do you want to argue with him? I think not." He stood. "I will make us some coffee. That will perk you up."

When we were finished, I offered to do the dishes but he held his hand up. "You are resting," he said. "That is your only job." He went to the sink and looked at me over his shoulder. "I brought a surprise for you." He reached into his canvas bag and pulled out a bundle wrapped in waxed paper. Inside the bundle there were two slices of cake. "My boss's wife," he said. "She heard what happened."

"You told her?"

He shook his head. "Not me," he said. "But she knew."

I thought of all the women whispering around Waukesha, heads bent together, talking about me. I imagined that Inge and Ella and Johanna had discussed and debated the merits of my choices for days. If they thought I was bad before, they must think I was even worse now. What woman would run away from her husband? I could already hear the story that Inge would tell the new girl about me.

Carl cleared the plates and forks and wiped the table. He brought two clean plates and two clean forks and set the slices of cake in their nest of waxed paper in the middle of the table. He poured the coffee. I looked at the cake, at its soft white icing.

"Here," he said. "Come on now. Have some cake. It will sweeten that temper of yours."

I smiled then and sat back and let him deliver a slice of cake to my plate.

"See?" he said. "It is working already."

I watched him eat, the crumbs that caught in his mustache, the way he licked icing off his thumb. When we were through, we sat in silence. The lamp by the bed buzzed briefly and went quiet. Outside, night fell. A faint breeze came in through the open window. I could hear the city in its relentless murmurings and whispers, the sound of the new age all around us, the machinery and the engines of progress and the clocks ticking us toward the future even as businesses and banks failed and tramps cast out from the mines and mills and lumber camps roamed the woods. I knew how I had come to this place but I had no idea what I was doing here. I only knew that there was no going back.

Carl patted his breast pocket, searching for his tobacco pouch, his expression mild and thoughtful.

"Why are you helping me?" I said abruptly, and as soon as I said the words, I knew I had been trying to find the courage to ask ever since the day I moved in.

He inclined toward me very gently and then he reached over and laid his palm on my hand. "Because we are family," he said. "Because your mother was my sister. Because not everyone in this world is bad. Although I do not see how you could know that."

I thought of my father, who was out there somewhere, beyond the coal smoke and the long train tracks, the rocketing cars of the interurban and the dark woods. I began to weep.

"No," Carl said. "Now look. You are safe here. Why do you cry?"

I shook my head.

"You can tell me," he said. But I could not. All I could do was listen to the sound of heavy wheels down in the street. The strike of a church tower's clock, somewhere out of view.

Carl wrapped the last of the cake. A long time passed. Finally he asked me again. He spoke softly, and kept his face turned away from me. I breathed in and then out and then in again. My father's house stood in another town and yet it was still with me. August did not know where I was and yet he was here by my side, his tender face, his crushing fist.

I put my face in my hands and sobbed. "I am sorry," I cried. "I am sorry. I am sorry."

"For what?" he said.

"It is all my fault," I sobbed. I jammed the heels of my hands into my eyes. The world an explosion of color.

"Why is that?" said Carl.

I could not look at him.

"You do not think the fault belongs elsewhere?" he said.

I gulped air but all of my breath disappeared. "I am bad," I sobbed. Then I lay my cheek on the table and cried harder.

He stood and came to me and knelt down and wrapped his arms around me. I felt wobbly and unstrung, as if I had said aloud the worst truth in the world and now found myself on ground so unknown and unsteady that it could at any moment upend and turn me out and flatten me.

"You are not bad," he murmured. "Bad things have happened. The stories they tell about you are bad. But stories are only stories. Things are only things. None of that makes you bad."

I cried for a long time and he held me. The smell of coal smoke coming through the window. Behind that, the smell of the lake, watery and wild. The night outside swimming with stars, if only I cared to see.

When I was finally empty, I sat up. He stood and reached into his pocket for a handkerchief and gave it to me. He told me that it would be better now and I should wipe my face.

"It is so easy for us to forget that you are still a child," he said. I opened my mouth and he held up one hand. "I know," he said. "I know. You are a married woman. You have been out to work. But you are still very young and I think you have found the world to be a different place than you imagined. As we all do. And this always comes as a shock to us but the shock is worst when we are young." He tapped his fingers against the tabletop. "I thought your beginnings might have given you greater protection from this," he said. "I thought you might already have seen enough so that things would be clear. But that is not the case. Perhaps those beginnings in fact made it possible for all of this to happen. Perhaps the things you saw made you blind." He studied me gravely. "You are healing. You are lucky. You are alive. Your face may not show any scars." He walked over to the window and looked out at the street. "It is a pretty night," he said. "You can see the lake from here. There is a steamboat out on the water."

I did not rise. I sat at the table with my sticky face in my hands.

"Do you know why I came to this country?" he said, turning back to me.

"Because my mother and father were here." My voice broken and bare.

"Well," he said. "Yes. Of course. That is what you would know. You know where we come from and you know what things were like there," he said. He looked at me. "No? You do not?"

"My mother told us stories about Rügen," I said.

"What kind of stories?"

"About bells in the ocean and a golden seagull," I said. "Dwarves." I broke off.

He smiled. "Elise loved those stories. She had a great feeling of being connected to a long-ago world. Some people get over the hard times in their lives by looking ahead. Your mother was not one of them. She looked behind her to a place she had never herself stood. A time of giants and magicians and talking animals and men roaming the countryside under the spell of a curse. Which could always be broken." He came back to sit at the table.

"She was not wrong," he said. "For a very long time, the land had been a land of haves and have-nots. There were very rich men who owned castles and then there was everyone else. They worked for the rich men in the fields and on the roads. No better than peasants. Not even as good as peasants, if you want to get right down to it. Nearly everyone lived in mud huts with thatched roofs. The water came in and the mud cracked and the floors were dirt or split wood and they cracked, too. You would have children and the children would sicken and die. Your mother lost her first child just that way. A boy. I remember him. He had a narrow face and sunken eyes and he never looked right. His ears were low on the sides of his head. And then they put him in the ground three months later. She was afraid after that, but then Martha was born and Martha was different and she lived. Just like that. One is here and one is not. Elise said there was no explanation, but in fact the explanation was that no one had enough food and the work was hard.

"Everywhere you went was the mark of the rich men. They lived to keep everyone else down. This is why socialism is so popular in our towns here. The people remember what it means to live in a world where there are those with everything and those with nothing. They ask very reasonable questions, if you ask me. Why is there not enough to go around? Why can't we share? Why is it that the rich get richer and the poor get poorer? But they do not understand that things work differently here. Here a man stands on his own two feet and whatever he has is what he has gotten for himself. So no matter what they think, socialism will never catch on in America. If you are ground down here, it is because you refuse to rise. Of course there are things that conspire against you, and some people have more advantages than others. I do not mean to exclude these things from the picture. But in the end, you do not have centuries of ownership by an aristocracy that believes you are more like a beast in the mud than a man, that believes you have no purpose other than to make the prince rich. Here you are your own man." He patted his pockets and then stood up and went to a hook by the door, where he had hung his coat. He went through the pockets until he found a tan cowhide pouch and his pipe and his matches. He stood by the window and tamped tobacco into the bowl of the pipe and then lit the pipe and drew a few breaths. Blue smoke wavered in a spiral around his head.

"The same does not hold true for women," he said. He turned to face me. "That is unfortunate but true. A woman can never rise. She will always serve two masters. And there is nothing she can do about that. She can join the socialist party and I see them at the meetings but she cannot vote and she cannot hold her own belongings as her own." He pulled smoke between his teeth and then exhaled.

"My mother and father—your grandmother and grandfather—had a house just outside of Garz," he said. "This was near the southeastern coast of the island. It was an old market town. Our father was a farmer. We were luckier than most because we had a long-term lease on the land. We grew fruit. Long lines of apple trees in the orchards. Grapes growing on wooden frames that we built ourselves. This island is in the north so this fruit had to be tough. Like us," he said, and smiled. He pulled deeply on his pipe and exhaled. "The house was a little bit luxurious because it had two rooms and it had a lean-to in the back for cooking. My mother kept chickens. The foxes got into them but she always had chickens. Your mother slept on a pallet at one end of the main living room and I slept on a pallet on the other end. In between, all the brothers and sisters. Our parents kept the other room for themselves and they kept some animals in there from time to time, too. Rabbits. Other things they were raising to sell. Once a small pig but he did not stay small long.

"This life was very hard. The apples were hard and green and sour. The grapes failed. The animals were filthy. My mother was very superstitious and kept a place in the main room where she prayed all of the time to some old god who came before Christ and was just as useful to her as I imagine Christ is to those who believe he will make their lives better."

He set his pipe down on the table and leaned it against his saucer. "And there were lots of children of course. This is the way, is it not? They say we have them to work the farms. They say we have them because we do not know better. They say we have them because we are no better than animals. Well. I cannot tell you about any of those things. You are free to make up your own mind. But there were lots of children. And some lived and some did not. I do remember that my father took a stick to my mother and because of that, the last baby came too early. My father walked the hill line with that burlap bundle under his arm and a spade over his shoulder. He buried the bundle in the orchard. He told me once that he would have thrown it down the well but he was afraid it would contaminate the water.

"My mother died after that one. It took some time, a few days, maybe a week, but she died. And we were sad, but I think we all knew that women die because they cannot fight being women. That is one thing they are helpless to stand against.

"At just that moment, Elise decided to marry. Herman had been coming around and she had put him off and put him off, but when our mother died, she said yes. She was young. Sixteen. Seventeen. Not old. But old enough to know that she might be better off elsewhere. And I saw the way she changed. She became very serious. She took to walking in the fields. She would stand at the top of the orchard and look back at our house and see our brothers and sisters in the dooryard and the smoke standing straight like a stick out of the chimney. Perhaps she waited to be kidnapped by dwarves. Perhaps she meant to disappear. She never spoke of these things so I do not know. But I think it is fair to say that once she decided, there was no going back. Herman was tall and handsome and he teased her and made her laugh and our father approved of their courtship. So one day Herman came for her and carried flowers and she wore a dark red dress and they walked down into the village and met my father in front of the church and they got married just like that. The neighbors came. They ate cake. Elise had her picture made. And my father paid Herman a dowry in cash, which meant that they could get a start. It was not much of a dowry but it was something.

"No one thing made them decide to come here. The first baby died. Martha was born. I think they just took the temperature of the place. The winds were blowing. The Germans were not so easy on the Pomeranians. The people of Rügen felt that they had stood apart for many centuries but now they had to knuckle under. And then things had not been happy for the Lutherans for fifty years or more. For many years, whole parishes would pack up and come to start towns in Wisconsin. You would hear the name of the place in the streets and in the taverns. Wisconsin. Wisconsin. No one had any idea what the word meant. But there was the word, wherever we went, and it began to be something real, and of course it told a story in its very utterance. And many people had already gone and that made it seem like anyone could leave. That you could survive leaving.

"One night Herman met a man who had been to Milwaukee and that man said that everyone spoke German in Milwaukee and everyone was free and all of us would be equal. There was plenty of work and a man could get a house and land without any problem. Money flowed like water in Milwaukee. Not like Rügen, where the only constant was the lack of everything. Poverty and dispossession level the world that way. Herman thought about a farm. That is what I remember. He wanted a dairy farm of his own. That would not be possible on Rügen, I can tell you. So it was all decided. They packed their things. They sold their furniture. Elise took our mother's watch fob with her and her wedding picture. A man is always what he carries but we usually think the opposite. This makes us feel powerful in the face of our own helplessness.

"A year later I came, too. My father had died and I felt his death like a door being unlocked. I decided it was time to move from there and I felt that the way someone young always feels that, which is to say, I did not know what a terrible thing it is for a man to leave his own country. A country is something that you do not leave behind. But I came on a ship with a big, promising name, the *California*, and I watched the ocean as we went. Never had anything seemed so far as land. When I got to New York, I walked up and down the city streets as if I was in a dream. I saw that people here were very wealthy. Buildings like cliffs everywhere around me and women wrapped in furs. After a few days, I took my sack and my case and went to Grand Central Station. I stood in the middle of the marble lobby as if I were in a church, and all the people passed me on the way to the platforms and they were like shadows running away from me, neither here in the present or part of my past. I went to a window and bought a ticket and walked down a set of stairs and stood next to the tracks until it was time to get on a train bound for Milwaukee. When I looked out the windows, I saw farms that were better than the farms on Rügen. And these were the common farms. These were the farms that any man might own. And I saw timber and open land and I had some ideas.

"When I got here, I took a job as a farmhand. The job came with a place to live and three meals a day. These are not things to be overlooked, as you know. And I liked getting up early in the morning and standing in the yard next to the barn and listening. First you hear the crickets and then they get louder just before the sun rises and then you hear the cows, whose first sounds of the day are grunts and moans, not the sounds you think they will make. And you stand there in the last part of the night and the air is fresh and sweet and none of this belongs to you so you can really just enjoy it. Really just take in all the newness around you.

"Some people might say we were raised like animals. My father was a very hard man. But in the end, that is your father, too, and you did not live in a house with a pig. And your husband. Very hard, as you were quick to find out. For my part, I thought we might have left this sort of thing behind. I did not think I would see Elise the way I saw her on the day we buried her. I did not think I would see in Herman something I had seen in my father. I do not know what I imagined. That we would get off of a ship and really believe that we were all equal? We say that we do. Do not try to tell any man in this country that he may not do as he pleases. Do not try to take that away. But a man believes in his own personal freedom and he believes in his own desires and in his own rage. He says that we should all be free. But then he goes home and bloodies his wife. If you mention it at all, he will only say that he is outraged by your complaint and unquestionably not to blame. That he has to live hard to put bread on the table and this is what happens when men are held down. He will look at you with the face of an angry child when he says this, as if he has no ability to decide his own actions for himself. He wants it both ways and we usually agree with him. Poor man, we say. He is not to blame. In my opinion he cannot have it both ways. But that is just my opinion. It is not a popular one."

He stopped. We sat in a silence for a long time.

"What happened to my mother?" I said at last.

He looked at me and then looked at the pipe in his hands. He set the pipe on the table. "What does it matter?" he said.

"It matters to me." I felt my words as small things taken by an empty sky.

He sighed. "What if I told you that I do not know?"

"I would say I do not believe you."

"But belief has nothing to do with it. This is bigger than belief. That is why it is so hard to see."

"That means you know." I reached for his arm.

He picked up his pipe and pushed his thumb into the bowl and patted his shirt pocket and then picked up his matches from the tabletop. "Well," he said. "If I were to answer that, it would suggest some certainty that I do not think I have."

"Martha said it was a terrible accident."

"It could have been."

"But was it?"

I knew I sounded like a child demanding a piece of the adult world, as if I was entitled. But I thought that after everything that had happened, I had earned this one thing, this fact that stood beyond me, that my uncle Carl knew and must tell me.

He struck a match and held the flame to his pipe and again drew deeply. The window in the building across the street went dark. I rested my head against my hand and watched smoke coil around the lamp.

"So much damage has been done and yet so little is said," he said then. "Even at the funeral, he said nothing." He fiddled with the box of matches and then put the box in his breast pocket. "No one can know for sure," he said. "Herman would have to say and Herman will never say. Elise never spoke to me of these things and I was not welcome in your father's house." He paused.

"I saw her one day on the street and she wore a scarf tied around her hair the way the women did in Rügen," he said. "It was a beautiful warm day. Just after a rain. When I got close, I saw the marks. Those you cannot hide. So I think I knew then. But we stood in the street and talked about you and Hattie and Martha. She thought that Martha would marry that boy and she said she was glad of it because George was so soft. She said he was a good boy and quiet and peaceful. I knew that what she meant was that he was not hard like Herman. Or the rest of them." He lifted his pipe and looked into the bowl and set it down again and looked at me. "Do you understand what I am telling you?"

I nodded. There was nothing new in the thing he described. My mother had fallen before my father and he had chased her into the yard. He had held her down and used the buckle end of a belt. He had taken up a piece of firewood from the bucket by the stove and used it on her head. Anything in our house could be used against her. And sometimes in the morning Martha would have a welt on her face. And sometimes I would stand before him in the front room with my throat closed, waiting for my turn. All he ever said was that he had to do this because he loved me.

Carl tapped the bowl of his pipe against his palm and fine ash fell to the floor. He looked at his palm and clapped his hands together and looked at his palm again. "It was the world," he said. "Here. There. All the same. It was the world that killed her."

I sobbed once and brought my hand to my face and held it palm flat over my mouth, as if sorrow was a thing that once come could never be contained.

He considered me. "It is a great deal to take in, and you have had a number of shocks already these days," he said. "But that does not mean I cannot help you. In fact, I think it makes me more inclined. I do not want to see you end up like my mother or my sister." He turned his pipe in his hands and then unlaced his tobacco pouch and tucked the pipe inside. He sat at the table and fastened the laces, and the leather made a sound as he drew it through the eyelets.

We sat in the trailing light. Then he slapped his hand against the tabletop. "We like to talk, right?" he said. He stood up. "But what can you do? Still there is the world."

I stood and walked to the wall switch and pressed the button. The room went dark and the window glass shimmered silver. I crossed to the window and Carl came over and stood next to me. I felt his presence. His kindness like a river. But when he stood next to me, it was as if he stood on the shore of a far distant land. And then I knew that if I felt marked it was not just because the people we passed on the street had stared at me, my swollen head as bulbous as a seedpod on a stem. It was not just because August had so changed me. I wrapped my arms around my waist and my uncle put his arm around me and I leaned against him. Over the horizon the moon rose through pale clouds and the wind moved dark clouds over the brilliant light and we stood together and looked far off into the invisible distance.

21

There weeks later the weather turned cool. I rose and washed my face and hands. I pinned my hair. I opened the wardrobe and shook out my green dress. I moved carefully, like someone who is afraid she is about to fall into pieces. I pictured myself on the floor in bits and parts, where the breakage would be obvious to anyone who came along. Elbow over here. Vertebrae over there. My head split in two.

Bertha met me at the corner. She paced beneath the street lamp and walked toward me as soon as she saw me. I touched my face nervously and she smiled. "You look fine," she said. I knew she wanted to comfort me but I wanted to hold my arms out and show her how all my bones had exploded, as if I were a girl made of shattered glass.

Jared Thompson stood when I came into the room. He told me that this was the time for me to tell my side of things, officially and for the record. He asked me if I was ready. He said that he would take down everything I said and then he would write the whole thing up and take it before the judge. He said that August would have a chance to answer and we would not be able to do anything until we had that answer. He explained that I must be truthful in everything I said. This was my statement and I would be under oath.

This last part made me squirm. I no longer believed in God and I had also begun to realize that I had never believed in God, at least not a god who set things up so that I would suffer at the hands of men. So I looked Jared Thompson in the eye and said that I would tell the truth, for the truth was all I had, but I could not swear to God to tell the truth because as far as I could tell, God had never done much of anything for me. Jared gave me a funny look and told me that I must swear nevertheless. And I gave up. If this was what it took, I would have to go along. All of these rules belonged to the world that did not belong to me and this particular rule was no different than any of the others. The skinny clerk with the green baize eyeshade came through the door and took a Bible from the drawer. He held it before him like an offering on a plate. "Raise your right hand," he said.

Jared Thompson asked me how long I had been a resident of Waukesha and how long a resident of Wisconsin. He asked me when August and I had married. He asked me for the exact date. He asked me to describe the amount of money that August had given me each week and he asked me to name the last time I had been given that amount. He asked if I had been given any other amounts. He asked if I had received money from other sources. He explained that he needed to know if I had a job or if others gave me money to help with my support. I told him that I had been very hungry so I had gotten a loan from Martha but it was really some of the money I had earned at the laundry and the same money that my father had taken from me and kept from me so that I was for all practical purposes destitute in his house. Jared Thompson held his hand up and said, "One thing at a time, Mrs. Bethke." He wrote furiously on his pad.

He wrote for a long time and then read what he had written. He struck a line through a sentence in the middle of the page and added a note in the margin. Then he looked up at me and asked me to describe how August had treated me. I told him he knew that. He shook his head and explained again that I needed to tell him this now so that he could write it down in a way that was particular to the law. I explained that ever since our marriage August had treated me in a very hard way. That he had belittled me. That he had struck me again and again. That he had spent all of our money on drink and had come home drunk or had not come home at all. That he had threatened me with his fist and with his razor and with his gun. That he had struck me so violently about the head and face that I had fallen. That he had kicked me until my ribs were broken. That the men who lived near us had to come and pull him off of me or he would have killed me without fail. That the injuries to my face were so severe that my jaw did not work and I could not chew any food. That my neighbor had taken me in to her home and protected me and nursed me until I was well enough to walk again. That August had come at night and stood on the lawn and screamed things at the front of the house. That one day while he was at work my friends had taken the things from our house, a bedstead, some bedding, the kitchen knives, the cups and plates, a washstand, everything they could carry, and placed these things in a wagon and had taken me to live in a room my uncle Carl kept in the city of Milwaukee. That they had done this so that August would not be able to find me. That they had done this because August had told the neighbors he would kill me. That my injuries were terrible. That I was in fear for my life. That I was sure my life was over, and if not my actual life then everything that had passed for my life before this and would never pass for my life again.

I stopped. This was the moment I had feared, and I waited

for Jared Thompson to tell me that he did not believe me or that it was my fault or that this was all normal and to be expected. That I had brought all of this on myself. I waited for all the things I had been told until now to come up and provide the cause for Jared Thompson to put me out of his office, me and my fissured, fragile self, broken into a million homeless shards.

But he said nothing. He wrote and turned the page and filled another page and then wrote another page. I looked out the window and waited. I could hear his pen on the paper, a scratching like small birds in a yard. I could hear him breathing. I could hear the rolling wheels of carts in the street. I wondered how the operations of court could ever work on my behalf. It did not seem that either law or justice would find me a fit contender. Yet here I was.

When I could not stand it any longer, I said that I could have no life if I remained bound to August Bethke. No man should be able to do what he had done. I wanted my freedom and I could never go back, because August would kill me. And then I said that some people might think that it was all right for August to kill me, but they would not want August to kill our unborn child and that would be the result if August ever got ahold of me.

At this, Jared Thompson stopped writing and lay his pen down. "What do you mean?" he said. When I did not reply, he asked again and then told me that I must tell him what I meant and that I must explain how I knew this. He knew that this was a very private thing for a woman. He would respect my privacy. He would ask no questions for which he did not need answers but that this would be important, if true, and it was not something to hide.

I looked hard at the peeling pine boards of the floor. Surely they had come from up north. Surely they had come from the deep woods. Perhaps they had even had my brother's hands on them. Willie who had disappeared, gone like he had never existed. That would not be me. Jared Thompson waited and dust turned in the air and then without lifting my gaze from the floor, I said in a very soft voice that I had stopped bleeding and this had been for several months now and when the baby came, I would have to keep it away from August. I felt heat rise to my hairline. There can be nothing more embarrassing than to think that someone has imagined you doing things with your husband in bed. I waited for the questions that I thought must come. How did he touch you, Mrs. Bethke? What exactly did you feel? And I thought that if I had to answer these, I would reveal how much I had wanted August to touch me and how wrong I was to ask for a divorce. How much I was at fault. How little August could be blamed.

But all Jared Thompson did was ask if I was sure. When I said that I was, he turned the page over and wrote something on the back. Then he asked me to tell him again about the night that August tried to kill me. He asked me if there were men who had seen this. He asked me their names and he asked me if I remembered their addresses. He asked me to be patient with him because the law required that he collect this information and make certain that all of it was right. Finally he said that he understood that I was an unhappy woman and that my unhappiness had led to my rejecting God but that we would have to set that aside for now. What he needed now was for me to swear again when the documents were all typed up. I would need to swear that I had read the complaint and that the contents were true to my own knowledge except for any matters stated as a consequence of information and belief, and as to those, I would need to swear that I believed all of them to be true. He asked me if I understood. I nodded and he sent me outside to wait in the room with the clerk. He told me that it was all right to wait and not to worry too much about the clerk, whose bark, he said, was worse than his bite.

I could not deny that Jared Thompson gave me hope. He wrote so meticulously and he spoke so kindly to me that I believed he wanted to help me. I knew that women did not go to court, but I thought Jared Thompson could speak for me and make sure things turned out right. This was America, after all, and no one could be possessed by someone else. The country had fought an entire war over this proposition and the question had been laid to rest. But I also knew that the things that were said about America were often not true where women were concerned.

I stood on the sidewalk in front of James Pulliam's place. Dark shade, dark grass, dark windows. The sun would be down soon. Around me the sounds of fall, unseen wagons moving harvest to market on the nearby roads, the racket of geese as they scissored in great waves overhead. There was very little wind, but still nuts and leaves and small dead branches fell onto the grass. Far up in the blue sky a single white cloud turned on a deep spiral of air.

When I got to the porch, no one answered my knock. I stepped back and looked up at the windows, where the shades were drawn and nothing moved. I wanted to say thank you but Edwin did not appear.

In the middle of October, I returned to Jared Thompson's office, where he gave me August's response. This is how the law works. You make your complaint and the person against whom you have laid your claim has an opportunity to tell his side. August had admitted we were married and admitted to being twenty-one years old and admitted that if there were to be a minor child of our union that he was the father of that child.

As to every other allegation, matter, or thing described in my statement, August denied each and every one. He said that he had always provided for my comfort and well-being. That he had only treated me with kindness and forbearance. That he had turned over all of his wages to me save for those he needed for his own expenses. That he had even provided for my family by giving my sister Hattie Reehs a place to live. He said that I had become angry when he told Hattie that she must pay for her board or else leave our home and that I had threatened to leave him if Hattie Reehs were compelled to leave the house. He said that I had without warning or notice removed all the household furniture and fixtures and utensils, all of which he said was worth five hundred dollars and had been given to us at our marriage by his generous relatives. He said that I had gone to live with a married sister residing at 746 Clarence Street in the city of Milwaukee and had resided there ever since. He said that he had come to me every night with the sole purpose of persuading me to come back and live with him at our home but that I had refused to do so until Hattie Reehs was permitted to come back and board with us. He said that he had steadfastly refused to allow this without money for board. He said it was my own fault that I had not come home. He said that he was ready and willing to provide for me and our child and eager to do so. He was a carpenter able to earn the sum of two dollars and sixty cents a day but that he had for some time been in ill health and so had lost wages because of an inability to work steadily. He said that he had no money, property, or income whatsoever except such as he was able to earn when he worked. He prayed that my complaint would be dismissed.

Jared watched me as I read. When I was through, I looked up at him. His gaze was steady and neutral.

"Do you want to tell me where you live?" he said.

I had read August's words as if they were claims made by a stranger. He told his story so earnestly that it sounded like it was true. He seemed reasonable and calm. He was only worried about an extra mouth to feed. He was only concerned about the welfare of the household. About my welfare. The welfare of our child. He had done everything he could.

I realized this was not the first time August had told a tall tale. If I had been paying attention, I would have known that I had heard it all before, and would just keep hearing it, again and again. I wanted to punch the wall. "I live in a room kept by my uncle," I said, my tone defiant, as if I dared Jared Thompson to take August's side.

"The address?"

"I do not know. I just know where it is."

"No number? No street sign?"

I shook my head. No one told me when I started that August would be able to tell lies about me. I thought he would come to court and tell the truth and I would tell the truth and it would be as simple as that.

"And your married sister? Where does she live?"

"I do not have a married sister," I snapped. "I have two sisters who live with my father. And I live in my uncle's room."

"If I asked you to, would you be able to take me there?"

I nodded.

"And your sister? Hattie Reese?" He said her last name the way an American would, hard and long, as if in the speaking he had spelled it differently and changed her. "Where does she reside?"

"With my father."

"Has she ever resided with you and your husband?"

"No."

"Mrs. Bethke."

"No," I said. "Never."

"So these are just lies?"

"Yes," I said firmly. "All lies."

22

It rained all night the night before the trial. Carl came at six and we sat at the table and ate. He told me that he had been back in Waukesha on an errand for his employer. He had seen Edwin in the woods walking quickly away from the streets. He had called to him but Edwin had not turned and had not looked back. He had moved on and disappeared into the trees. I nodded and said nothing. Carl set out an apple pie that he bought at the bakery because this was a special occasion. He smiled when he cut into the pie and said that some parts of this country were very sweet. He slid a plate across the table to me. "If not for you, then for the baby," he said, and nodded at my round lap. I had not said anything to him but it was easy to see. When he left, I lay down and watched the light of the fire fade behind the door of the stove and the rain spill down the sides of the building across the street.

In the morning I saw yellow leaves flat like hands against the windowpanes. Downstairs, the street was cold and gray. I rode the interurban back to Waukesha across gloomy fields, the trees in the distance a dark blur, the river when we came upon it a dark slash, the bluffs dark shapes against the dark gray sky.

So this is what comes of love, I thought, and felt that everything I had known could be held in a cup marked with that word and the cup itself was something horrible to behold. I saw August as soon as I started up the stairs to the courthouse. I wanted to be strong but my breath caught and my heart leapt. He was still August, after all, hatless, with the wind blowing his hair into his eyes. When he saw me, he stepped toward me. Our eyes met. I started to raise my hand. I do not know what I thought. That we would touch? My arm seemed to have a life of its own and it seemed something outside of me was driving me toward him.

But before he could speak, a man took August by the elbow and headed him toward the door. August pulled away and turned back toward me. He took a match from the box and struck it and then tossed the match in my direction, the flame a brief blue butterfly that vanished in the morning air. I stepped back. He laughed.

We all stood when the judge entered the courtroom. Once I saw August say something to the man next to him. Once I saw him turn and look at me. Jared touched my arm and leaned close to me. He told me to look away. He told me that August would try any number of tricks to unnerve me. I turned damp-eyed to the backs of the heads of the men seated with their hats on their knees in the row in front of us.

I was the only woman in the courtroom. Carl and Bertha had wanted to come, and Bertha had sent word that Hattie had wanted to come, but I said that a courtroom was no place for a child. I told Carl and Bertha that I had to do this by myself. But when I looked at the back of August's head, or thought of the match he sent sailing at me through the air, I wished I could take it back.

We heard cases of disorderly conduct and cases of petty theft and a case involving a land dispute. This last took a great deal of time because men will fight hard over the ground they think they own. When they finally said it was our turn, I stood and followed Jared Thompson to the table behind a wooden balustrade that stood between the courtroom and the judge's bench. He pulled a chair out and held it for me. He faced the judge and explained why we were there. Then the attorney for August stood up and explained why they were there. Each story entirely different and August's story only a set of pieces strung together and in none of those pieces did I find anything true.

When I took the stand the men who had been coughing and clearing their throats and shifting in their seats and whispering among themselves went still. I stood up and came across the room in front of the judge and felt the quiet of the courtroom rise behind me, as if I had slid underwater. Then the rosy-cheeked bailiff brought the Bible to me and I hesitated and my cheeks went hot. But I remembered what Jared Thompson had instructed me to do and put my palm flat on the book and swore whatever it was the bailiff wanted me to swear. I took a step up and sat in the wooden chair and forced myself to ignore the men gathered on the benches like vultures. I looked for Jared, who walked up to me and asked me to tell him my name and where I lived and how long I had lived there and then as best as I could recollect, and no more than that, what had happened on the night August tried to kill me.

It took me about twenty minutes to explain everything. I did not look at August. Jared asked me questions about the day August and I got married and what the marriage had been like and had there been any reason before I married to suspect that August Bethke would attack me? Had he struck me during courtship? Had he spoken to me indecently? Had he been known to brawl? He read Bertha's affidavit aloud and asked if the description she provided regarding the severity of my injuries was true. He asked the judge if he could enter that document into evidence. The judge said, "Duly noted."

I had a hard time speaking. The questions were familiar but my answers felt confused. I thought I could not form any words at all, and then it seemed that my own language had run away from me. And when that happened, I felt that I had forgotten the things that were true about my life or else could not lay claim to them. But I had a job to do and I meant to do it. And Jared helped. He nodded after each of my answers. I started to look for that nod. If it did not come, I tried to say more. If it came sooner than I expected, I stopped.

Before I left the stand, Jared Thompson asked me about the other times that August Bethke had struck me. I recounted them slowly. He asked me to describe the demeaning way that August Bethke had spoken to me. Tears came to my eyes. Jared repeated the question. In the long silence that followed I could hear the mixed sounds of the street outside, where men went about their days unfettered. Jared walked up to the witness chair.

"Mrs. Bethke," he said.

How could I say these things out loud in a place where I was not wanted? In a world where no one believed me? It seemed the only way that August could defend himself was to attack me, to say things that were not true, to disregard the facts until all that was left was a tale he thought worth telling. In his story, I was the guilty one.

The courtroom was still. I took a deep breath. And then I said that August had called me a bitch. And then I said that he had called me a whore. And then Jared said, "Is that all?" And I looked up at him and my face burned but I found a way to say out loud that August had called me a cunt. The word rolled out over the stillness of the courtroom and Jared did not ask anything else. He waited and I waited and the word hung in the air and even the men in the seats before me kept quiet. And then I realized that underneath everything else he said, *cunt* was August's word for me.

After that Jared asked me about the money I had been given by August Bethke to cover my keep and provide for my creature comforts. He asked me to describe the exact amount of food that I'd had available to eat. When I said that I did not have any food at all, he asked me how I had managed not to starve. And so I explained that I had been forced to go home to my sister and beg her for whatever money she could spare.

When I was done, I glanced at August. He sat with his elbows on the table and his head in his hands as if he were reading a newspaper spread out on the table before him. His attorney tapped him on the elbow, and August dropped his hands into his lap and sat up. He crossed one leg over the other and then crossed his leg back.

When August's attorney rose and came to me, he smiled. He was shaped like a violin, with a pinched waist and pants that sagged at the crotch and a high voice that would have been silly had he not been so serious. He said his name was Walter Meyer and he was sorry for the court proceedings we were all forced to undergo that day. No one wanted to cause me further harm. That in point of fact he more than anyone in that room wanted to protect me from further harm. He thought that I had probably been injured enough.

He spoke like a schoolmarm reading the rules to a test, but he was lying. Of course he wanted to cause me harm. August wanted to cause me harm so his attorney would naturally want the same thing.

He told me that his sole purpose in this was to get to the truth of things and he felt certain that he would. But he wanted to be sure that I understood the depth of the compassion he felt for me. He had seen me himself, walking to and from the woods. He personally knew men who had come to me in the forest. He knew what a fine business I had kept out there, out under the trees, out where I thought no one would ever find out.

Jared Thompson stood up and objected and the judge said, "Sustained." Walter Meyer just smiled again. He said that he intended no disrespect, of course, and he was happy to meet me at last, since I was so notorious and he was well acquainted with my exploits, since others had told him all about me. And Jared Thompson stood up again and Walter Meyer just waved at him as if he were waving at a float in a parade or a friend or a swarm of gnats. "All right," he said. "Withdrawn."

He asked me where I had been employed and I told him. He asked me if I had been a regular worker. I said yes. He looked at me. "Always at work?"

"Yes."

"Always? Never missed a day?"

"I missed one day," I said. The sound of the wind in the trees rushed through my head.

"Just one day?"

"Yes."

"And you were always on time to work?"

I studied the railing that ran in front of the witness stand. "No," I said.

"No? But you were a regular worker?"

"Sometimes I was late." A flush rose to my hairline. I remembered the heat of the laundry and my wet skirt dragging across the floor. August on the river at night.

"Sometimes you were late. How many times?"

"I do not know." I shifted in my seat. I tried to count. I tried to remember. But somehow my mind had become like a land stripped of signposts and roads.

"You don't know or you won't say?"

"I do not know." So hard to answer when one is terrified. A simple statement that only begins to tell the tale: not even that will come.

"Was it five times?"

"I do not know."

"Ten times?"

Jared Thompson stood up. "Your Honor," he said. "This has been asked and answered."

The judge waved him off. "One or two more questions in this vein will be fine," he said. He glanced down at me and then gazed off above the crowd of men before him.

"Was it more than ten times?" said Walter Meyer.

"No," I said.

"So you do know."

I looked at him. Behind him the men in the courtroom like a tableau. Unmoving faces as if they even failed to breathe. August at his table with his gaze on me like a man with an intention known only to him. He leaned forward.

"You didn't worry about your employer on such occasions?" said Walter Meyer. He widened his eyes as if I had just said something very shocking.

"I did what I was supposed to do," I said. I tried to keep the hurt out of my voice and I told myself not to cry.

"So you did worry about your employer. But still you came late." He looked around the courtroom with an aggrieved expression on his face. "That doesn't seem right to me. Just not right at all." He walked up to me. "Who was your employer?"

"William Oliver," I said.

"And would Mr. William Oliver agree with your assessment of the way things stood between you?"

"I do not know," I said softly. I thought of all the ways that William Oliver and I had not agreed, and of the one thing on which we had not agreed most of all. I tried to picture him standing before us, admitting the thing he had asked of me, the thing I would not do, the thing he had done. I could not see how this would ever happen.

"What was that?" Walter Meyer had been walking up and

down in front of the men in the benches with his hands crossed behind his back, playing to them as if they were the jury. Now he cupped his palm around his ear and leaned toward me.

"I do not know," I repeated.

Jared Thompson stood up. "Your Honor," he said. "Relevance."

Walter Meyer turned to the judge. "I'm merely trying to establish whether or not we have before us a credible witness. Whether or not her word can be trusted. She comes to this court and asks for relief and claims her husband, whom I know to be a kind and loving man, tried to kill her. That's a big statement. A very big statement. This is not a common occurrence, as you well understand. Men don't kill women. The very idea is preposterous. And it's even more preposterous to imagine that this man, who has a gentle spirit, would kill this woman, who does not. So we need to find out how she ticks." He looked earnest and sincere. "Right now, it's her word against his. We don't really know what went on behind closed doors. So I need to come at this thing any way I can. I need to do this part of my job."

"Your Honor," said Jared, but the judge held up his hand. "Go on," he said to August's lawyer.

"Mr. William Oliver," said Walter Meyer. "You worked for him for how long?"

"Five months."

"Five months."

"Yes."

"And what was the nature of your relationship with Mr. William Oliver?"

I thought of his hands in my hair as he bucked against me in the alley, the smell of his breath. The bulk of his body crushed on mine. "I worked for him," I said quietly.

"And that's all?"

"Yes." My very breathing nearly ceased with the thought of him.

"Nothing else you want to say about that?"

"No." I looked at my hands. The anger I felt at just that moment was provoked even more by impotence than by Walter Meyer. I could not bear the things he said about me. I could not bear that he said them in this courtroom. But there was nothing I could do about it. When we were preparing, Jared Thompson had told me the other side would get mean. But he had not told me how they would get mean or what they would say or how they would come after me. Perhaps he knew all of these things and therefore assumed that I knew them, too. But I did not and now I had to learn in front of a room full of men.

"In those five months you never left your place of work to seek him out in his private rooms?"

"No." I clenched my hands. Walter Meyer glanced quickly at my lap. Jared Thompson had told me, above all, to remain calm. To answer the questions with as few words as possible, and not to give my emotions away. I forced myself to let my fingers go limp, as if I could take back the clenching and therefore take back my rage.

Walter Meyer walked toward me. "No?" he said. "You didn't go upstairs and stay there for many hours on end?"

"I went where he told me to go," I said. I looked at the floor, at the way two boards in the floor held themselves together with black nails, at the nails themselves.

"He told you to go upstairs?"

"Yes."

"So you did go with him to his private rooms."

"To his office," I said, and hung my head. Shame was a nail that could have staked me to the very floor, and yet Walter Meyer did not seem to mind.

"His private office?"

"I guess," I said slowly.

"And what did you do there?"

"He talked to me."

August frowned.

"About what?" said Walter Meyer.

"I do not know." I wanted to bolt from the chair, bolt from that room, bolt from the stares of the men who no longer read their newspapers or talked quietly to their friends but merely gaped at me as if I were some kind of marionette on a string, a carnival act, a freak in the middle of a dance only she could do.

"Mrs. Bethke. You have to try to remember."

"But I do not," I said. I straightened in my chair.

"You don't."

"No."

Walter Meyer sighed deeply. He acted as if he was very much put out by my incompetence. He gave me a hard look and then he turned back to the courtroom and opened his hands before him, as if pleading for understanding.

"Mrs. Bethke," he said, walking back to me. "What if I told you that I have witnesses who will testify that you went to William's Oliver's office and stayed there for very long periods of time and enjoyed a special relationship with him? That would all be true, would it not?"

I shook my head. I glanced at August, who sat back hard in his chair as if surprised. He stared at me.

Mr. Meyer leaned toward me. "What did he say to you, Mrs. Bethke?" he said in a slippery voice. "What was it that you were given to understand?"

Someone in the back of the room coughed and I could have sworn the smell of his breath came to me.

"Mrs. Bethke," Walter Meyer repeated.

"You will answer the question," the judge said. He sounded bored.

"He wanted me to have a relationship with him," I said. I looked at August.

"A relationship."

"Yes."

"I see. And did you?"

"No."

"Are you sure?"

"Yes," I whispered, and wiped my eyes on my sleeve. Jared Thompson left his seat and came up to me where I sat. He handed me his handkerchief and nodded encouragingly.

"What kind of relationship are we talking about?" Walter Meyer said. "Did he have work he needed you to do?"

"No." *Please stop*, I thought.

"Was it a romantic relationship?"

"That was what he wanted," I said, Jared's handkerchief balled wetly in my hand. I wiped my eyes again.

"He wanted a romantic relationship and you said no and that was the end of it?"

"Yes."

August coughed and coughed, as if he wanted to get my attention. When I glanced at him, he picked up the glass of water that had stood untouched before him. He raised it in my direction.

Walter Meyer nodded briskly. "Very good," he said. "Your Honor, I have an affidavit here signed by Mr. William Oliver, who has sworn that he conducted a consensual romantic relationship with the plaintiff, for which he supplied her sums of money. He is sorry to have to say these things in public but that is the way it is. I also have a sworn statement from Mrs. Inge Braun, a coworker in the laundry with Mrs. Bethke, describing Mrs. Bethke's business in the woods, her constant tardiness at work, and her outright absences on many occasions. I would like to enter both of these documents into evidence."

I felt the turning of the world, all the stars spinning away, the ground gone beneath me, the great tides pulling me, and the room but a space for the pulsing of blood in my head.

"Your Honor," said Jared Thompson. "If he has witnesses, let him bring them to court so they can testify. Let these individuals be available for cross-examination."

The judge leaned back in his chair. He was a tall man with yellowing white hair. Behind him, the flag of the land, run up on its pole, an eagle clutching the golden ball that rested at the top, wings outspread and beak parted and askew, just like the eagle I had seen in the justice of the peace's chambers the day that August and I got married.

He tipped forward. "Mr. Meyer," he said. "Are these witnesses available to come to court?"

"Mr. William Oliver is a prominent local businessman. Mrs. Braun is his employee. They prepared sworn affidavits because they prefer not to come to court themselves. They prefer not to be associated with such a sordid set of events as we have before us. They are good and decent people with fine names. They do not wish to be dragged into this."

"Once you sign an affidavit, you cannot claim that your sensibilities are too fine to get involved," the judge said. "Do they know that?"

"I believe they do," said Walter Meyer. "I believe that fact is well known to them."

"Can you produce them?" the judge said. His chair squeaked as it turned, a sound like a shrieking wheel on a rail, and the judge glanced down and then looked up again. "Can you get them into court today?"

Jared Thompson gave me a tortured look, as if he had known all along that this was what they would do to me and there was nothing he could do to stop it.

I looked at Walter Meyer. He stood before the bench. He

had composed his face so it would seem neutral and frank. "I do not believe they will come," he said.

"The court can compel them," the judge said. "You know that."

"I do not believe they will come."

The men in the court shifted in their seats. A door banged as one of them left the courtroom. For a moment I could hear voices in the hallway.

"Let me get this straight," the judge said. "I just want to be sure I'm hearing all of this correctly. You want me to enter into evidence affidavits from witnesses you claim are central to your case but who will not come to court and who will not respond to a subpoena? Who would stand in contempt? Is this what you are telling me?"

"Your Honor," Walter Meyer said. "This is a painful case. Surely you can understand my impulse to protect these fine citizens from someone like Mrs. Bethke. I promised them that they could swear to the facts as they knew them but would not have to come to court. I gave them my word. My word is my bond."

"Your word is your bond," said the judge. He eyed the attorney.

"Yes."

"I'm afraid that's not the right currency here," the judge said. He cleared his throat. "I can tell you that I'm inclined to agree with Mr. Thompson. These are grave charges and cannot be entered into the record without thorough examination. So I am going to deny your request unless and until you produce these witnesses for cross-examination. If you have anything else, I'd like to hear it. If not, I'm going to disregard this testimony and move on."

"Your Honor."

"That's my final word on the subject," said the judge. "What's next?"

Walter Meyer stared out across the courtroom, as if he wanted to give the impression that he was a reasonable man, a man who must be given a minute or two to think things over, who must be allowed to organize his thoughts, who only wanted to follow the correct course of action. But when he turned back to me, he came at me with a broad smile. "Mrs. Bethke," he said. "You said that your husband tried to kill you. I'd like you to explain this to the court. What was his reason?"

I clutched my wet handkerchief and looked at Jared Thompson, who stood up and said that I had already given this testimony.

"Agreed," said the judge. "What's your point, Mr. Meyer?"

"If we agree that her testimony is already in evidence," he replied, "then certainly it's permissible for me to ask her one or two more questions in this vein? For the sake of refinement and clarification?"

"I'm not going to run your case for you," said the judge.

"I just want to be sure I don't misstep," said Walter Meyer. "A man's reputation hangs in the balance."

I blanched. It did not seem that Walter Meyer was much concerned with my reputation except as he could further ruin it.

"Ask your questions, Mr. Meyer," the judge said. "But bear relevance in mind or you will surely hear from our friend over here." He nodded once at Jared Thompson and then looked away and gazed out the window as if he had lost all interest in the proceedings. The gray morning had cleared and the courthouse square stood under a bright white sky. I felt myself sag just a little.

"Mrs. Bethke," August's attorney said. "Is it your testimony that your husband changed overnight from a kind and loving boy into a brutal and heartless man?"

"Yes," I said.

"And that he would walk into the house after a hard day's work and just strike you out of the blue?"

"Not out of the blue," I said in a tight voice. "He usually had a reason."

"Which was?"

"It was always different."

"Give us one example."

I thought. "If he thought I looked at him the wrong way," I said.

"And that would be it?"

"Yes."

"That's all? A wrong look?"

"It was when he thought I looked at him the wrong way," I said tensely. "It was not that I actually looked at him the wrong way."

"So now he makes things up?"

I felt the baby move, a faint fluttering. I sat up as straight as I could and looked at August's attorney and said, "Yes. He does."

"I don't know as that's the way I would see it," Walter Meyer said. Again he delivered his broad smile, as polished as a bare jaw bone on a plate. "I don't know that at all. But that's the way you're asking me to see it. So let's hear more about it. You say that your husband came home from work and walked into your house and tried to kill you. For no reason other than that he was a heartless man with evil in his soul."

"I did not say that."

"You didn't say that your husband tried to kill you?"

"The rest of it," I said fiercely. "I did not say he was evil."

"So he's not evil?"

"He was drinking," I said angrily. I paused and tried to calm down. "He was angry. That's not the same."

Jared Thompson got to his feet. "Your Honor. Where is this going?"

Walter Meyer paused and again opened his hands before him, palms up, as if the judge could answer his questions for him. "The question is: How big of a liar is she? We see that she twists the truth to her own purposes. First he's an evil man. Then he's a drunk. Now he gets in a killing mood over something as insignificant as a wrong look. I ask you. Which is it?"

The judge held up his hand. "Enough," he said. "I have been listening carefully. And I have looked at the things that have been legitimately brought before me. If you want to know the truth of it, I don't like to hear a case like this one. Makes me want to give up on my fellow man. But what it all comes down to is that I don't see much here beyond a lot of pretense and innuendo."

"Your Honor," said Jared Thompson.

"Hold on there, Mr. Thompson," said the judge. "I didn't mean that the complaint is a bunch of lies and nonsense. I meant that the defense strikes me that way."

"Your Honor," said Walter Meyer. "I haven't even put my client on the stand."

"And you are not going to," said the judge. "These are just shenanigans, from where I sit."

"Your Honor."

"Mr. Meyer, I'm not sure where you think you're practicing law. I know you are new to our city and I know that things are often different out west. Isn't that where you come from? Out west? The place of endless promise? The land of milk and honey?"

"I was in Texas before this," said Walter Meyer. He sounded defensive and small.

"Texas. Hot there, isn't it? No trees?"

"There are trees in Texas," said Walter Meyer. "Your Honor."

"But I'm sure you could find parts of Texas where folks haven't ever seen a tree and aren't likely ever to see one."

"In the western parts, down south, perhaps," Walter Meyer said. He looked confused. "That area is mostly arid and desert."

"But if you had me on the stand and wanted some judge to believe that it was too hot in Texas for trees to grow, that's what you'd ask me to say, isn't it? You'd count on the fact that up here in Wisconsin there are mighty few people who've spent a lot of time in Texas. You could weave any story you want, practically, and make it sound as valid as the day is long. Am I right?"

Walter Meyer looked bewildered. "That would depend upon the case," he said.

"That's all it would depend on? The case?"

"Naturally I would want to win," said Walter Meyer. "That would be my goal. So the case, yes, that would be the primary motivator."

"You don't have an interest in truth?" said the judge. "In justice? These things are not factors for you?"

"Again, it would depend upon the case," said Walter Meyer. He stiffened. "A case like this one, justice needs to be served. The truth has to come out."

"But in some cases, these things are less important to you? Is that what I'm hearing?"

"In every case, I serve my client and the court," Walter Meyer said in an acid tone. "That is my duty and my obligation and I accept it fully."

"Thank you, Mr. Meyer. I think I have a good idea of what that means," said the judge. "Go sit down."

"Your Honor?"

"The witness is excused. I'm going back to my chambers. We'll convene after dinner. You'll hear my ruling then."

We walked down into the courthouse square. Jared Thompson suggested that we eat in the tearoom that stood across from the courthouse. We sat at a table under the front window. He ordered a plate of sausages and a basket of rolls and a pot of mustard and a plate of dill pickles and a plate of sauerkraut. He told me that I might as well have something to eat, since there was no telling when the judge would return and he didn't want me to faint halfway through the afternoon. When I made no move, he picked up a roll and split it with his knife and sliced sausage into it and then laid sliced pickles and a spoonful of kraut across the top. He put the sandwich on my plate. "Eat," he said. Outside, preoccupied men in business suits made their way along the street and the sky turned a brighter white.

The judge came back at two thirty in the afternoon. Walter Meyer sat so that his hand rested in the middle of August's back, giving the impression that August was a man in need of comfort. I tried to swallow the lump in my throat. Jared smiled at me when we sat down and patted my arm. I know he meant to show me that everything would turn out fine, but he kept his attention on the judge the way another man might watch a sniper on a parapet and so he failed to set me entirely at ease. On the one hand, it all seemed built on words. On the other, I knew what words could build, the stories that made the world.

The judge called us back to the front of the courtroom, and we took our places at the long tables in front of his bench.

"This is my courtroom," the judge said. "And this has been my courtroom for a number of years now, probably eleven, although Mr. Meyer here would be alarmed to hear that I can't readily swear to an exact number without thinking about it. And in matters such as these, I have discretion. I can decide what I'd like to hear and what I'd like to leave be. There is no jury in a divorce trial and no worry about reasonable doubt, the way you would have in a criminal matter. I can weigh the evidence as I see fit. So this is what I did. I had some dinner sent up from a place down the street. I sat at the desk in my chambers, and I looked at the materials before me with a great deal of caution and care. My chop grew cold, I can tell you that, and I don't know if it was because it had to travel to get to me or because I wanted to be careful and be sure, based on what I saw before me, and I let it lie too long. Wouldn't be the first time. And what I saw in the record suggested to me that there is an answer for these two parties before me. Like most answers you get in a courtroom, it's not going to satisfy either party. But it's a fair disposition of the case as I understand it, and I don't think there is more to understand than I already do. Mr. Meyer here can save himself the time and trouble of bringing more information forward. I don't think there is any more relevant information to be had and I am prepared to rule." He held his hand up. "Keep your seat, Mr. Meyer. I am finished with you." Then he looked down at a sheaf of papers that lay on the bench before him and began to read aloud. "I find that these parties were residents of Waukesha, Wisconsin, just as they described, and lawfully inter-married. I find that the plaintiff has not made a sufficient case that Mr. Bethke starved her or failed to provide for her creature comforts and the defendant is not guilty of these acts and I dismiss those charges."

Tears came to my eyes. I should have known better than to ask justice for redress, for justice belonged to men and men alone. But Jared kept his gaze trained on the judge and said in a low voice, "Wait. Wait." I wiped my eyes with the back of my hand and then wiped my hand on my skirt. The judge cleared his throat.

"However," he said. He rubbed his eyes briefly and then straightened and looked out over the courtroom again. "However. I find that the defendant was guilty of cruel and inhumane treatment of the plaintiff as alleged in the second cause of action, that his conduct toward her has been such as may render it unsafe and improper for her to live with him; that on or about June 17, 1907, the defendant unlawfully and cruelly assaulted the plaintiff and knocked her down with his fist, to her great hurt and injury, and kicked her on that same occasion such that she suffered grievous bodily harm; that on other occasions, the defendant also assaulted the plaintiff and shook his fist at her in a threatening manner and at other times held a knife to her and on one occasion threatened her with a gun. That he told the neighbors that if she misbehaved again, he would 'lay her low at his feet' and showed these neighbor men a revolver that he kept for his own protection. I further find that when the plaintiff left the defendant, she took with her, and continues to hold in her possession, a bedstead, bedding, with other articles of household furniture and property, all of which she needs the use of and that the same does not exceed in value the sum of one hundred dollars. She is ordered to retain these with no molestation or interference from the defendant. I find that the plaintiff is entitled to a judgment of divorce from the defendant, forever dissolving the bonds of matrimony existing between the two of them. Further, I find that she is entitled to the future care, custody, and possession of the issue of this marriage until further order of the court, with permission to said defendant to visit the child at the plaintiff's home and take the child out walking. I also find that the defendant's answer to the plaintiff's charge of cruel and inhumane treatment is not proven or true. I further order that neither party shall be free to marry again until one year has passed from this date, and that the defendant must pay the plaintiff's court costs and attorney's fees."

Jared put his hand on my arm again. "You see?" he said. "It pays not to be too hasty."

As soon as the judge finished, August turned toward me with a choking expression on his face. I would not meet his gaze but watched Walter Meyer put his arm around him. Then they both stood. August looked at me and looked at me, but Walter Meyer pulled him away and propelled him up the aisle between the benches. The men who waited for justice watched him go. Then they stared at me as I walked up the aisle behind him. Our reverse wedding march in this church with its own sacraments.

My light-headedness settled when we came outside into the fresh air. The courthouse square looked different, too, each corner sharply focused, each pure block of fading sunlight alive. Even the lilac dust that rolled up from the gritty curb was fresh and spotless, as if the moment when the judge believed me had made the whole world true.

Jared set his black leather case down next to his feet and turned to face me. He told me that I was a free woman now.

"You should be proud of yourself," he said. "Not many women would have the guts to go through with that."

I shook my head. I did not know if I could speak or what words I might be able to say. He smiled at me as if he understood.

"To walk into a room and stand up against the man who is your husband in a room full of men to be judged by men, with not a friendly face in sight," he said. "That takes some backbone." He smiled again. I had never noticed before that he was good-looking and had a kind of warmth around him.

"Thank you," I said. My voice was hoarse and my words sounded exotic, like the words of someone speaking in the language of a new country. "I know that you did not have to take this on."

"Oh," he said. "I thought we might have a chance. We had to go at it through the divorce. That was the channel that was open to us. I'm glad we had the presence of mind to see it and to take it." He spoke amiably, as if it was the legal challenge of the case that had interested him.

A small wind blew leaves across the pavement.

"It was all lies," I said. "Did you know it was going to be all lies?"

He looked away from me. After a time he said, "In my experience, the question of truth has everything to do with the perspective of the person telling the story. It's very easy for that perspective to get caught up in other things. Desire, for one. Rage, for another. The things people want that they don't even know they want. The things going on around them that are invisible to them even as they pursue them. We are blind to our own blindness. People are complicated, and the way they come to believe the things they come to believe is never clear to them. They'll fight you if you point it out. I've seen people who were outright liars take the stand and speak with all the sense of entitlement of an aggrieved party. They can get so they believe the things they're saying."

"So you do not believe in the truth?"

"I believe that a woman who walks into my office with her face smashed to pieces has encountered something very real, even if no one else thinks so. I think that's about as close to the truth as we can hope to get. And I'm satisfied with that." He picked up his case. "My wife will have supper waiting," he said. "Can you find your way home?"

I nodded.

"Now look," he said. "The court will have Bethke pay my fees and then the court will hand those over to me. So don't worry about that. It's between the court and your ex-husband now. If he doesn't pay, they will chase him down and take the necessary steps. There is nothing left for you to do. But when that baby comes, you come and see me. We'll bring Bethke back for custody and support. And we'll make him pay for that, too. Do you understand?"

I nodded.

"Fine," he said. "That's fine, then." He put his hand out and I shook it. "Good luck to you, Mrs. Bethke. I will see you before spring."

"My name is Marie," I said.

He smiled. "Yes," he said. "I'm sorry, Marie."

I passed through the courthouse square. Down by the town hall, a crowd of men in filthy work clothes came along the street. They carried canvas workbags and bottles of beer and yelled as they walked. I stepped to one side to let them pass and listened to the sound of shoe leather on pavement and hard voices and shouts. They stopped in front of the building where the copper companies kept their local offices. I made my way through the back of the throng and then passed into the next street. A breeze came up and then over the horizon, a break in the overcast and the single gleam of the first star. I smiled and put my hand in my pocket and counted the change by touch.

23

Every morning I rose in the dark and sat on the edge of my bed until my eyes adjusted. Then I turned on the light and dressed and ate a slice of bread. I went to work at the tearoom at the end of the street. At first, I took orders and carried trays of food, but then the woman who ran the place noticed that I knew how to cook. She asked if I would like to make the breakfast menu. I kneaded dough for sweet rolls and bread and shaped the loaves and laid these into pans and slid the pans into the oven. When the bread was half-baked, I cut the rolls and twisted them and set them on a rack above the bread pans so everything would come out together. I made coffee and fried sausage and eggs on an iron griddle that lay like a slab over the stove. The first customers came in with the light.

I liked the process of making something out of nothing, the dough that rose from the flour and yeast, the loaves that took shape in my hands. The newspapers were full of stories about the strikes and then all of a sudden the banks failed in a wave. After that, men came to the front of the tearoom and looked in the window and stood there for a long time. They watched the customers eat and then they walked away. The women came to the back door. They stood in the frozen mud and hung their heads. Some of them lifted their faces when they saw me and tried to act as if they were there by accident and that none of this had happened to them. I always gave them food. They thanked me or said nothing or said something to someone who was not there and walked away as if they moved in the disconnected landscape of a dream. I found two circles carved into the doorframe and I knew that we were marked as a place that was kind to the weary traveler. It did not take much for me to imagine myself in their shoes. It did not take much for me to know that any one of those women could have been me, for we all stood in a river that threatened at any moment to overtake us.

Late one morning toward the end of November I looked up to see Martha and Hattie on the sidewalk outside. Martha had bare hands but she wore her blue hat with the netting. Hattie wore my mother's old coat with the piece of rope tied around the waist. They shaded their eyes against the morning sun and tried to look in the window. When they came inside, Martha hugged me and gingerly put her hand on my belly, as if she had never seen a pregnant woman before. They sat at a table next to the stove. I told them to bring their chairs closer and get warm. Martha's hands were red. She folded them under her armpits to warm them.

"We have been so worried," she said. "You never sent word."

I sat down. "Hattie knew," I said, confused. "Hattie came with the wagon and then she came with me to Milwaukee to Carl."

"We knew that," Martha said. "We just never knew anything else."

"What else was there to know, Martha?"

She reached up and fiddled with her hat and then took it off and set it on her lap. "I do not know," she said at last. "Something."

"You did not come," I said. "Hattie could have shown you the way. Or Carl."

"How could I have come?" she said. "It was all the way in Milwaukee." She made it sound like I had asked her to travel to a foreign land, not to a city she had been to many times before. And here she was in Milwaukee today, a fact she chose to ignore.

"Do you want something to eat?" I said. "You look hungry."

She glanced at the rolls piled in baskets on the counter. She shook her head.

"I do," said Hattie. "I could eat a horse."

"Hattie," Martha said. She used her warning voice.

I stood up. "I will put something on the table. In case you change your mind."

"I said I was fine."

"I know," I said. I felt a ripple of kindness toward my older sister, rigid and thin as a straight line. She must have thought I planned to charge her. "But you can have the coffee and rolls for free," I said.

They ate in silence. The tearoom was empty and I could sit with them. I could feel the pleasure of being back with my sisters again, even if Martha and I never saw eye to eye.

"Has August been to see you?" Martha asked suddenly. She shook her skirt to dislodge the crumbs.

"August?" His name came to me like a word I did not want to say.

"Does he understand your situation?"

"What situation?" I gave her a quizzical look. I knew what she meant but I wanted to see if I could get her to talk about it.

"Your circumstances," she said delicately. She waved her hand in the air over my stomach like a magician trying to do a trick. "I want to know if he is taking care of things and treating you well," she said.

"What difference would that make?"

She sighed. "It is time for all of this to stop," she said. "It is time to mend fences. You need to go back to him. You must do whatever it takes to set this right. You have more than proved your point."

Hattie set her roll on her plate. "Don't do it," she said to me. "I mean it."

The stove creaked as it cooled. I stood and took wood from the kindling box and dropped it inside. I poked the fire to make sure it would flame. Martha finished her roll and put her hands in her lap and sat there looking at the top of her hat and then ducked her head and reached for the basket and helped herself to another roll. She would not look at me as she ate. When she was through, she put her hands under her armpits again as if she had to work to warm herself.

Hattie spread another roll with butter. "Do you like it here?" she asked.

I nodded. "I like the work," I said.

Hattie took a bite and chewed. "We don't have good bread at home now," she said after a minute. "But that's all right. It's better that you're here."

I felt a rush of warmth toward her, my little sister who only wanted the best for me.

"Just tell me," Martha said, her voice as reedy as the sound of wind by the river. "Are you ever going to go back to your husband?"

I did not reply immediately. I wanted to give her the courtesy of pretending to consider this, to think that she could provide advice. Eventually, however, I had to say something. "I do not think so," I said. I looked up at the ceiling as if this thought had just come to me out of the air.

"I am sure he is sorry by now."

"I am sure you are right."

"That doesn't matter," said Hattie.

"Come back with us," said Martha, ignoring her. She put her hand on my knee. "We can get your things from Carl's room next week."

"No," I said, the word blunt and firm and final.

"It is not just you now." She dipped her chin at my belly as if I might have forgotten that I was pregnant.

"I know that."

"I do not understand you," Martha said.

I nodded. "I know," I said.

She cleared her throat and rubbed at an invisible spot on the table. I felt sorry for her. I knew she did not want this gulf between us any more than I wanted it, but I could not see how to cross it. I am sure she felt equally at a loss. "So," she said. "You will never go back to him?"

"You shouldn't," said Hattie.

Martha glared at her. "Shush," she said.

"I will not," said Hattie.

"No," I said. "I will not go back to him."

"But what about us?"

"I can see you," I said. "You can see me. That will not change."

"You know that he will never let you back into the house," she said. I knew who she meant. We were not talking about August now.

A log fell in the stove and she turned ever so slightly toward the noise. "The shame you have brought on us by running away. He cannot get over it."

"If you come back, you know what will happen," said Hattie.

"I am sorry," I said. "I did not intend to bring shame on anyone."

"You are hard-hearted, you know that?" Martha would not look at me when she spoke.

"No more than you," I said.

She sat back and looked a little offended at having to say all of this out loud. I did not really blame her. We each had our own truths and they would never match.

We sat without speaking. I watched a team of huge gray Percherons pull a wagon by the shop, their hides rippling and their blond tails flying. The thunder of the wagon wheels faded as the horses pulled away.

After a while, Hattie kicked the table. "I think you should stay here," she said.

"You are a child," said Martha.

Hattie shrugged. "I think she's safe here," she said. "And that's what's important."

When had she gotten so grown up? I thought of her as she helped to load the wagon outside of the house I shared with August. I thought of her on the train to Milwaukee. She had taken her braces off. She had stood on her own two feet. Martha and I had tried to protect her by standing between her and our father. She would grow up and see things a different way, as if she had grown up in a completely different family.

"Sometimes when bad things happen, you have to take care of yourself," I said. I spoke to my older sister as if she was a child, and who was to say she was not? "So I got a lawyer and I went to court and I took care of this. This is my job. I live down the street. You can come see me here anytime."

"What are you saying?" Martha said. She grabbed my arm. "What do you mean, you got a lawyer?"

"I got a divorce," I said. It was not so hard to say the word now that it was a reality, and I saw that what it really meant was a world in which no one hit me. "It's all right," I said. "It's fine."

"Oh God," she cried. She clawed at my sleeve. I pulled away.

"You are hurting me," I said.

She stood up and looked at Hattie. "Put your coat on," she said. "We are leaving." Then she scowled at me. "It is not all right," she said. "It is not fine. You ought to be ashamed of yourself." She stabbed at her hair with her hat pin. "Try as I might," she said, "I do not understand how you can be so selfish."

Hattie hugged me and promised she would come and see me when the baby came. But Martha stood buttoning her coat and would not look at me. Before she left, she paused in the doorway and told me that I might as well know that my father had been keeping company with a woman who owned a dairy farm in Price County. She was a widow. Along with the dairy farm, she owned a small hotel and kept a herd of pet deer penned in the yard so that visitors could see something wild. She had her own hunting permit and used it. Then Martha said our father had decided to marry this widow and she thought that his marriage would happen soon. He would move himself and the last of their household to Price County, and Martha and Hattie would go with him, at least until he could secure work for them.

It did not take much for me to picture it, the white house sitting atop a rise, the long, undulating pastures of rich grass, the chasms in the earth where water rolled, the horizon of expectations now real, the idea of the land he had always wanted hurtling at me like a wall I would hit at high speed. My mother was gone and everything of our family could be wiped out with a new marriage and a signature on a deed. This was the reason, I thought, this and no other. I wondered how long it had taken him to decide after he met her. My father had always wanted land. My father had always felt that land was his destiny. He had not crossed an ocean to come up empty. Martha had her hand on the doorknob and Hattie had tied her rope into a sash, knotting it at the waist to keep her coat closed.

"What is she like?" I asked.

Martha shrugged. "I have not met her," she said. "He always takes the train there."

When they were gone, the tearoom was very still. I went back to the icebox and leaned my head against the door and thought of my mother dead in the ground and of my father and his terrible crime and his terrible plan. And then I fell weeping to the floor. When the woman who owned the tearoom came in, she saw me lying wet-eyed and heaving in the flickering light from the stove. She knelt down and put her arm around my shoulders. She told me that everything was all right and I should go into the back room and lie down, for clearly I was overtired. For a time I lay on a cot set up beneath the shelves of canned beans, but I could neither sleep nor could I rest. I stood up and went back to work.

You have known girls like me. You might have been a girl like me. We are all the same under the skin, girls who pick up leaves and stones and have hopes for the future and who are taught that we must marry and obey and love. Our mothers told us, *It's not his fault. He doesn't know how to touch you the right way.* Our mothers told us to forgive him. Our mothers told us it was our fault. *You should have seen it coming,* they said. *You should have known that he would do that. You should not have made him angry.* And so we are shamefaced and still and silent and scared. We are afraid of him and afraid that no one will save us and sure that we cannot save ourselves. These things should be as familiar to you as the song you sing when you do the wash. You know us and you have been us and you might be one of us yet. It might not be a hand or a brick or a blade. It might be a word or a look that promises the course of the cane. It might be a darkness that you cannot name but which you know is with you and has been with you for as long as you can remember. Perhaps these ideas are too common even to bear repeating. And yet they must be repeated because every day the papers are filled with the stories of women who have been thrown from windows or shot with guns or lost in the night, a long, terrible story that is as familiar as the air we breathe. We have not seen the last girl. She has not yet walked among us.

24

Some nights my mother told us a story about the Princess Svanvitha, whose father had once been a powerful king on Rügen. I believe this was my mother's favorite story, for my sisters and I could count on her to tell it once a week. For our part, we never tired of it and I imagine it gave my mother great pleasure to have us nestled around her, our heads on her knees or on the pillow behind her back, where she could smell our hair and look into our faces as she spoke.

Princess Svanvitha was a beautiful and pure girl. She lived with her father the king in her father's castle in a town not far from Garz. Her mother had died long ago and her father had never remarried, so the girl lived with her father as if enchanted by the spell of his power. Years passed, but soon enough she came of age and many suitors came from across the land, hoping to claim her hand.

The prince of Poland wooed Princess Svanvitha for a long time and tormented her with his suit, but she always declined him because she did not like him. She chose the prince of Denmark instead, who seemed to her to be a kind boy and a boy who would care for her. Her father was happy with her selection, and the people were happy because they knew there would be a wedding. Perhaps they thought it would be a wedding as perfect as a wedding in a fairy tale, which is the most perfect kind of wedding you will ever find. My mother described Princess Svanvitha's bridal gown at length, the exquisite stitching of the lace, the weight of the satin, the abundance of pearls, the jewels that adorned the bodice and the skirt. Her veil was to be so ethereal that it would appear as if wings had sprouted from her back and she had become a fairy princess before the eyes of the onlookers. My mother pointed out that only a beautiful princess could wear such a dress, and Princess Svanvitha was so slender and lovely and pure that the people called her the King's Lily. My mother made us think that no title would be more apt for us, either, and we should not aspire to any other.

Despite Princess Svanvitha's choice, the spurned prince of Poland never gave up his suit. He still insisted that he was the better man. He tried to tempt Princess Svanvitha with the promise of riches, if only she were to change her mind. But on the very eve of her wedding, when joy and celebration spread across the land, the prince of Poland was forced to accept that Princess Svanvitha really would marry another. And so his heart conceived a wicked plan. By his arts he managed to convince her father and everyone else that Princess Svanvitha was not the modest young lady they all believed her to be. He told of her improprieties and her flirtations and he intimated that more than that had passed between them, so much more that he dared not speak the truth aloud.

Immediately, the prince of Denmark mounted his horse and departed, taking with him all the dukes and duchesses and kings and queens who had come to Garz to attend the wedding. The harpists and bagpipers and other musicians who had been preparing for the festivals and tournaments also disappeared. The castle was left sad and deserted and the disgrace of the poor princess was bruited about everywhere, even though she was as innocent as a newborn babe.

The king her father was beside himself and nearly out of his mind and wanted to kill himself over the humiliation Svanvitha had brought on the royal house. Days passed while he ranted in his chambers. But when he was again in his right mind, he became merely furious and called out to have Svanvitha brought before him. For her part, she stood trembling before him and did her best to protest the lies. But the king would not listen. Instead, he tore her hair and ripped her dress and struck her. Then he commanded that she be removed from his presence and taken to a secret chamber so that he would never have to set eyes on her again. Around this room he caused a strong, dark tower to be built, into which neither sun nor moon could shine. The chamber itself was a small and barren place, with neither bed nor chair nor carpet and only a tiny hole through which her keeper could hand her food. Svanvitha had to sleep on the hard floor and go barefoot. She could not comb her hair nor play music nor wash herself. In time, her fine clothes became nothing but rags.

Thus passed three years. The poor princess was but a young girl—just seventeen—when her father banished her, and she would have died of her misery had she not had the certainty of her innocence to keep her spirits up. This she clung to like a rock. She knew her father had put her in the tower so she could reflect on the terrible shame she had brought to his family. It was true that during those dark days she had nothing but time for contemplation. But she did not spend one minute thinking of her own disobedience, for that was nothing but the lie of the suitor she had spurned. Instead, she waited for her father to come to her and tell her he was sorry for all that he had done against her. Sometimes she imagined that one day the king would call for her and her very innocence would be proof enough to set things right. But her father never requested a second audience and Svanvitha had no chance to tell her side of the story.

My mother told us that Svanvitha was at her most pitiful when she thought the king might call for her. Anyone could tell that he would never do that. He would never listen to her side of the story. He would never admit that he had made a mistake. He would never apologize for having done wrong.

One day Svanvitha lay on the floor in a corner of her chamber. She rested her head on cold stone. She tried to remember Garz as it had been when she last saw it. She could see herself picking flowers near the temple of the ancient goddess and walking in the shadow of the battlements. All of a sudden she sat bolt upright and jumped to her feet and began to pace up and down. After all of these lonely months, she had suddenly remembered the legend of the parapet. When a pure and chaste princess walked the rampart between twelve and one on Midsummer's Eve, naked and as God made her, the earth itself would open and reveal a secret chamber filled with treasure. That treasure could be removed. That treasure could be brought to her father. That treasure would prove that the prince of Poland had lied. The only thing she would have to watch out for was the gray ghost that guarded the cavern and sometimes turned himself into a snarling black dog.

If she was not chaste, not modest, and not a virgin, the ground would remain sealed shut and no glittering cavern would appear.

Svanvitha pushed her fingers through the tiny hole in the wall of her chamber and got the attention of her keeper. When he drew close, she cried, "Dear keeper, go to the king, my lord and yours, and tell him that his poor daughter wants to see him and speak to him, and pray that he does not deny her this last favor."

And the keeper agreed, for he had never been completely convinced that Svanvitha was as immodest as the Polish prince had said she was. The keeper thought she was good and pure and that it was possible a terrible mistake had been made. But he was a subject of the king and merely the keeper of the tower. He knew he had to keep these thoughts to himself.

And so it was that the keeper went into the presence of the king, who grew wrathful when he heard the request his daughter had made. He cast the keeper out and said that he must not speak the girl's name again or he would find himself in prison, too, and no one would ever know what had become of him.

So the keeper returned to the tower and told Svanvitha that the king had denied her request. And Svanvitha fell crying to the cold floor. But after a time she picked herself up and told herself that sooner or later she would have an opportunity to try again.

That night, the king had a very beautiful dream, which he could not remember when he woke in the morning. But the dream must have changed something in him, for he sent for the keeper and ordered him to bring Svanvitha before him. The keeper brought her just as she was, a thin girl with tattered clothes that hung on her like airless sails. When he saw what had become of his daughter as a result of her imprisonment, her rags and her wasted body, her pallor and her haggard face, the king went as pale as the whitewashed wall behind him.

Svanvitha bowed low before him and said that she was suffering innocently of the charges concocted by the evil Polish prince and she knew of a way to prove this and to improve her father's fortune all at once. She begged him to listen. When he did not interrupt, she reminded him of the old legend about the ramparts at Garz, which said that a pure and chaste princess who walks the rampart between twelve and one on Midsummer's Eve, naked and as God made her, will cause the earth to open and reveal a chamber filled with treasure. She wanted to say more, but the words stuck in her throat and she sobbed bitterly. But she saw that the king had been moved by her speech, or perhaps he'd seen a way to increase his wealth. Either way, he nodded once and said that she would have her chance.

Forty days had yet to pass before Midsummer's Eve and during that time, the king sheltered Svanvitha in his castle. She bathed and had fresh clothes and ate the food he had prepared for his own table. She walked in the garden and took in the air. She watched the birds she loved and felt taken up by the wind that stirred her. She looked far out at the forests where she had played as a child and imagined herself as she had been, before she learned her true value to the king.

On the morning of the day of Midsummer's Eve, the king had a servant deliver a beautiful gown to Svanvitha so that she could appear on the rampart in a style that befitted a true princess of Rügen. But Svanvitha told the keeper to put the gown away. She would ride to the tower dressed as a boy so there would be no danger of anyone recognizing her.

Just before she left, the princess went into the chamber of her father the king and bade him farewell. He bowed his head and wept, and she held to his knees and let her tears fall into his lap. Then she disguised herself for the journey to Garz, which she made alone and on horseback.

The road between the king's castle and the ramparts at Garz was not long, and Svanvitha made good time. No one recognized her, so they could not call her the terrible names they had used when the prince of Poland spread lies about her. The night was dark, but she was not afraid and in the shadows saw the promise of her liberation. Never had the air smelled so sweet, and never had she looked on the cottages she passed with such tenderness of feeling.

When she got to Garz, she took the saddle and the bridle from her horse and laid these on the ground. She turned to the horse, which she had ridden since childhood, and rubbed his muzzle and whispered in his ear. Then she slapped him on the haunch and watched him gallop away into the night. She climbed the stone steps to the parapet, unbuttoning her shirt as she went, and loosening her hair from her cap. Then, as the clock struck midnight, she stripped and stepped out onto the rampart. She walked backward, beating the battlement behind her with a St. John's wand, just as the legend said she must. She had not gone too many steps when the stone gave way and the earth opened below. As predicted, she fell as gently as if in a dream into a huge hall lit by a thousand lamps and wax lights, with walls of marble and diamond mirrors. She landed on a heap of gold but she was not hurt. She looked around in wonderment, for the room was filled with more riches than she had imagined the world could ever hold and so much that there was hardly room to walk among the treasure.

In the corner, the gray ghost waited but he made no move to harm her. Instead, he merely nodded as if he was happy to meet his descendant. And then he rose and faded and in his place stood a retinue of servants, who turned toward Svanvitha, ready to do her bidding. She was dumbstruck for a moment, but then she collected herself and showed them that they were to fill their garments—their pockets and their cloaks, their breeches and their gloves—with all the gold and jewels from the chamber. This they did while Svanvitha looked on. And all the while she thought how she would please her father and he would have to let her go free because she had proven her innocence and brought him great wealth. But she knew that the night was short on Midsummer's Eve and she felt a great urgency to finish her task and lead the retinue of servants out of the underhall. And yet she wanted to make sure she brought her father enough wealth so that he would be sure to pardon her for the crime she had not committed.

At this part of the story, my mother always said that it is easy for a girl to start to feel guilty for something she has not done when everyone else believes that she is guilty, and Svanvitha just wanted to be sure she was never sent back to that terrible tower room. Anyone could understand her plight. Anyone could see that she had only one way out. She had to take her time and make sure she got this one thing right.

So it was that daylight had begun to break when Svanvitha started up the steps to the top of the rampart. She could hear the cock crow and she could see that the sky had grown brighter in the east and she grew afraid that the servants with the riches in their pockets would be left behind. So she turned to urge them on. But as soon as she turned, the staircase that had risen to take her to the door fell away beneath her and the servants and the treasure disappeared and the door above slammed shut with such a thunderous sound that she cried out. She fell to the floor, where she lay breathless in the dark. Eventually, her eyes grew accustomed to the gloom and she saw that a huge, snarling black dog stood on the stone steps and blocked her way.

When she did not return, her father the king decided that she had deceived him and had used the legend as an excuse to slip away. He ordered that she be brought to him the minute she was found so that he could once again lock her in the tower. But of course he was wrong.

It is said that poor Svanvitha stays in the dark, empty chamber to this day and she is not alone. The great black dog is there lest she should take it upon herself to try to find a way out. And, too, every so often a strapping young lad will go missing from the village and never be seen again. The villagers all know what has become of him. He is with Svanvitha, in the dark below-ground. She might have been innocent once but she is surely innocent no more.

My mother always explained the outcome this way: You are not supposed to turn around and look back over your shoulder at the spirits of the underworld, for then they will have you in their power. You must never speak to them, or they will hold you in their power forever.

At first I thought she meant to teach us that we must always obey our father and never go against him and never rebel or disobey. Later, I realized she meant something else: Even should you obey your father in every way, he will still do with you as he pleases. And if you try to get away, you will be beset by things that you never knew about or dreamed. The world is full of rooms guarded by snarling dogs. If you do not wish to live in darkness, you must be prepared to fight with all that you are worth, for the world will never agree that you are simply to be free.

25

In early December it turned warm and then it rained and went cold overnight. The roads iced over, and black sheets of frozen water lay glassy on lawns and sidewalks. In the tearoom we had little business after two in the afternoon, and the owner put her coat on at two fifteen and told me to close up shop if things stayed slow. She opened the door and the air that came in when she left had the tang of snow.

Just before four, I banked the fire in the cookstove and turned the lights out and pulled the shades in the front windows so they rolled down to the sills. I took my coat from its hook in the back room and left it unbuttoned over my belly and stepped out into the snowy street. Down by the corner, a man in a long dark coat stood in the shadow of a building. He leaned and smoked and then cast his cigarette into a dirty pile of snow. He turned and looked up and stared at me as I came along. We were alone in the dim street and no lights shone in the windows overhead and no one else was near. Even the tavern lay still behind us. He walked up to me and said my name and looked searchingly at me. Then he fell to his knees and wrapped his arms around my legs and pressed his face into my thighs. We stood in the shadows and a cold wind came up. I shivered and then began to cry. He sobbed and tightened his grip and I lay my hand on his hair. The scent of him like the memory of a ghost.

After a time, I pulled away and he got to his feet and wiped his eyes.

"Marie," he said. "Marie."

I stood teary-eyed before him. Then I bit my lip and told him I was late.

"I am sorry," he cried. "I am sorry. I am sorry."

"Thank you," I said.

He held my arm. "Is that all you can say to me? Thank you?"

"I accept your apology," I said. I pulled my arm away.

"Then you will come home?" He waited. When I did not say anything, he said, "We can fix the divorce. It is only paper. We know how we feel."

I shook my head.

"I have to go," I said. "I cannot stand here with you." I stepped away from him and turned to go up the street. A woman opened the door to the building on the corner and looked outside. She looked at us and then whistled and whistled again. A sallow brown dog bolted out of the alley and made for the stone steps. When the dog was inside, the woman stepped down into the street and looked up and down again, as if she expected something to march past, and then she turned and went into the building. The door closed with a thunk.

"Please," he said. "Please."

"No," I said. "I cannot." I remembered the feel of his mouth on mine and the weight of him and I swayed a little in the street, as if I would fall toward him and fall back into him and fall back into the life I had left behind. He caught my elbow and told me that I should sit down. But I shook my head and took a step back.

"You should not be here," I said. "The judge told you to keep away."

"But this is not what we want," he said. He began to walk beside me.

I stopped walking. "August," I said. "This is what I want. I am not going to change my mind."

"But we have a baby now," he said. He put his hand on my belly but I brushed his hand away. He flinched. "Everything will be different," he said. "I will not drink. I will get used to being married. I will make sure you have what you need. So. Like that. We can go on."

"No," I said.

"You love me," he said. "I know you do."

"Yes," I said. "Well. That does not seem to be the point anymore."

The lamplighter passed and touched the street lamp on the corner with his frail torch. It began to snow. August looked at me with a strange expression, his mouth wet, his eyes shadowed in their sockets. The light from the street lamp moved and his expression shifted in waves. I did not see myself in his gaze, only his own desperate longing which could not be my longing anymore. Then I told him it was time for me to go, and he said that he would walk with me wherever I was going and keep me safe. I paused and saw that he would follow me to my little room at the top of the stairs and he would know where I lived. So I nodded and walked as far as the house on the corner, where I stepped up to the wooden door. Someone had painted it a glossy black and a tarnished brass oval was screwed to the center panel. I lifted the door knocker and let it fall three times. The sallow brown dog barked somewhere inside and the woman who had whistled for him opened the door. She looked surprised and said, "Yes?" I looked at her very hard and she looked past me at August, who waited in the street behind me with a distraught expression on his face. "Come in," the woman said. "It's so very good to see you." When we were inside, she turned the deadbolt in the door and told me to have a seat in the parlor. Then she walked to the window and watched through a slit in the shade until he was gone.

There came a number of days when it snowed and snowed and business disappeared. The woman who owned the tea shop and I sat at one of the tables and played cards. She taught me to play double solitaire and poker. We bet buttons from a jar she kept under the kitchen counter. She thought it was amazing to see how many people lost buttons in her tearoom. Her name was Olga Jensen and she had come to Wisconsin from Sweden when she was a very little girl. Her father had died on the ship coming over, and her mother had been sent to Mendota in the first year. She did not know what had happened to her after that. When she was a child she heard nothing at all, but when she was older she heard that her mother had died almost right away in an influenza outbreak on the wards. Then she heard that she had been sent to work in the hospital laundry, for what other occupation might a crazy person pursue but laundry, and had been killed there in a terrible accident. Then she heard that she was free and walked the city streets like any woman who was sane and had remarried and had forgotten all about her daughter. So Olga, who was small and frail, grew up in a foundling home with neither brothers nor sisters nor aunts nor uncles. It was as if she had been dropped onto this earth from a hole in the sky. When she went out to work, she found a job in the kitchen of a boardinghouse. Right away she began to save up. She knew she wanted a place of her own. She had been married twice and had buried two husbands and was about to marry for a third time. It was her next husband's idea that she would leave Milwaukee with him and go up to Price County and start a farm. But she had no intention of doing any such thing, for it meant leaving her tearoom behind and she had learned how important the tearoom was if she wanted to stand on her own two feet. She was not about to change her mind about that. So she thought she might learn to like the train, which she otherwise thought dirty and filled with people who smelled bad, and just see her new husband on weekends. Or she might let someone she trusted run the place for her a good deal of the time. She was sure whatever needed to happen could be sorted out. But she could not relinquish her freedom, of that she was very sure, for without freedom, a woman was nothing but a slave.

We played cards until we were tired of cards, and then Olga laid the deck in one of the drawers behind the kitchen counter. We looked at the pots and she handed me a rag and a tin of polish and together we polished the pots and then the forks and spoons and knives. We mended the holes in the kitchen towels and cleaned the cookstove. Still it snowed, and the drifts began to come up as high as the windowsills, especially where the wind blew. When that happened, Olga went outside with a shovel and moved the snow from the sidewalk into the street. She wore no hat and her hair grew white with snow and then her eyelashes. When she looked at me, working inside, she laughed and wiped her runny nose with a white handkerchief she kept in the sleeve of her blouse. She had given me some old clothes to wear, and in the evenings I sat and let the waistbands out as far as they could go. Time had passed and now I wore the skirts with their plackets gaping open and belted by a long piece of rope that I pinned to the plackets on either side. Over that, I wore a loose smock that had once been some big man's shirt.

Late in the day, a tall young man in a short tan coat came to the window and looked in at us. He'd jammed a flannel porkpie hat on his head like an afterthought, and his hands were bare and raw. When he saw me, he tapped his fingers lightly on the glass. I stood and went to the door and held it open and asked him to come in. But he shook his head. "You come out," he said, and I smiled and went to the back room and got my coat.

We walked away from the tearoom and away from the center of town. We passed away from the narrow streets filled with machine shops and tobacconists and greengrocers and shabby stationery stores. The snow thickened over us, and when I looked up it spiraled down in a fluttering wind. Edwin walked slowly so I could keep up. He looked at me and said my name and reached over and brushed snow from my hair. He smiled and I smiled back at him. He took my hand and I let him and he tightened his grip. It was very cold and yet we breathed as we walked and our clothes grew damp. We came to a park where the socialists had gathered on warm summer nights and told each other what it would mean when they had at last escaped their chains. Under the snow, the gazebo they used for a stage was a shrouded place, overhung with the bowed branches of evergreens. Black needles. Blackening sky. The snow driven down now in a straight line and the wind dying down. We came up the stairs under the dark branches and sat on the little wooden benches that ran around the inside of the gazebo. Here the afternoon was muffled and we were hidden from the street. Edwin sat down first and he put his arm around me. I lay my head against his shoulder. His coat was cold but his arm was warm and I felt myself fit to him. We stayed like that for quite a long time and then I closed my eyes and felt the wind rise and felt a spray of icy crystals against my cheeks. Out before us, a silent city made empty by snow, the quiet of a deep northern plain, the lake a still gray presence iced over and gone motionless at the shoreline. White land and white water stretching away over the horizon and not even the boats at the docks able to move, not steamship nor barge, nor ice cutter nor rowboat.

And at dusk the sinking sun new and strange and at the place where the land met the deepening blue sky a glowing redness and the trees gone in a selfsame blur. Beyond the city lay the woods, their dark and shrouded trails, their limpet pools and hidden deer, the rising birds and the deep ferns of spring and the dusty dry leaves of fall, the long, deeply windswept places beneath the trees where the limestone rose and the river fell away and away and the earth itself turned under us like a place that could be home after all.

ACKNOWLEDGMENTS

The End of Always is a work of imagination but it rests on real events. To uncover Marie's story, I used the court documents that recorded her divorce, including affidavits from Marie and from August, responses from their attorneys, rulings from the court, and later documents detailing August's failure to comply with court-ordered child support. These records were retrieved from the Wisconsin Historical Society and I thank the archivists for their help.

I used standard genealogical practices in working with primary records (i.e., state and federal census lists, city directories, ship's manifests, military records, and death certificates and newspaper obituaries regarding the deaths of Alvin and Elise Reehs) to establish the Reehs and Bethke family histories. Newspaper accounts from 1890–1910 allowed me to recover the stories of the real young women who were killed, beaten, maimed, lost, or abandoned during that period and which I reference in the novel. Some of the stories were drawn from the newspapers of the time, while others came from those collected in Michael Lesy's stunning *Wisconsin Death Trip*. I have been obsessed with this extraordinary work since I first opened the book in 1973. I owe him a huge debt of gratitude.

I am also profoundly grateful to my parents for giving me my copy of *Wisconsin Death Trip*, and to my mother for her willingness to share what she knew of her family history, including the very thin file kept by her father, the child of Marie and August. I am also grateful to Dana Henning, Hattie's granddaughter, who generously shared her memories of the Reehs family. And I thank Friederike Seeger for her beautiful translation of the Reehs family Bible.

The individuals described in Edwin's boardinghouse are historical individuals whose stories appear in *Wisconsin Death Trip*, but Edwin is a work of a fiction. The fairy tales Elise told her daughters are based on the true fairy tales of Rügen, compiled by Ernst Moritz Arndt as *Fairy Tales from the Isle of Rügen*, first published in Berlin in 1817. I consulted the 1896 edition. Finally, the tale of the brown dwarf is based on John Greenleaf Whittier's poem, "The Brown Dwarf of Rügen," which was originally published for children as a cautionary tale about keeping bad company. The poem draws on the story of John Dietrich, Rügen's best-known fairy tale adventurer, and was included in the 1888 book *The Complete Poetical Works of John Greenleaf Whittier*.

I am endlessly grateful to my brilliant, generous, and patient agent, Julie Barer; my wonderful, supportive editor, Deb Futter; and the incomparable Brian McLendon and Libby Burton at Twelve. I also want to thank those who have provided unwavering support, now and across the years: Tobias Wolff, Lynn York, Anna Gemrich, Michael FitzGerald, Joan Gantz, John McGowan, Aaron Shackelford, and Kathy Pories, as well as all of my friends and family. I owe a special thanks to Nizar Chahin, whose relentless encouragement has made so many things possible.

As always, and above all, I owe my greatest thanks to Chase and Haley, my beloved children, who are endlessly tolerant of my reading and scribbling.

ABOUT THE AUTHOR

Randi Davenport is the author of *The Boy Who Loved Tornadoes: A Mother's Story*, the winner of the Great Lakes Colleges Association New Writer's Prize for creative nonfiction and a finalist for the Books for a Better Life Award. Her short fiction and essays have appeared in the *Huffington Post*, the *Washington Post*, the *Ontario Review*, the *Alaska Quarterly Review*, and *Women's History Review*, among others. She earned both an MA in creative writing/fiction and a PhD in literature at Syracuse University. She has been a Summer Fellow of the National Endowment for the Humanities and a Public Fellow at the Institute of Arts and Humanities at the University of North Carolina at Chapel Hill. She has taught and/or served in administrative positions at Hobart and William Smith Colleges, Duke University, the University of North Carolina at Chapel Hill, and elsewhere.

READING GROUP GUIDE
A Conversation with the Author

Marie seeks love throughout *The End of Always,* but power and violence seem to thwart her every step of the way. How do you balance these big ideas while telling a tale like this?

I didn't start by thinking that I was going to write a novel about power and violence, that's for sure. I started with Marie. Marie Reehs was my mother's grandmother, which makes her my great-grandmother. She was born in America but her father, mother, and several older siblings were born in Germany, on the island of Rügen. This is where the family came from when they immigrated to Waukesha, Wisconsin. The only thing I knew about Marie when I started was that her name was connected to a deep family mystery. I set out to solve this. When I did, I discovered the events that inspired *The End of Always.* And those events eventually led me to the issues of power and violence you mention. But I couldn't start with those, just as I couldn't write a novel that was just a literal transcription of my great-grandmother's life. Either choice would have taken me on a fool's errand. It's important to remember that the novel is a story, first and foremost. It's about one young woman whose life, I suspect, will feel achingly familiar to many readers. If I've done my job, Marie's experiences cannot help but tell us something about ourselves. Perhaps that's where the things you call "big ideas" come into play. But I didn't write the novel trying to nail those concepts. I wanted to get at the heart of Marie's life. The "big ideas" about power and violence are inescapably central to her world. As they are to women everywhere.

Tell us about the origin of the stories from Rügen that Marie's mother tells her.

The tales are specific to Rügen, an island with a long history of changing political affiliations. The island's original Germanic inhabitants were dispossessed by Slavic people, who were in turn dispossessed by the Danes. In 1648, the island fell under Swedish rule and did not become part of Pomerania, in Prussia, until 1815. Because of the island's remote location, its diverse past, its long history of paganism, and its relative late-coming to Christianity, the island retained its fairy tales of giants and goddesses and mysterious dwarves well into the time that Herman and Elise Reehs lived there in the nineteenth century. Even Hattie's real-life granddaughter, who was born in Wisconsin and lives just outside of Philadelphia today, remembers Hattie scaring her with tales about dwarves and the terrible calamities that would befall children who stepped out of line. Ernst Moritz Arndt collected the stories in 1819 and I discovered them as I was researching the island. Arndt gathered the tales from the people he knew on Rügen, transcribing the stories he was told and then creating the volume as a gift for a young friend. The tales are quite different from the (now sanitized and profoundly revised) tales we know from the brothers Grimm. For one thing, the fairy tales from Rügen are transparently prescriptive (although perhaps this is Arndt's hand at work) and lead to resolute lessons about good citizenship. As soon as I found them, I knew I had to use them. I thought they might give me a way to say some things aslant.

Talk a little about the title *The End of Always*. What does this phrase mean to you?

In the most obvious sense, the title refers to Marie's fight to escape the brutality that the women in her family have always endured. For her, at least as far as the world of the novel is concerned, *always* comes to an end. But the end is hard won. It may not last. We don't know. More broadly, the title refers to the *always* that women in America experience. Even women who insist that they have never experienced violence and perhaps believe that it's not all that pervasive know what a risk they take when they walk in a parking garage alone at night or on an empty street in an unfamiliar neighborhood. They know what it might mean if they run out of gas on a country road or fail to check the backseat in their car when they get into it at the mall. They have seen the things that men they know do. Deep down inside, we all know where we live, even if we say otherwise. The title is less hopeful on this score. Could there be an end to that *always*? I'm forever optimistic, but I'm a realist, too.

At the end of Chapter 23, you address the reader directly, writing: "Every day the papers are filled with the stories of women who have been thrown from windows or shot with guns or lost in the night…We have not seen the last girl. She has not yet walked among us." Why did you choose to break the spell of the book this way?

Throughout the novel, Marie speaks in little asides to the reader. These moments are often subtle, but taken together, they suggest that Marie is narrating the story from a place in her adult life—that is, she tells her story retrospectively even if there is no formal device (a setup involving a letter written to a grandchild, for instance) to signal this. In terms of the psychological integrity of the character, it made sense to let Marie speak directly to us. To give her a chance to sum up why her story matters. To let us hear her voice from a time well beyond the afternoon when she and Edwin set out together in the falling snow. To have her remind us that we still have a very long way to go.

Discussion Questions

1. Does the fact that *The End of Always* is based on actual events shape the way you think about the story?
2. Describe the story. What happens? What do you know about the different characters? What do you know about the town of Waukesha? About the events of the time period? How does the author bring the time period to life?
3. Is there a passage in the book that struck you? Share it and explain why you were so taken with it.
4. German myths and stories are sewn into the narrative of *The End of Always*. How did these stories contribute to Marie's ideas about the world? How have fairy tales and fables contributed to yours?
5. Marie and her sister Martha have a complex relationship. Do you think that Martha has Marie's best interests in mind? If you were Martha, what advice and guidance would you have offered Marie?
6. Is the death of Marie's mother at the hands of her father truly an accident, a time when his violence went too far, or is it something more calculated and sinister?
7. Almost as soon as she goes out to work, Marie begins to hear stories about young women who have met bad ends. Are you familiar with stories like these from our own time? Do the stories of 1907 and today have anything in common?

8. August's love for Marie seems to be partly rooted in the reality that he cannot have her immediately and must try to find her. For her part, once they meet, Marie falls under August's spell so easily. Why does August seem to equate love with making Marie his own? Why does Marie fall in love with him so fast?

9. Throughout the novel, men exert their control over women in many ways: Martha is forbidden to see George; Hattie is forced to wear leg braces she does not need; August has Marie quit her job and does not provide food for her. There are many other examples. How do you feel about these instances? Do some men still try to control women in the same way today? Why do you think some of the men in the novel control the women closest to them?

10. Rather than witnessing violence in *The End of Always*, we often see evidence of it on the bodies of women in the novel, including Marie and her mother. Why do you think the author focuses more on the aftermath of violence than on depicting detailed scenes of the violence itself?

11. What does America look like in *The End of Always*? Does it seem familiar? Why or why not?

12. The day after Marie spends the night with August, Inge simplifies an important power dynamic at work in the book: "A girl has one thing and one thing only and when that is gone, it is gone. There is no getting it back." Do you think society's relationship to virginity has changed since the early twentieth century? How? Is it easier to be sexually active as an unmarried girl or woman today? Does a girl still have "one thing and one thing only?"

13. Not all of the men in *The End of Always* are bad. Marie encounters some men—either directly or by proxy—who show her kindness. Who are they? Does the fact that these men have more power than the men in the immigrant community make a difference or are they, too, just exercising their control? What do you make of Marie's uncle Carl?

14. Could Edwin ever exist as a love interest for Marie? Or is he something more important?

15. Bertha is a kind and generous friend. What is it about her presence that aides Marie in escaping her situation?

16. Marie is born into a violent home. Despite her best efforts, she continues in that tradition. What do you think accounts for this cycle? Do you think the cycle can be stopped?

17. Does Marie change over the course of the book? If so, does she change for the better or for the worse? Do you think she could have found another way out? What do you think of the choices she made?

18. What sort of future do you see for Marie and her child? Do you believe the ending is hopeful or resigned?